The Essence of Whiskey and Tea

Stacey Wilk

The Essence of Whiskey and Tea

by Stacey Wilk

Heritage River, Book 3

This is a work of fiction. Names, characters, places, and incidents are either the product of the author's imagination or are used fictitiously, and any resemblance to actual persons living or dead, business establishments, events, or locales, is entirely coincidental.

The Essence of Whiskey and Tea

COPYRIGHT © 2024 by Stacey Wilk

Print ISBN: 979-8-9872613-9-2

Digital ISBN: 979-8-9872613-5-4

Cover Art by *Diana Carlisle*

Publishing History, 2019

Wild Rose Press

First Mainstream Women's Fiction Edition

Print ISBN 978-1-5092-2819-5

Digital ISBN 978-1-5092-2820-1

Heritage River, Book 3

Published in the United States of America

This book is dedicated to the real Kiki.

She's not a fork stealer.

And, to Toni—who is.

Chapter One

JT Davies made his own luck.

He'd spent the better part of his adult life making opportunities happen. He relied only on himself. Except for his dad, no one had given him a single thing. His dad had given him a ton of love, even when JT didn't deserve it, and now the deli, Eat At Jake's.

He didn't want the deli. He did want his father back, but God had him now. Lucky bastard. Jake Davies was the best man he'd ever known.

He didn't plan on a permanent return to Heritage River, but there he stood in the house he'd grown up in, with his fifteen-year-old daughter glaring at him.

"Do you want to come with me to the deli?" He patted his pockets, looking for his keys. Every room in the house was filled with cardboard boxes labeled with room names. The oversize furniture from their last house didn't seem to fit against any of the walls in the modest Queen Anne-style home. The beds needed clean sheets. The

1

fridge was empty, but he had to take some measurements at the deli. After that he'd begin the settling-in process.

Maddy scooped up his keys from the top of a box that read *Office,* even though they were in the living room, and swung them back and forth. "Is there food at the deli? Because I'm starving. You promised after the movers left we'd get something to eat."

How did teenage girls perfect that scowl? What had happened to the little girl who thought her daddy was pretty cool? He was still cool, wasn't he? He was older, had less hair and more aches and pains, but he could still pull off some cool.

Not according to Madeline Elizabeth Davies. His beautiful, tall daughter had become a snarly, still beautiful, still tall, and smart—too smart for her own good—teenager who would rather live with an alligator than him. Good thing alligators didn't rent rooms.

"You know the deli isn't operational." In fact, it was gutted. "But we can try to find something else."

Maybelline's Bakery had closed hours ago, before the sun had a chance to set. Except for the ice cream shop, no other dining establishments existed on Main Street, which was part of the reason he wanted a Whiskey Bar to go in the place of Eat At Jake's. He planned to open his fifth Whiskey Bar, this time right in Heritage River. Once the bar started making money and Maddy graduated from high school in two years, they'd hit the road.

Heritage River had done nothing for him, but he was glad to take their money, and he was very good at making money in exchange for good food and great whiskey.

"Does this town have a vegan place?" She flipped her head upside down and tied her hair into a knot on the top of her head.

He also didn't understand why anyone would be a vegan. He was convinced Maddy claimed to be a plant eater just to piss him off. "I doubt it."

"You were here like nine months ago. Didn't you notice?" The scowl returned. She flopped down on the couch and pulled out her phone.

"You were with me the last time I was here. Did you see one?" He hadn't noticed much of anything when he was in town the last two times.

His dad had called and told him about some tests the doctor wanted him to take. JT flew in to be there with him because his stepmother was good for just about nothing. He got lassoed in to helping out one night at the deli for some fundraiser to save the music and art programs at the high school. He flew out the next day. He had come back for the funeral, but that was it.

"How about a pizza?"

"Yeah, Dad, like cheese isn't dairy. Thanks a lot for respecting my choices. Forget it. I just won't eat." She returned to her phone. Her fingers flew across the screen.

He seemed to have lost another battle.

"Why do you have to go to the deli tonight anyway? You promised you'd spend less time at work if we were here. That's the only reason why I agreed to come to Heritage River and get dragged away from my friends and my school."

"Giving up those friends is no loss. Trust me." He

grabbed his wallet and shoved it in his pocket. "I am going to work less once the Whiskey is up and running. I need to make a quick stop before the contractor comes over in the morning. I want to do that now so I can drive you to school in the morning." He was going to try to work less, but if he was going to get the Whiskey Bar operational quickly, he'd have to put in more hours than his child would want. "Are you coming with me, or should I bring you back a salad?"

"Bring me a salad but make sure it doesn't have any cheese or eggs on it. Can't I skip school tomorrow? What's the big deal if I start a day late?"

He needed to be at the store tomorrow and didn't want her sitting around the house all alone. At least at school, someone would be able to keep an eye on her. "Tomorrow. Drop it." He was working on the tough-love thing.

"This school isn't going to be any different, you know. You can't fix me by moving me around from county to county. I hate school, and I'll hate this one too."

He had hated school too, when he was her age, but he was smart enough to know not to tell her that. He couldn't be the one to tell her about the things he used to do because then he'd lose all his parental leverage. But the truth was, he'd been a real pain in the ass as a kid, and so was his daughter. "You might not hate it so much if you tried a little to like it."

"Oh, so I don't try? Is that what you're saying? I'm just a big loser who doesn't give a shit about anything, right, Dad?"

"I didn't say that. You're not a loser. Why would you think I'd say something like that about you? And stop cursing." The whole situation spun out of control.

"You curse all the time, and you did say I didn't try, which is the same thing as saying I'm a loser. I'm going to set up my room." She pushed off the couch and unfolded her thin body cloaked in black, tight pants and a top that showed off her stomach. He shook his head. He'd have to buy a gun to keep the boys away, especially after the last time.

"I could help you when I get back."

"No, thanks." She marched up the steps, giving him her back and probably the finger.

Yeah, that went well. He snagged his keys and headed out. First, he'd stop at the deli, and then he'd try to find his vegan daughter an acceptable salad. He'd also buy himself a pint of whiskey. He needed it.

JT parked on Main Street right outside the old Eat At Jake's. Cast-iron lampposts lined the street and spilled their white glow on the sidewalk. Many of the shops were closed up tight for the night. Main Street went to bed early, but he'd change that. The dumpster had been dropped off in front of the store instead of the back lot. He'd probably get hell from the other store owners. Tough shit.

Of all the Whiskey Bars he owned, this location

meant the most to him. Here he would prove to himself and everyone who said otherwise that he had made it.

He shoved his way out of the truck and stopped. When had that popped up? A sign hung above the last shop on the street. Savannah's Tea Room. *Savannah?* He stood under it and looked up.

"Nice, isn't it?" A man with white hair and a belly hanging over his waistband appeared next to him, licking a melting ice cream cone.

"What's nice?"

"The sign. The flowers and teapot are nice, aren't they?"

"I guess." He didn't care what the sign looked like. A tea shop two doors down wouldn't hurt his business any. May's bakery had more to worry about than he did. "Who owns this place?" He'd known a Savannah a long time ago.

The man licked his cone. "Savannah Savage. Well, she's Montgomery now, or maybe she went back to Savage. I don't know which."

His Savannah owned that store? Well, she wasn't *his* Savannah. They had lasted all of five minutes, but she had stuck her claws in him all the same. Savannah always liked to run things, to call the shots. Tell him what to do.

He'd shut her down.

He owed her that much.

Chapter Two

Savannah Savage Montgomery lived by the rules, rules set by her late father, small-town society, and herself. She couldn't finish raising three kids alone and make her new business a success without the rules she imposed. Rules gave order to life, and order made sense.

She packed two school lunches in her dimly lit kitchen, one with hummus and carrots and the other with an overstuffed sub too big for anyone's jaw except for maybe her fifteen-year-old son's. She folded napkins into thermals that would keep the food cold for five hours and checked *making lunch* off her list.

The sun wasn't quite up yet. She liked that time of the morning when the kids were upstairs getting dressed, and she was alone in the kitchen listening to the local morning show on the radio. The day stretched out before her, filled with possibilities. Those thirty minutes were truly hers before she had to turn her time over to her children, her job, her responsibilities.

She poured hot water into her favorite green mug with no handle and steeped the Earl Grey Cream tea. "Ten minutes. Hurry up. I don't have time to drive you in today," she yelled up the steps.

She was anxious to get to work. A line of fall-flavored teas was due to arrive, and she wanted to unpack them herself. She hoped the new teas would bring in additional business. She needed more customers—and a little luck. The bills wouldn't wait. Unfortunately, she had plenty of bills.

Caroline and Grey pounded down the steps, punctuated by laughter and conversation of silly social media posts. Grey was taller than she was now and looked so much like his father she found herself sucking in a breath every time he entered a room.

She missed her husband. If she was going to survive being a newly widowed working mother of three, even though her oldest was at college, she had to stick to her plan. She had to put one foot in front of the other and provide a safe and happy life for them. Sticking to the plan was how she'd survived the loss of both of her parents, the fight with her brothers, and Adam's death before Christmas last year.

Caroline had pulled her dark hair back in a ponytail, coated her eyelashes in tar, and smoothed her lips with a pink shimmer. She wore Adam's sweatshirt again, which hung practically to her knees, but the worn-out cotton with faded lettering from his college on the front made her little girl feel better.

What little? Caroline had entered the teen years and was ready to skip ahead to adulthood. Her eighth grader thought she was ready for flight from the nest. Savannah sighed. Sometimes children could tire out that little pink bunny that never stopped moving. She was certainly more tired these days.

"Car, are you ready for your science test?" Math and science were not her daughter's best subjects. Many a tear had been shed over failed tests. She handed each child their lunch.

"I studied. I think I'm ready."

The test would tell them. Caroline struggled in math, science, and Spanish. Savannah couldn't figure out what was happening. The child needed better study skills. They'd have to work on that. She'd add *study with Caroline* to her to-do list.

"Grey, did you do all your homework?" The tea had grown cold. She didn't have time to make another cup. The morning was off and running, and she had better keep up.

"I forgot my AP English assignment, but I'll have time during lunch. It's no big deal."

"Sounds like a big deal to me."

"He wants to get into Uncle Colton's detention." Caroline laughed and shoved her lunch bag into her purple backpack.

"I don't need to get into trouble to go to that. He lets everyone in."

Her older brother had become the music teacher at the high school. No one was more surprised than she was when that happened. Also not surprising, Colton's charm had quickly made him everyone's favorite teacher, even if they didn't take a music class. Most people fell victim to that charm, including her. And who wouldn't want a rock star as their teacher? Well, sort of former rock star, but that was another story.

"If your grade drops, Greyson, I'm taking your phone." She would ensure he did his best in school. She didn't want him skating by just because school came easily to him.

"My grade is fine, Mom. Stop worrying. I'm doing my best, and I have an A in that class anyway. Even if I forget to hand in my homework, nothing will happen. The stupid teacher doesn't even check half the time."

"I don't care about whether or not the teacher checks. And don't call her stupid." The teacher was stupid, but it wasn't southern to voice it. "Do that homework. I'll be checking."

He hung his head. She'd made her point and didn't feel any better for it.

"Okay, the bus will be here any minute. Go have good days. I love you both." She pulled each of them into a hug and sent them out the door.

She rinsed her mug and shoved it in the dishwasher. The radio DJ said something about an upcoming guest and then segued into another song. She stood a little straighter at the sound of a melody from her high school days that catapulted her back to her graduation party.

10

The one *he* was at, the he who had been everywhere at the time. The *he* she couldn't seem to shake from her memory no matter how old she became. Something tiny nudged her heart. That night was better left forgotten, even though visiting there once in a while was nice.

Grey had left his lunch. She let out a long breath and pushed her hair off her neck. She should let him starve because he refused to buy food at school. The last thing she needed was an extra stop at the high school before she made it to work.

She checked her list. The to-go cups never arrived from the distributor, which meant a trip to the warehouse store to buy more, and a phone call to the distributor for a refund. She could swing by the high school and drop off Grey's lunch then. Somehow she'd juggle it all. What choice did she have? She didn't have a partner to pass off to any longer. She shot Harley a quick text to let her know she'd be late.

Running her own business wasn't what she'd thought it would be, and now her funds were all but nonexistent. The Heritage River one-hundred-sixtieth black-tie dinner was the answer to her problems. She'd have to win it first.

Her phone rang. She checked the screen and almost let it go to voice mail, but what if there was a problem? "Hey, Rae. Please tell me the milk didn't spoil again."

Sometimes Rae helped out at the tea shop when Harley couldn't cover the opening. She knew the morning routine.

"Relax. Everything here is fine. Harley has scones

11

coming out of the oven, and she brewed up some teas. However, the dumpster is still in its unwanted space on the street. More importantly, I saw a hot guy in tight jeans down at Jake's."

The end of Jake's broke her heart. Jake Davies had been a good man and a permanent fixture on Main Street her entire life. Whoever had that dumpster on the road blocking parking spots couldn't be half the decent man Jake was.

Still, the neighborly thing to do was bake cookies and pack a jar of green-and-white infusion tea leaves as a welcome to the street. She added that to her list.

"Ooh. Ooh. There he goes," Rae whispered into the phone.

"Who?"

"The hot guy. I'm standing out front of your store, pretending to clean the windows. This is the first sexy guy I've seen around. Except your brothers. My God, does Colton have a nice ass."

"Rae, he's engaged, and his fiancée is only yards from you." Colton engaged—another surprise.

"I call it like I see it. Hurry up and get down here. You're missing all the fun."

She used to be fun. Spontaneous even. An impulsive side had existed a long time ago, before marriage, before kids, and during... She stopped. Lately, she'd been thinking a lot about her life before the real world took ahold of her. Life couldn't move forward if she kept looking back.

So why was the view better in that direction?

"Take a picture of your hot guy because by the time I get there, he'll probably be gone." She ended the call.

She wasn't interested in any guys. Sure, admiring a handsome man didn't hurt anyone, but her life couldn't juggle a romance. Adam hadn't been gone long enough for her to begin dating. How would that look to the people in town?

She and Adam hadn't set any world on fire with their predictable, practical romance, but wasn't that what life was all about after almost twenty years of marriage? She had no right to expect more.

She shoved her wallet, phone, and keys into her tote, then reached to turn off the radio. The singer's voice stopped her. It was another song from her life before marriage. Another reminder of who she'd been once and what she longed for snuck in and shoved her off balance.

"...even after all these years, when life is good, and he's around, I can't forget the way you made me feel. It's you I long to hold even after all these years," the singer crooned.

Her mind clicked backward to the night of her graduation party. She had put pain in the eyes of the young man who had set the world on fire for her once. The words had dripped from her mouth. "Don't tell my brothers."

He promised he wouldn't tell, and he never did.

Not in twenty-four years.

He'd left her instead.

Chapter Three

JT barked orders at the construction crew. He had a ton of things to accomplish and couldn't get a single one done. His phone rang all morning. He fought with the glass manufacturer about the price for the old-fashioned and pint glasses, and unpacked the lighting fixtures to discover half of them were broken.

Maddy had picked that morning to argue again about his long working hours. The opening of any new establishment took time. She didn't understand that. She also didn't understand why they couldn't leave Jake's as it was. She loved her grandfather's deli. She would understand some day. He hoped.

His phone chirped again. He pulled it out to find a number he didn't recognize. He almost let it go to voice mail when he realized the town underneath the number read Heritage River. Who from town had his number?

Then it hit him. The school.

"JT Davies."

"Dad, I need you to come pick me up."

He checked his watch. It was barely nine in the morning. "What happened? Are you sick?" She had better not be faking it again.

"I got dress coded. I have to go home."

"Dress coded? What's that?" He should know the school terminology by now. He'd been the only parent most of her fifteen years.

"Can you just come get me? I'm not allowed to stay."

"I don't understand. I'm working. I can't come get you unless you're sick. That's our deal."

"Hold on."

"Mr. Davies, this is Joann Humphreys, the school principal. Madeline has received a dress-code violation. Her attire is inappropriate for school. You will need to retrieve her. She isn't allowed to stay. She cannot return until tomorrow, will receive an unexcused absence, and cannot make up any of the work she misses."

This woman sounded like uptight Mr. Viking who'd been principal when he went there. "Mrs. Humphreys, do you think you could give Maddy a pass this one time? This is only her first week at your school. She probably isn't familiar with the dress code." He couldn't remember what she'd left the house wearing. She'd refused to take the bus, so he drove her, but his mind had been on the Whiskey Bar. He was pretty sure she had on clothes that covered the important stuff. He'd have to pay better attention next time.

"I'm sorry, but we don't bend the rules here. If I do

that for one student, I'll have to do that for all the students. I take the dress code very seriously. You have twenty minutes to get here. Thank you." She ended the call.

What else would go wrong today?

Heritage River High School made JT sweat even at his age. He wiped a hand over his face, adjusted his black cowboy hat, and opened the first set of glass doors. The sign on the inside door read "Please show your driver's license." He pulled out his license to announce his arrival.

Even Heritage River had succumbed to the need for heightened security. Thanks to the rest of the world, his small southern hometown had lost some of its innocence. But the town was a good one to have Maddy in. She needed roots, more discipline because he'd been slacking in that department, and a sense of home. He hadn't done a very good job of providing that before. Hopefully, this move worked out better than the last one.

"Come on in," the female voice inside the black, plastic box on the door said.

The hallway spread out before him. The place smelled like wax and popcorn. The auditorium was on the right and the nurse's office on the left, if memory served him correctly. He also had been very well acquainted with the principal's office.

He approached the red-haired woman behind the

reception window. She smiled up at him, spreading her freckles across her cheeks. Her name tag read Tess. "Howdy, I'm JT Davies. I'm here to pick up my daughter, Madeline."

"Do you happen to know what class she has now? Or I can check."

"I think she might be in the principal's office." He lowered his voice. He was also used to retrieving his daughter from the principal's office.

"Oh. Well, let me call down and find out for you." She pushed a few buttons and waited. "Do you have a Madeline Davies? Her father is here. I see. Okay." She returned her gaze to him. "Mrs. Humphreys would like to speak to you."

Whatever happened to old Mr. Viking? Was he even still alive?

"Second door on the right." She handed him a visitor's pass he stuck to his shirt.

He passed through the door into a large office with a counter-high desk splitting the room in two. Windows lined the back wall. A digital clock on the wall offered the time in red numbers, as if it were an exit sign. Oh yeah, he wanted out. Two women sat at desks covered in papers and binders. They stared at computers.

One of the women turned to him and frowned. "Can I help you with something?"

"Dad, in here." Maddy's voice cut through the office.

He slid away from the reception area and entered the principal's office. He pulled his shoulders back and reminded himself he was not the teenager in the room any longer. He stuck out a hand. "JT Davies."

"I'm Mrs. Humphreys. Thank you for coming." The woman's gray hair was tied into a knot that had to be pretty tight. Her face stretched back as if it were a slingshot ready to fire. The large amount of dark shadow painted around her eyes gave her a zombie kind of look. He forced his smile to remain in place, and his gaze locked with hers because he wanted to bend over and laugh. Yeah, she looked like one of the undead. Okay, sometimes he was still the old JT.

Maddy slumped in the chair, her hands fisted in her lap.

"Hi, Mads."

She looked up at him from under her lashes and curled up her lip in a snarl. "Hi, Dad."

"Mr. Davies, as you can plainly see, Madeline isn't wearing school-appropriate clothing. I wanted to point out to you the place in the student handbook where dress code is discussed. Because you just moved into town, I'm sure you haven't had an opportunity to read through the handbook thoroughly." The principal handed over a paper handbook with the page opened and highlighted.

He ignored the handbook and scanned Maddy's clothes. She had on jeans with tears in the legs. He didn't understand why he had to spend fifty dollars on jeans that came with holes in them. He could rip through the denim with his good pocketknife for free. She also had on a tank top that scooped a little lower than he'd like, but she was his little girl after all. "What's wrong with what she's wearing?"

"Clothing with rips aren't allowed. And the straps of her top are too thin. The straps must be two fingers wide." She dropped the book on the desk.

"I don't love the jeans either, but everything that should be is covered. As for the top, you're kidding me?" They'd pulled him away from a job to discuss tank tops? He was losing money every second they stayed there. He shook his head. "I don't have time for this. Your dress code is noted. Can she go now?"

"Well, if I could have another moment?"

"Hi, Debbie. I wanted to drop off Grey's lunch. He forgot it. I also brought over our new scones for everyone to try." A female voice drifted into the principal's office and distracted him from whatever the zombie principal said.

He'd never forgotten that voice. He'd tried by drinking it away, by filling his head with the voices of other women, by avoiding his childhood friends, but he couldn't forget the way his stomach flipped every time he heard her.

"Mr. Davies, did you hear what I said?"

He turned toward the outer office, ignoring Mrs. Humphreys.

"Dad?"

The voices died away. The room disappeared around him. Only the digital clock on the wall behind her kept time. He hadn't seen her since that night at her graduation party. *Don't tell my brothers.* Savannah's words had cut him in half, but he promised.

And then he'd left.

Now she was ten feet from him. And he didn't give a shit.

She might still be beautiful, but she was used to controlling everyone and everything around her. Well, not him. Not anymore. And if her little tea store suffered in the process, so be it.

Nothing personal, after all. Just business.

Chapter Four

Joann Humphreys said something that grabbed Savannah's attention. She turned away from whatever Debbie said to get a better listen. Her heart jumped into her throat. The travel mug filled with vanilla-cranberry tea fell out of her hand, bounced open, and splashed on her legs. She looked down and then right back up. Her eyes played tricks on her. They had to be.

"Savannah? Are you all right?"

Who was talking? Was that Debbie? Bees buzzed around her brain because standing only feet from her was a man she'd known once, and not just any man. He was tall, with solid shoulders and a thin waist. He still wore a cowboy hat. But the dark brown eyes that hid all his emotions were the giveaway. She had searched those eyes a thousand times for something that told her how he felt.

He was older than she remembered, but he'd transformed from a boy into a man with a strong jaw, crinkle lines around his eyes, and a goatee over textured skin. He still made her insides turn to a liquid mess.

"JT?" She found her voice.

Debbie ran around the office counter with paper towels and stooped down by her feet. "Bless your heart, you spilled your drink."

"I did?" So she had. When did that happen? She ran a hand through her hair. Had she remembered to put on makeup that morning? *God, he looks great.*

The man stepped into the main office. A young lady followed, with her gaze jumping between the man and her. JT didn't have children, did he? Wouldn't she have heard? He didn't say anything. He stared at her with eyes as empty as coal.

Had she been mistaken? "I'm sorry, but you look a lot like someone I knew." She needed to pull herself together. Of course, this wasn't JT. Why would he be in Heritage River on the day she'd been thinking about him?

"Holy shit, it's JT Davies." Colton barged into the office right past her and gripped the man in a hug. "What the hell are you doing here?"

"Mr. Savage, please. How many times do we have to tell you not to use language like that?" Joann called out from her office.

Colton waved her away. Joann didn't have a lot of power over Colton because, well, because he was Colton and because he donated back his entire salary.

"Savannah, why didn't you tell me and Blaise that JT was in town? Did you move back?"

Her tongue strangled her words.

"Hey, Colton. Good to see you, and yeah, this is my daughter, Maddy." He nodded in the young lady's direction. "I moved into my dad's place. I'm in a bit of a hurry, but we'll catch up soon."

Colton shook the girl's hand. "I'm Colton. Your dad and I go way back."

His daughter? Maddy was tall and thin like JT. She had his dark eyes and pretty blonde hair falling to her waist. Her clothes weren't school appropriate. Joann probably dress coded her for it. That woman was such a tight ass.

"It's nice to meet you." Maddy smiled like her father.

Savannah's heart knocked on her ribs.

"Blaise is going to shit when he finds out you're here. You've got to come over, and we'll jam. Well, we'll jam, and you can carry our stuff around. Savannah? Are you all right?" Colton narrowed his eyes.

Her tongue gave up its grip. "It's nice to see you, JT." She leaned forward to hug him hello, but he backed up.

"Uh-oh," Colton muttered. "I've got to get to class. Call me. I know Blaise will want to see you." He jotted his number down on a piece of paper and handed it to JT.

"Thanks." He shoved the paper in his pocket. "If you'll excuse us." He nodded to her and brushed past as if he didn't know her at all.

She watched as he retreated through the door. Heat filled her cheeks. Who did he think he was, ignoring her like that? He'd been the one who walked away without so much as a goodbye. He'd never wanted a relationship with her. She would've been glad to give them a chance, but he couldn't get out of town fast enough, and now he was going to snub her. Hell no. She took her mug back from Debbie, who stood there holding it out.

"Do you know him?" Debbie's smile touched her ears.

"I knew him once. He was good friends with my brothers. Sometimes he'd roadie for them, but I haven't seen him in years." Twenty-four to be exact, but who was counting?

"He's cute."

"He's trouble."

"I could use a little of that kind of trouble in my life these days." Debbie laughed. "I don't think he's married. His daughter's records only listed him as the parent. Maybe his wife died?"

"That would be sad." She'd have to do some investigating. "Enjoy the scones."

Out in the parking lot, she sent a text to her brother Blaise.

JT Davies is in town. And living in his father's old house.

Her mind skipped. The dumpster outside of Jake's.

Was he the one renovating?

Her phone pinged.

I heard.

Colton had wasted no time telling Blaise.

Did his wife die?

If he'd lost his wife recently, she had some good books

that had helped her get through the first month of Adam's death.

Dumped him. A long time ago. You want a date?

Shut up.

His wife had dumped him? Her heart squeezed a little, but she stopped it. JT was none of her concern. He'd made that clear when he forced her to live without him.

She had gone on with her life. It had been a good life. Warm. Safe. Reliable. Predictable. She'd followed the rules, while her brothers broke them. She'd done as a good southern woman was told to do.

She slid into the minivan and kicked over the engine. The inside filled with another love song, something about the dangers of loving someone too much. The sting of JT ignoring her inside the high school still burned her skin. He'd been the one thing she couldn't have and the one thing she'd always wanted. She wouldn't allow him to disrupt her routine existence.

He would be down the street from her tea shop. She'd been trying for years to get him out of her mind. Now he'd be her neighbor.

She'd have to do what she always did—put a good face on it. As long as everything stayed professional, he'd never know how she'd felt after he left.

Nothing personal.

Just business.

Chapter Five

Five years ago JT and Maddy had found themselves alone. His wife, the mother of his child, left a note on the kitchen table while he was at work and Maddy was at school. She wrote that she'd resigned from her job as mother and wife. She no longer wished to cook, clean, drive Maddy around to her activities, or do laundry. She felt entitled to a midlife crisis, and she was going to have it because damn it, she had earned it.

In the note, she'd confessed that all the nights she spent at the gym were lies. She'd been having an affair with her personal trainer, and she was in love with said trainer. JT would have to figure out how to parent on his own. She loved Maddy, but she loved herself more. She didn't love him at all.

The first year he and Maddy had done fine. The second year Maddy developed a wild streak inherited from him. His life had become quite complicated since then. He knew the insides of several principal offices because they'd moved so often. Maybe that was part of the problem.

He stole glances at his daughter as he navigated the streets of Heritage River until he returned to Main Street and the construction of what would be the Whiskey Bar.

"Maddy, I need you to follow the rules this time."

She stared out the window.

"Maddy, did you hear me?" He parked on the street.

She turned with tears in her eyes. "This is your fault. If you didn't pull me out of my school, I wouldn't have gotten in trouble today. Nobody dress codes in a real school, but in this small town they have nothing better to do."

Something tightened in his chest. This was his fault. He stared out the windshield. The truck's engine ticked to cool down. "I'm sorry for the hundredth time. This is what's best for both of us at the moment. Grandpa wanted us to live in his house."

"I don't understand why you care. You never cared about that house before. Or the deli. Grandpa always came to visit us. Why didn't you sell it and let us live where we were? I had friends. You're not supposed to move in high school. These are supposed to be the best years of my life."

"Who said that?" They certainly hadn't been the best years of his life, and he didn't want them to be the best years of her life. That's all she'd need, to peak in high school. She'd end up pregnant, married to the quarter-back, and living in a double-wide with no future and no money.

"Everyone says that. You know, stay young and stuff like that." She rolled her eyes.

The sun cooked the inside of the truck. He turned over the engine and eased the window down, hoping for a breeze he didn't get. "Does this have to do with your mother being gone? I can find her if you want me to." He hadn't bothered to chase Audrey down after she left. She hadn't wanted any alimony. She only wanted freedom.

He didn't want her either. He didn't need her. He tried to be enough parent for Maddy. He certainly had made enough money to support them. But if Maddy wanted to know where her mother was, he'd scour the earth looking for her.

"No. I hate her."

"Mads, you don't mean that." He wouldn't lie. The fighting side of him took that statement as a victory.

"I do. If she loved me, why did she leave me?"

"I don't know." He couldn't imagine leaving his daughter for anything. From the first minute he held her in his arms, he was hooked. She had reached up with a closed fist and batted his jaw. It was as if she'd reached inside his chest and gripped his heart in her little hand.

"Just promise me no more trouble, okay? You can't go back to school dressed like that. I don't have time to get called down to the principal's office." He closed the window again and turned off the engine. He had to get inside and get some work done.

"I should be able to wear what I want. It's a stupid rule."

"You want to settle in and make a good impression."

"Or what? Are you afraid I won't amount to anything if people don't like me?"

He was the wrong person to answer that question. "I want you to stay out of trouble until you're old enough to bail yourself out. Can you do that?"

"I didn't get in trouble for drugs or having sex. I don't know why you're making such a big deal about this. I could be a drug addict, you know. There's a heroin epidemic in this country."

"Madeline, just promise me you won't do it again." Frustration slipped into his voice even as he tried to keep it out. He ran a hand over his face. He might actually call Colton and have a beer with him and Blaise. He needed a night out.

"Fine. I'll wear a nun's habit to school tomorrow."

He took a risk and gathered her in his arms across the seat. Sometimes he missed when she was little and climbed into his lap to show him her stuffed animals. This time she accepted the hug. "Make sure it has one of those chastity-belt things too."

She groaned. "Dad, your stupid hat is hitting me in the head."

He laughed and threw the thing in the back. He eased her away so he could see her face. "Your mother's leaving isn't about you. That's on her."

"Do you have anything to eat in that place yet? I'm starving. I didn't get to go to lunch." She shoved open the truck door and closed down all her emotions. Just like him.

He pushed out into the hot day too. "You can get something at the bakery." He reached for his wallet.

"What about that Tea Room? That looks nice."

If he protested too much, she'd go straight there. "Don't know anything about it." He handed her a twenty. "I'll be inside. Be polite to Mrs. Lewis if you go to the bakery."

"Like I wouldn't." She rolled her eyes, turned, and crossed the street toward the bakery. He let out a long breath. At least she stayed out of the tea shop.

He couldn't call his old friends even if he wanted to. Getting anywhere close to Savannah would only stir up trouble. She might start asking questions he couldn't answer.

Parker stuck his head out of the deli's door. Correction. The Whiskey Bar's door. "JT, you ever coming back to work? We've got a problem."

Savannah filled small mason jars with tea leaves. The smell of apple, cinnamon, mulled spice, and pumpkin floated around her. She needed people to buy these new fall flavors and fast because she had that tiny problem of running through all of Adam's life insurance money.

Now she couldn't pay for Jud's college. In fact, she didn't have the money for any of the kids to go to college. She wasn't sure if she could make the mortgage payment on the store, buy the dresses for her brother's wedding, and meet a myriad of other expenses. The Tea Room had taken more capital than she'd realized.

If she could win the spot as caterer for the Heritage River one-hundred-and-sixtieth-anniversary, black-tie dinner, her problems might be solved. That kind of exposure would bring in customers. If she could wait that long.

"You're spilling tea leaves." Harley leaned against the doorframe into the back of the shop, which was basically the small kitchen. She had her hair pulled up in a messy bun that looked perfect, a look she could never seem to pull off.

"Don't you have an art class to teach?" Her mind had been on the dark eyes and tight jeans of her past instead of packing tea without making waste. Guilt sat down on her chest.

She should be thinking about her late husband. But like sunlight spilling through the cracks in a wall, JT seeped into her thoughts over and over. She'd thought about him so much over the years sometimes she wondered if she was being fair to Adam. How could she have a life with one man, a good life, and relive memories of another man whenever her mind was lost for something to ponder on?

"I do have a class." Harley bit into a cinnamon bun from May's and scooped her big tote onto her shoulder.

"You're eating at the competition's."

"I know. I'm sorry. I can't turn down anything from May's. I'm an addict. I hung up three new paintings out

31

in the table area. Thank you again for allowing my students to display their stuff in here. Eventually, I'll get the gallery fully running if Colton would ever stop giving me his two cents."

She raised an eyebrow. "Are you sure you want to marry my very challenging brother?"

"Never more. He's the love of my life. Plus, the easy-going one was already taken." She laughed. "Don't tell him I said that. He'll get mad. You know how competitive he is. Oh, you and I have to talk about the wedding menu."

"We will. He's very lucky to have you, and so am I. Now scoot. I've got work to do, and you have minds to inspire and murals to paint."

"Are you worried about whatever is going in at Jake's?"

She kept her gaze on the butcher-block table covered in flour. "I heard his son owns it now." It was the only thing that made sense.

"Rae went snooping earlier. She said it looked like a bar was going in. Colton mentioned once or twice that JT owned some bars now, but I haven't seen him anywhere on Main Street. Could be him." Harley finished the last of her bun and licked her fingers.

How that woman could eat so much junk food and never gain an ounce was beyond her.

"We won't have any problem with a bar. Our clientele is completely different. I'll go down later and say hello to the owners. Welcome them to the street." The Tea Room focused on lunch, salads, wraps, soups. They provided a lighter fare that went well with tea. Completely different from bar food. See? Everything would be fine.

But if he wanted to compete in the anniversary dinner competition, that could be a problem. She hoped she had the catering opportunity in the bag because the caterer had to be from Heritage River. May only made baked goods. Jake's was gone. Their little town didn't have a lot of restaurants, and many of them were participating in the parade. The rule was a restaurant couldn't do both.

"I'll see you tomorrow." Harley hurried from the shop. The bell above the door escorted her out onto the street.

Savannah began the daily closing routine of pulling all the food that didn't get sold. She fixed a box of scones to bring home, one for each brother and their families and one extra. She couldn't sell them after the day they were baked, but she wouldn't waste them. Sometimes she brought them to the neighbors who needed a pick-me-up. She swept the floor and sanitized all the surfaces.

She went into the dining room and navigated around the small tables set for two or four. Each table was made of mahogany and covered in a simple lace tablecloth. Four crystal chandeliers hung from the ceiling. They were an extravagant purchase and ones Colton told her not to make. He'd stuck his nose in her business too. He was a smart businessman and talented musician, but she chose to do things her way.

On the sidewall was an old-fashioned buffet that

displayed antique teapots. She turned out all the lights. She loved this room.

She gathered her boxes of scones and threw her tote bag over her shoulder. With her free hand, she locked the front door, then mustered up the energy to go greet the new neighbor. The stupid dumpster took up too many parking spots. How had the town allowed this? Maybe she should make an anonymous call to complain.

Warm September air helped her down the street. The sky was the brilliant blue that only happened that time of year. Hopefully, the next few weeks held the weather. The parade would be nicer on a day like this.

The town council hadn't announced the small events leading up to the black-tie dinner. Those could be outside too, but they had organized the painting of a two-paneled mural on the side of the old feed mill that had once been the place for local farmers to get what they needed for their farms but had been shut for two decades. Harley and her students were handling that project.

The door to Jake's swung open, nearly hitting her in the face. She jumped back and dropped the boxes of scones. "Hey," she said. If she hadn't been deep in thought, she might've noticed the door.

"You've got to be kidding me." JT dumped a full trash bag into the dumpster. He had on a black T-shirt pulled across broad shoulders that showed off a cobra tattoo on the inside of his left bicep. His hair was cut close, but he still kept his sideburns a little longer. They blended right into the scruff on his jaw. He looked better standing there than he had when they were young. He'd grown into himself.

"You almost hit me with that door. You should be more careful." She squatted down to pick up the scones. She had to chase a few that rolled away. She must look like a mad frog. Was her butt sticking up? Did she look fat? She stood. *Forget the damn scones.*

"Did you come down here to offer me your dessert as a welcome-to-the-neighborhood thing? Savannah Savage, always the perfect neighbor. You probably run the welcome committee here in town too."

She had run a few welcome committees over the years, but that wasn't the point. "I was doing no such thing. Don't flatter yourself. My minivan is over there." She pointed past his shoulder and lifted her chin, hoping he'd believe the lie. "Why are you still acting like a petulant child?"

"You're right. I'm exactly the same as I was. I turned out to be the garbageman after all." He pointed to the dumpster.

"I don't get it." Then his words hit her. Mr. Viking, the old high school principal, had hated him. With good reason, unfortunately, but the man's mean words "someone has to be the garbageman" had cut JT and left a scar. "I never thought that."

He stepped closer and leaned in. He smelled like oak, and heat rolled off him. "You did and probably still do."

"Don't go accusing me of things I didn't say." She had believed he could be anything he wanted if he had only tried. Other than hanging with her brothers and dragging their equipment from one backyard party to another, he hadn't seemed to have a goal. But she always knew he had potential. He never saw it in himself.

"Take your boxes back to your tea shop, Savannah."

"I was just trying to be friendly." Maybe they could find their way to being friends. She'd be happy with that. They had been once.

He yanked open the door to Jake's, then stopped. "Oh, nothing personal, but there isn't room on this street for both of us. You'll have to go."

She flinched. "I beg your pardon? Are you talking about my tea shop?"

"Yes, darlin'. I eat the competition for lunch. Just thought you should know."

"Is that some kind of a threat?" The businesses could exist on the same street, but if he wanted a competition, he would get one.

"Not a threat. Just stating a fact. Once the Whiskey Bar is up and running, you won't stand a chance. By Thanksgiving you'll be taking your sign down."

"Good luck with that. The Savages are part of the fabric of this town. Your father was a part of that too, but you're the outsider. This town has its loyalties. I'm not worried about the patronage of my shop, but if you want a fight on your hands, you've got it. I'm not afraid of you, JT Davies. You don't scare me. Never did."

He stormed into the store without another word.

She kicked a rogue scone into the road. He might not scare her, but he sure as hell made her blood boil. Damn him and his ability to get under her skin. She should be over him, not have a care in the world for him.

But here she was, trudging down the street with JT Davies snarled in every thought.

She'd show him. She could compete with the best of them.

She hoped.

Chapter Six

JT wanted to kick himself. Instead, he kicked the empty shipping box and stuck his foot in it. *Outsider?* Did Savannah really think he didn't belong in Heritage River? Of course she did. They had always been from different sides of the tracks. It didn't matter that he had been friends with her brothers. She had been the shooting star, and he had been the garbageman. The argument had been his fault. He told her he was coming after her business. Real smooth.

"Hey, easy on the cardboard." Parker materialized from the back room, reviewing sheets on a clipboard.

He tugged the box off his foot and stomped on it.

"Having a bad day?" Parker smirked.

He had met Parker more than a dozen years ago at college during a business class. Parker had sat beside him and asked a lot of questions about the bar business because he'd been bartending to make ends meet.

Together they'd invested in their first Whiskey Bar and never looked back. Parker knew him better than most.

He ran a hand over his face. "Why are women so much trouble?" Every woman in his life had him spinning in circles, from his stepmother, to his ex, to that beautiful woman with long, dark hair and eyes the color of steel. He thought he was over her, but as soon as he could smell her sweet scent, which hadn't changed, he wanted to pull her into his arms and kiss her until she begged him for more.

He hadn't meant to be such an ass to her. She deserved better than that, and especially from him, but he couldn't stop himself. She'd rejected him that night with those four little words, and he'd been pissed off about it ever since.

He hadn't been good enough for her then, but he'd show her. He'd turned himself around, made something of himself. So why did he want to put her out of business? To prove a point. To win. *Grow the fuck up.*

"Are you seeing someone?" Parker pulled a bottle of Jack out from behind the bar and held up two glasses.

"None for me, thanks. I've got to get Maddy home soon. And no, I'm not seeing anyone. I've got enough on my hands at the moment. I don't need to get tangled up with a woman too."

"Then who has you spitting nails? Was it that attractive lady you were talking to on the sidewalk?"

Yes. "No. I knew her a long time ago. She came by to say hello. Her brothers are in the band Savage. In fact, they are the band Savage."

"You're kidding? Do you know them too?"

"When we were kids, before they hit it big, I used to help them out with equipment and stuff. We used to be tight." Until he slept with their little sister. He couldn't exactly look his buddies in the eye after that for fear Blaise would be able to read his mind and punch him in the face, which he would deserve. Even today.

"You've got to get them to play here. Maybe as a grand opening or something. Do you know how many people we'd draw with Savage playing?"

"I don't think they're that popular anymore. Blaise ended their last tour about a year ago, and they never went back on the road. I think his brother is teaching at the high school." He had been shocked to see Colton in the school. When they were kids, Colton had skipped school whenever he had the chance.

The story floating around the internet was that Blaise had ended Savage's last tour because his son got arrested. He should have called Blaise to check on him, but he hadn't, and when he was home around Christmas, he hadn't even knocked on their doors.

"If Colton Savage is a teacher, he'd be glad to get back on stage. He was the ultimate front man. Can you ask them? What would it hurt to ask? All they can say is no. Think about it. Whiskey and Savage. Goes perfect together. If you don't want to ask, I will, but the request will probably be better coming from you. I can see it now. We could Facebook Live it." Parker stared off, looking at some image he'd rather not think about.

How was he going to ask Colton and Blaise to play

for him? He'd just told their sister he was going to put her out of business. He really needed to learn to shut his mouth. Still the old JT, no matter how much he tried to run from it.

If he didn't call Colton, Parker would. Better he made that call and felt things out first. "I'll ask, but no promises."

Maddy pushed through the door. "Dad, I love that bakery across the street. It's adorable. The woman who owns it—her name is Maybelline, but you know that. She wants you to stop by and say a 'proper hello.' That's a quote. She told me she knows all kinds of stories about you when you were young. She promised to tell me. Hey, Parker."

"Afternoon, Maddy."

He'd make sure to go across the street and have a chat with Maybelline Lewis. Maddy did not need to hear about his younger days. "I'll go over soon and say hello."

She pulled a folded piece of paper out of her back pocket and handed it over. "Did you know the town is celebrating its hundred-and-sixtieth anniversary? That's old. Like you." She laughed.

Parker snickered behind his hand.

"Funny." He scanned the paper. The town had several events planned to commemorate the anniversary. All of which would lead up to a black-tie dinner catered by a restaurant in town.

"Mrs. Lewis said the bakery is going to be in the parade." Maddy unraveled her earbuds from her phone.

"I don't really like parades, but I might want to see what she puts together."

May had made an impression on Maddy. Not surprising. Everyone loved May and her big hugs. She had often watched out for him when he was a kid, offering advice whether he wanted it or not.

"Why didn't you bring me here when Grandpa was alive? I like this little town."

She changed her mind the way fire moved in the wind. He'd never brought her to Heritage River because he was busy with work, and his dad was willing to come out to them for holidays. Jake always had a good staff he could trust to mind the store while he was away. His step-mother might have been good for nothing while his dad was sick, but she knew how to watch the register at least.

"What was it like growing up here? Was it great?"

He'd never told her any of his stories. He figured it was better she didn't know too much about his bad choices. His dad had been all too happy to hold those stories close to his chest. He appreciated that. Hopefully, he'd told his dad how thankful he was for keeping his secrets.

He glanced over at his daughter. Should he tell her about the time he crashed the boat? Or the time he got shot with a BB gun? He could also tell her about how no teacher thought he'd amount to much and how maybe bringing her to Heritage River was a big mistake because some people would judge her because of him. Or he could tell her Savannah thought he was an outsider who would never be accepted in this town.

"Yeah, kiddo, growing up here was great. Can you finish up today, Parker? I'll unpack the rest of the liquor tomorrow." He folded the flyer back up. A black-tie dinner? Some ideas smoldered in his mind.

"Sure. I'm the partner that does all the work anyway."

He gave Parker the finger, but he only smirked in return.

"Dad, you just flipped him off."

"You didn't see that. Let's hit the road." He had some plans to make, and they included a town's fancy dinner.

He would show the people of Heritage River. If he won that dinner, they'd have to say he'd made something of himself. He wouldn't be an outsider any longer.

Savannah held a broom over her head. Something had been scurrying around the attic for a week, and she'd been too afraid to come up and inspect. In the past, she would've sent Adam, but he wasn't there, and Jud was away at college. Grey and Caroline were afraid of spiders. A creature with clicking paws on wood was out of their realm. She could call her brothers, but they'd laugh at her until she was old, blind, and deaf. No thanks. The broom would have to do. She teased her foot on the plywood lying over the beams in the floor. The last thing she needed was to fall through the ceiling.

A critter had left tiny poop pellets as a gift. *Gross.*

The unwelcome guest had also chewed on her insulation and the plastic coating around the pipes. She'd have to poison the thing to get it out of her house permanently. The internet had to provide instructions on how to kill a squirrel or raccoon. She couldn't afford an exterminator. YouTube would have to do. She could handle a simple poison job. She'd handled everything else life threw at her.

Whatever was in her attic wasn't there now. She shoved dusty boxes away from the crime scene, not wanting this unwelcomed guest to chew on her possessions.

A plastic container tucked in the back corner away from everything else, including the sunlight that streamed through the two windows in the attic, caught her eye.

She dragged it back over the plywood and under the lightbulb suspended from the beam above her. Adam's grandmother had saved Christmas ornaments from when she was a little girl. Their family didn't have much, but they cherished spending Christmas together.

His grandmother had kept the ornaments as a special memory of her childhood. It wasn't fair that he'd never get to see them on the tree again.

"Mom, I can't figure out my homework. Can you help me?" Caroline yelled up the attic steps.

"I'll be right down." She put the box back and left the broom behind.

Caroline held her laptop in one hand and a piece of paper in the other. She'd piled her hair into a knot on the top of her head. She'd swapped her jeans for pajama pants but still wore Adam's sweatshirt. Savannah would need to sneak that thing away and wash it soon.

"Let's go in my office. What are you working on?" Her desk was a mess of papers, candy wrappers, and half-drunk mugs of tea.

"Pre-algebra. I stink at math. I'm the worst kind of student. Jud and Grey are smart, but I'm not. All my friends are smarter than I am too. They're all in advanced math. Why do I even have to take math?"

She made room on her desk and waved Caroline over. "You are smart. You just have to find another way to study. Show me the problem." She wasn't sure if she could help with pre-algebra, but she'd try.

"I'm not smart. My grades are terrible. I'm going to fail math and science. And did you know I haven't passed one Spanish test in the past three years?"

"That isn't true. You never failed Spanish class. Have you tried the flashcards?"

"Flashcards don't work. Maybe I didn't fail the whole class, but that was because of my classwork and group projects, but I failed every single test."

"You have to keep going over the material until you know it." The second half of last school year, she hadn't been paying attention as much to the kids' schoolwork. She'd walked around in a fog, adjusting to losing her husband, but she'd pulled herself together and started a new business. Maybe she should have been more focused on Caroline.

Unfortunately, before she could really get her footing, her past showed up and smacked her in the jaw.

She'd always wanted to see JT again just to talk and make sure he was okay. She'd never imagined they'd have a fight at their first reunion.

"Mom, you're not listening. You know what? I think I'll Facetime Gretchen and see if she can help me with math."

"We haven't even started. I can help you." How long had she checked out? Or was this another one of Caroline's teen mood swings? She hated to say this, probably would never say it out loud, but girls were much harder to raise than boys. *Harder* wasn't the right word, not after what she'd been through with Jud. *Different*. Girls were *different* from boys in a more challenging way.

"It's okay. You have something on your mind. Gretchen is in Algebra One. She'll help me study."

"I want to know you know the material. Why can't you study with me?"

"I don't want to study with you. Dad was always the one to help me with math. I want Dad back." She blinked away tears.

The pain on Caroline's face crushed her heart. "I'm sorry, honey. I wish he was here too, but it's just us."

Caroline rolled her eyes with the skill of a pro. "Yeah, I know it's just us. I live here." And she marched out of the room.

The anger was to be expected. The school therapist had said as much. She couldn't find a private therapist within an hour's drive who took her insurance, and she couldn't afford the out-of-pocket expense.

Her shoulders dropped a little now that she wouldn't

have to deal with eighth-grade homework. Wanting that cup of tea and some alone time turned her stomach sour. She was a bad mother for wanting time away from her kids.

Grey never asked for help with his schoolwork, and she could hardly help him now that he was a sophomore. If he became really stuck, he'd call Jud. The boys were close. They reminded her of Colton and Blaise growing up. Sometimes she felt a little on the outside of two brothers joined by their love of music. She loved music too and could play the piano as well as her brothers because her father had insisted they all learn, but she'd never been a part of their dream to make it big.

Instead of following music, she followed her father's rules. He didn't want his children involved with modern music. Colton and Blaise had frustrated him, often times angered him. She wanted to please her father so he'd continue to look at her as if she were the most special child in the world. She'd pushed her interests aside for approval. Every one of them. Including JT.

Did Caroline ever feel like an intruder to two older brothers? Savannah had never asked. Her heart was heavy. She wanted to put her feet up and read a good romance novel if she wasn't going to get any in real life. She needed to recharge. In the morning, she'd feel ready to take on the world again.

Her computer pinged. A new email appeared in her inbox from Caroline's teacher. She had to read it twice:

I believe Caroline has a visual-processing problem... checked out by an eye doctor...might explain her focus and learning issues...won't be ready for high school...intervention.

She jumped up from the chair to ask Adam's opinion and then remembered and sat down with a thud. Adam's absence was most noticeable at times like these. Did he think Caroline had a visual-processing problem? Did he think the teacher was a kook because she kind of did?

Was the teacher saying Caroline wouldn't be able to go to high school? That was ten months away. She just needed better study skills, that's all. What did the teacher know? She hardly knew Caroline.

Could her child have a visual-processing problem? A medical condition would explain a lot. Was poor visual processing even a medical condition? How had she missed this until now? What kind of a mother misses her child's suffering? Her head pounded with each question.

She didn't know where to begin to fix this. A response to the teacher might be a good place to start, but she didn't have the energy to search for the right words. Tomorrow. She'd respond tomorrow when her mind was fresh and after she Googled visual processing.

Maybe she should call Harley. She might've heard about this during her years of teaching art at the high school. She picked up the phone and tapped at the screen.

The phone rang and rang. She was about to hang up. "Hey. What's up?" Colton's voice boomed across the line instead of Harley's.

He had moved into Harley's place at Christmas last year, after he asked her to marry him. She had a beautiful

48

old house on acres of land on the edge of Heritage River. Harley was good for Colton. She kept him grounded and sober, something she and Blaise appreciated.

She'd like a house with lots of land and space to roam around. She bit back a laugh. Talk about big dreams. "Is Harley home?" She looked inside the mug closest to her. Empty.

"What? You can't talk to me?"

"If I wanted to talk to you, I would've called your phone. Is she out?" She gathered the mugs and went into the kitchen. She left them on the counter beside the sink full of dirty dishes.

"She's in the shower. I saw it was you, so I picked up. Are the kids okay?"

"The kids are fine. I just wanted to ask her opinion about something." She leaned against the counter and tugged on her necklace.

"I have opinions."

"Yes, Colton, we all know you have opinions, but I want to talk to Harley. Can you have her call me?"

"Savannah, it's me. You can tell me if you need anything."

Growing up without their mother had bonded her and her siblings together. Even when she was being a giant bitch to him, Colton always loved her. "Thank you, but I'm fine, really. I want to ask her a teacher question."

"You definitely don't want me for that." He laughed.

"You are a rather unorthodox teacher."

"Shit, yeah. I'm Colton Savage, baby. How about running into JT Davies? That was a blast from the past.

He called Blaise. Said he wanted to see us. What do you think that's about?"

As long as it wasn't about her, she didn't care. She put a kettle of water up. "He wants your autograph? Wait a second." He wouldn't dare, would he? "Don't you even think about playing at his whiskey bar."

"So he is putting in another one of his bars. Cool. Hell yes, I'll play. As long as I can get Blaise and Cash to do it. Knox will say yes in a second. I don't have to worry about him. He is all Savage. I love that kid." Not only had Colton found true love last year, he found out he had a son too.

"Colton Thomas, you can't play for JT Davies. He threatened to put me out of business. He said there wasn't enough space on the street for both of us. He's still the same asshat he was." He also still had a really nice ass, not that she looked.

"*Asshat?* Those are fighting words. What is it between you two? I never understood why you couldn't get along with him. He wasn't that bad. I was a hell of a lot worse than he was."

"You're my brother. I'm stuck with you." *Oh, and that thing between us, we slept together on my graduation night, and he broke my heart.* That was just a minor detail neither brother knew about.

"You might be stuck with me, but that doesn't explain why you can't get along with JT. Did he really threaten to run you out of business?"

"Yes." She stood up straighter. "Please tell me you'll say no if that's what he wants."

"Let me see what he says first. Blaise might want to help an old friend out. You know how he is."

She did. Blaise would say yes, and Colton could never pass up a chance to have people clapping for him.

"When are you meeting with him?"

"Tomorrow night."

"Don't agree to anything until you talk to me first." She needed to find a way to convince Blaise not to help out JT. She could tell him about that night. Her virtue would be something her big brothers would take seriously. Even now. Cavemen, both of them.

"I don't know. This might be music business. That's me and Blaise. You know how it is. It's nothing personal, but a gig is a gig."

"What about solidarity amongst siblings? We stick together. Why can't you do this for me? Just call me first."

"Something's going on here. Did he do more than say he wanted to put you out of business? Did he touch you? I'll kill him."

"Settle down. I just don't like having my new business threatened."

"He's hardly your competition. Are you sure you two didn't have a fight about something else?"

"I'm sure. Just have Harley call me when she can, okay?" She needed to steer the conversation away from JT.

"Yeah, I will."

"I'll see you for Sunday dinner?" She had started a new tradition after Adam died and Colton returned to town.

"Harley wouldn't let me miss it."

"She's a keeper." She envied the relationships her brothers had and they way they were with their women.

Blaise always kept Grace within his reach, placing a hand on her low back when they walked into a room. He'd smile down at her, and her whole face lit up, as if his smile were a special gift just for her. Colton always had an arm around Harley or was whispering sweet words in her ear that had her blushing.

She and Adam had never been like that. They'd never shared public displays of affection. He hadn't looked at her as if she were the only woman in the room. He'd grown to take for granted that she kept his house clean, his laundry done, and the groceries stocked. More times than she liked to think about, he barely heard a word she'd said because his face was in his tablet or watching television. She wanted a man to see her the way her brothers saw their women, not as his personal assistant.

"You don't have to tell me Harley is the best. I'm the luckiest bastard in the world," Colton said, dragging her back to the phone call.

"Remember to talk to me before you say yes to JT." She ended the call, not waiting for another response, and turned off the burner.

Forget the tea. She needed a drink.

Chapter Seven

"**D**ad, you promised we'd watch a movie together."

JT dropped the pen on the table. Maddy stood in the doorway to the dining room with her arms crossed over her chest, her phone in her hand, and his snarl on her face. How did his father put up with his attitude all those years? *I'm sorry I barked at you so much, Dad.*

"I need five more minutes." Papers covered the dining room table like trampled confetti. He needed to organize the bills and receipts. The shipment of gin had been short, and he couldn't find the original invoice. Industry magazines begged to be read. He had made copies of his liquor license and then spilled coffee on them. He needed to run off more tonight.

"You said that ten minutes ago. You promised we'd spend more time together if we lived here."

How could he forget? She reminded him every

chance she could. He should be glad she demanded his attention. At her age, all he ever wanted to do was go out with Blaise and stir up trouble. *Blaise.* He needed to call him back and move the time they were meeting. He tried not to growl.

"I'm trying. Once the Whiskey Bar is up and running, things will slow down." He needed to hire a manager to run the place. His bartending days were over, even though he liked talking to customers. He was the partner out in front with the crowd. Parker was the analytical one, the behind-the-scenes one. They had plans for more Whiskey Bars around the state. Wait until Maddy found out about that. They weren't moving for the time being. Whether he liked it or not, Heritage River was his home again.

She plopped down in the chair next to him and scrolled through her Instagram account. "The school is putting a float in the anniversary parade. There's a committee of students working on it."

He punched numbers on the calculator. "Did you join it?"

"I don't know anyone on that committee. They aren't going to want someone new."

"That might not be true."

"Dad, you're not even looking at me."

"Sorry." He pulled his gaze away from the spreadsheet and held hers.

"I met a boy in class today. He seemed okay. He helped me with some of the notes because I wasn't in class the other day. Afterward we walked together. I didn't know where I was going, so he showed me how to get to science."

"I'm glad you're making friends." He'd rather she made a few girlfriends. He knew what boys that age usually wanted. He had certainly wanted it. "Who is this boy?" He wagged his eyebrows, hoping for a smile.

He got the scowl instead. "Dad, it's not like that. We're just friends. His name is Grey. He plays soccer, and he's in my AP history class. Are you going to watch the movie with me, or should I start it without you?"

"I just need to make a quick call."

"Fine." She huffed and pouted.

Before he could pick up the phone to dial Blaise, his phone woke up with Parker's name on the screen. "What's up?"

"I was about to close up for the night. I think you need to come down here."

"Why?" They weren't even open, and they had problems.

"Your stepmother is here, and she won't leave."

Fuck.

JT parked in the back of the Whiskey Bar and let himself in through the kitchen entrance. The sounds of his footsteps were muffled by the anti-fatigue mats on the floor used to help with the hours of standing his employees would do.

He'd renovated Jake's old kitchen and built a wall to

block the view of the patrons, unlike his dad's place where everyone who entered Jake's had a front-row seat for the making of the food.

The butcher-block prep stations waited for their first day of business. Skillets, sauté pans, and saucepans hung from the ceiling. He'd kept the wood beams his father loved so much and had them restained in a dark finish. All the storage and appliances were a high-polish stainless steel. Even in the dim light, they shone.

He passed into the front of the restaurant, where his stepmother sat at the distressed mahogany bar. Her hair had gone a few rounds with too much peroxide and lost, and her skin, once smooth and firm, now had pores he could drive his car through and more lines than a detailed road map. Parker poured a beer into a glass and handed it to her.

"Shirley, what are you doing here?" He debated on taking that glass from her.

She turned her head in his direction and stared at him with milky eyes. "Jakie, is that you?"

Shirley was the only person on the planet who refused to use his nickname and gave him one she liked better. Which he hated. "Yeah, it's me. Parker, I've got this if you want to go."

"Night, Shirley." He planted a kiss on her cheek and headed out the front door.

"Good night, sweetheart. Thanks for the beer."

Just the two of them. Lucky him.

"Did you drive here by yourself?" he said.

She'd moved out of the house she shared with his father, the one he lived in now, when Hoke Carter told her Jake had left the house to him. She'd been ripe with anger and refused to go until Hoke showed up with Sheriff Jones. His father had left her plenty of money to buy a new house. She wanted her old one. He'd thought about giving it to her. For a minute.

"I miss him." She turned the beer glass in small circles. "I came here to feel him around me, and Jake's was gone. I think I overreacted." She sniffled.

Great. "What did you do?" This time.

"I banged on the windows and doors. I might've been yelling too. That bakery bitch across the street called Sheriff Jones on me, but Parker came out and saved the day. I'm sorry, Jakie."

"JT."

"JT. You were always so difficult about that. What's wrong with a term of endearment from your mama?"

Stepmother. "You know you can't keep coming here and doing stuff like that. We talked about this. I don't want anything to happen to you, but this is my business now. I'm going to have customers in here soon. I can't have them being upset."

"It isn't fair that you got the house and his store. He didn't leave me anything."

It wasn't true, but he wasn't going to argue with her. "I can help you invest the money if you want." He went around the bar and poured himself a shot of whiskey. He needed help finishing this conversation.

"You?" She laughed. "You aren't any good with

numbers. That sweet and handsome Parker handles the money around here. You're just the muscle."

He tried not to flinch. "Do you need a ride home? I can call you a cab."

She waved his offer away. "You're the expert on drinking, aren't you? How many times did your father have to come haul you out of a jail for drinking and getting in fights? I'm fine to drive."

She could never stay off memory lane. "How many drinks have you had?" He could put her up in a hotel if she wouldn't go all the way home tonight. But he wouldn't let her drive if she'd drunk too much, no matter what she said about him.

"First one." She pointed to the still-full glass. "I'm not a drunk, even though you told your father I was. I'm just sad. He wasn't supposed to die and go and leave his deli to you. You didn't earn it. Always in trouble growing up. If it wasn't for me, you'd be in prison now, and what's the thanks I get? You leave me homeless." She shoved the glass. It tipped, spraying the beer all over the bar and onto the floor. He lunged for a towel to clean up the spill.

"I'm sorry, Jakie, but you made me so angry I forgot myself for a second."

"For Christ's sake, my name is JT. When are you going to figure that out?" His voice echoed off the brick walls.

She recoiled and almost fell off the barstool.

"The reason why I'm not in prison is because of me." He stabbed his chest. "You didn't have one goddamn thing to do with it. My father, Jake—say his name when you talk about him—is gone. That's it. He left you plenty of money to buy three houses, but your head is so clouded from all your drinking you can't read the bank statements. Now get out of my bar and don't come back, or I'll call Sheriff Jones myself."

Her eyes widened with a clearness he hadn't seen in a while. She covered her head with her arm, as if he'd tried to hit her, and slid from the barstool. She pushed through the door and out into the night without another word.

"Fuck." He threw the beer glass against the wall. It shattered into a thousand pieces. He walked into it every damn time. When was he going to learn?

He went to the supply closet to retrieve the broom and dustpan. His hands shook as he swept up the glass, but with each stroke more glass ended up on the floor than the pan. His dad had promised him that Shirley knew his wishes, said he'd taken care of it, but that didn't seem to be the case.

Shirley had hated him his whole life. She'd always wanted him to be someone he wasn't and resented him because she'd never had a child of her own. She couldn't wait to see him go. She had said as much the day he shoved some clothes into a duffel and left.

The door swung open. He hung his head. "Shirley, please go home."

"It's not Shirley."

He turned in the direction of the voice. A slow burn

crept up his neck and across his face. "Savannah, I'm having a really bad night. Can you just go back out and leave me alone?"

She stepped farther inside and let the door swing shut. "How dare you think you can put me out of business? You come back to town, and you disrupt everything with your dumpster in the street blocking my customers from parking. You were rude and inconsiderate when I was trying to be neighborly. And if all that wasn't bad enough, you ask my brothers to play at your bar. My brothers."

He fumbled with the broom and the glass. "Now isn't the time."

"Now is exactly the time. Whatever your problem is with me, deal with it. My tea shop isn't going anywhere and certainly not because of you." Her eyes smoldered like hot coal.

"Are you out of steam yet?"

"What?"

"Well, woman, you come barreling into my place yelling at me. I'm waiting for you to stop before I try to speak." He bent to pick up the glass, and a piece slit his finger open. "Fuck."

"Did you cut yourself?"

"I'm fine." He grabbed a towel and wrapped it around his finger.

"Let me help you." The fire burned out of her eyes, turning them to ash.

"I don't need your help. I'm sorry about the dumpster, but the company won't come back to move it. I'm paying a fine if that makes you feel any better." The towel slipped. He reached for it and knocked the broom over.

"It does." Her gaze drifted around the bar. "Oh, for goodness' sakes, let me help you." She marched over and picked up the broom.

He could handle her tilted chin and defiant glare, but he couldn't deal with her softer side tonight. The side she'd shown him in small steps trying to trust him. The side of her who laughed at his jokes, who took his hand and navigated the wet rocks in the stream so she wouldn't fall, who'd held her arms out to him because she saw something in him no one else had. He had been wrong about that.

She tucked her hair behind her neck. If he got a whiff of her sweet scent, he might crumble. Her skin was creamy, and he wanted to run his tongue over it. "Only you would walk into a place you've never been and take completely over."

She flashed him a quick smile. "Some things never change, I guess. I saw you throw that glass. I also saw Shirley walking down the street. She wobbled a little. Do you want to talk about what happened?"

"No."

"Of course not." She swept up the last of the glass with ease. "It looks great in here. I like the chalkboards with the drink lists. That's a nice testament to Jake. He would be proud."

"Thanks. I like to think so." His father had kept the

deli menu on a chalkboard hanging above the meat counter. He never had paper menus, and when someone in town wanted to make an adjustment to a sandwich or salad, Jake just added it to the chalkboard. Every Whiskey Bar had the liquor listed on chalkboards in his dad's honor.

"Your dad always sang your praises." She dumped the glass in a plastic bag and put it in the garbage. "Do you want me to look at your hand?"

If she touched him, he'd burn from the inside out. "No, thanks." He scratched the back of his neck with his good hand. "Listen, I'm sorry I said I wanted to put you out of business. I shouldn't have said that."

"No, you shouldn't have. Well, I said my piece about my brothers. I want it on the record I'm against them playing here, but Colton will do what he wants anyway. I'll be going now." She turned for the door.

"Savannah, wait." He held up the bottle of whiskey he opened earlier. "Do you have time for a quick glass?" He should let her go, but she was the fire he always wanted to play with.

Her smile lit up her gray eyes, and something pulled low in his belly. He took that smile as a yes, poured two shots, and passed her a glass.

"Thank you for coming in here and cleaning up."

He'd screwed up when he left without saying good-bye. They'd gone their separate ways. She'd moved on without him and done fine for herself, which was exactly what he thought she would do and had every right to do.

"Are you sure you don't want to talk about what happened between you and Shirley?"

"Why were you walking up and down Main Street at this hour?"

"Changing the subject. That's fine. I needed to get out of the house for a little while, didn't know where to go, and found myself sitting in the minivan in front of the Tea Room."

He held up his glass. "Here's to avoiding conflict." The whiskey burned a line down his throat.

"This stuff is terrible." She shook her head and grimaced.

"Are you out tonight because you don't want to be home with your husband?" He didn't see a ring on her finger, but she'd been at the high school. She must have kids there. He could ask Blaise when he saw him, but he didn't want Blaise sniffing anything out.

"I lost my husband nine months ago." She took a tentative sip.

"Wow, I'm sorry. I didn't know. Are you okay?"

He leaned his forearms on the bar, putting him eye to eye with her. *Back up, dude.*

She had lost her husband before his father died. When he had been in town, his only mission was his dad. He hadn't bothered to ask around about the old gang. He should have.

She held his gaze but drank more. "I miss him late at night when the house is quiet, the kids are sleeping, and it's just me."

"How many kids do you have?" He wanted to know

63

everything about her. What had she been doing since he left? And he wanted to smooth out the crease between her brow while she spoke about her hurt. Big mistake. This woman was off limits for many reasons.

"Three." She emptied her glass. "This stuff kind of grows on you. Can I have a little more? Is it just you and your daughter, or is there a Mrs. JT hiding someplace?"

He splashed a finger size in the glass for her. "No missus for me. Divorced now about five years. We got the fastest divorce in history." It was hard to put up a fight when his wife left him and his daughter for her trainer. Audrey wanted nothing from him. She'd changed her name as soon as the ink was dry, tried to see Maddy the first Christmas they were apart, but after that she'd made herself scarce.

"Are you back in town for good?" Her words slurred as if they were coated in oil, or whiskey. "Can I have some more of that, please? My purse is in the car. I can pay for these drinks since we're not friends anymore."

"I think you may have had enough to drink." He'd never take her money.

She pointed to the glass. "A little more. I haven't been this relaxed in...I don't know how long. How long have you been gone?"

The tightness returned to his belly again. She hadn't forgotten about their time together. How often had she thought of him? He poured a splash more and put the bottle away. The last thing he needed was for her to tell Colton and Blaise he'd gotten her drunk. Never mind they were consenting adults.

"You didn't answer my question. Are you now a permanent resident of Heritage River?"

"I am. This is a good town for Maddy to be in. She needs roots and stability. Something I've struggled with giving her because my work always has me moving around." He'd said way more to this woman than he meant to.

"I'm glad. The place hasn't been the same since you left." She downed the rest of the booze. "Whoa. I think the room just took a turn on the dance floor." She slid off the stool and held her arms out as if she were on a tight-wire.

"Looks like I better call a ride for you." He pulled out his phone.

"You don't want to give me a ride home?"

He wanted to drive her home and take her to bed too, because for all the years he'd been gone, it had been Savannah's face he'd seen. "That's not a great idea. Stay put. I'll be right back." He ran into the kitchen, pulled a water bottle from the refrigerator, and ran back.

She dropped into a chair at one of the tables and held her head in her hand. "I don't think I feel so good."

"Drink this." He twisted open the top. "You still can't hold your liquor."

She looked up at him with a question in her eyes. "You remember that?"

The space between them heated up. She reached out and traced a finger over his chin, setting him on fire. He wanted to run his fingers through her silky hair, but he stepped back and let the space around him cool down.

"I'll be fine in a few minutes. Maybe if I just put my head down. Why don't you have a couch in here?" She looked around for a place to rest.

He went for his phone again and searched his contacts. He waited for the call to connect. "Hey, it's JT. I need some help."

Chapter Eight

Savannah needed to get out of the bar, but her legs stopped doing working. She couldn't get out of the chair. Why had she walked into this place? Her heart had dragged her in. Stupid heart.

JT sat across the room at another table with his hands folded and watched her. He'd looked so damn sad when she saw him throw that glass. She only wanted him to be happy. Now she was a tad too drunk to get in her car.

He'd smelled so good—like whiskey and tobacco, not cigarette smoke—when he'd brought over that bottle of water. The drunk part of her brain had told her arm to move and touch his chin. Her body had burned when she'd felt his scruffy beard against the pads of her fingers, but he must have been grossed out or mad about it because he'd jumped back. Clearly, he hadn't spent the last twenty-four years thinking about her the way she had replayed their memories.

"Can you give me a ride home?" Heat filled her cheeks, and she had to look away. She would never drive in this condition. How was she going to face her children like this? What kind of a mother gets drunk with her children waiting? "You know what? Where's the bathroom?"

He jumped up. "Are you going to be sick?"

She shook her head. Bad idea. "I don't think so."

The door swung open, bringing in much-needed fresh air. And her brother. *Great.* "Did he call you?" Her tongue tripped over her teeth. She tried to shoot JT a stink eye for ratting her out, but she wasn't sure her face worked any better than her legs.

Blaise shoved his hands in the pockets of his jeans and laughed. "You're shit faced."

"Give the man a trophy." She swung her arm and sent the room spinning again. JT and Blaise dove for her. "I've got it under control. Relax." Men—they overreacted.

"How much has she had to drink?" Blaise tucked an arm around her waist.

She rested her head on his shoulder. Finally, a place to lay her head. "You smell like laundry detergent. Grace is so lucky to have you. I wish I had someone like my brothers. Harley is lucky to have Colton too. You're a good big brother. You're my favorite brother. Did you know that? Don't tell Colton because he thinks he's everyone's favorite."

"She's had a few shots."

"A few? I'd say more than a few with all that rambling."

"Why are you yelling?" Her head hurt, and the lights pierced her eyes like a chef's knife.

"Sorry, man. My fault. We were talking. I didn't realize it was going to her head until it was too late."

"Okay, Sis, time to get you home. Thanks for the call and keeping an eye on her."

"Could you stop talking as if I wasn't in the room? You're pissing me off."

"That's my sister." Blaise's laugh shook his body.

"Stop shaking the room." She really needed to lie down.

JT followed them to the door. "Savannah, thanks for stopping by."

She waved her fingers but couldn't seem to pull her head off Blaise's shoulder. He led her out onto the sidewalk. The click of a lock said JT was done with her.

The night air cleared her brain a little. "I need my purse. It's in my minivan."

"I'll get it." Blaise opened the door to his truck and helped her inside. He returned and belted her into the seat because she was losing the battle with the seat belt.

"Do you want to tell me how you ended up drinking with JT?"

"I most certainly do not." Her head started to spin again. She'd spare JT the embarrassment of telling his story about Shirley. The poor man had had two drunk women on his doorstep in one night. "Could you open a window?"

Every turn sent the contents of her stomach sloshing.

She clamped her lips shut to keep the whiskey down. "I'm a mess." Tears burned the back of her eyes.

"Yeah, you kind of are right now, but not usually. You're our family director. You keep us all in line."

"I don't want that job anymore." *Here comes the whiskey.* "Could you drive a little slower, please?"

"What do you mean you don't want to be in charge anymore? You love bossing everyone around. You've been doing it since you could talk."

She leaned her head back against the rest and looked out the window at the houses tucked in for the night. Comfortable. Safe. "I'm tired of being responsible. I want to have some fun and say to hell with the rules. Why can't I do that?" She turned back to him.

"Caroline and Grey, for one. But who says you can't have any fun? I think you had some fun tonight." He winked.

"I made a complete fool of myself in front of him." Her throat tightened, and her eyes burned with tears. She had wanted the first time she and JT spoke after all those years to be special. She'd imagined seeing him in the grocery store or coming out of Jake's, and they'd stop and talk. He'd look at her with a twinkle in his eye and swoop her into a hug.

He'd tell her how great she looked and would want to take her for coffee so they could catch up, and by the end he'd tell her he regretted leaving without saying goodbye and if he could do it all again, he'd be more honest with her. He'd ask for her forgiveness and want to call her to try again.

Instead, she'd nearly puked in his bar.

"JT has been in worse condition than you are. He isn't going to judge you for a few drinks. Me, on the other hand…" He laughed again as he pulled into her driveway.

She wanted to swat him but was afraid the sudden movement would have her losing the contents of her stomach in his truck. Grace would never forgive her for stinking up her boyfriend's vehicle. Blaise, her sweet brother, had fallen in love with a wonderful woman who adored him. Would she ever be that lucky?

He ran around the front of the truck and helped her out. "Easy now. I'll help you into the house and check on the kids. You need to take two aspirin, drink plenty of water, and get to bed."

At the front door, she shoved her purse at him. "My keys are in there somewhere." She leaned her head against the house, but the spinning wouldn't stop. The dark porch gave her some courage. "Blaise?"

"Yeah?" He didn't look up from his task of searching for her keys.

"I can't get him out of my head."

"Who?" His gaze met hers. "Adam?"

She opened her mouth to tell him the whole truth about that night when she'd made JT promise not to say anything about them. She'd been so afraid Blaise would be mad at them both, and she didn't want her brothers to hate JT. The whole thing had been her idea.

She'd had a few too many drinks that night too. She'd never told JT that. He would never have slept with her if he had known she'd been drinking, and all she wanted that night was to forget about the rules. She wanted his hands all over her. He'd made his way into her heart, and she didn't know how to make it beat the right way anymore. Sadly, she still felt that way.

Instead of the words that would free her, and maybe get her head to stop thinking about him for five minutes, the acid of whiskey burned a trail up her throat, out her mouth, and on her feet.

The alarm clock shattered the silence and dragged Savannah from the depths of sleep. "Ugh." A hammer smashed her skull from the inside out. She slapped at the clock and flopped back down on the pillow.

What day was it? A school day. She needed to get up and make sure the kids were getting dressed, but the ringing in her ears made that slightly impossible. How stupid had she been last night?

She remembered it all. Embarrassment burned her neck and face. She'd never be able to look JT in the eye again. *Oh God. The porch.* She threw the covers back and stumbled out of bed. The sudden movement had the hammer slamming into her skull again. She stopped and squeezed her eyes shut. One step at a time.

She tugged the bedroom door open, and voices drifted up the stairs. The kids were up, but another voice tangled and intertwined with her children's. She eased down the steps.

Blaise cooked eggs in his wrinkled T-shirt, jeans, and

bare feet. The sulfur smell made her stomach turn. Caroline and Grey sat at the breakfast bar hanging on his every word.

"What's going on?" Her throat scraped the words out.

"Good morning." Blaise handed her a cup of coffee. "I was just telling the kids you were at the tea shop last night and started not feeling well. You called me for a ride home. Since I was concerned you had the flu, I slept on the couch because I'm the nurturing brother." He winked just for her to see.

"Uncle Blaise is making us eggs, and he said he'd drive us to school today." Caroline jumped off the stool and wrapped her arms around his waist. He hugged her back and dropped a kiss on her head.

She had to turn her attention to the coffee mug, or the tears would spill and give her away. What was she doing allowing her heart to drive her mind and thinking about JT all the time? She had children to raise, a squirrel to capture, a competition to enter, and a store to make successful. She didn't have the time for childhood fantasies.

"I can take them to school. I just need a minute to wash my face."

"Let me do it. I haven't had a chance to spend much time with them lately, and you could use the time for yourself before you go to work."

"Don't you have someplace to be?" She took a small sip of the coffee. Her stomach accepted the offering.

"Not until noon. Perks of the job."

He still played gigs with Colton and their sons, but they'd added a whole new repertoire of music Colton had fought every step of the way. Blaise had been stubborn or smart enough to wait him out, and now they were selling out small bars and coffeehouses. He also mentored young musicians, which paid the bills.

"I can drive them." She didn't need him to save her. She had made a mistake, but she could handle her responsibilities. It was her job to take care of her children, not anyone else's.

"I know you can. I would like to, if that's okay with you."

"Please, Mom," Caroline said. "Everyone at school thinks it's lit when they see me with Uncle Blaise."

"How do you argue with that?" Blaise held up his hands.

"Fine. You take them to school. I think I left something on the porch. I'll be right back."

"Took care of that too." He turned back to the eggs and slid them onto plates. "But your shoes have seen better days."

"Caroline, are you ready for your science test?" She dropped down into a chair. Blaise held up a plate of eggs. She shook her head. He smirked.

"I think so. I knew it all last night."

She should have stayed home and reviewed with Caroline. What was wrong with her, walking her way into JT's place? He'd had her raging mad, and before she knew it, she wanted to help him ease the pain clearly

74

sketched in his eyes. She could not control herself around him. She needed to be near him and away from him at the same time.

She finished her coffee and tossed a slice of bread in the toaster.

"Grey, man, you dating any ladies?" Blaise slid on his boots.

"Blaise, please. You sound like Colton." She popped two ibuprofens. Maybe the hammering in her head would quiet down to the thump of a bongo drum.

"What? He's half Savage and a sophomore in high school. We're pretty good with the women. Why shouldn't he be? He's good looking, smart, athletic. Plays music." Blaise drummed an old Savage tune on the table with his hands.

Grey knew the whole song and joined him. He had always admired his uncles and had been playing drums, guitar, and piano since he was about eight. Caroline kept time on the juice glass with her fork. Her talented children needed more music in their lives.

She should have gone against her father's wishes and played music with her brothers. Music was in their blood. Now that she was in her forties, the dream was a thing of the past. She wasn't nearly as good as Colton and Blaise, who had made music their lives despite the family fights it caused. Why hadn't she been as brave? Because she had disguised fear to look like disinterest and control.

Her head pounded more as they played, but she didn't have the heart to stop them. All three of them held smiles that rivaled the sun. She picked up a spoon and tapped along. Blaise swung his gaze in her direction and nodded. The tears pricked her eyes.

Blaise ended the song with a bang. "Come on, Grey. There must be some girl that turned your head." Grey shrugged his backpack over his shoulder. "There is a girl I kind of like. She's in my AP history class. She seems okay."

He hadn't mentioned this to her. Who was this girl? Was he wishing his father were around to share news of a pretty girl with? Would sharing with Blaise be enough?

Blaise spun his keys on his finger. "If you ever want to talk girls man-to-man, you can call me, okay? Don't call Uncle Colton, though. He always gives bad advice when it comes to women." He winked.

Her brother always seemed to know what everyone needed.

She forced hugs on her children as Blaise escorted them out of the house and into his truck. She watched until his taillights turned the corner. Ozzy, with his wild white hair and plaid shorts, waved from his patch of boxwoods across the street. She waved back and returned to her much-needed coffee.

The empty house seemed to expand around her. Without the comforting noise of her children filling the rooms, she wanted to be somewhere else. She quickly changed and headed to the tea shop.

She'd make sure to ignore the Whiskey Bar as she passed.

"Would you like more tea, Kiki?" Savannah reached for the ceramic teapot covered in a floral cozy. She served every customer their own pot filled with the tea of their choice.

"Yes, and could you bring me another cranberry-and-orange scone? Thanks." Kiki, in her white designer suit and hair coated with enough hair spray a tornado ripping through Tennessee wouldn't move it, tapped the mug on the table.

She couldn't figure out why this woman insisted on bringing her own mug from home when they had perfectly good cups right here.

She counted the forks at the table. Three, the number that had been there when Kiki sat down. Kiki stole forks. Savannah hadn't witnessed it first hand, but she was pretty sure.

She returned to the kitchen, refilled the teapot, and added more pecan-pie green tea to the filter.

Rae leaned against the counter with a mug of tea in her hand. Her black-and-gray scarf draped around her neck with perfection. "Want to tell me what's bothering you?"

She turned in Rae's direction. "What makes you think something is bothering me?"

"I know you better than most. And the dark circles around your eyes. What gives?"

She waved her hand in the air. "Oh, just life. You know. I have kids, a house, and a job. Nothing everyone else isn't faced with." Her response was rote. She wouldn't share how she really felt, not even with her best friend. She needed to keep the appearance that she had it all together. Her problems were her own.

"Don't believe you. I'm here if you want to spill."

Rae pushed off the counter with her hip and put her mug in the dishwasher. "I have to get Amanda at school. She has play practice and doesn't want to take the late bus home. Will you be okay closing up?"

"I'll be fine. Go." She shooed Rae out of the kitchen.

"Okay, I'll see you tonight at six."

"You don't have to be there. I can handle it." The town council would hold the meeting tonight to discuss the dining events for the anniversary. She would put her hat in for the black-tie caterer.

"I'll be there, and you'll get it. I can feel it." Rae retied her scarf.

"We don't know who the competition is yet."

"Doesn't matter. I'll meet you there." Rae left without waiting for a rebuttal.

"Where's my sister?" A loud voice bounced off the walls and landed next to her in the kitchen.

She ran to the doorway and smack into Colton and Harley. Colton wore his confidence as if it were an expensive three-piece suit. Harley in her floral blouse and jeans with high boots shook her head at the man in her life, but her smile lit up her brown eyes. Their hands were linked. "Excuse him."

"Must you announce your arrival like a walking PA

system?" She led them back in the office and closed the door. "My guests are trying to have lunch."

"Your guests are a bunch of white-haired old ladies who probably can't hear anyway." He pulled up the chair next to Harley and stretched out his long legs, taking up most of the space in the room.

"Don't be so cranky. They are nice women who enjoy having tea with lunch. Except for Kiki the Fork Stealer," she said.

"What the fuck is Kiki the Fork Stealer? Can I smoke in here?" He patted his shirt pocket.

"Absolutely not. And Kiki is a customer. She was out there in the white suit. You walked right past her. She comes in here, orders lunch, and takes a fork every time. She doesn't think anyone notices. She does it to May too."

"Is that the homeless woman who sometimes sleeps on the gazebo in the center of town?" Harley sat on the edge of her seat. Her engagement ring caught the over-head light and splintered rainbows on the wall.

"No, that's Mildred. Kiki lives in the next town over in one of the big mansions. She has more money than Colton does. She likes stealing forks."

"Why don't you have her arrested?" Colton said.

"For stealing a fork? I think she's lonely. She doesn't have anyone. Her husband died, and her children scattered. She wanders around that big house all by herself. So what if she likes to take a fork once in a while?"

"She's still a thief and cutting into your profits." He crossed his arms over his chest.

Colton had a lot of flaws, all of which he owned up

to, and he'd made more than his share of bad choices, but he would not tolerate lying, stealing, and harming a family member.

"I can handle Kiki. Let's talk food. I have some ideas for the wedding." She turned her computer to face them and pulled up the file she'd created with pictures of the finger sandwiches, fruit platters, teapots in coordinating colors to Harley's bridesmaids, which included her, Grace, and Harley's best friend, Ella. Caroline would be a junior bridesmaid. The slideshow filtered through croissants with melted brie, soups, and salads.

"That's chick food." Colton scrunched up his face.

"It's beautiful. I love it." Harley rested her hand on his arm.

"Babe, I know I said my only request was no Christmas music, but we can't have chick food at our wedding. The guys are going to want something to sink their teeth into. How about steak?"

"Because the wedding is in the late afternoon and at your house, I thought a lighter fare would be appropriate. I included the soups, lobster bisque and French onion, because the day may be cold. Anyone can have steak. This menu is elegant. Don't be so closed minded." She tugged on her necklace, trying to keep her frustration in check.

"I'm not closed minded. I like what I like. And I like meat and potatoes. The soup is okay, but not those tiny sandwiches."

Savannah took a deep breath. Arguing with Colton would get them nowhere. She'd let Harley work her magic on him. "Harley, I'll email you the file. Take a look at it. You don't have to decide today. And if your fiancé wants steak, we could add a french dip sandwich."

"I want to eat with a fork and a knife."

"Shut up, Colton," she said.

He stood. "You can't talk to your clients that way and expect to keep getting more business. They're going to say bad things about you."

"I know, but I can talk to you anyway I want." She stuck her tongue out at him.

"She's got you there." Harley laughed and planted a kiss on his cheek. He beamed, grabbed Harley, and kissed her full on the mouth.

"Seriously, get a room." She shooed them toward the door, envious of their obvious love for each other. "I have to run anyway. Tonight is the town meeting to discuss the anniversary event. I'm going to submit a bid for the caterer. Cross your fingers."

"Do you want me and Blaise to come with you?"

"Me too. I'll come," Harley said.

She tugged on her necklace again. "Thank you both, but I can handle the meeting by myself."

Colton surprised her with a hug. "We know you can handle it. That wasn't the point. Call me if you change your mind."

"I won't." She needed to make the Tea Room a success by herself. This was her second chance at a new life.

Harley wrapped her in a hug of honeysuckle. "Thank you for the menu. It's perfect."

"You two are going to gang up against me." Colton wagged a finger between her and Harley.

"Already happened," she and Harley said together.

The town hall had been in Heritage River for one hundred and sixty years and was Savannah's favorite building. She let out a long breath and went inside.

It had started out as the town courthouse, but the structure had gone into disrepair in the seventies. After the scandal in 1979 when the mayor embezzled fifteen thousand dollars from the town, a committee of Heritage River residents petitioned to have the town hall demolished in hopes a new business would pop up in its place. One of those committee members included her father. He was never one for nostalgia.

The McGee family had fought to preserve the courthouse as a national landmark and paid to restore the building to its former glory. Rowan McGee, a third generation McGee, was the current town mayor and now banged a gavel to quiet down the roomful of people.

Savannah scanned the crowd. Maybelline Lewis sat with her husband, Pete. She might want to cater the event too, but the bakery only sold sweets and breads. That wasn't exactly a meal, and rumor had it May wanted to put a float in the parade. Beau Carroll was up front with Hoke Carter, their heads pressed together. Those two old men were probably cooking up some scheme or another. Billy Lewis, Pete's brother, stood to the side, talking with Sheriff Jones. She knew everyone in the room on some level, but her nerves still had her stomach twisting into braids. She needed this opportunity, or the Tea Room might flop. The experts said most restaurants failed in the first year. She couldn't be one of them. Too much was riding on her succeeding.

Rae slid onto the bench beside her. "Sorry I'm late. Some crowd. Don't be nervous."

"Who says I'm nervous?"

"Your bright red neck. You've got this." Rae patted her leg. "Hottie ten o'clock."

She turned to look over her shoulder, and her mouth went dry. JT sauntered in and up the aisle to a bench near the front. He had on a white button-down shirt with the sleeves rolled to his elbows, showing off his strong forearms but covering the tattoo that made her core heat up. His butt looked pretty good in the black dress pants. He slid in next to Pete Lewis, shook his hand, and removed his black cowboy hat. His daughter followed close behind.

If he was here for the catering spot too, she might not stand a chance against a whiskey bar. He was barely in town five minutes, and he couldn't stop himself from competing. That competitive streak of his ran long and thick. The town council wouldn't award him the dinner. Would they? "He's not so hot."

Rae raised an eyebrow. "Have you gone blind? He's not my type. I kind of think his partner, Parker, and his blond locks are more my thing. But there's something

83

about that JT Davies that makes women fan themselves when he smiles."

The bad boys always seemed to have that effect. She crossed her legs.

A tap on her shoulder turned her around. Her swollen heart choked the breath from her lungs. "What did ya'll do?"

"Like we'd miss this." Blaise gripped her shoulder.

The bench behind her filled with all her reasons for getting up in the morning. Caroline slid into the row beside Blaise and the ever-elegant Grace. Caroline smiled and waved. Grey followed Caroline in and gave her a salute. Cash flashed that dimpled Savage smile and took a seat beside Grey. Knox, complete with earbuds hanging from his ears, sat beside Cash. Colton and Harley rounded out the end. Colton gave her a thumbs-up and mouthed *kick ass*. The only person missing was Jud. Hot tears spilled down her cheeks.

Rowan called the meeting to order. The council discussed the plans for the anniversary event. Plenty of activities had been planned, including a tailgate party and an afternoon luncheon on the library lawn. But the biggest event, the one she coveted, was the black-tie dinner dance on the hundred-and-sixtieth anniversary of the town right after Thanksgiving. Catering that event would take the Tea Room to the next level. Customers would come for miles with the kind of publicity she would get from this contest. She'd have the money she needed to pay the mortgage, Jud's college bill, and keep the Tea Room running.

"At this time, we'd like to take all the submissions for the caterer. The person must be from Heritage River. The town council will attend each of the events and decide on the winner. Who would like to go first?" Rowan searched the crowd for the first response.

She wiped her hands on her legs and stood. "Savannah's Tea Room would like to be considered."

Clapping and shouting resonated behind her. Colton whistled. Pairs of hands patted her on the back. Rae nodded and clapped too. Other people in the crowd smiled and applauded as well. She let out a slow breath.

The noise simmered down. She searched the crowd for another submission, but no one else seemed to move. Maybe JT hadn't come to compete after all.

"Anyone else?" Rowan said.

Several rows ahead of her, JT stood. Her sight clouded over. She shook her head, but nothing cleared. He held his hat in one hand. "The Whiskey Bar would like to be considered for the catering position. Thank you."

"Mr. Davies, your establishment isn't open yet, and are you technically a resident? Will you be able and ready to participate? As the mayor, I can tell you this anniversary is very important to us."

JT placed a hand on Maddy's shoulder. "Madeline and I are glad to be a part of Heritage River. She recently started at the high school. The Whiskey Bar will be open this weekend and more than ready to be the caterer for any of your events. My father would've wanted a chance to help out a town he was very proud of. My submission is as much for him as the Whiskey Bar."

The crowd applauded the mention of Jake. *Nicely done.* She dropped back down into her seat. How could she possibly compete with the memory of a deceased man everyone loved? The air in the room pressed against her, forcing her to take slow breaths.

"Does anyone else wish to throw their hat in the ring?" Rowan waited for a response, but none came.

How could there be no one else who wanted to cater? She craned her neck to look for Enzo who owned the pizzeria. He must want the opportunity to compete, but as far as she could tell, he wasn't even in the room. She couldn't lose this chance to JT. She could've had the whole thing to herself.

"Well, then we'll have a contest between the two businesses. The council was concerned something like this might happen. In fairness to both businesses, the council will appoint someone to cater the tailgate and someone to cater the luncheon. Those two events will be used in the determination of the black-tie formal. Look in your emails for the decision on those particular events. We will hold another town meeting right here to announce the winning caterer of the black-tie dinner two weeks prior to the event. Thank you for your interest and good night."

People started filing out. She stood and met JT's dark gaze as he approached. He gave her the smallest of nods. The competition was on. He would never back down, and neither could she.

"Hey, Sis." Colton grabbed her shoulder, forcing her to unlock her stare.

"Yes?"

"Do you think you have a chance against JT? No offense, but booze versus tea?"

She straightened her shoulders. People were watching. She couldn't let on that fear turned the contents of her belly to ice water. She could not lose. "To quote you, you bet your ass I can win."

Chapter Nine

J T stared at his Mac, hoping the words would scramble and the email from the town council would say something else. No matter how many times he shook his head, the email still read the same:

Congratulations. You've been chosen to cater the luncheon on the library lawn.

He'd wanted the tailgate party. Booze and bar food went a lot better in a parking lot with a bonfire than with a bunch of ladies in white pumps and high-neck blouses sitting on wrought-iron chairs.

The noise of people talking and laughing over silverware clanking drifted into his office from the front of the Whiskey Bar. They'd opened right on time because if they didn't, heads would roll. The place had been packed every night. The bar was new, and people were interested. In a few weeks, the place could be empty. He'd never had that problem. He had more whiskey options than any other bar did. He had his father's signature pulled pork the locals would recognize. That dish had given him regulars in his other bars.

The lunch crowd was a little light, but most people wanted to drink with their meal in his place, and even the biggest drunk tried to wait until five. He'd checked Savannah's website. She offered a nice lunch. Understandably, patrons would want to go to her place for lunch, but her menu would never satisfy a tailgate crowd.

Anyone at a tailgate expected hot dogs, burgers, and wings, food that greased up fingers. He'd win fair and square. Nothing personal, because he did not want to take her business.

When he won the black-tie dinner, he planned to feature his finest whiskeys. The ones usually out of the average budget. He also had high-end beers and wines most people glossed over when looking at the drink menu. At one time, he wouldn't have known the first thing about these drinks. He would've been glad to down a two-dollar beer to get a buzz on. But that was then. He'd show the people of Heritage River he'd learned a few things.

A knock on his open door pulled him away from his rambling thoughts.

"Hey, man. It's great to finally catch up." Blaise Savage crossed the room in two steps and gripped his hand in a firm shake.

Blaise hadn't changed much over the years. His hair was speckled with gray, and the lines around his eyes deepened when he smiled, but the rest was still his old friend.

"Good to see you." He pounded Blaise on the shoulder.

"Thanks again for the other night with my sister. She doesn't usually drink like that, but she's been through a lot this year."

"No judgement. I just wanted to make sure she got home okay. She didn't want a ride from me." He hadn't wanted to be in a car with her, because he didn't trust himself not to wrap his hand around hers and pull her close. She intoxicated him. He needed her out of his thoughts, not in his bed.

"She didn't want a ride home from me either, but that's Savannah. If she isn't running the show, she isn't happy."

Savannah had walked into his bar and started moving around as if she'd been doing that for years. She fit in his space, and he liked it even if he shouldn't.

Although they were a lot older now, and everything with Savannah was the past tense, he still had to force himself to look Blaise in the eye. "Have a seat."

"Your bar is great. Congratulations." Blaise shrugged out of his leather jacket and tossed it on the back of the chair. "I was surprised when you called and said you wanted to talk. What's it been?"

"Too many years. Can I get you a bourbon? That was your drink, wasn't it?"

"I stopped drinking a while back. I saw what it was doing to my brother. Someone had to be sober on stage."

He hadn't known. "A soda?"

"I'm good. Looks like you really made something of yourself. I read your website. This is what, your third Whiskey Bar?"

"Fifth. You didn't think I would ever make it?"

"I didn't think any of us would."

"How would you feel about playing here? My partner and I want you to play a once-a-month kind of thing. Friday nights. What do you say?"

Blaise scratched his jaw. "I really appreciate the offer, but we don't play our old stuff out anymore unless we get a special request from the audience."

"Why not? You guys were the best."

"Ancient history. They were good times, but they didn't last. We've got a whole new sound now. Troy and Patrick tour with other bands."

"I didn't think anything would break you guys up."

"Life changes. We aren't the same people we used to be. For me, I'm glad about that. I didn't have anything to prove anymore."

He still had something to prove, but did he need Savannah's brothers to do it? Savage's playing would hurt Savannah. She had marched right in here and demanded he not hire her brothers. She wanted him to stay away—again. Even if Savage could drum up business, he would honor her request and let it go. He should have realized that before now.

Parker shoved the door open. "Hey, JT... Blaise Savage. I don't believe it. I'm a huge fan." He pumped Blaise's hand.

"It's nice to meet you." Blaise unfolded himself from the chair and clapped Parker on the shoulder.

"I love your music. Your drum solos really rock. Can we take a picture? I can put it up on social media."

"Parker, leave the man alone."

"It's fine. I don't mind. I like meeting fans." Blaise's smile never wavered. He was always a professional.

"Get in here." Parker waved him over as he tried to position the phone to snap the best shot.

"I'll let you two take the photo." He backed up with the phone.

"JT and I would love Savage to perform a few nights. Would you be interested?" Parker took the phone back and tapped away.

"Parker, I already asked. He can't do it."

"I'll talk to my brother. I have to run. JT, it was great catching up. I'll be in touch." Blaise grabbed his jacket.

"I'll show you out." He pointed to the door and led Blaise through the crowd and out to the quieter sidewalk. "Thanks for stopping by."

Blaise shoved his hands in his pockets. "I didn't want to say anything, and this doesn't have anything to do with whether or not we play here, but how did Savannah end up in your bar the other night?"

"She walked in." He held Blaise's gaze this time.

"It's none of my business, and she'll rip me a new one if she knows I even asked, but I was curious. She doesn't go out much, and she ended up pretty wasted."

"I understand. You're looking out for your sister. I would too, if I had one. Forget I asked about the gig.

You've done enough for me over the years. Just stop by some night and bring your lady friend. I saw you with her at the town hall meeting. Dinner's on me." He should not have called Blaise and asked him to play. It would only stir up trouble.

"You know what? We'll do it. We'll play. We're booked the next few weeks, but then our calendar clears out. I'll text you the dates. Thanks for thinking of us. It'll be fun. And you can help me set up my kit. Like old times."

Much like he didn't want the library luncheon, he didn't want Savannah to be mad at him.

When she found out her brothers would play, she was going to be as furious as a rattlesnake disturbed from its hiding spot.

And he had no one to blame but himself.

Chapter Ten

The tailgate?

Savannah closed her laptop and paced the small office at the Tea Room with a mug of black lavender in her hand. She had wanted the library luncheon. That event was a perfect fit. She had been the head librarian for years until she quit and opened the store.

Grace had taken her job, which gave her a family connection to the event. Savannah could picture Blaise on the lawn in his Sunday best, with Grace on his arm. If Blaise came to the library, she could imagine him dragging Colton along. She had an elaborate plane to drop a few hints around town that her brothers would be there. Maybe even beg them to play a few acoustic songs. Everyone attending would have loved it.

What was she supposed to do with a tailgate party in the high school parking lot before a football game? Tailgates were not exactly the place for pots of tea. Unless that tea was spiked with whiskey. *Whiskey.* Now was not the time to think about JT.

The Tea Room had been open for an hour, and the only one in the place was Kiki, who had ordered the vegetable soup. Grateful for a dish requiring a spoon, she took the forks away before Kiki could slide them in her purse.

"Do we have any reservations?" She checked the reservations book at the front desk, where Harley straightened the menus. They used the old-fashioned book up front because it went with the antique chairs at every pedestal table and the lace curtains she'd found online. In the back, those reservations were kept on the computer.

"Not today. But we do have a party of four coming tomorrow at noon for a birthday."

"That's something." Not enough. "I'll be right back." She pulled her apron over her head and hung it on the hook in the kitchen.

"Where are you going? Not that you have to report to me. I'm just curious." Harley leaned in. "I really don't want to be left alone with Kiki."

"She isn't going to do anything except sit there all day and drink tea. She isn't a trained criminal, and I'm pretty sure she isn't packing. I'm going down the street to get my library luncheon."

"Oh crap. JT won the luncheon?"

"Not for long." She pushed out of the door onto the sidewalk. The sun baked the concrete while the blue jays sang as they chased their mates. Even the birds were in love.

She marched down to the Whiskey Bar, opened the door, where the air conditioning greeted her hot skin with a kiss that did nothing to cool her. The bar smelled of pears, coconut, and wood. Patrons deep in conversation filled the tables. Whiskey glasses and beer bottles decorated every surface. Four men sat at the bar, eating lunch and staring at the television in the corner.

She forged up to the bar, ignoring the envy in her veins. A young lady with her black hair pulled back and tattoos on her neck poured a beer from the tap. She'd thought about getting a tattoo herself as a midlife-crisis kind of thing, or at least part of her effort to reinvent herself.

"Excuse me, is JT here?"

The woman handed over the beer to a man in a greasy baseball cap and slid cash into the register. "He's in the back. I'll get him for you."

Savannah went to the pool table and ran her fingers across the red felt. The noise of conversation washed over her, and her mind wandered to a time when she thought everything was still possible. Now she just wanted to get from one hour to another and pay her bills.

"Did you want to play pool?" JT's voice startled her out of her thoughts.

He crossed his arms over his chest. His white T-shirt stretched against his muscles and tucked into his thin waistband. His jeans were faded and ripped at the knees. The brass buckle on his belt was as big as her hand.

Her breath caught in her throat, and every sensible word she possessed disappeared. Why had she come over here? "I haven't played pool in a long time." Adam had never liked pool, and once the kids arrived, a Friday night out consisted of watching a movie on the couch.

"You were pretty good at it." He tapped on the corner of the table and shared his smile with her.

"It's not hard to beat three drunk guys." They'd often played pool at the Stargazer three towns over when Savage had gigs there.

By the end of the second set, her brothers and JT had been pretty wasted. She'd always stayed sober because she was underage and had to beg her father to let her go. She'd taken every chance she could to be near JT, hoping he'd notice her as a person and not Blaise's little sister.

He ducked his head and let his gaze trail away, but he laughed at the memory they shared. "True. Did you come for lunch?"

If he was on the menu. "I'm working, but I needed to speak with you."

"About?"

She straightened her shoulders. "I'd like to make you a proposition."

He shook his head and backed up. "Stop right there."

"No, no. I didn't mean it like that." Heat filled her cheeks. What was wrong with her? "I wanted to know if you would trade me the library luncheon for the tailgate party."

"What's the matter? Is a tailgate party below your fancy-tea sensibilities?"

"Of course not. The library is a better fit for me, that's all, and I thought your customers would appreciate your bar menu at the tailgate."

"So my customers aren't good enough to come to the library luncheon. Is that what you're saying?"

"What? Why would I say something like that?"

"You just did."

"Well, it wasn't what I meant. You're twisting my words."

"Okay, what did you mean, then?" He hooked his thumbs inside his belt and rocked on his heels.

"I only meant that I have a connection to the library. I was the head librarian for several years." She needed to look at something other than his hips.

"Why does that not surprise me?"

"What does that mean?"

"You always were the stuffy type."

"Stuffy? I am not." Okay, maybe she was a little these days with her to-do lists and backup calendars, but she wasn't always. And she didn't even own a cat.

"Okay, bossy, then. How about that?"

She was bossy. She couldn't argue with that. "Will you switch with me or not?"

"Nope." His lips curled into a slow smile.

She let out a long breath. He enjoyed this. "Why not?"

"For one, I want to see your cucumber sandwiches at a tailgate, and for another we're not allowed to switch. I guess you didn't read the entire email."

She had not. Pretty stupid on her part. But he knew

she served cucumber sandwiches. He must have read her menu. Heat filled her cheeks again, and her lips curled up, as if she were a schoolgirl finding a note from her crush stuffed in her locker.

"We could go to Rowan and tell him together. The council would have to let us switch if we presented a united front."

"Why would I do that? I'm not worried about serving my food and beverages at a luncheon. Did you take a look around? I have customers for the lunch crowd." The cash register at the bar rang.

And she didn't have customers. Plain and simple. He knew that too. "The library committee, whom I'm sure will be in attendance, does not drink whiskey or eat food that drips down your chin."

"You have far more to worry about than I do. I can serve wine because it's already on my menu and salads they'll eat with a fork. Easy. What's your plan?"

She didn't have a plan other than to walk down here and ask him to switch. Foolish to think he'd do her a favor. Why should he? He'd never done anything for her except steal her heart and run away, though he didn't know about the stealing-her-heart part. If only he'd asked her how she felt about him back then. Their lives could've been very different. Not that she regretted her choices. She didn't. She'd been holding on to a "what if" for so many years it seemed as real as her real life did.

"If you don't want to switch, fine. I wish you luck because you're going to need it. I will win that black-tie dinner." She'd have to figure out a way to make the tailgate work. She could do it. She'd handled bigger challenges than this. She brushed past him.

He grabbed her arm. His touch ignited her skin or maybe it was the way he licked his lips that set fire to her veins.

"I might be older, but I still don't turn down a healthy competition."

"I see you aren't any smarter. Prepare to lose." He had to lose because she couldn't. She needed to stay in business or sacrifice everything.

"I never lose." He leaned in and whispered. His hot breath sent chills down her neck. He released her arm and eased away.

"We'll see about that." She held her head high and marched out, ignoring the continued ring of the cash register as she did.

Chapter Eleven

J T let himself into the house and shut the front door with a quiet click. Maddy was probably asleep because he'd sent her a text hours ago telling her to go to bed and not wait up; he couldn't get home when he thought.

All he wanted was to heat up the supper he'd brought home from the Whiskey Bar and catch the highlights of the Braves game on the MLB app. The night had worn him out. First, Savannah stopping by and then a list of other things he didn't want to revisit.

He popped open a beer, shoved the flatbread in the toaster oven, and rolled his neck on his shoulders to loosen the knots. What he wouldn't give for a good massage from a beautiful, feisty brunette with the eyes the color of storm clouds.

"You're late." Maddy flipped on the recessed lighting in the kitchen.

The stark white light hurt his eyes. "Why are you still

up?" He turned off the lights. The soft hue from the microwave eased the pain.

"You promised you'd be home early. You said you'd hire someone to take the night shifts. I hate being in the house all by myself."

"You're fifteen. I'd think you'd want to be alone as much as possible."

She dropped onto a stool at the island. "The house makes weird noises. Do you think Grandpa is haunting it?"

"If he is, you don't have to worry about him. He'll probably figure out a way to make you a sandwich." The toaster oven dinged its completion.

"Hilarious. Will you be home tomorrow?"

"I'll try. Why don't you come to the bar after school for a few hours? You can do your homework in my office, and then we'll go home."

"No, thanks. Can I hang out with a friend after school?"

"Who's the new friend?"

"Grey. The one I told you about from history class."

He didn't remember her mentioning a new friend. "Where are you going to hang out?"

"I don't know. Does it matter? Would it matter if I was hanging out with a girl? I'm not going to sleep with him."

He tried to pull the flatbread out of the toaster but burnt his fingers on the rack. He shoved them in his mouth, then under cold water. "For Christ's sake, Maddy.

Do you have to talk like that?" He really couldn't handle having a teenage daughter who liked boys.

"I know what sex is. They taught us about it in, like, the fourth grade." She snagged a piece of his flatbread. He really wanted that.

"I don't like thinking about you knowing about it." He knew what boys that age wanted. He'd wanted it and gotten it on most occasions. He wanted to lock his daughter in a tower and throw away the key until she was thirty or he was dead, whichever came first.

"I'm almost an adult. Does that freak you out?"

Hell yes. "You're supposed to grow up. That was the plan. What do you know about this boy?" He leaned against the counter and chugged some of the beer while she continued to nibble like a rabbit at his food.

"I don't know. We get along. He's funny. He plays soccer. He doesn't have soccer practice tomorrow, so he asked if I could hang out."

If he said no, he'd be the bad guy again. If he said yes, what was he agreeing to? He should probably ask to meet the boy so he could be standing at the door innocently holding a... baseball bat.

"I want you home by six, no going to his house, and he can't come here if I'm not home. If you can't find a place to *hang,* come to the Whiskey Bar. I won't bother you while you're with your friend, but I don't want you wandering the streets." Two teenagers with nowhere to go could be a surefire way to find trouble. He knew about that too.

"That's fine. I love the bakery. We could walk there after school."

So the boy didn't have a license. Good to know.

"The bakery is only open until three."

"We could sit at the park."

"Absolutely not." The park was surrounded by the woods with walking trails. Those trails had too many places to make out.

"Why not?"

"No parks. A public place. Go to the pizzeria if you don't want to come to the Whiskey."

"Fine. Will you be here when I get home?"

"Yes." He hoped so.

"Thanks, Daddy." She slid off the stool, kissed him on the cheek, and sashayed out of the kitchen.

She only liked him because he'd said yes.

What was left of the flatbread was cold again. He ate it anyway and searched his tablet for the sports app. His mind couldn't stay on baseball. Images of Savannah standing in his bar, only inches from him, kept playing on repeat. Her eyes were filled with challenge, and her chin tilted up at him. Her tough exterior captivated him, but he wanted to see her softer side too. He could still feel her arm under his touch. His fingers flexed at the memory.

His phone vibrated against the counter. He debated on ignoring it. Whatever it was could wait, but he eyeballed the screen anyway.

"What are you still doing up?" He took his food and his beer and eased into his leather chair in the family room. The moonlight spilled in through the bay window, splashing waves of soft gray light on the floor.

"Jacob, a man my age is up ten times a night to visit the comfort station." Uncle Harlan's voice was low but held a hint of humor.

"Sorry to hear that."

"No sorrier than I am. My old bones might be well past the use-by date, but my mind is as young as ever."

"Nothing is ever going to stop you. You're like a good scotch."

"Damn straight, young man. I'm sorry to burden you with this call after you probably put in a long day, but I don't want you finding any surprises in the morning."

Oh shit.

"Shirley paid me a visit earlier tonight."

The beer went sour in his mouth. "What did she want?"

"Asked me to read over my brother's will. She's looking for a loophole."

"Dad left her plenty of money. If she'd let me help her, I could invest it and she'd be set for the rest of her life. Maybe move to Florida and leave me the hell alone." He pushed the flatbread away.

"I think she's lost, is all. Can't find her way back, and lost people are scared sometimes. Her world doesn't look right."

"What am I supposed to do about it?" He clenched his fists.

"Nothing you can do. Finding the right path is on her, but she's going to come back looking for you to make things right. I don't want you going and losing that temper of yours. You've got a good life now and a daughter who needs her daddy. If Shirley keeps coming around, I want you to send her to me."

Harlan didn't need to fight his battles for him. "I'll set her straight."

"Jacob." The warning coated Uncle Harlan's voice.

"I'll keep my cool." He had bigger things to worry about, like winning the black-tie dinner. Shirley would go away with a little shove. Figuratively speaking, of course.

"I'm here if you need me."

"Do you want to come to dinner at the Whiskey tomorrow night?" He missed his uncle and needed someone on his side for a change.

"I would love to, but my cigar club is meeting tomorrow night. How about a rain check?"

"Sure." The weight of the day sat back down on his shoulders. "Thanks for the call."

"G'night."

He leaned back in his chair. The darkness around him, the beer, even the call couldn't get the memory of Savannah to fade. He had tried most of his life to get over her, but she was around every corner. For years, he'd hoped she'd walk up to him in a coffeehouse or a bar and give him her bright smile.

He wanted his heart to turn cold so he wouldn't feel so alone. What was she doing about then? Was she curled up with a book? She used to love to read. Did she ever think of him? Maybe she did when an old song came on the radio, one that played when they'd been together. She had never given him a second look until that night. He had tried to impress her, but she had her head turned the other way. Then his wish had come true. She had slid up alongside him, and his brain fried. He had taken what she offered and had never given her anything in return. What would she want with him now?

He pushed out of the chair. Enough. He needed to get some sleep. Still, the image of her hands all over him invaded his thoughts. He couldn't shake her, but he needed to find a way.

The tables at the Whiskey were filled, and it was three o'clock. JT wiped down the bar with a smile. The library luncheon was a few days away. He was ready. Savannah didn't have a chance to win the black-tie dinner. He wished the competition were with someone else, but he reminded himself this was business. Nothing personal.

The door swung open, bringing in the scent of fresh air and Maddy—with a boy. This must be the new friend. He was tall and thin, made up mostly of arms and legs. He had dark, wavy hair and wide eyes.

Maddy beamed when she saw him behind the bar and dragged her friend over. "Dad, this is Grey."

Grey stuck out his hand. "It's nice to meet you, Mr. Davies. Your restaurant is nice. Different from Eat At Jake's, but I liked Jake's. I didn't mean anything by that."

At least the kid had manners. He gripped the boy's hand in his own. Strong grip. He made eye contact. So far so good. "Howdy, Grey. I miss Jake's too, so don't worry about that. Do you kids want something to eat?" He tried to play it cool, as if it were no big deal his little girl brought boys around.

Maddy took one of the seats at the bar, and Grey followed. They dumped their backpacks on the floor. "Can you make me a salad without chicken or cheese?"

"Yes, your highness. Grey, do you want some real food? I've got burgers, pulled pork, wings. Name it."

"Um, I promised my mom I'd be home for dinner, so I better not eat too much but thank you."

He mixed the salad for Maddy and grabbed a bowl of chips for Grey. The kid seemed nice enough. There wasn't any reason Maddy couldn't have a guy friend. Maybe the kid was gay, and that would solve all his problems.

He came through the kitchen. Grey yanked his hand away from Maddy's when he saw him. Okay, probably not gay. He placed the food in front of them.

"Dad, you went to high school with Grey's uncle."

He leaned forward on the bar. "I did? Who's your uncle?"

"Blaise Savage." Grey chomped on his chips.

His hands slipped, and he almost clocked his chin on the bar. "Blaise is your uncle?"

"Yup. Do you remember him from high school? A lot of people know him because of the band."

"Sure do remember. So Savannah must be your mom?"

Grey's face lit up. "Do you know her too? She was a couple of years younger than my Uncle Blaise, I think."

"Sometimes she hung out with the band when they used to play parties. I met her a few times. We didn't run in the same crowd at school. She was smart. I was lucky to pass study hall. Y'all enjoy your food. I've got to take care of something in the back."

He closed the door to his office and leaned against it. Of all the kids in school, his daughter had to get involved with Savannah's son. Well, that couldn't happen. He'd have to put a stop to it.

Now.

Chapter Twelve

Savannah closed the register and filled out a deposit slip. Sales had been low again. Other than the birthday party, no one had come in for lunch. Not even Kiki.

She struggled with a menu for the tailgate party. Egg salad would be an option because that was already on her menu, but what else? She should have offered sodas as an alternative to tea, which Colton had suggested before she opened, but she didn't want to listen.

The whoosh of the door announced someone had come in. "We're closed. I'm sorry." She hadn't bothered to lift her head to see who it was. She didn't have the energy to put on a good face at the moment.

"You shouldn't turn customers away." JT filled up the small foyer area with his broad shoulders and long legs. He crossed his arms over his chest. His T-shirt rode up over his large biceps, and the corner of his tattoo peeked out at her. His beard was thicker than the other day. It looked good on him. Of course, it did.

"I closed out my register." She held up the blue moneybag. "Did you want to buy tea or to take a look at my menu for the tailgate?" He certainly hadn't come by for lunch.

"I don't care about your menu. I came by to ask you to keep your son away from my daughter."

"Excuse me?"

"You heard me. Your son. I don't want him hanging out with Maddy."

The girl Grey wanted to spend time with after school was Madeline Davies. Didn't it figure? She couldn't agree more, but she wasn't about to give him the satisfaction. "Are you saying my son isn't good enough for your daughter?"

He opened his mouth but clamped it shut. "I don't know anything about your son, but considering our history, I don't think it's wise for our children to become friends."

"But you're okay with asking my brothers to play in your bar? Our history would have nothing to do with that?" At least they were admitting there had been a history. She didn't know how much longer she could see him around and act as if nothing had ever happened between them.

"Your brothers playing some music for me and our children becoming involved are not exactly the same thing." He crossed the foyer in two steps.

Nothing but the small reception desk stood between

them. His beard had specks of gray mixed in with the brown. He still had the hole in his left earlobe from when he'd tried to pierce it with a needle and an ice cube one summer.

"My family is good enough to make money from but not good enough to date. Is that what you're saying?" She tilted her chin up. She'd be damned if he'd get the upper hand.

"You of all people should know I don't think it's a matter of who's better. If Maddy and Grey start dating, I don't want that to cause any trouble."

"What kind of trouble would it cause? Grey is a responsible young man. He wouldn't try to get your daughter pregnant." And she'd kill him if he did. "If they enjoy spending a little harmless time together, I don't see the problem."

"We're the problem, Savannah." He lowered his voice.

Her heart tried to climb up her throat. She had to swallow to push it back down. She didn't want to spend time with him at Sunday dinners and holidays if their children became serious, and she couldn't go on pretending he didn't take up every corner of her mind. Grey and Maddy together would be a problem for her if JT still regretted being with her.

"We aren't a problem, because there is no *we*. Never was. Now if you'll excuse me, I need to get to the bank." She zipped up the moneybag. The words hurt to say, but she had no choice. She needed to be on higher ground, and he needed to believe she hadn't given him a second thought since he clearly hadn't been pining over her all this time.

How could she have so foolishly believed she might have meant something to him? She'd been nothing more than a conquest he forgot about as soon as he won it. It was as if someone had tied a rope around her chest and pulled.

"You aren't going to tell Grey to stay away from Maddy, then?"

"Nope. And if I were you, I wouldn't do it either. The more you push them apart, the more they'll want to be together. They're not even officially dating. You're probably overreacting anyway."

"They were holding hands at the bar before I came down here to talk some sense into you."

"You have apparently wasted your time. And holding hands doesn't exactly have them walking down the aisle, now does it? They could sleep together, and even that wouldn't guarantee a relationship, now would it?" She couldn't stay away from picking at that scab.

"Your son better not try to get into bed with my daughter." A vein pulsed on the side of his neck.

"A woman's chastity is only your concern when it's your daughter?"

"Well, who the hell else would I care about?" He threw his arms in the air. The space between his eyes creased. "Are you...hold on... Savannah, do you think?" His words seemed to stick together and tumble over one another.

"I don't think anything at all." Her emotions raced

ahead of her and out of her grasp. She had stopped talking about the kids and was somehow talking about them.

He came around the reception desk and met her gaze with his. "You came on to me that night. You said—"

She put her hand on his shoulder and looked away. "I know what I said. I was a child pretending to be a grown-up."

He moved her hand and wrapped his around it. His touch was warm. "You were eighteen, and I was twenty. We were both kids, but nothing we did was pretend."

"Ancient history, right?" She forced herself to look him in the eye.

He let go of her hand. "Right."

She instantly regretted making that last comment and extinguishing the touch. "I'll talk to Grey about using good sense and not rushing into anything." She kept her hands busy with the deposit bag.

"Thanks. I'll do the same with Maddy."

"Problem solved, then." She needed him to leave before the tears that burned the back of her throat gave her away.

"I guess so."

"Then you can go back to your bar." Being in love with him wasn't rational, but dear Lord, he'd always been in her heart.

Guilt tugged at her thoughts of love. She'd been married to a good man who had shared a good life with her. It hadn't been enough. She had wanted more and never thought she would have it. Who had the right to complain about a decent life? Who had the right to be so greedy? But she needed JT the way she needed breath. It had always been him.

He turned to go, and that rope around her chest loosened. He turned back, and before she could say anything, he placed his hands on either side of her face and pulled her to him.

Had he read her mind?

He kissed her as if the last twenty-four years hadn't happened. Her lips remembered the way back to him. His beard rubbed against her skin and heated her core. She wrapped her arms around his neck to pull him closer and feel his chest pressed up against hers.

He laced his fingers in her hair, and she opened her mouth to him. He tasted like cinnamon and sugar. Her body caught fire. He pulled slightly on her hair to tilt her head back and take the kiss even deeper. The flames licking her skin threatened to devour her.

Her tongue chased his as he traced her teeth and her lips. The thoughts in her head bounced between wanting more of him and putting a stop to this kiss. They hadn't talked about that night. Hadn't reminisced about the years. Hadn't flirted even, but here he was setting her world on its head with that tongue.

"Holy shit." The voice broke them apart.

JT jumped back. Her heart pounded to get out of her chest. She tried to smooth her hair back into place.

Colton covered his eyes. "Are you done kissing my sister?"

"I'm sorry. We were—"

"Stop. I don't want to picture it." Colton dropped his hand.

"Colton, go away." She crossed her arms over her chest and tried to discreetly wipe her mouth. "It's not what you think," JT said.

It wasn't?

"I don't care what it was. None of my business, but I don't like seeing some guy try to swallow my baby sister's face, even if that guy is you. Look, if you two dig each other, great. Fine by me, but get a fucking room. I'm going to go outside, take a walk, and have a smoke. When I come back, I don't want to see any more of that shit." He pointed a finger at the two of them. "I'm scarred for life." He closed the door behind him.

JT ran a hand over his face. "Does he know about what happened between us?"

"I never told anyone." Not like she hadn't wanted to, but when she found out he was gone two days later, she had been too embarrassed to even share her secret with her best friend. She had carried that memory around all by herself. She'd spent years missing him, and no one had ever known.

"Well, at least your brothers won't try and beat the shit out of me."

"Why would they do that? What happened was in the past."

"I'm sorry I kissed you. I shouldn't have done that. I don't know what made me do it."

She wasn't sorry, not one bit. She did want to yell at her brother for interrupting what had been the best kiss

116

she'd had in ages. That thought stopped her. She didn't want to be unfair to Adam. Dear, sweet Adam had built a good life for them. She had loved him. Still did.

But she'd loved JT too, and as deceitful as that sounded, she did. She'd loved him her entire life. She'd just tucked those feelings away and only brought them out when she had time to sit with them privately. She'd never searched for him. She'd never asked Blaise how he was. She hadn't wanted to ruin the life she did have over a man who'd walked away from her as if she were day-old scones.

"You regret kissing me like you regret sleeping with me." She might as well get it all out in the open.

"Now isn't the time to talk about this. Colton is going to come back, and I don't want to be here when he does. I'll call you." He stormed out.

Famous last words.

She shoved the deposit bag into her tote and pulled out her keys. She flipped out the last of the lights in the kitchen. She forgot to lock the front door, tossed down her tote and keys, and marched back. Colton pushed open the door. She forgot about him too.

"Did he leave?"

"I'm leaving too. Did you need something?"

"Harley wants that chocolate tea. She said you'd know which one she likes. Are you dating him?"

"Come in the kitchen." She pulled down a mason jar of the chocolate-raspberry tea and handed it to him.

"We're not dating."

"How much do I owe you?"

117

"Nothing."

"You can't make money giving your products away." He shoved a fifty at her. "If you aren't dating JT, then what was happening here? When I saw you two at the high school, you didn't look as if you liked each other much, and now you're sucking face in your store. What gives?"

She handed the money back. "That's too much. Nothing gives. I don't know what happened. He came here to tell me to keep Grey away from Maddy, and then he kissed me."

"Grey likes his daughter? Good for him. Keep the damn money. Replace the forks that nut keeps stealing."

"She's not nuts."

He threw his hands in the air. "You women drive me crazy, you know that? Every time I turn around, Harley adds something else she wants for the wedding. It was supposed to be quiet, simple, just the family, and now somehow my old producer is on the guest list. And I wanted simple food, a backyard barbeque, and you've convinced her to go with that other stuff, and she won't let me have my damn hamburgers. This all from the woman who eats cheese puffs for breakfast."

"Maybe you should ask JT to cater your affair if you can't appreciate the finer things in life. He has hamburgers and pulled pork and greasy wings. All the manly food you think is so important."

"I think you like him." He glanced at her sideways, then leaned against the counter.

"That kiss was a mistake." Best mistake she'd made in a long time.

"I might be pigheaded, but I'm not stupid." Colton draped an arm around her shoulders. "When did this start?"

She shoved his arm away. "I don't like him. That kiss won't happen again. I'll talk to Harley for you."

He pushed off the counter. "Nah. She can have her girlie food if it makes her happy. I'll use my charms for something else." He wagged his eyebrows.

"Gross."

"What? You were just sucking face in public. I only said I was charming."

She locked the door and walked with him through the parking lot. "Besides Harley, whoever said you were charming?"

"Every woman I ever met, but Harley is the only one who counts. She's the best thing that ever happened to me, and I want to shout it from the biggest stage in the world. I'm pretty sure I've been on that stage too."

"Do you know how to capture a squirrel?" The stage comment didn't warrant a response. It would only encourage him.

He narrowed his eyes. "Is that a trick question?"

"I have a squirrel in my attic. I can't get rid of it. It's eating my insulation."

"I'll come by and take a look." He pulled out a pack of cigarettes.

She shook her head, and he shoved them back in his

pocket. "I can take care of it. I just wanted to know if you had any ideas."

"You don't have to trap a squirrel by yourself. Blaise and I will come by."

"No. Thank you. It's not a big deal. I'll throw some poison down."

"Is that squirrel eating something besides the insulation?"

"Does it matter?"

"It could. You can let us help once in a while. It won't kill you." He tried to hand her the fifty again.

"This from you?" She pushed the money away and unlocked the minivan.

"Hey, I've been sober for over a year. I know how to ask for help when I need it."

Which was never. "Thanks. I've got it under control."

"Are you going to the parade and watch our amazing float?"

The parade would be right after the library luncheon. "I don't think so. I'm not in the mood to stand in the sun and watch the floats go by." She had numbers to crunch. Jud's school would be billing for the next semester soon, and she didn't know where the money was coming from. "I also have a squirrel in my attic I need to evict."

"That isn't going to take all day. A little sunshine might do you good."

"Sun is going to wrinkle my skin." She also didn't want to risk running into JT. She placed a kiss on Colton's cheek and squeezed his arm before sliding into the van.

She wanted the unbridled love from a man that Colton felt for Harley, but not just any man. She wanted the sexy man up the street with the salt-and-pepper beard, the tattoo on his left arm, the smile lines around his dark eyes.

Problem was his amazing kiss didn't mean he really wanted her. History had proved he never had.

And he never would.

Chapter Thirteen

The empty blue sky stretched out uninterrupted until the tips of the Smoky Mountains broke the view. The heat was thick enough to cut through with a meat cleaver. JT stood on the back porch of his new old house with a mug of coffee in one hand and his phone open to the weather app in the other. The forecast called for thunderstorms around noon. He checked the sky again. Not a single cloud. Meteorologists knew shit. He wished he could be wrong half the time at work and still have a job.

The library luncheon was in a few hours, and everything was on schedule. He had this event in the bag, and he'd get that black-tie dinner too. Then everyone in three counties would know he'd made it.

He shoved his phone in his back pocket and scratched at his jaw. Would the tent hold if a thunderstorm did roll in?

At least he had a tent. If a storm hit during the tailgate, they'd be screwed. No tent had been ordered for them. Savannah would do a dance if the rains poured down on their heads this afternoon. If she didn't want him to fail before, she must now. He hadn't called since that kiss. *Coward.*

He also hadn't mentioned anything to Maddy about Grey, but he had his eye on her. If they ended up together, it would be what he deserved. Simply because he was unhappy with his current state of confused feelings didn't mean Maddy shouldn't have a little fun. She grumbled at him a little less for being at work when she was with Grey.

"Maddy, we're leaving in thirty minutes. Make sure you're ready."

"Going where?" She sat at the island eating cereal, with her hair piled up on her head, wearing an old T-shirt of his and faded plaid pajama pants. Her face was planted in her phone. As if it would be anywhere else.

"You're coming to work with me today. The library luncheon? Please tell me you didn't forget."

"I can't work with you today. I have like a ton of homework, and I promised Grey we would hang out later."

"You're coming with me because the ladies at this luncheon will like seeing you way better than me. I want you to help serve. I only have Georgia working with me."

The guest list was forty, and he had decided to serve a mixed green salad with citrus, avocado, and almonds topped with grilled chicken or shrimp sautéed in a bourbon barbeque sauce. He wasn't giving the ladies a choice for lunch, because everything else he served might offend their delicate palettes.

"I hate serving. I'm not ever going into the restaurant business."

"I need you to put out the appetizers while I grill up the food. Georgia will serve the drinks." They'd set up a small bar. Georgia was the best bartender he ever hired. "You can handle refills and coffee." He also had hot tea, but no one would want hot beverages on a sticky day. The comparisons of his tea to Savannah's wouldn't exist.

"Can't you hire someone?" She dumped her cereal bowl in the sink.

"When I was your age, I worked in the deli all the time."

"Yeah, I know." She dropped her gaze back to her phone.

He covered the screen with his hand. She jerked her head back up. "You're working today, or that phone disappears. You now have twenty-five minutes."

She marched out of the kitchen, but her words trailed back at him. "I refuse to spend my entire life working like you do. There's more to life than working."

Was he the only parent who thought he screwed up everything? How did Savannah do it with three? He should have made Maddy get a job at a greasy fast-food joint where she'd have to mop bathroom floors and stand over the fryer until her face was an oil slick. Maybe then she'd appreciate working for her father where all he made her do was put on pretty clothes, makeup, and smile as she sat guests. And that was only when he was desperate.

He employed twenty people at every bar. He didn't make her work so she could focus on school. And what thanks did he get?

He dumped his cold coffee in the sink. The doorbell rang. He wasn't expecting anyone, and they had about ten minutes before they needed to leave. If Shirley stood on his porch, he'd have to shut the door in her face. He didn't have time for her this morning.

He checked the side window and let his shoulders drop before he opened the door. "Uncle Harlan, what are you doing here?"

The old man had slicked back what was left of his white hair. His face always had a rosy glow. He'd put on a dress shirt and one of the two ties he owned. "I'm coming to your lunch." Harlan gripped him in a bear hug and pounded his back.

"I think you want a chance to charm some of the ladies."

Harlan straightened his tie. "I can't help it if the ladies find me irresistible."

"I'll get Maddy, and we'll go." He turned for the stairs.

"Jacob."

The tone in Harlan's voice as he used his given name made him stop short. "Is something wrong? Are you sick?" He couldn't bear to lose his uncle so soon after losing his dad.

"Nothing like that. It's Shirley."

"Save it. I don't want to know what she's up to. I've got to kick ass at this luncheon so I can beat Savannah

Savage for the black-tie dinner." He wished it were someone else he had to compete with. If he won, how would she ever forgive him?

"You need to hear this now. Shirley wants the bar."

"My bar? Impossible. Dad left the building and the business to me."

"She says you stole it from her. She's hired herself a lawyer."

"Not Hoke Carter?"

"Nah." He pushed the air with his hand. "Hoke told her over his dead body would he go against Jake's wishes. She had to go a few towns over to find some city slicker with a shiny suit."

JT paced the hall. "They'll have to pry that bar out of my cold, dead hands before she gets it." Shirley would have one hell of a fight from him if she thought for one second she'd take away his success.

"Now, don't go doing anything foolish. I'll go with you to talk to Hoke. He called me this morning and said he'd represent you free of charge since he wrote up my brother's will. He didn't want to bother you about it today with the luncheon and all, but I knew if you didn't hear about this right away, you'd only go off half-cocked the later you found out. You can't afford to lose your temper. Don't give her any ammunition against you."

Shirley had plenty of that, but nothing that would matter now. He'd straightened up the minute he left Heritage River and joined the army. He'd gotten his degree after that, and then he had Maddy. And if nothing before had taught him to get his shit together, the minute he held his newborn baby girl in his arms, all red and screaming at him as if it were his fault she'd been dropped into the cold, cruel world, he knew he had to be the best man he could be for her.

He clapped Harlan on the shoulder. "Thank you, but you don't have to come with me. I'll call Hoke first thing Monday. I promise."

He had one other call he needed to make too. But first, he had to kill it at the luncheon.

The sky was filled with gun-metal-gray storm clouds. A wind had picked up and billowed the sides of the tents as if they were sails on a boat. The fans brought in to keep the space inside the tent cool worked overtime to shove the humidity away. JT checked the weather app. Storm right on schedule. Damn.

The smoke from the grill burned his eyes, but he always loved the smell of meat and fish cooked over an open flame. He never tired of flipping a steak to watch the fire shoot up around the grate and sizzle the meat to the right temperature.

"Dad, I need help." Maddy had pulled her hair into a ponytail that went halfway down her back. She wore a black skirt and white blouse. The blouse was stained, and her feet were bare.

"Where are your shoes? You can't serve food in bare feet. I'll probably get some kind of violation for that."

"My heels keep sinking in the ground. I almost fell twice. We're outside. Who's going to care?"

"The health inspector? Do you have sneakers in the car?"

"No."

He heaved a huge sigh. "Can you ask Georgia to help you?"

"Georgia is too busy running drinks back and forth from the bar to the tables because no one over the age of fifty wants to get up and get their own drinks. And it's hot as hell in that tent. Everyone is sweating. Dixie Bordeaux looks like she's going to have a heart attack."

He had about two minutes before he needed to pull that chicken and cut it into strips. "What do you need? It has to be quick."

"I can't get the door to the library open. It's stuck. And the rest of the appetizers are in the refrigerator. Those ladies want their food. They don't like waiting. You'd think they'd never had a meal before."

He took a quick look into the tent. Women fanned themselves. Most were huddled in conversation with scowls painted on their faces along with too much eyeshadow and lipstick. Harlan made a group of four women way north of the retirement age sitting in the corner laugh. But the side tables were empty of the chopped vegetables, dips, and fruits. The town council stood in a huddle with their heads together deep in conversation. Rowan McGee pointed an anxious finger in his direction. Things didn't look good. He spotted his solution.

"Watch that chicken. Don't let it burn."

"I won't touch the chicken. I'm still vegan," she yelled after him.

He hurried through the tables. He wasn't exactly dressed to be seen out in the front. His apron was dirty with sauce stains. His T-shirt was drenched in sweat. He should have trimmed his beard too. But none of that could matter. He needed the couple walking into the tent from the other side.

"JT, do you have a second? I'd like you to meet someone." Rowan blocked his path with his greasy, slicked-back hair and beady eyes.

"Can I get right back to you?"

"This will only take a second." Rowan gripped his shoulder and led him toward the group standing off to the side. "This is Charlie Ash, Rose Bostik, and Fred Grooms. They all preside on the council with me, and we're the deciding votes for the black-tie formal."

He shook hands with each of them but kept his eyes on the one way to get the library door open. Maddy waved at him from the back of the tent, but he could only shake his head.

"It's a real pleasure to meet y'all. I'm running the kitchen today and don't normally come out from behind my grill. Would you give me a minute to finish up back there? Then I can come out and give a proper hello." He always hated sounding like a southerner, but today he played that drawl for all it was worth.

"How's the food coming? A lot of people are hungry," Rowan said.

"I'm just dying to stop by your new place. I do love a small shot of whiskey on a Friday night." Charlie Ash clapped his age-spotted hands.

He needed to get the hell away from these people. He tried to find Maddy, but she'd ducked back behind the tent. Uncle Harlan hurried to the back of the tent too.

"You come by the Whiskey any Friday night, and I'll fix you any drink you want. On the house. The food will be ready in just a minute. I'm sorry for the delay. If you'll excuse me." He ran off before they could say another word.

He searched the tent and found what he was looking for. He hurried past Lorraine Haywood waving at him. She used to live behind his dad before she hit the lottery on the pick six and moved into the McGee estates up on the hill.

He dropped into a chair at the table occupied by the couple he'd wanted. They both startled at his sudden appearance. "Blaise, boy, is it good to see you." He stuck out his hand.

Blaise shook it with a firm grip. "Hey, man. Great event. This is Grace. I don't think you two officially met yet."

"It's really nice to meet you. I'm sorry to ask for a favor about two seconds after I interrupted you, but we can't get the library door open. Do you have the key?"

Grace stared at Blaise. "I didn't bring my work keys. I think they're at home on my desk."

"Are you sure the door is locked?" Blaise turned back to him.

"I think so. Maddy couldn't get it open. It must've locked after someone shut it earlier. I need to get inside to the fridge now." He should have insisted on having keys to the library. Stupid move. But Arlene, who worked at the library, had opened the door for him and took off for her bag party. Whatever the hell that was.

"I'll run home and get my keys. You go with JT and see if the door is stuck. It does that sometimes in heat like this." Grace looked toward the sky. The clouds took on a horror-movie quality. "I hope this weather holds."

Blaise handed her his keys, and she ran off.

"Thank you. She's nice."

Blaise smiled. "Yeah, she is. She was a big surprise too. I'll have to tell you all about it over a big steak. Let's go see this door."

Maddy intercepted him and Blaise. She still had nothing on her feet. "Dad, you need to come look at the chicken. Hello, Mr. Savage."

Blaise nodded. "Nice to see you, Maddy."

"Is Uncle Harlan with you? Ask him to pull it off the grill and cut it in strips. He knows what to do. I'm trying to get the library open, and for Christ's sake, put on some shoes."

"I don't have any shoes I can put on. I'll go back to the chicken, but don't say I didn't warn you." She marched off.

"Why doesn't she have shoes?" Blaise pulled his phone out of his pocket and tapped at the screen.

"She's a teenager. That's why."

"I think I actually understand that."

They ran around the outside of the tent. Blaise tugged on the library door. "I don't think it's locked, but it is definitely stuck. When Grace comes back, she can unlock the front doors. You'll have to bring the food through the stacks of books."

He fisted his hands on his hips and hung his head. This day was a shit show. "I just need to plate some food for these people before they start eating the tablecloths. Thanks for coming. I didn't think I'd see you here."

"Because you're my sister's competition?"

He laughed. "Yeah, I guess so."

"You're also helping my girlfriend's library. I was sort of stuck in the middle on that one. Piss off my sister or piss off the woman I sleep next to."

"Screwed either way."

"You got that right."

Maddy jumped up and down and waved him over. "Dad, the chicken."

"Go see what she needs. I'll wait here for Grace." Blaise shoved his phone back in his pocket.

"Thanks, man. I owe you."

"Take it off my tab."

He ran over to the grill. Uncle Harlan had abandoned his tie, unbuttoned the top button of his dress shirt, and rolled up the sleeves. He stood over the cutting board, staring at the chicken.

"What's the matter? Is it burned?" Cajun wasn't exactly the flavor he was going for, but he could pass off blackened chicken as that if he had to. Maybe no one would notice if he drowned the salad in dressing.

"The burned part ain't the full problem. The chicken had a fight with the ground. The ground came out a few points ahead." Uncle Harlan kept staring at the food.

"Why are you staring at it like that?" And where was Grace with those keys? Did he just feel a raindrop?

"I'm wondering if you can see the dirt that stuck to it when it fell. You don't have enough chicken to start over." Harlan shrugged and sliced the chicken into strips.

"You can't serve food that fell on the ground," Maddy said.

"You'd be surprised what kind of food gets served in certain places. Never my bars, but today, I'm desperate. Those people are hungry, the town council is here, and we have about ten minutes before the skies open up. Maddy, start plating the greens. I'll get the other ingredients."

"JT, I'm out of iced tea and seltzer." Georgia stuck her head through the back entrance of the tent. "I called Parker, but he's at the Nashville location. I tried Gil. He said he'd send more, but he's swamped over there. It might be a while."

"Will they drink soda?" He tossed almonds into a bowl.

"Only diet. Cranky old ladies." She turned without another word.

"Where's the shrimp?" He turned in circles.

"I think you forgot to cook it." Maddy dumped mixed greens onto plates with the finesse of a street fighter in a ballet dance.

"Shit," he shouted. "I'm screwed. The shrimp is in the library fridge. What the hell was I thinking?"

As if to answer his stupid question, the wind picked up speed. Was that another drop?

Grace and Blaise hurried across the lawn, each holding a tray. "We brought these, and we'll help you get the rest," Grace said. She pulled a bag off her shoulder and dug out sneakers. "Hi, Maddy. I'm Grace. I don't know if we're the same size, but Blaise said you needed some shoes. I also brought socks."

"If you weren't already dating this guy, I'd kiss you full on the mouth. I swear I would." Instead, JT kissed her cheek.

"That's enough of that." Blaise shoved him away but laughed.

"Let's hurry. We'll get the rest of the trays." Grace tugged on Blaise's arm, and they ran off.

"Maddy, go with them and get the shrimp. Hurry." Maddy shoved her feet in the shoes and followed.

"Can I save this lunch?" He turned back to Harlan.

"I think you can. The chicken is ready. Good thing you're serving a cold meal. Cover those salads while you cook up the shrimp. When you're ready, I'll help you serve to get the plates down faster. Ask Blaise and his pretty lady to help too."

"I can't ask them. She runs the library. I'm not supposed to have help from the library."

"You already do. No point in stopping now."

Maddy brought him the shrimp. He tossed them in bourbon sauce and grilled them up. Harlan, Maddy, and

Grace brought out the appetizers. Every guest darted for the food tables.

"I think we might pull this off." He dropped shrimp onto the salads.

Lightning split open the gray sky. Thunder marched in on its heels. The wind gave one final yell, and the clouds pushed out all that water they'd been holding on to. Rain came down fast and heavy, sinking the top of the tent and putting out the grill. The power went out, stopping the fans and anything still on in the library.

Forty people yelled and ran for cover. Rose Bostik slipped on the wet grass and nosedived as if she were stealing home plate. Charlie Ash's toupee couldn't handle that much water. It slid off his head and landed in a mud puddle before he could grab it.

Rain soaked through JT's jeans and T-shirt. Maddy was sodden, and Grace and Blaise dripping. Harlan managed to get under the corner of the tent in time. A car turned into the lot. The driver honked its horn.

Gil hopped out and grabbed something out of the trunk. He ran over to where they all stood in the rain. "I have the seltzer." He held up the case like a prize in a horse show.

If the whole scene wasn't so damn pathetic, he'd laugh.

JT checked his watch. Inside of thirty minutes, the dangerous downpours, sky-to-ground lightning, and tornado-like winds dropped on their heads and then screamed their way out of town as if they'd never been there. The sky in Heritage River had returned to a vast blue filled with promises of great things to come. The earlier signs of clouds made of black cotton and despair were gone.

He sat under the part of the tent still standing. The other half of it hung low to the ground, the poles broken from the weight of the rain. He wanted to stay in that spot by himself until he became young again.

Here had been his big chance to prove he was more than the kid who failed classes, who wasted time chasing after his friends with the real talent and were the ones going places, who broke just about every rule put in front of him because he could.

Word would get to Savannah, and she'd say she'd been right about a loser like him all along. Jacob Tyler Davies was nothing more than a fool with a fool's wish.

Everyone in attendance had left without a single thing to eat. No way would the town council award him anything. He might as well as step out of the competition now. Not that he would. He'd be damned if he'd concede to a loss.

His phone vibrated in his pocket. He took a quick glance but shoved it away. The Whiskey would have to do without him a few hours more. Georgia and Gil would figure things out, whatever was wrong.

He needed to clean up the grill area, pack up the trailer, and return his shit to the Whiskey. He also needed to get home to Maddy. She expected him to have supper with her since he'd forced her to work today. He owed her more of his time, but five more minutes of sitting wouldn't hurt anything.

"You going to stay there all night?" Savannah ambled up and took a seat opposite him.

Her dark hair fell in loose waves over her shoulders. Sunglasses hung in the low-cut collar of the white shirt, showing off her smooth skin and the tops of her breasts. He wanted to run his finger under the thin black rope around her neck that ended in a silver charm and dangled dangerously close to those sunglasses.

"Did you come here to gloat?" He turned his gaze away from the eyes that could look at him and undo him in seconds.

"I saw the tent and someone sitting under it. Thought I'd warn them the whole thing might come down on their head. I was halfway across the lawn before I realized it was you."

"I've been warned I'm sitting under an unsafe structure. You've done your good deed for the day. You can go now."

"Do you have to stack the tables?" She responded as if she hadn't heard the bite in his tone.

"I do. The rental guys will be back tomorrow to pick everything up." He'd be there longer than he thought.

"I can help you."

"I don't want your help. I want you to go." A flame of humiliation cooked his insides. He could handle just about anyone in town seeing him at this moment but not her. He needed his feelings for her to go away. Instead, they only intensified because he couldn't wipe his memory free of her.

"You are as stubborn as they come. You'll be here for hours cleaning up. We can put our differences aside for now. Let me help you."

What he wanted was for her to stay and smile at him, to ease the grip on his chest because she had been the only one who could do that, and at the same time—he wanted her to go.

"Maddy is going to be mad at me again." He pulled out his phone and typed a quick text to tell his daughter he'd be late. He'd have to unload the trailer back at the Whiskey, and he'd probably get pulled into something the second he stepped inside. He wouldn't get home until after Maddy went to sleep.

"Why?"

"She wants me to work less. I think it's because of the move. She's having trouble making friends, so spending time with her is my punishment. That's how she sees it, that she's punishing me by keeping me from the thing I'd rather be doing." He pushed out of the chair and started closing up the tables.

"She thinks you'd rather work than be with her?" She followed his lead, breaking down other tables and stacking them under the part of the tent still standing.

"I've had to work. I'm the only parent, and I had to make a living, didn't I? I couldn't make myself fit into an office job with a better schedule, and believe me, I tried. Running a bar worked for me, and until recently she didn't seem to mind my hours."

"I'm not judging you." She stopped securing the legs of another table and stared at him.

"Sounds like it." He turned away from her and rolled a table to the stack.

"Hey. Don't turn your back on me. All I asked is what Maddy thinks."

He pivoted back around. That low flame of humiliation grew into an angry fire. The anger wasn't for her, but he didn't know where to put all his frustration.

She glared at him with eyes of steel.

"You know what I want to know? Why do you think you need to manage everyone?" He wanted to push away all the hurt inside him, and all he was managing to do was piss her off.

She cleared the space between them and tilted her chin up. "Because I get things done that way when I can't rely on other people to hold up their end of the bargain. A lot of people promise things and then don't come through."

She meant his leaving town on her, but he couldn't go there. Not while he was mad enough to hit something. Not her. Never her or any woman. He had that much sense. "I need to pack up. I don't have time for this conversation."

"Fine. Do it yourself." She turned on her heel.

He should let her go. She was nothing more than an old fling, an old friend at best. She was better off without him. He wasn't ever going to change. Today proved that. "I'm sorry."

She stopped. With her back to him, she said, "You are an ass, JT Davies."

He went to her and placed his hands on her shoulders. She turned under his touch and faced him. The anger cooled down and was replaced with the warmth of wanting her because no one could see through him the way she did. "Do you know what really makes me an ass?"

She narrowed her eyes. "What?"

"This." He shoved all reason out of his head and cupped her face in his hands. He wanted to taste all of her.

He pulled her close and pressed his lips against hers, but she resisted, and he almost backed off until she yielded to him and opened her mouth. When her tongue found his, the anger destroying his insides turned to smoldering ash. Kissing her set his world right.

He ran his hand down the side of her neck and traced the skin under her rope necklace with his fingers until he found that charm. He cupped her breast through her shirt, and she let out the tiniest of moans.

His heart pounded in his ears as she wrapped her arms around his waist and her hands trailed up his back. He'd wanted to kiss her again every second since the last time in her store. He couldn't get her out of his system, and he was afraid the more he tasted, the more he'd want. Even though she responded to his touch, would she walk down the street with him for everyone to see, or was he still her best-kept secret?

He eased back. She stared up at him with wide eyes.

Her lips were swollen and red. Her chest heaved against his, driving him mad. "Savannah, I don't know why I keep kissing you."

"You are being very forward."

"Do you like when I kiss you?"

"I shouldn't. What would people say if they saw us?"

He stepped back and let his arms drop at his waist. "Go home."

She flinched but righted herself. "I shouldn't like kissing you because my husband died nine months ago. I'd think a woman with a little self-respect would wait longer to want to kiss a man out in public."

"Who cares what other people think. I like kissing you. Besides, Colton already saw us."

"I care what people will say. I have three children to think about. You weren't supposed to walk back into my life and remind me of who I was before I was married. I don't know how to handle how I feel when you kiss me. And as for Colton, I don't want him thinking we're a thing."

She didn't want her brothers to know about them like before. Her words stung now as much as they did back then. "I won't embarrass you."

"I didn't mean it like that." She crossed her arms around her middle and stared at the ground.

"I think you did, lady. Now go. I have work to do."

"JT, that night when I said—"

"Save it."

"You are the most thickheaded man I've ever met. Even more so than my brothers, and that's saying something. Do you know nothing about me at all? I know we haven't kept in touch, but do you have any idea what kind of a person I am?"

"You don't want the people of Heritage River to have a reason to gossip about you, and being with me would give them a lot to chew on. Is there anything else I need to know?"

"You know what? Never mind. But I will tell you this." She pointed a finger at him. "If you ever kiss me again, so help me God, I'll wrap your tongue around your head and choke you with it." She marched away.

He couldn't let her walk away now. He'd stuck his foot in his mouth again, let his anger fog his brain. When would he learn? "Savannah, wait."

She had one word for him, and all she had to do was point up.

Chapter Fourteen

Savannah checked the price tag of the bridesmaid dress for the third time and smothered a groan. The cost of her dress plus the cost of Caroline's junior bridesmaid dress would stretch her monthly budget until it grew ugly, red, swollen stretch marks and then exploded wide open in a bloody mess.

She had to make it to the black-tie formal. With the publicity from that, she'd bring in customers and she'd be okay. She had to be. She had no other plan.

Harley and Grace scoured the racks of dresses at I Now Pronounce You for the perfect dress for Harley's wedding. She pretended to search too, but her heart was stuck in her checkbook. She couldn't be happier for Colton and Harley, and she wanted to support them in every way, including being in the wedding, but she needed to support her three children and keep the roof over their heads too. The wedding came at a bad time, is all. She sipped the champagne left for them by Carrie, the owner, who was off helping a bride try on wedding gowns.

"What do you think of this one?" Grace swooped out of the dressing room and up onto the platform in front of the three-way mirror.

She wore a full-length gown in navy blue with lace arms and a sweetheart neck. The mermaid-style dress flattered Grace's curves, and the dark blue brought out the blue in her eyes.

"You're stunning." Harley clasped her hands together. "Thank you both for coming with me today. I wanted a special day for just the three of us, like sisters."

Harley had no siblings, and her last relative had passed away a year ago, leaving her only Colton and their son.

Grace waved her hand in the air. "I'm thrilled to be included. I never had a family at all, except for Chloe, until Blaise walked into my life and shared his with me, so thank you for including me. I haven't been in a wedding in a very long time."

"Are you and Blaise ever going to get married?" Savannah made a show of lifting a dress off the rack, holding it against herself, and putting it back. Next week she'd have enough money for the deposit for the dress, if more customers came into the shop.

"We talk about it, but if I remarry, Larry gets out of the alimony. I want him to choke on those checks a few more years." Grace shrugged, stuck out her tongue, and crossed her eyes. "I like things the way they are right now. I get to spend as much time with Blaise as I want, and then he goes home and does his own laundry. I never want to wash and fold a man's underwear ever again. Now getting him out of that underwear is another story."

"Amen to that." Harley held up her champagne glass. "I'm having the best sex of my life, but I told Colton when he moved in I wasn't his personal assistant. He could wash his own underwear."

"Ladies, I don't want to hear about my brothers' boxer briefs off or on, if you don't mind." Savannah gulped down some of the champagne.

Grace ran her hands along her arms. "I do like the sleeves. The lace is so pretty."

"I don't know. The dress is pretty, very pretty, but I think it's going to accent my middle." She squeezed the extra skin spilling over the top of her jeans. No matter how many crunches or hours on the elliptical she accumulated, she couldn't seem to flatten out her middle. "Maybe something a little less unforgiving?"

She wanted to run from the store because her motives to get Grace out of the dress were selfish and had nothing to do with her thickening waist. She swigged the last of the champagne.

"Savannah, you have a great body, but if you don't like it, we'll find something else. I want everyone to be happy because I'm so happy I have to pinch myself sometimes. I never dreamed I'd spend the rest of my life with Colton." Harley held up a long-sleeved, dark-gray chiffon dress. The designer name on the tag told her the price could crush an elephant. "Would you mind trying this one on?"

She forced a smile on her face, wanted to pour herself more to drink but didn't, and took the dress from Harley. "I'd love to."

The dress had spaghetti straps and sleeves that hung loosely off the shoulders, creating a dramatic and chic cold-shoulder effect. The material pleated in the middle, hiding any of her earlier concerns about extra weight, and the long slit up the front made her legs go on forever. The dress was perfect. She checked the price and tried not to hyperventilate.

"Savannah, do you need help?" Grace called from the other side of the wall.

"Coming."

She stepped around the wall between the dressing rooms and the front of the store. Harley sucked in her breath.

"Wow," Grace said.

"You look amazing," the bride trying on her dress said from the platform on the other side of the store.

"That's the perfect color for you with your dark hair, and the way it brings out the silver in your eyes... Grace, would you wear that dress?" Harley walked in circles around her.

"I'd wear that if it made me look half as good as it does on Savannah."

"Are you sure?" She needed to derail this a little. "We could try on more. You still have plenty of time to decide. I don't want you to choose a dress because of me. It's your wedding, and you'll have to look at the pictures. Maybe we should come back next week with Ella."

"I think we found the perfect dress," Grace said. "Ella is going to rock that dress anyway. She works out every day doing that online program thingy."

Savannah poured more champagne with a shaking hand. "I guess we found the dress."

"Carrie, we need measurements, and lunch, ladies, is on me. Well, it's on Colton." Harley waved a credit card in the air. "I thought we'd go to the Whiskey Bar. I haven't been there yet. Colton says it's major league. Were you two going to go on Friday night to watch the guys play?"

"What? My brothers are going to play at the Whiskey Bar?" She banged her leg with her fist. "Those jerks. I asked Colton to talk to me first, but he did what he always does." She deposited the glass back down on the table, almost knocking it over. She needed something way stronger than champagne.

"I'm sorry, Savannah. I thought you knew. It's only for one night," Harley said.

"They only need one night. It doesn't matter that they aren't the original Savage anymore or that they play mostly new music. When Colton and Blaise step on a stage anywhere, people still come. The roof will blow off the Whiskey Bar if they play there."

"You could ask them to play at the Tea Room." Grace turned her glass in her hand.

"I asked Colton. He said rock music and tea don't mix."

"You went to the wrong brother." Grace winked. "Ask Blaise. No offense, Harley."

Harley waved her hand in the air. "None taken. I love him, but you're right. He's a big fat pain in the butt when it comes to his stage presence."

Her phone came to life with the intro to the Savage song "Rockers Lullaby." One of her kids was calling. Blaise wrote the song for her after Jud was born. Grace was right. Blaise's heart was easier to find.

"Hi, Jud."

"Mom, something is wrong with my account. The school is saying I have a balance." His voice rang in her ears. "I can't do early registration, and I need to get the class I want next semester."

Savannah pushed through the door of the bridal shop. No one else needed to hear this conversation. The afternoon heat met her on the sidewalk. "I'll check into it when I get home. When does registration close?"

"Tomorrow."

Figured.

"Um, Savannah, honey, you're still in the dress." Carrie popped her head out the door with a crease between her brows and a clenched jaw.

She covered the phone with her hand. "I'm sorry. I'll only be a second." She turned her back on Carrie so she'd get the hint. What did the woman think she was going to do, run away? She wasn't a criminal. She was just someone who preferred her private life stay private.

"Jud, what were you saying?"

"I thought Dad left enough money for all of us to go to school. You said money wouldn't be an object."

"He did. It's probably just a mistake. I'll make sure

the money didn't land in another account. I'll text you when I know something. How is school going otherwise?" The only account the money went into was the one she used to open the business. She would have to pay for the deposit on the dress with a credit card that was almost maxed out. She'd have to take out another loan to pay for Jud's school, and that was if anyone would give her one.

"Fine."

"How are your classes?"

"Okay. I have to go."

"Love you."

"You too." He hung up.

She leaned against the warm brick of the building, then jumped away before she put a snag in a dress she couldn't afford. She and Jud had made such progress after last year's disaster when he and Cash went head-to-head, but after Adam died, Jud pulled away again, and sometimes she couldn't steer him back.

She took a deep breath. She would have to wrestle her situation under control. She had to make it to the black-tie dinner. The publicity would bring customers in, and then she'd be fine.

What if JT won the dinner? Part of her wanted him to win. He worked hard to build a successful franchise. She had Googled him after he came back to town. Before he showed up, she had made a promise with herself not to search him out and find where he lived or worked. That wouldn't have been fair to Adam.

But it didn't mean she hadn't thought about JT and remembered what life had been like with him in it. No matter how hard she tried, she could never stop loving him. The people of this town needed to see what he'd made of himself.

That kiss on the library lawn had nearly done her in. She hadn't been able to erase the feeling of his lips on hers or his calloused hands against her face. He'd given her more reasons to wish he'd make love to her.

Harley shoved her head out of the door. "Carrie is ready to take your measurements and the deposit, and then we'll go to lunch. Are you sure you're okay about the guys helping JT out? You looked a little flushed."

She forced a smile on her face and straightened her shoulders. "Great. I'm great. No problem at all."

Nothing money, strangling her brothers, and a new heart couldn't fix.

Chapter Fifteen

JT poked his head around the corner. He had a straight shot over the bar and to the table where three pretty women sat. The one with the bright eyes and the dark hair that curled past her shoulders had his jeans feeling slightly uncomfortable. She had that necklace on again, and he had to admit he was a little jealous of that silver charm hanging between her breasts. She drove him crazy. He needed one night with her, and he would show her he was worth her time.

He couldn't control himself around her. After the last kiss, she hated him more than she had before.

"JT, what are you staring at?" Georgia said over her shoulder as she shook a cocktail for a customer at the bar.

"Lower your voice. I'm going to take an order."

"We have servers for that." She shook her head and laughed.

Okay, so he was pretty obvious. Voices mixed with

laughter and the clank of silverware swirled like brandy in a glass. He had a pretty good size lunch crowd.

"What can I get you ladies?" He leaned on the edge of the table.

She snapped her head up from her phone and ran her gaze over him. He put his hands behind his back to give her a better look. She stopped at his belt buckle then found something else to look at. He bounced on the balls of his feet, hoping to keep the smirk off his face. She'd liked that kiss as much as he'd hoped.

"Hi, JT. How's Maddy?" Grace glanced up from her menu.

"She's great, thank you. And thanks again for your sneakers. I'll get them back to you."

"Sneakers? What's that all about?" Savannah played with her necklace. "Were you two hanging out?" She placed the charm between her teeth.

He wanted to be that charm.

"I lent Maddy my sneakers the day of the library luncheon. I'm sorry I couldn't do more to help."

"Can't control the weather." But he was pretty sure Savannah had tried. She liked to control everything.

"I'll have a salad and an iced tea," Grace said.

"I want a cheeseburger and fries. And a Coke." Harley handed the menu back.

"What about you?" He risked a glance at that necklace hanging back in its place.

"I'm not hungry, thanks." She folded her hands in her lap.

"Savannah, you have to eat. This is our special lunch," Harley said.

"Don't spoil the special lunch." He clapped her on the shoulder because he needed to touch her. "Your future sister-in-law wants to have lunch with you. Stop being cantankerous." He handed her the menu.

She turned to Harley. "I'm sorry I'm being such a grouch today. I'll have the salad, too, and a beer."

"What kind?"

"What kind what?"

"Savannah, I have twenty different beers here. Which one do you want?" He pointed to the chalkboard.

She waved him away. "Surprise me."

He leaned in, and she smelled like summer. "Be careful what you challenge me with."

He hurried into the kitchen and placed their order. Behind the bar he poured a pale ale and scribbled a note. He would ask her out on a date. Something he probably should have done before he took advantage of her that first time. But he'd been young, stupid, and head over heels for the girl who had the world on a string. Savannah was everything he wasn't. She was smart and had a future. He never dreamed someone like her would look twice at him. When she slid off those shorts, he had been a goner. And a coward. He'd make up for it now, if she'd let him.

He would slip the note in her hand and watch her face as she read it. Maybe she'd know then how much he needed her.

The door swung open, bringing in the heat and

Rowan McGee with Rose Bostik and Fred Grooms. He stopped on the way back to Savannah. What were they doing there?

"Rowan, how nice to see you again. Welcome to the Whiskey Bar. We'll get you a table in a minute." He shook their hands. The pale ale sweated in his other one.

"We thought we'd come to your place for our taste test. Seemed unfair the storm came in and swooped the library luncheon into its funnel. You can't control the weather."

His words exactly. "Thank you. I appreciate it. Why don't y'all have a seat at the bar? Georgia will take good care of you until a table is ready. Whatever you want is on me." He guided them to the bar and helped Rose onto the stool. The woman's legs dangled inches above the footrest.

"Where you headed?" Rowan said.

He held up the drink. "Bringing a customer their drink. I'll be right back." The bar might be crowded, but he was understaffed, the kitchen line had been behind schedule all day, and Parker was in Nashville. He couldn't afford to lose this group again. He still wanted that black-tie dinner.

He glanced over at Savannah. He wanted her too. Could he have both? No. If he won that contest, he would lose her. She had her own reasons for wanting to win. He could probably guess what some of them were. Her store was new. She needed the foot traffic. Her lunch crowd was light. He'd never seen any restaurant survive who couldn't keep a lunch crowd. Selling tea leaves in glass jars wouldn't be enough to keep the lights on.

"Mr. Davies, is this your entire menu?" Rose's dried-up voice dragged him out of his thoughts.

"Yes, ma'am, it is."

"Your father offered far more in the way of food options." She dropped the menu on the bar.

"This isn't my father's place. I specialize in whiskey, but I don't want my customers drinking without food. His pulled pork is on the menu. You could order that."

She scrunched up her birdlike face. "I don't see how you'll ever make a success out of a place that condones so much drinking. Liquor is the gateway to sin."

"Rose, you're not being fair now." Rowan tried to laugh off the comment, but it stuck.

This woman was like everyone else. "I'm afraid I don't agree with you, and the four other Whiskey Bars I own agree with me." No matter how many places he owned or how much money he made, women like Rose would never change their minds about him. He looked at her and saw Shirley.

"You're selling sin. I'm not sure I can recommend you for our event. Our town has a moral reputation to uphold. What would Heritage River look like if the caterer for an event that boasts our accomplishments is really a sinner?"

Fred Grooms tried to hide in his menu. *Yeah, good luck with that, dude.*

His phone vibrated in his pocket, but he couldn't answer it. "You know what? You're right. I am a sinner. A big one. I even masturbate. But then so is everyone in this place, and if I had to take a guess, so are you."

Rose almost fell off the stool.

"Now if you'll excuse me." He forced himself forward toward Savannah, or he might kick that old lady right onto her butt. Uncle Harlan would not be pleased with him if he did that, and when word spread he'd spoken to Rose inappropriately, Harlan would try to box his ears. It didn't matter he was a grown-ass man now.

He took a deep breath and placed the beer in front of Savannah. "It's a pale ale and has peach undertones. I thought you might like it. You always liked peaches, didn't you?"

She opened her mouth, but only a squeak came out. He slid the note into her hand. She looked down at it and back at him.

"Read it."

His phone vibrated again. He dug it out of the front pocket of his jeans. Maddy.

Savannah rummaged through her big bag and pulled out her phone. "Grey, are you okay?"

"Maddy, what's up? I'm kind of busy."

"Dad." She sobbed into the phone. "You have to come to school. I've been suspended."

"Suspended?" Savannah yelled into her phone. "I'll be right there." She shoved her way out of her seat.

"Do you want us to come?" Grace said.

"No, no. Stay. I'll call you if I need anything." She slapped her head. "I have to get Caroline to dance practice."

Harley waved her hands in the air. "We'll get her there."

Savannah glared at him. His heart sank.

"Grey is with Maddy. They're in trouble," she said.

"I'll drive you." He reached for her hand.

She pulled away. "You did this."

"They did this. Let's go find out the details first."

"Fine." She marched away.

The note sat crumpled on the table.

Chapter Sixteen

Savannah ran into the high school, not waiting for JT to even park. What had those two kids done? They could ruin their future. She pulled at the second set of glass doors. Her body went forward, but the door didn't budge. Her shoulder collided with the glass and a pain shot up her neck.

She scrounged for her wallet in her tote, fought to get her license out, and shoved it against the black box. JT ran up beside her. "Get out your license, and hurry."

He pulled and tugged until his wallet came loose from the front pocket of his jeans. "Here."

The door buzzed, and she flew past the reception desk. Tess waved the sign-in sheet at her, but Savannah didn't stop. Too damn bad. She wasn't signing in.

"Where is he?" She stood before the main counter in the office.

Debbie looked up at her with a mug halfway to her

mouth. She pointed to Joann Humphreys' office. The door was closed. "Colton is in there with him."

She let out a long, slow breath. She wanted to get in there and handle whatever was happening.

JT ambled into the office and looked around. "Where are they?"

"Your daughter is in the principal's office too. Mr. Savage is in with them."

"Can your brother handle this?" he whispered in her ear.

"My brother can handle anything. Can we go in?"

"I'll let her know you're here." Debbie picked up the receiver and punched the numbers.

JT flopped into a chair and stretched out his long legs.

"How can you sit at a time like this?" She tugged at her necklace.

"You seem to have the pacing under control. Not exactly enough room for both of us to do it."

"This is no time to be cavalier. Our kids are in trouble. Grey never got into trouble before." What was happening in her family? Everything was falling apart. Couldn't she have a moment where everything was running smoothly? If it wasn't Grey, it was Caroline's grades or the money for Jud.

"Kids get in trouble." He ran a hand over his jaw.

"But suspended? This could ruin his chances for college. He could blow his whole future on one stupid move. This is my fault. I'm not paying enough attention. I'm too busy trying to run that Tea Room, and that's falling apart. I should've stayed home and kept a better eye on him."

He jumped back and up and grabbed her by the shoulders. "Hey, this isn't your fault. Sometimes kids make mistakes. Let's see what the principal says. Maybe it won't be so bad."

"It's bad. They're getting suspended, and I don't even know what for."

"I got suspended. They'll be fine."

"Things are different now. When you got suspended, it was a vacation. You went fishing or worked with your dad. You weren't even counted as absent. They'll lose credit and have to repeal to get it back. Suspension goes on their permanent record. This is a disaster."

The door to the office swung open. Colton came out, shaking his head. "I tried." He leaned in. "But that woman is one uptight bitch." He patted her shoulder, shook hands with JT, and left.

"Mrs. Montgomery, Mr. Davies, please come in." Joann Humphreys, with her gray hair pulled into its migraine-causing bun, ushered them to the end of the gangplank.

"You have to be kidding me." JT couldn't help it. He laughed, and the acrid principal stared at him with puckered lips and eyes the size of brandy snifters.

"Mr. Davies, I don't see what could possibly be amusing here. Your daughter and Mr. Montgomery were caught with vaping devices in the locker room when they should have been in class. They were in possession of a smoking apparatus, and Madeline has already been disciplined for a dress-code violation.

Our three-strikes policy indicates the punishment is extended detention. Madeline must report to three consecutive detentions immediately after school for three hours. During that time, she'll have to participate in a community service project. You should be taking this seriously."

"JT, could you sit down, please?" Savannah pointed to the empty chair beside her while managing to glare at him.

"I think I'll stand, thanks. Okay, I'll give you the smoking thing is a problem. I don't want her smoking because it's unhealthy and gives you cancer and shit. But a three-hour detention for three days because she cut class? That's a bit over the top, don't you think? How about one day detention, and we call it even?"

"This isn't a negotiation. Considering your line of work, she could have easily been in possession of alcohol. That would have indeed been cause for suspension. Why the children called you and said they were being suspended was beyond me. I do apologize for that miscommunication. I believe Mr. Savage riled them up."

"Hold on." Savannah put a palm up to Pucker Face. "My brother would never do that."

"Mr. Savage has problems following the school policies. He seems to think the rules don't apply to him or those he cares about."

"You couldn't be more wrong about that. I'm not saying Colton doesn't bend the rules so far they look as if they'll shatter, but truth and honesty are codes he lives by. You don't know my brother at all. Don't go blaming miscommunication on him. Now what's going to happen to Grey?"

"Greyson will serve two lunch detentions. Cell phone usage will not be allowed during that time. If he is caught using the phone, it will be confiscated and you will be required to pick it up at the end of the following school day. I have copied the discipline action from the handbook." Humphreys handed Savannah a piece of paper highlighted in several places.

"How come he gets off easier than Maddy?" Was his daughter being treated unfairly?

Savannah shot that glare at him again and dropped the paper back onto the principal's desk. He wanted to smooth the line between her brows, but he had to know what happened with the kids. "I'm sorry. I don't understand the school rules." He kept his back to the principal and met Savannah's gaze so she'd know he meant what he said.

"Greyson isn't in the habit of getting into trouble. Madeline took the blame for possession of the smoking device. She claims Greyson had nothing to do with it. She showed him what she had, and the physical education teacher walked in on them." Humphreys tapped her fingers on the desk.

He turned to look back into the main office, even though the door was closed and the kids were out there waiting for them. What the hell was his daughter thinking? She stuck up for her friend. She wasn't a snitch. His heart did a little tumble in his chest. She was all him, and thank the liquor gods for that. Sometimes that was good; other times, not so much. He'd have to talk to her about that after he read her the riot act for smoking and cutting.

"Give Grey the same punishment as Maddy." Savannah stood and tilted her chin up.

"That's not necessary. Greyson doesn't have the same history."

"Savannah, you don't have to do this." He gripped her arm.

She turned to him. Her eyes had darkened to the color of smoke-filled clouds. "It's not fair. They can serve together. A little community service won't hurt them."

His chest did that tumble again.

"I have one request. Whatever community service they serve over the next three days, I want Colton to be the teacher supervisor."

"He isn't slotted for extended detention."

She pulled out her phone and began tapping away.

"Why?" He read over her shoulder as she typed.

Colton sent a text back.

Hell yes.

"Because there won't be any miscommunication if he's there."

"I can't allow that," Joann said.

"Of course, you can. He's a teacher here, no matter how much you hate it. The kids and the parents love him, and he works for free. You're going to do this." Savannah turned on her heel and yanked the door open. "Greyson, let's go."

Her bossy, run-the-show attitude was kind of a turn-on. He followed her out.

"Maddy." He nodded in the direction Savannah and Grey went.

She scurried after him. "Dad, I'm so sorry."

He stopped on the sidewalk. "Save it. You're grounded. You've got some detention-community service thing for the next three days, and then for a week it's straight to the bar after school until I take you home. No hanging out with friends. Just be glad I don't take your phone. And the only reason why I'm not is because I'm proud of you for not snitching out Grey." He threw an arm around her and pulled her close.

She rested her head against his chest. "I really am sorry. I won't do it again."

He eased back. "Don't smoke. You'll give yourself lung cancer. And don't drink, and don't do stupid things that could get you killed. Where'd you get that ecig?"

Savannah and Grey had made it to his truck parked at the end of the lot. She pointed a finger in his face while he stared at his shoes.

"I can't tell you."

"It's his?"

"Dad, I can't say."

"Madeline Elizabeth, if you don't tell me how you are in possession of a vaping device, you won't see that phone until I'm dead."

She tucked her hair behind her ear and glanced over

at Grey, who was getting reamed by his mom. "He paid a senior to buy it for him. He wanted to try it. Thought it might be cool. I was trying to talk him out of it when Mr. Holmes walked in. I tried to say it was a USB stick, but Mr. Holmes knew. I took the blame. But you can't tell Mrs. Montgomery. Grey doesn't want her to worry. She's been upset about something lately, and he doesn't know what it is."

"Is Mrs. Montgomery upset because of her husband?"

Savannah had pushed him away because she thought she should still be grieving for her husband. He hadn't really considered how she felt about losing her spouse. He'd allowed his anger to cloud out what she needed. He should give her space, and when she was ready, she could come to him. If she even wanted him. He regretted giving her that note. She didn't want to go on a date with him. He was just jumping first and thinking later.

"He doesn't think that's it. He says she misses him, but she seems to be handling things well. It's something else."

Would Savannah tell him what was bothering her? Did she trust him enough to let him help her? "Wait for me in the truck." He unlocked the doors.

"Dad, you can't tell her."

"I'm not." He was a lot of things. But he was no snitch.

Maddy slid into the back seat of the truck without another word.

He strode up to Savannah and stopped her in mid-sentence. Grey's face was the color of a Red Bush label. "Are you ready to go?"

"You don't have to give us a ride. I'll text someone to come get us, but thanks."

"Grey, go wait with Maddy." He ignored what she said, which was going to piss her off, but he needed her alone for a minute.

"Excuse me? I just told you we don't need a ride. Don't you dare go telling my son what to do."

Grey bounced his gaze between the two of them. "Mom?"

"I want to take you home or back to your minivan or wherever you want to go. I'm trying to help."

"I don't need any help, thank you very much."

"Grey, can you give me and your mom a minute, please?"

Grey jumped into the truck beside Maddy.

Savannah stared at the sky and blew air out of her nose.

"JT, I don't have time for this. I have to go home and deal with a son who's in trouble at school. Then when I'm done with that, I will argue with my thirteen-year-old about her homework, make dinner, prepare for my work-day, do the laundry, and pay the bills all before I collapse into bed."

"You're not afraid of anything, are you?" He took a risk and rubbed the ends of her hair between his fingers. She gave so much to her family. She provided for them, supported them without asking for anything for herself.

She helped others, but she did not want to be the one granted help.

"What are you talking about?" She backed up.

"You stand up to whatever is in your path, and you deal with it." He stepped closer. He didn't want her running away from him.

"I can't wait for someone to come around and take care of what needs to be done, or nothing will get accomplished." Tears filled her eyes.

"Hey." He pulled her against him, and she didn't fight him this time. Her hair smelled like strawberries, and his blood rushed south. "It's okay. Grey will grow up and become an upstanding citizen. I promise."

She pushed away from him and swiped at her face. "Nothing is okay. Every time I think I've turned a corner, something else falls apart. I'm not sure how much more I can take."

He wanted her back in his arms, but her rigid posture said stay away. She needed to do this alone.

He ran a hand over his face. "I know you're upset right now, but just talk to Grey. Don't yell at him or lecture him. Maybe the vaping has to do with something else."

"Are you telling me how to parent my son?" She fisted her hands on her hips.

"I wouldn't dream of telling you what to do. You're a great parent. I'm making a suggestion. Giving you another point of view."

Her shoulders dropped. She scooped her hair away from her face. "Do you find it hard to be a single parent?"

"Every day, darlin'."

She gave him that smile that turned his insides to liquid. "Thank you."

"For what?"

"For being the quiet voice of reason in my otherwise chaotic head. I'll talk to Grey. Calmly."

"Good." He wanted her to get to the bottom of what might be bothering Grey, but he wouldn't give Maddy away in the process. "Are you ready for that ride home now?"

"One second. What was on that note you gave me earlier? I think I dropped it someplace. I'm sorry."

Him and his stupid ideas. "Nothing. Forget it. I'll take you home now."

"Oh no. You don't get to write me a note and not tell me what was on it."

"It doesn't matter. Let's drop it."

"What if I don't want to drop it? Maybe I want you to tell me. Or are you backing down? The JT I used to know didn't back down from anything."

"Dad, are we going?" Maddy stuck her head out of the truck and shouted.

"Coming." This conversation needed to be shelved anyway. He wasn't going to take her challenge.

"Tell me." She gripped his arm and tilted her chin up at him. "What are you afraid of?"

He turned to her and cupped his hand behind her neck. "I'm afraid I'm going to start something I shouldn't. I was asking you out on a date to make up for the kiss.

Not that I'm sorry I kissed you. I'd do it again if you'd let me."

She moved his hand away but met his gaze. "I'm sorry, JT."

The dull ache filled his chest again. "Sure. I get it." She'd always be sorry around him.

"I'm sorry for what I said at the library about the kiss. I kissed you back. I was as much at fault. I just—"

"Drop it, please." If she didn't want to be with him, then he needed to start getting over her. He hadn't planned on wanting her when he came back home. He'd figured she would be married and off limits. But every time he saw her, the old feelings were there and he couldn't stop the need to pull her in his arms. Except she wasn't going to be his. He needed to let her go. And no civil conversation in the high school parking lot was going to change that.

Chapter Seventeen

Savannah cuddled a hot cup of English Breakfast tea against her chest and stared at her bed. She only ever slept on her side of the bed, and that was the side that needed straightening. The other side, Adam's side, hadn't been touched. She wasn't the kind of sleeper who rolled around trying to find the perfect spot. That had been Adam. When was the right time to start packing up reminders of her married life?

Her plan to start over wasn't working the way she thought. The Tea Room was supposed to be her second chance to find herself. She thought a business of her own would give her what her life lacked. She needed her own identity. She didn't recognize who she was and hadn't for some time. The problem was she was lost and didn't know where she'd taken a wrong turn. She tugged the comforter into place.

What had Grey been thinking using a vaping device

at school? Or smoking at all? What was happening to her middle child?

"Mom, what time is Uncle Blaise coming?" Grey stood in the doorway of her bedroom. His shirt collar was twisted, and the hem had a hole in it.

Blaise was picking up the kids for the anniversary parade. He and Colton had made a float. They would play with Cash and Knox and had asked Grey to play the bongos and Caroline the triangle.

"He'll be here in about an hour. We need to talk."

"You're not letting me go to the parade because of yesterday, right?"

She should take that away from him, but the mother guilt she wore like her silver charm necklace stopped her. "You can still go, but what were you thinking? Smoking that stuff is dangerous and against school rules. Do you want to ruin your future?"

"My future is fine. You worry too much. I wanted to try it, but I didn't even get to."

"Thank God for small favors. Do you want to try crack too?"

"No. I don't know what I was thinking, okay? It seemed like a cool idea at the time. I know it was stupid. Maddy tried to talk me out of it. She grabbed the vape away from me. That's when the teacher walked in." He tucked his head into his shoulders as if he were a turtle.

"So that thing was yours?" The reality of what happened soured her stomach. The world seemed to slip through her fingers. He was a young man trying to be a grown-up too soon.

"I didn't know she was going to take the blame. I started to tell Mrs. Humphreys it was mine, but Maddy just started talking over me like I wasn't even there. Then Uncle Colton walked in because he was in the office and saw me. I never had the chance to correct the mistake. I'm sorry. It's all my fault. Okay?"

As she'd told JT, nothing was okay. Her life was about as stable as a rickety old house in a high wind. She took a deep breath. "What's really going on with you?" Her son had never done anything like this before. She wasn't naïve to think her child was perfect, but this wasn't him.

"What's going on with you, Mom?"

She flinched. "What are you talking about?"

"I know you're upset about something, and I don't think it just has to do with Dad. Are you sick too? Are you going to die?" He took a deep breath, as if those words cost him effort.

She put the mug down and wrapped her arms around him. She didn't care if he was too old for affection. "Oh no, honey. I'm fine. Really. The shop has been keeping me busy, and I'm worried about Caroline's grades, but other than that we're all okay."

"If you say so."

He was too smart to believe her, but she would not burden him with her problems. "Greyson, you don't have to worry about me. I'll take care of us. I promise. About the vaping thing...you are now in charge of mowing the lawn. I'm not paying you because of yesterday. You start this weekend." She had to fire the landscapers she'd hired after Adam died. The yard had been

172

his domain, and now she couldn't afford to keep the service.

"Come on. That's not fair."

"Life's not fair. I think you've seen a small sliver of that by now. If you argue or don't do it, I take your phone and you're grounded until Christmas. End of discussion." She took her mug and left Grey before he could say another word.

She made a detour into the mudroom closet and grabbed rat poison before climbing into the attic. She had a squirrel to extinguish.

Heat oppressed the space, blocking her path as if it swelled against the wood beams. Sweat broke out on her neck and between her breasts. She put the tea down on a box and swiped her hair into a knot.

More insulation had been chewed on since her last visit. *Little bastard.* She shook the box. "Like I told Grey, life's not fair. Prepare to die."

Animal-rights activists would probably be mad at her for trying to kill a squirrel. Too bad. The rodent was eating her wires. The activists weren't going to pay for the electrician she would need soon.

Still, guilt twisted in her stomach. She put the poison down on the top of the Christmas ornament box.

She pushed the ornaments aside and crawled under the eave for the light blue box she hadn't looked at in years. She dropped down on her butt and lifted the lid. Time traveled backward.

Her fingers trailed over the memories. There she was in high school in her cheerleading uniform, sitting on top of a fence, looking off into the distance. She couldn't remember who'd snapped that photo.

Then she stood with her brothers and JT. Colton positioned himself slightly in front of them with his arms wide. JT and Blaise sandwiched her on either side. They were all laughing. The program for the battle of the bands where JT had shared her soda was faded and discolored, but it still held the power to make her heart squeeze.

She'd known she was in love with JT that very night. She'd told herself he'd be hers and they'd live happily ever after. She'd been a child with childish dreams. She hadn't been brave enough to go against her father, and he didn't like JT.

"Going nowhere. Worse than Colton. At least Colton has talent, even if he was wasting it. JT has nothing except a father who doesn't know how to control him and a stepmother wrapped up in herself. His momma had been the only good thing in that boy's life. If she had stayed alive, he might've had a chance. Stay away from him, Savannah Gale," her father had said.

What would have happened if she'd just told JT how she felt instead of coming on to him? She had known one night with him wasn't going to be enough. It had only fueled her feelings for him.

At the bottom of the box was the notebook paper Colton and Troy had scribbled on with lyrics and musical notes. She'd kept them not because she knew her brothers were going to make it big someday. That thought had never crossed her mind that night. Colton's scratches on paper were nothing new to her and didn't impress her at all.

She only wanted something to hold that would tie her to that night because JT had disappeared like morning fog. She needed something tangible to know their night had actually happened.

"Mom, JT and Maddy are here." Grey's head popped up through the opening in the floor.

She jumped. "Who?"

He rolled his eyes. "Mr. Davies and Maddy. You didn't tell me they were coming over."

She shoved the lid on the box and pushed it back in the corner. "I didn't know they were stopping by. I'll be right down. Offer them something to drink and don't let them sit outside. The patio furniture is dirty. Make them comfortable in the kitchen."

His head dipped back down. She left the poison. She'd find another way to deal with her unwanted tenant.

What the hell was JT doing here? She unknotted her hair and shook it out before running into her bathroom for a swipe of lip gloss and spray of perfume.

The photo of her and Adam from their honeymoon stopped her on the way out of the bedroom. She said a silent prayer for forgiveness because, God help her, she wanted the man downstairs.

Voices drifted toward her from the kitchen like the smell of freshly baked scones. JT swung around as she approached. His smile spread across his face and lit up his eyes.

"You look fantastic." He placed a kiss on her cheek and stepped back. "And you smell great."

He smelled like oak, and she gripped the counter to steady her weak knees. "How nice of you both to stop by."

JT and Maddy held glasses. Maddy's had water in it, and JT's looked like the iced tea she'd made this morning. Grey had managed to give them both a lemon.

"We wanted to know if y'all want to go to the parade with us." JT's gaze never wavered from hers.

She soaked in the white T-shirt and faded jeans that hugged him in all the right places. The tattoo peeked out and winked at her. She needed to sit.

"Caroline and I are going with my uncles." Grey jumped up on the counter.

She shot him a look, and he jumped down.

"That's cool." Maddy turned her gaze away and ran her finger up and down the glass.

"Yeah. They were asked to put a float in the parade. Uncle Blaise said yes right away. Uncle Colton said he'd do it only if they played. He asked me and Caroline to play too. And he invited the seniors from the orchestra to join in. It's going to be great."

The doorbell interrupted their conversation.

"Anyone home?" Blaise's voice sang out to them.

"In the kitchen," she said.

"I'm ready." Caroline ran in wearing Adam's sweatshirt, her backpack slung over one shoulder and a smile that could power the state. She jumped into her uncle's arms.

Blaise ruffled Grey's hair. "It's a party." He shook hands with JT and Maddy. He weaved around the crowd and pulled her into a hug. "Hey, Sis." He kissed the top of her head, and she held on for a second longer, needing his strength.

She reached for her wallet. "Okay, here's some money if you two want lunch or a snack or something."

"I've got it." Blaise pushed her money away.

"That's not necessary."

"Don't argue with her, Blaise." JT laughed.

"She does like to boss everyone around, but I can treat my niece and nephew for the day." He turned to her. "Don't insult me."

"I wasn't trying to insult you."

"So put your damn money away."

"Stubborn Savage man." She shoved the money back in her wallet. She never wanted her brothers to feel as if they had to take care of her. Sometimes she forgot their pride was involved.

"Stubborn is you, darling sister. Maddy, if it's okay with your dad, you're welcome to come with us. There's plenty of room on the float, or you can ride in the truck with Harley."

"I know we planned on spending time together today, but can I, Dad?" Maddy's face shone. She had JT's eyes and crooked smile.

Savannah understood exactly what Grey saw in this beautiful young lady. Her heart melted as JT looped an arm around his daughter and pulled her close. He rested his chin against her head and closed his eyes.

"Go have some fun." He let her go. "Be respectful." He fished his wallet out of his jeans pocket. "Thank you, man."

Blaise shoved JT. "Jesus Christ, what did I just say to my sister about money?"

JT nodded and slid his wallet back in his pocket.

"Thanks, Mr. Savage," Maddy said.

"Let's hit the road. Colton doesn't want us to be late." Blaise grabbed Caroline's backpack and slung it over his shoulder.

Her big brother herded the kids toward the door like a pro. They laughed and talked over each other like puppies playing in a pen. Sunshine and a day filled with possibilities met them at the door.

"Have fun." She shouted to their backs and tamped down the envy for their carefree natures. *To be young again.*

Blaise closed the door behind the noise, shutting her and JT in loud silence.

He rocked on his heels. "So that leaves us."

"I guess so." She searched for a place to rest her gaze and decided on him.

He smiled at her again. "Do you want to go to the parade?"

She could get lost in that smile. "Oh, I don't know. I wasn't planning on it. I have some paperwork to do for the Tea Room, and the patio furniture needs attention. This is my only day off. And there's laundry."

"Do you ever breathe?"

"When I have the time."

He laughed, deepening the lines around his eyes, and the tension eased its way off her shoulders.

"It's a nice day, and my daughter ditched me for a couple of old rock and rollers and her new friend. I have nothing to do now. What do you say?"

"I should really stay here."

"As friends. It's okay for us to be friends, isn't it? We were that once, weren't we?"

She missed his friendship and the way he made her laugh. She missed the way he ran into the world head-first, and she could never get enough of the way he looked at her. No one would deny her a friendship, even if she secretly wanted more, would they?

"Let me get my purse."

The residents of Heritage River laughed, talked, and waved into three deep rows on Main Street. The sun and clear blue sky gifted them their warmth, like a new neighbor bringing apple pie to their door. Every store front hung a red, white, and blue pendant with one-hundred-sixty anniversary in gold script. Customers moseyed in and out of the Whiskey Bar.

JT wanted to link his hand through Savannah's but shoved them in his pockets. She shielded her eyes, even though she wore sunglasses. Her hair hung loosely down her shoulders. He remembered its silky feel between his fingers. He needed to think about the floats passing by instead or risk giving himself an erection and really embarrass her.

"Would you like an ice cream?" He leaned in and whispered in her ear. He wanted to be near her. He didn't give a damn about ice cream.

Like the sun, she gifted him her smile. "Right after the kids come by. I don't want to miss them. Thank you asking me to go to the parade. I'm having fun."

She was letting him in and giving him the chance to make her day better. He couldn't have asked for more in this moment. "My pleasure. There's no place I'd rather be."

"Jakie." The shrill voice pierced his eardrums. Shirley pushed her way through the crowd and stood beside him, smelling like cigarettes. "I hoped I'd run into you here."

"Shirley, we don't have anything to discuss." She wanted his bar, and he wasn't going to give it to her. Period. He promised his uncle he'd keep his cool, and he would because of that promise. He didn't want to embarrass Savannah by starting a fight.

"Hello, Shirley. It's very nice to see you." Savannah held out her hand, but Shirley ignored it.

"Are you here with him? Is that appropriate? What do your brothers think?"

Savannah stared at Shirley. He expected her to say something, but she stood there mute.

"We're friends," he said instead, hoping to ease the crease between her brows. She didn't owe Shirley an explanation.

"Yes, yes. We're friends, Shirley. You know that."

"I know nothing except my son took everything from me."

Anger locked his jaw tight. His fists clenched at his sides. Now he was the one who went mute. The words on his tongue were hot, and he couldn't let them out.

Savannah leaned closer. "I don't think now is the time or the place for a family conversation, do you? I'm sure JT will be happy to speak with you at a later date."

If he didn't want to kiss the hell out of her before, he did now. "Thanks" was all he managed.

Savannah smiled up at him. His jaw unlocked some.

"Now is as good a time as any." Shirley lit a cigarette and blew smoke right at him.

"Please go. If you have something to say to me, call Hoke Carter." He waved the smoke away to keep it from Savannah. Shirley was like waves in a storm because she wouldn't let up where he was concerned.

"Look who I found." Harlan smacked him on the shoulder. "Y'all enjoying the parade. Miss Savannah, I hear your talented brothers have a float coming by soon."

He'd never been happier to see his uncle and planted a kiss on the old man's cheek.

"Harlan, it's a pleasure." She gave his uncle a hug. "You are correct. Blaise and Colton and my children will be along any minute, and Maddy joined them. You don't want to miss it."

"Shirley, take a walk with me. I need something refreshing to drink, and that revolting Beatrice Adler has been chasing me up and down this street, trying to ask me to supper. She'll stay away if she sees your scowling face." Harlan's belly shook with laughter.

Savannah covered her smile. JT laughed too. He couldn't help it.

"I'm not done with you yet, Jakie." Shirley pointed a finger at him as Harlan ushered her away.

"The boy prefers JT, woman." Harlan's words carried back to them in the wind.

"She's hideous. I'm sorry. Your father was a saint to stay married to her."

"Can't pick your family." He wondered how Savannah could speak the truth, and yet she still worried about appearances. He couldn't figure her out sometimes.

"Here they come." She clapped.

The loud music arrived first. He'd recognize that tune anywhere. He'd been to more Savage gigs than he could count a hundred years ago when his hair was still thick and his attitude was made up of vinegar. This time the tune was a little different.

In addition to the fiery sound of Colton's guitar and Blaise's bad-ass drumming, an orchestra filled in the spaces beside them. A black Ford pickup pulled a trailer with thirty kids playing string instruments plus Blaise and Colton. The two young guys playing bass and guitar had to be their sons. Maddy sat beside Grey on a bale of hay while he pounded the bongos. Grey pointed to her, and she smacked one too. He had to blink away the emotion trying to strangle him.

He whistled between his fingers, and Maddy looked

up. He waved, and she waved back. Savannah jumped up and down beside him, clapping and yelling. They watched until the music faded away and other floats had blocked their view.

"Do you still want to get that ice cream?" She played with the thin black rope around her neck, rocking the charm back and forth.

"Yes, ma'am."

"The kids were great, weren't they?" She ordered vanilla with rainbow sprinkles in a cup.

He wasn't surprised. She probably didn't want to make a mess. He went full force with a double chocolate in a large waffle cone.

"Yeah, they were. It was nice of Blaise to include Maddy."

She flipped her hair off her neck. Her skin was smooth like the ice cream and his memory could recall its sweet taste. Even in a crowd of people, only the sight of Savannah interested him.

"Blaise is a good guy. Colton, too, especially where the kids are concerned. He's such a good teacher. No one would believe it." She licked the back of the spoon.

He should look away or focus on the cone in front of him, but his gaze stayed on the spoon in her mouth. He cleared his throat. "Not me. Let's sit."

"What is Savannah Montgomery doing with Jacob Davies? They aren't together, are they?"

He swung around at the sound of the words. Whoever had said them wasn't trying to be quiet, but the crowd was thick around Cream and Sugar. Even though he could see over most of their heads, he couldn't find the culprit.

Savannah's neck and face had turned red. She shoved her spoon back into the dish. She'd heard too.

"Hey, don't listen to them." He didn't want her to be hurt by someone else's stupidity. She wasn't doing anything wrong by being with another man. She wasn't cheating, and still the old birds of this town couldn't wait to gossip.

His own pride was bruised, but he was used to it. He'd hoped winning the black-tie dinner might change their minds about him. That would never happen. His own stepmother thought he was dirt.

"Savannah, are you okay?" He wanted that smile back on her face.

"We should go. The kids will be home soon. I want to be there when they get back."

"Let's take a walk. Just you and me."

She dumped her unfinished ice cream in the trash. "Another time. If it's too much trouble to take me back, I can get Grace to give me a ride home. She's at the library."

Was she really going to let one sentence from someone they didn't know get between them? "We aren't doing anything wrong."

"I know we aren't. I'd like to go home. Should I text Grace?"

He tossed his ice cream too, and tried to hide the disappointment taking hold. "I'll take you."

He wasn't going to give up. He wanted to be the reason for her smile again. Those old bitches could go fuck themselves.

Chapter Eighteen

Savannah paced past the front window of the Tea Room. "Kiki, I'm closing up now. Would you mind taking care of your check?"

"Sure." Kiki smiled. At least it looked like a smile. The woman had gone one too many rounds with Botox. Now her lips barely moved.

She kept an eye on Kiki as she fumbled in her over-size Michael Kors bag. Diamond rings covered both ring fingers. They had to weigh ten pounds each. What she could do with the money those rings must cost.

She counted the silverware on Kiki's table. A fork was missing. Colton was right. This woman cut into her profits. She'd lost twenty forks in the last month. What did Kiki do with them all? It wasn't as if the lady couldn't afford to buy them. She'd have to do something about the stealing, but not tonight. Tonight she wanted to go home and get into a hot bath and forget about her problems for a while. She didn't want to think about money, Grey, or

Caroline's problems at school. And she definitely didn't want to think about JT.

She couldn't get the hurt on his face out of her mind when those stupid women were gossiping about them. She shouldn't have let what they said bother her, but it did. She should have taken a better stand with Shirley, but she couldn't find the right words. She wasn't ready to take on the world. Still, she owed him more than standing there tongue-tied.

"I'll get the door for you."

"I love your tea shop. I'm so glad you opened it. I feel like it's my own special place. No one is ever here except me." Kiki reapplied her lipstick while she walked.

Her words splashed a little too much cold reality on the afternoon. "Thanks for coming." She waited for Kiki to take a final look around, as if she may never return, and then left. Well, at least the forks would be safe.

Her phone buzzed. Colton's face popped up on her screen. She locked the door and swiped at the screen.

"Hey, what's up?"

"Harley and I are at your house."

"Is everything okay?" Her mind went right to accident, fire, and broken bones.

"Chill. Everything's cool. We stopped by to see what you were up to, is all, and drop off more ideas for the wedding menu. We're going to take the kids for burgers and then back to our house to play Rock Band on the video-game machine Knox has. Cash is coming over too. You want to join us?"

She took a deep breath. Everything was fine. "Caroline has math homework. She has to do that."

"Harley is already helping her. Caroline says she's failing math. Is that true?"

She needed to finish researching the visual processing problem. That's what she'd be doing when she went home. The bath would have to wait. "Absolutely not. What would make you think such a crazy thing?"

"Ease up. I'm just asking."

"Sorry. Thanks for taking out the kids. I'm going to skip this time. I have stuff to do around the house. I can use the time without them home."

"Your loss, little sister. I'll bring them back before morning."

"Colton, don't keep them out too late. It's a school night."

"Like I don't fucking know that. This teaching job sucks. I hate getting up before noon."

"You love teaching."

"Don't go spreading that rumor. They'll never let me out. See ya." He ended the call.

She didn't want to go home to an empty house filled with her old life. She sat at her laptop and started researching visual processing. If Caroline needed a doctor, she'd have to find a way to afford it. Their health insurance didn't cover eye doctors or glasses.

Someone banged on the front door. She dragged herself away from the computer. She should ignore it, but the frantic pounding had her curious. She pulled back the lacy curtain, and her heart stopped.

No one should have that much effect on her, but he did, and every time she saw him, she had to try to get over him all over again. It wasn't working. She opened the door to the man who occupied every waking thought.

JT's black T-shirt matched the sexy cowboy hat. The short sleeves stretched against his biceps, showing off his cobra tattoo. The shirt was tucked into the waist of his jeans, and right in the center was his big belt buckle. She made a fist to keep from trying to take the damn thing off right there.

"Hi." He smiled down at her.

"Hi yourself." He always smelled so damn good. Her hands begged to be let loose on his chest. She shook the thoughts away.

"I was in the neighborhood and thought maybe we could take a ride."

"Now isn't a good time."

"I thought you might say that. Here's the thing. No time is ever a good time. Someone or something always needs your attention, right? We have to make the time, and there's no time like the present. No thoughts. No planning. Just you and me and a ride. The sun is going to set soon. I thought we could watch it go down at the lake."

"Don't you have to get home to Maddy?" How could he so easily toss aside responsibilities? She never seemed to know how to let go. The to-do list was long, and it constantly wrapped itself around her neck. If she wasn't planning and working the list, nothing ever got done.

When the kids were out of the house, she could slow down. If she even knew how.

"Maddy and Uncle Harlan are at our house having supper together tonight. The Whiskey is running like the tight ship it is. Georgia and the crew don't need me. Parker is in Nashville. I thought maybe you could ask Blaise or Colton to watch your kids, or you could send them to my house."

He had considered her children. Her heart nudged her. She should lie and tell him they were home waiting for her. He'd never know the truth. But she didn't want to lie. She wanted to be with him. "I'll meet you there."

"Miss Savage, let me take the reins tonight."

"You know I'm not Miss Savage anymore." She had stopped wearing her wedding ring, but that didn't make her *Miss* anything.

He leaned in. His beard scratched against her cheek. His scent of amber and ginger made heat pool in her core. "You'll always be Miss Savage to me," he whispered.

He placed his hand on the small of her back and led her to his truck. His soft touch made her feel special. He helped her slide in and ran around the front. They drove in silence as he weaved his way out of town. He turned off the main road leading to Highway One and onto a side street only the locals knew.

"Nice night for a boat ride, don't you think?"

She turned in her seat. "You have a boat? Did you steal it?"

"Hey, I'm not that kid anymore." He narrowed his eyes.

She laughed. "I'm joking. I know you wouldn't steal a boat. Whose dock did you borrow?"

"I have friends in the right places."

Someone who would know they were together. She stopped the panic before it took hold. They were friends. As long as she kept it that way, there wasn't a problem.

"I never had a chance to ask you. How did things go with Rowan the other day?" She had almost forgotten Rowan and the town council had come into the Whiskey Bar to check it out since the library luncheon had been a disaster.

The tailgate event was coming up. She might as well know where she stood in the competition.

"I'm not going to lie. I'm at an advantage in the competition now that they came to my place. Your tailgate is going to struggle unless a tornado comes and sucks it all up in its funnel." He smiled and winked.

"Has Colton been giving you lessons in arrogance?"

His laugh came with ease. He always knew how to let go and have fun. That had been the thing she missed most.

"If I were him, I'd be arrogant too. He's earned every bit of success he has. He built one of the best rock bands ever."

"The king did fall from grace, you know."

"Nah. Not Colton or Blaise. They just shifted careers, had a few bumps in the road, but they've accomplished more than most people dream about."

"It looks like you've done okay for yourself." Her

brothers' shadows casted long and far, even over her sometimes.

"I've come farther than the garbageman."

"You need to stop referencing what some idiot said to you thirty years ago."

"Easier to believe the negative stuff." He held out his hand, and she took it, letting the weight of it sink against her skin. Friendship didn't feel like standing on the edge of a cliff ready to jump.

He parked in the sandy area in front of the lake. The sun spread its pinks and oranges through the trees. Before long the moon would cast its shimmery light against the surface like a blanket of diamonds. Warm air soothed some of her nerves. "JT, I think there's something we should talk about."

She wasn't a fool. They were at the lake, the sun was setting, and she was so far in love with him she couldn't see straight. There were things they needed to get out in the open before she lost all decorum.

He met her at the front of the truck. "Later. Now is for fun. You've got that crease between your brow, and that only means you're about to make a list or convince yourself to be responsible. You don't have to do any of that right now. Trust me for a few hours."

As if it were that easy.

"We need to walk from here." He grabbed a cooler from the back before he slid his hand over hers.

"You brought drinks?" Maybe this trip wasn't so spontaneous.

He shrugged. "I own a whiskey bar."

"Are we going to Billy Lewis's place?"

"He's got the dock and the boat."

"Does he know we're coming? Because if he doesn't, he's liable to come out with his shotgun."

His laugh was full and rich, like a well-steeped Earl Grey tea. "I had Harlan call and ask for me."

"Were you planning on something that might be misunderstood as suspicious?"

"Not me." His cocky smile spread wide.

They climbed the slight incline to Billy's property and made their way through his driveway and toward the backyard. A set of weather-worn wooden steps led down to the dock and a small boat.

"JT Davies, is that you?" Billy Lewis called from his back porch. The light inside the house lit him from behind. He swatted at some bugs hovering nearby. His shotgun was nowhere to be seen.

"Yes, sir. Thank you again for allowing me to borrow the utility boat."

"See to it you return her in the shape she is at the moment. I've got some fishing to do this week. Howdy, Savannah."

"Hi, Billy."

"Next time Colton comes for a visit, you come with him. Bring those children of yours along." His voice creaked out each word like an old rocking chair.

"I will. I'll bring you some scones too."

"My stomach is growling already. Night now." The back door slapped shut, leaving them alone again.

"Do you want to race to the bottom of the steps?" JT took off, not waiting for an answer.

"You're nuts, you know that." She kicked off her wedge sandals and ran after him.

He waited in the boat and held a strong hand out to her. "Give me your hand." The tattoo slipped out from under the sleeve of his T-shirt.

Her heart did a flip and landed on its head. She climbed over the side of the aluminum boat and took a second to find her balance. "You can wipe that smile off your face. I won't fall in the water." She settled in opposite him.

"Never thought you would, darlin'." He pulled the cord on the engine and got them underway toward the middle of the lake.

When he found a spot far enough out that Billy's house became sugar-cube size with golden lights in the dusk, he shut the engine down and opened the small cooler.

He pulled out two snifter glasses and a bottle of Midleton whiskey. He poured some and handed a glass over to her. "Hold it in your hand and swirl it around.

The warmth from your hand will cause some evaporation, but the top of the glass will trap it so when you drink, you'll also smell the vanilla and oaky scents. It makes for a richer flavor. Take your time with it."

The whiskey left a warm trail down her throat and in her belly. She needed to go slow with this drink and stay in control. No repeat performances of the first time in his bar. "Why did you pick whiskey to be your signature product?" She inhaled the intoxicating scent.

"From the first time I drank it, I felt like I made it, even though I wasn't close. In fact, I hated it when I took that first sip, but I knew what message whiskey sent to everyone else. That was the message I wanted to send." He looked off into the dark distance at something only he could see.

"You wanted people to know you were special."

"Right." He looked back at her. His dark eyes soaked her in.

Her belly twisted in response. "You are special." The whiskey gave her the courage to say what she'd been thinking.

"I'm trying, darlin'." He tipped his glass at her.

They sat in silence and sipped their drinks as the sun's orange rays burnt out the rest of the day. The lake glittered good night and faded to black. Cicadas began their bedtime conversation. She'd dreamed of a chance like this. Why was her heart trying to break her ribs in a mad dash out of her chest?

He rummaged around inside the cooler. A whoosh and the scent of sulfur hit the air. He held two sparklers. Their white light sizzled and crackled, illuminating his face and the darkness around them. "Here."

She reached for the pinwheel of light. "I haven't had one of these in years. Maybe when the kids were little."

"That's what I've been waiting for."

"What's that?"

195

"That smile on your face. The one that lights up your eyes so bright I want to jump in. Those women gossiping at the parade came along and stole it from me."

"JT—"

"Don't say anything." He knelt in front of her. "Let's just enjoy the night."

She wanted to run her fingers through his hair and trace the line of his sideburns to his jaw. She was hopeless when it came to him. "Could you take off your hat?"

He tossed it behind him. "Anything else?" The cocky smile made a reappearance.

"I really need to say something because I'm battling with myself here."

He slid back on the bench. The shower of sparks made its way down the stick and fizzled out, a little like her nerve.

"When you get your mind made up, there's no stopping you." He leaned his elbows on his thighs and focused his stare on her.

"I promised myself if I ever got the chance, I'd ask you one question." Their knees touched, and the warmth from the whiskey spread through her whole body.

"Why did I sleep with you?" He ran a hand over his face and scratched at his jaw.

"I hope you wanted to be with me that night. I've been kind of hanging on to that, so please spare me the embarrassment of finding out you regretted it."

"I've never regretted that. I wish it had been a better experience for you. I should've taken you someplace nicer."

"Please stop talking."

"You are one bossy lady." The smile remained.

"I need to get this out." She took his sparkler stick with hers, dipped them in the water, and placed them inside the boat. They could throw them away properly later. She forced her gaze to meet his. "Why did you leave?"

He sat back and stared off into the distance. "You didn't want me around."

"I never said that." Had she? She'd played that night over in her head so many times the memory had become three-dimensional, as if it had happened yesterday instead of twenty-four years ago. She remembered every detail. Those weren't the words she'd said. She would have remembered telling JT to leave because she had desperately wanted him to stay.

"You made it clear I wasn't enough for you, and you were right. You had a big future ahead of you. You were going off to college. I had barely graduated from high school and was floundering with that pathetic land-scaping business. Back then when you spoke, your big words would trip me up. I'd think how ignorant I must sound to you. You were going to tire of someone like me who dragged your brothers' equipment around. I wasn't special like they were. I wasn't anyone important."

"You were the brightest light. You made people laugh. Took chances I could never. I'd watch. Everyone hung on your every word, and I'd think please look my way. I kept hoping you'd notice me as more than Blaise's little sister."

"You barely spoke to me."

"You scared me."

He laughed. "Me? What's so scary about me?"

"You fought the system every step of the way. You didn't care if you got suspended or into a fight. You were friends with my brothers, and they were the biggest troublemakers. Even though I loved them, I knew I couldn't keep up with them. My father always had stricter rules for me because I was the girl. I couldn't believe you'd want someone who did her homework, followed the rules, planned to go to college instead of standing on the stage with Colton and Blaise. It took four beers before I got up the nerve to even approach you that night."

"You were drinking?" His eyes shot open wide.

It was her turn to laugh, and the release was like a delicious cup of tea. "You didn't know?"

"What do you take me for? I would never have made love to you if I knew you'd put away four beers." He scratched at his jaw again. "Christ. I swear I didn't know that."

Made love. Better not to read too much into those words. "I still don't understand why you left without saying goodbye."

"I should've said something to you. I was a coward. But after what you said, I had to get out of town. I didn't know how else to handle my anger."

"I said not to tell my brothers." She finally understood.

"When you said you didn't want them to find out, I knew I had to make something of myself and then come back to you. I didn't want you to be embarrassed by being with me. You didn't want Colton and Blaise to know because I was nothing more than their roadie. I get it. It's okay. You were right."

"You're wrong." Her chest ached. She flexed her fingers to stop them from reaching out to him. All these years he'd thought the wrong thing. How different would their lives be if he'd only asked, or if she'd only said. "I was never embarrassed by you. I thought you were amazing. I didn't want Blaise to be mad at me. I'd just seduced his best friend. He and Colton had made it pretty clear they didn't want me dating their friends. Some of it was big brothers being protective, but the rest was just young men being stupid."

"Blaise will beat the shit out of me this minute if he ever finds out I slept with his drunk sister. He'd have every right to."

"It's none of his damn business. I don't report to him. I'm glad we did it."

"You don't regret it? Even after you married and started a family? Fell in love?" He leaned forward with arms on his thighs again. He tapped on her knees.

The ache in her chest spread up her throat and burned tears behind her eyes. "I've never regretted one second in your company. I've thought of you a million times over the years. Songs come on the radio that take me right back to us being young and hanging out together. I was so grateful for the band to use as an excuse to be near you. I wanted to make love to you, to feel your hands on my skin. I was in love with you then."

"What about now?" His voice grew husky. He spread his hands across her thighs.

She closed her eyes and took a deep breath. She had loved him her whole life. All the years she tried to shake him loose from her thoughts, but he stuck like honey. Here he was, the man she should compete against for the black-tie formal, the man whose daughter made her son's head turn and made him do questionable things.

Instead of running from him, she wanted to tell him her secrets. She wanted to hear his laughter, to watch him take life by both hands and give it a good shake. She wanted to undress him and feel the heat of his skin against hers.

"JT—"

He took her face in his hands and stared right into her soul. "Don't say anything. Just listen. You're the most incredible woman I've ever met. It's been you all these years in my head and my heart. I've wanted to come to you so many times, but I never thought I'd done enough to prove myself. I've wanted to be the only man in your life. I hated that you married someone else, even though it was me who sent you away and forced you to live a life that didn't include me."

She eased away from his hold and took another swig of the whiskey. She needed help to force the guilt away. *Too soon*, the voice in her head said. *Not responsible.* Another sip would allow her one night of being the person she was before marriage and motherhood, when she was still Savannah Savage.

"Kiss me and don't stop."

He took the glass out of her hand. "Did you have too much to drink?"

She traced the line of his jaw and shook her head, too afraid to speak.

His mouth was on hers. Hot and full of spice. She opened her lips to find his tongue. Her heart expanded until she couldn't breathe. He laced his fingers in her hair and gently tugged her head back to deepen the kiss. She moaned against his mouth.

He drew back. "That little moan drives me wild." He scooped her up and placed her on his lap. The boat rocked with the motion. His erection rubbed against her most sensitive spot. She would drown in her desire.

He kissed her again. The full-body taste of the whiskey lingered on his tongue. She wanted to drink him in. Every part of her ached for his touch. Needing to feel the flex of his back muscles against her hands, she tugged his shirt out of his jeans.

She would never stop loving him. If he walked away from her again, her heart would perish. She had waited for this moment, had prayed for him to find her again, and now he was back. He hadn't promised her anything, but she couldn't stop feeling more like herself when she was with him than when she wasn't.

He broke away and lifted his shirt over his head. His cocky smile returned. "Your turn."

Without hesitation, she did the same and tossed the fabric to the side. He cupped her breast over the black lace of her bra.

"You're beautiful." His words were a whisper.

She ran a finger down his chest to the top of his belt buckle. "So are you."

He let out a growl and kissed her again. Then he stopped.

"What's the matter?" She worried he would pull that engine string and take them back. Had she done something wrong?

"I can't make love to you on Billy Lewis's boat. What kind of a man does that? Let me take you someplace with a bed." He lifted her and placed her on the bench in front of him.

"There is no place I'd rather be." She reached over and unhooked his buckle. She'd wanted to do that for weeks.

"You deserve—"

She put her fingers to his mouth. "What I want is for you to make love to me right now."

"I didn't plan this. I won't lie. I hoped, but you're worth more than lying down with me on some shitty boat. Let me take you some place nice. I can afford a fancy hotel."

"I don't want to wait." She might lose her nerve. If they didn't do it now, they may never. Their real lives waited for them at home.

She unhooked her bra and dragged it over her arms. He reached for her. His thumb rubbed against her nipple, making it tingle and harden. He leaned in and took her into his mouth. His tongue left hot streaks against her sensitive skin.

She pulled him up and kissed him. Her fingers

memorized every muscle in his arms and torso. Her hands shook as she fumbled with the button of his jeans.

He laughed. "Allow me." He shimmied out of his pants. His full erection pushed against the soft material of his black boxer briefs.

The boat continued to rock with their sudden movements. They would probably end up in the lake, but she didn't care. He eased her back to the bow of the boat where they had more room to move.

She slid her hands inside the waistband of his underwear. He gripped her wrist. "You have to take your pants off too. It's only fair."

"Is this a competition?"

"Always, darlin'." He kissed her nose and moved to the side so she could get her wide-leg pants off.

She missed his nearness and pulled him back on top of her. She wrapped her arms around his neck, and he pressed against her, warming her up. The only thing between them was her lacy panties and his boxers.

He ran his fingers through the ends of her hair. "I love the way your hair feels."

"Just my hair?"

He yanked her panties off and tossed them. Hopefully, not in the water. He removed his own undergarments and positioned himself above her. The heat in her core would burn her up.

"Touch me," she whispered against his face and guided his hand down.

His mouth was on her neck, leaving wet trails to her shoulder. His fingers went lower until they found her center. His touch scorched her. A moan escaped her lips, and her hips moved with his rhythm. Her insides coiled with each stroke until she thought she'd never unwind with relief.

She dragged her hands over his tight butt and then around to his front where she stroked the full length of him.

"Keep doing that." He growled against her ear.

She needed him to fill her up. "Now, JT."

"Are you sure? I can hold out longer if you can." He nipped at her chin.

"Make love to me now, mister, or I'm throwing your ass in the lake."

He positioned himself against her and drove into her, stretching and filling her with his hardness. She took him in and wrapped her legs around his waist to feel all of him as he moved with her. They rocked with the sway of the boat. Small waves lapped against the sides.

The coil inside her twisted tighter until it broke in half, sending her end over end. Large, powerful waves of release crashed against her until she had nothing more. Her inner muscles flexed against him as he raced to the end and met her in seconds flat.

"Savannah." He called out her name again, kissed her neck, and held her close. His heart beat against her chest in time to hers.

She held on to him, afraid to let him go because he might disappear in front of her eyes. Tears stung the back of her throat. "That was wonderful."

"Exactly as I remembered it." He eased onto his side and brought her with him.

She snuggled against him, and he rested his chin on the top of her head.

"You're mine, Savannah Savage, and I want the whole world to know it."

That might be a problem.

Chapter Nineteen

JT parked beside Savannah's minivan at the back of the Tea Room. He still couldn't believe only an hour ago he'd made love to this woman sitting beside him. He did wish their first time together after all those years hadn't been on a small utility boat. He wasn't sure how he was going to look Billy Lewis in the eye ever again.

She hadn't meant to send him away. He'd been so young and stupid back then. He'd wasted a lot of time.

She also hadn't said a word on the ride back, only looked out the window. When they had returned to his truck, she had several text messages from her kids. They wanted to know where she was.

Was she regretting what happened? He hoped she'd forget the gossipers and see him for who he was now, but he never wanted her to do something she wished she hadn't.

He took her hand in his and kissed it. She turned to

him and smiled. He'd wait his whole life for that smile. He'd do whatever she wanted just to get her to smile at him like that. "When can I see you again?" No point in trying to play it cool. He wouldn't be able to.

"After the tailgate. I need the next couple of days to finish getting ready."

Her brothers were scheduled to play at the Whiskey the same night. Now he wanted to cancel them. Savage would drive the crowd to his place. Her tailgate could go under without anyone present, but he needed that black-tie to prove to the townspeople he'd made something of himself.

"Do you need any help?" He wouldn't be able to stand her pushing him away again, and yet the chill in her eyes said she was.

"Nope. I have it all under control." She eased her hand away.

"Of course you do." His breath caught in his throat. "Is everything all right?"

"Why wouldn't it be? Thank you for an unexpected evening." She dropped her gaze. "I need to get home, though." She reached for the door.

He grabbed her wrist. "Can I ask you something?"

She pressed her lips together into a white line. "Certainly."

"Don't shut me out, Savannah." That wasn't what he'd planned on saying. He wanted to know why winning the black-tie dinner was so important to her. Maybe he could let her have it if only she'd tell him.

She placed a hand on his face. "Tonight was wonderful. I have no regrets, but I need some time."

"Okay." He gripped her hand in his. He wanted to mean something to her, but he didn't want to rush her. She needed to be the one to announce them. If she still needed time or struggled with starting something new so soon after losing her husband, he'd take the back seat. As long as she allowed him to make love to her.

Please let her want him in her bed.

His phone buzzed, but he ignored it.

"Do you want to check that?"

"It can keep. I'm not ready to set you free yet." Even to himself, he sounded like a desperate teenager. "Can I ask why winning the black-tie is so important to you?" There. That was what he'd meant to say before.

She looked out the window, then back at him. "I need the exposure. The Tea Room isn't going to survive without it."

He could back out of the event now and let her have it. He had four other bars that made him money. The Heritage River location would be fine. He knew what he was doing. But he still wanted the people of the town to see it with their own eyes. He wanted Shirley to choke on the mean words she'd said to him over the years. Maybe he wasn't ready to back out just yet. More than once, he'd wished it wasn't Savannah he had to compete with.

"I could come by and work on your business plan with you if you want. You'll still need to retain customers long after the dinner is over."

She pulled her hand away. "No, thanks. Maybe

someday, but not just yet. I have to do this myself. The Tea Room is my chance to shine. It's my second chance, you know? I spent so many years being a wife and a mother I kind of forgot about what I wanted. I took a big risk opening this place. I need to make it a success by myself."

"You don't have to do it all alone. In fact, you shouldn't. Do you have any investors?"

"Nope. Just me."

"Your brothers didn't want in?"

"Oh, Colton did. He offered several times, but he wanted to do things his way, like always. I turned him down."

If her brother wanted to invest in her business, then he'd guess she had a good chance at being a success. Colton Savage's net worth was far north of the elite one percent.

She leaned over the center console and brushed her lips against his, sending a bolt of desire right to his middle.

"I have to go," she said.

"Let me walk you to your car." He slid out before she could point out she was parked a foot away. He opened the door for her.

"It's a minivan, mister. My own personal Mom Bus. Get it right." She tugged on her necklace and leaned against her *Mom Bus.*

He stood before her, positioning himself between her legs so she had to look up at him, and if he was lucky, put her arms around him.

She ran her finger over his tattoo. His skin warmed.

"I have wanted to run my fingers over that snake since I saw it. It's very sexy."

"I'll get another one for you. You can decide where I should put it."

"I know exactly where you should put it."

He gripped her hips and pulled her close so she could see what she was doing to him. "Want to give me a list?"

She wrapped her arms around his neck and tilted back his hat. Her fingers traced the spot where his hair met his forehead. "Another night."

She sent him some very mixed messages. He didn't know how to navigate this. Did he let his heart lead? She'd crush him if she left him this time.

She kissed him again, quick and soft, and settled in her van. He watched until her taillights were out of sight.

He hurried home to call her.

JT let himself into the house through the kitchen. The light above the stove was on, but the rest of the house was dark and quiet. He passed through the foyer to the family room on the other side. The blue light of the television flickered against the windows, but the sound was low. A movie about an out-of-control bus racing through the streets of LA played. Uncle Harlan snored on the couch.

He grabbed a blanket and covered the old guy, then turned off the TV. He wanted to call Savannah and say goodnight. Maybe she'd tell him what she wore to bed.

She had no idea how many nights he'd wondered what she was doing, how long he'd waited to touch her.

Tonight had only caused a spark that could start a wildfire. He wouldn't be able to stop spending time with her, touching her, loving her. Okay, he should slow down a little. They'd had sex. Not exactly something that made up for a lifetime worth of missed nights, though he sure as hell hoped it had.

He turned and stopped.

"Dad, you're home late." Maddy stood in the entryway to the family room, her hair piled on top of her head. A cropped T-shirt showed off too much of her middle and his sweatpants. She held a mug between her hands.

"Shouldn't you be asleep?"

Uncle Harlan grunted and rolled over. He ushered her into the kitchen.

"I was doing homework. I have a big project in my English class. I also wanted to hear how your date went with Mrs. Montgomery."

He didn't like the sound of Savannah being Mrs. anyone. "How did you know I was out with her?"

She raised her eyebrows. "Uncle Harlan told me. Are you going to take her out again?"

"We're just friends." He pulled a beer out of the fridge to avoid looking his daughter in the eye. No promises had been made tonight between him and Savannah. Even though her friend was the last thing he wanted to be, he'd do whatever she asked of him and still try to convince her they should be together at the same time.

"Did you date her when you were young?" She leaned against the counter and looked at him over the mug.

"She wasn't interested in me back then. Just friends. Like now." He focused on the beer. Easier to tell a lie while he stared at the bottle.

"But you liked her as more than friends?"

He'd liked her from that first moment he saw her in the cafeteria at school. He had been a junior, and she was a freshman. She stood with friends, laughing. Her whole face lit up, and her eyes sparkled like a tall highball. She hugged her books to her chest with one hand and flipped her long hair off her neck with the other. He had never seen anyone so pretty.

He asked his friend standing next to him who she was because he hadn't recognized the tall, dark-haired girl.

"Dude, are you stupid? That's Savannah Savage."

He had to pick his face up off the floor. Blaise's sister was hot. He didn't know how that happened, but he knew he had to stay away from her. She wouldn't be interested in him anyway, until the night she'd brought him behind her garage and blew his mind. Kind of like earlier on the boat.

"Why all these questions?" He pressed the cold beer to his head.

"Do you have a headache?" Maddy narrowed her eyes.

"I'm fine."

"I want to know what you were like when you were my age. You never really talk about your past. You don't try to bore me with stories like other parents do. The only stuff I know is what Grandpa used to tell me."

"Yeah, well, Grandpa was the storyteller. Not me. My past isn't worth dragging up. I did lots of stupid things guys that age do. I decided one day I needed something more, joined the military, and you know the rest."

"But what kind of stuff? Did you get in trouble a lot? Did you get extended detention like I did? Would Mrs. Montgomery know? Could I ask her?"

"I told you she wasn't paying any attention to me back then. I hung out with her brothers mostly, and we didn't have that detention then." He had been in detention plenty of times and suspended twice, not that he would tell her that.

"If you're competing with her for the black-tie anniversary dinner, why did you ask her out?"

"Okay, enough of the third degree. You don't spill half as much about Grey."

"You're no fun." She took her mug and headed for the steps.

He followed. Maybe he could still call Savannah.

"If I married Grey and you married Mrs. Montgomery, you'd be my dad and my step-dad-in-law. That's hilarious."

Hysterical.

In the darkness of the upstairs hallway, he edged near the subject they often avoided. "Sweet pea, I'm sorry you only have me to talk to about stuff like boyfriends."

Stacey Wilk

"I'm not."

"You deserve better, more, two parents." Maybe she'd get into a little less trouble if she had a mom like Savannah to watch out for her and not just a dad who worked late nights at a bar.

"She didn't love us, Daddy."

"I understand why she didn't love me but not you. You are special." The words twisted against his tongue. He wanted to say the right thing and didn't know what the hell that was.

"I am pretty special, but so are you, even if you work too much and stay out too late. She was dumb not to be in love with you. Grey thinks you're cool, and so do I. I bet Mrs. Montgomery does too." She kissed his cheek and turned on her heel. "Good night." And closed her bedroom door.

How'd he get so damn lucky? He didn't know what he'd done to warrant a daughter like Maddy. He thanked the stars for her and all the ways she drove him crazy.

He'd had a damn good night. With a little confidence puffing up his chest, he fished his phone out of his pocket and dialed Savannah.

He closed his own bedroom door and yanked his T-shirt over his head as he waited for her to answer.

She picked up slightly breathless. "It's late, JT."

The sound of her voice spread over him like a smooth scotch.

"I wanted to say good night." He dragged his jeans over his legs and pictured Savannah wrapped around him. He needed to think about taking out the garbage, or he'd have an erection.

"Good night."

"I know you said you needed a few days to get ready for the tailgate and you wanted time, but I was wondering if I could take you to breakfast in the morning. We both aren't open before eleven. We can make it quick, and we can keep our clothes on. Unless you want to take them off." He flopped onto the bed.

She laughed, which meant she was smiling, and all for him.

"I don't think so. I have a delivery coming in the morning."

"You don't have to play hard to get. I'm a sure thing."

"I'm not sure my children will handle me being with another man so soon. I'm not ready to make us public yet."

"Are you sorry about what happened tonight?" Is that what she was saying? Did she regret making love to him?

"I loved every minute of us on that boat. I want to take things slowly. That's all. Can it just be you and me for now? We can let other people in later."

"Where do your kids think you were tonight? Did you tell them you were with me?" He jumped off the bed and paced the room.

"I didn't tell them anything. Colton dropped them off, and they went to bed, which is what I should do. I still have to get up with them for school. Can we talk about this another time?"

"I want to talk about it now. I don't want to keep

anything a secret." So much for giving her space and time, but he couldn't seem to shut his big mouth.

"I wasn't expecting tonight to happen. It's not like I woke up this morning planning to be on a boat with you. I need time to process what's going on, and I have a lot of other things I'm juggling right now."

He continued to wear out the floor with his pacing. "What are you saying? You don't want to be serious with me? After tonight, I didn't think you'd want to date other people." He sounded like a Neanderthal, but he still couldn't stop himself. He'd waited years to hear her say she wanted him, and now that she'd rocked his world, he didn't want her to pull back.

"JT, relax. I don't want to date anyone."

"Including me?" He needed to shut up before he ruined everything between them. He was willing to wait forever for her, so why was he turning this into a fight? Because fighting was what he did best.

She breathed into the phone. "JT—"

"How long do I have to sneak around for?"

"I'm not asking you to sneak around."

"You're not asking me to shout it from my roof."

"Fine, shout it from your roof. I dare you."

"I will. I'll climb up there right now in my drawers and shout it out."

"First of all, stop using words like 'drawers.' You sound like a redneck that way. Second, don't try to kill yourself to prove a point."

He threw open the window. "I'm climbing out there right now in my drawers, sweetheart. You know what?

I'm going to video call you. I'm hanging up." He pressed the End button and redialed, using the video feature.

Her face filled his screen. "Have you lost your mind? You can't climb out on the roof. You'll kill yourself. I didn't mean to dare you. Please don't go out there."

He swung a leg over the sash of the window. The roof pitched right below. The deck was below that. He could hang from the gutters and drop down without a hitch. If he did fall, he'd roll onto the deck. He probably wouldn't break anything. "I'm going out."

"Jacob Tyler, get back inside that house this minute."

"I love when you talk dirty to me." He swung his other leg over. The asphalt shingles scratched his bare feet, but he stood and held the phone back to give her a better look.

"Oh my God, are you standing? Please go inside."

"Not until I shout from up here that Savannah Savage is my girlfriend."

"I'm hanging up on you. You're acting like a child."

He sucked in a deep breath so he could bellow every word. He'd wake up the entire neighborhood, and he didn't give a shit. He wanted the whole world to know this woman was his.

He puffed up his chest, ready to blow, and lost his balance. His arms circled. He dropped the phone. Savannah's scream trailed off. The shingles were slick. His feet slipped, and he went down on his side. Something scraped his skin. He rolled like a whiskey barrel to the edge of the roof and flew off. The air seemed to lift him up, but gravity had other ideas. He reached for the gutters. His fingers only skimmed the metal edge. He landed with a whoosh in the boxwoods, missing the deck completely. He bounced and crashed onto the grass. The ground knocked the wind out of him. He couldn't move.

"JT? JT?" Savannah's voice was somewhere in the distance. "Oh my God. I'm calling an ambulance."

Fucking great. He was still in his drawers.

Chapter Twenty

Savannah raced through the streets of Heritage River. No one was on the road at this late hour, thankfully. She came up to a red light, slowed down, looked both ways, and floored it. She had to get to the hospital.

She'd also had to wake up Grey and tell him she was going to the hospital to help JT. Grey had raised his eyebrows with a knowing look and flopped back into bed. Or guilt made her think Grey knew what she'd been up to on that boat.

She slammed the car in park, jumped from the driver's seat, and ran for the doors. The ambulance had to be there by now. "Excuse me, did an ambulance bring anyone in?"

The woman behind the registration desk looked up from the computer. She had long hair that may have once been black on its own but looked more like a freshly tarred driveway. Her olive skin was pocked and oily. "The paramedics just brought someone in."

"Was it Jacob Davies?"

"Are you his wife?"

"I'm just a friend, but I called the ambulance for him. He fell off a roof."

"I'm sorry. Because of the privacy laws, I can't tell you who was brought in if you're not his immediate family."

Fucking laws. She understood why Colton was always bucking the system. "Thank you." She marched right down the hall to the curtained area.

"Wait. You can't go back there," the lady with the bad dye job yelled after her.

She resisted the urge to flip her off. Most of the curtains were pulled open, revealing empty beds. At the end of the hall, one space was closed off by a green curtain. Voices drifted through to her.

"I want to go home." "

Dad, let the doctor see you."

Oh God. Maddy was there.

"Jacob, you're not going anywhere until the doc comes."

And his uncle. Heat burned her cheeks. Had JT told them what he was doing on the roof? She should turn around before anyone realized she was there. He didn't need her. He had his family with him. They'd take care of him.

The curtain rolled back on the metal track. Harlan

stared at her with hooded, dark eyes. His skin was flushed, and his white hair shaved close to his head.

"Hi" was all she could manage. Her heart had lodged into her throat.

" 'Bout time. Talk some sense into him, will ya? He wants to get out of here before he's checked out properly. I'm going to find a doctor. Madeline, come take a walk with an old man."

"Thank you for calling the ambulance, Mrs. Montgomery." Maddy scooted past her to join Harlan in the hall.

"Of course. And please call me Savannah." After tonight formalities weren't necessary. Heat burned her cheeks again.

JT scowled from the bed. The machines around him were pushed to the side, waiting to be needed by another patient. He sat up with his legs dangling over the side and both arms locked straight. Veins popped out on his strong hands fisting the side of the bed. He had on a T-shirt and shorts. His feet were bare.

"Are you okay?" She eased closer.

"Fine." He gritted his teeth.

"Does anything hurt?"

"Besides my pride?"

"No one told you to climb up on that roof."

"You dared me."

The set of his jaw reminded her of Colton when he didn't want to concede defeat. "I should know better than to dare you."

221

"My uncle found me in my underwear, on my back, in the grass."

"You kind of asked for that." She could joke because he hadn't broken his neck, and she wanted to ease the crease between his brows. He'd looked sexy in those boxer briefs, even if he was standing on the roof like a buffoon.

"I didn't get to shout to the world that you're mine." He reached out and pulled her close. The smell of rubbing alcohol drifted off him. He settled her between his legs and wrapped his arms around her waist. He grimaced.

"What?"

"My side." He eased up his shirt. His right side was scraped and dotted with dried spots of blood.

"You should get that looked at. You might have broken something."

"I don't need a doctor. What I need is to go home and wrap my arms around you."

She traced his hairline and pressed her hand against the scruff of his beard. Her insides warmed like water in a teakettle. "You probably need some ibuprofen and an ice pack more."

The curtain swung back. She tried to move away, but JT kept his hold on her. Doc Taylor walked in. He stood tall with a shock of white hair on the back of his head and his hands spotted with age. His paunch hung over his belt. Doc had treated everyone in Heritage River at least once who was old enough to remember when Elvis Presley married Priscilla.

"JT Davies, the nurses woke me up from a perfectly good sleep because your uncle raised holy hell in the lobby. I told him the young doctors knew how to stitch up a dimwit who falls off a roof in the middle of the night. But as it seems our only ER doctor is tied up at the moment, I dragged myself out of bed to quiet Harlan down."

JT stiffened. "I'm sorry if they bothered you. I'm fine. Savannah is going to take me home." He eased her back and slid off the bed. He tried to hide the pain movement caused, but he didn't do a very good job.

"Sit back down. Let Doc Taylor take a look at you. He's here." She pressed a hand on his shoulder, but he didn't budge.

"Savannah, do your brothers know where you are?" Doc grabbed the chart at the end of the bed.

"I was on the phone with JT when he fell. I came to make sure he's okay." She held the man's gaze. She didn't like where he was going with this.

"Why don't you wait in the hall while I examine him?"

"I'll stay." Because she had seen more of JT than that old chauvinist ever would, and she didn't like being told what to do or the old man's implication she had to report to her older brothers. She turned to JT. "Unless you want me to leave."

"Hell no. But I don't need a doctor. Let's go."

Doc tossed the chart on the end of the bed and blocked their path. "If you leave, it's at your own risk. The hospital isn't responsible."

"Fine." He pushed past her and stood toe to toe with the doc.

"Still the same JT. When are you going to learn? Aren't you a little old to be jumping off roofs? That wild act you've been playing since you were a boy is growing old. A man your age should start acting like a man and not a child. Aren't you raising your daughter? She's going to end up just like you, amounting to nothing, if you don't show her the right road. You need to get yourself to church on Sundays."

JT clenched his fists. She placed her hand on the center of his back, but he didn't release his fists. He was a good man who had a right to a second chance from the narrow-minded members of this community.

"Shut that trap of yours, Amos." Harlan stood in the entryway. Maddy peeked around his shoulder with wide eyes.

"JT, let's go," she whispered and gripped his arm.

Doc Taylor turned to Harlan. "I was just telling your nephew he needed to get on the straight and narrow. I'm not embarrassed to say I voted against his liquor establishment. A shame he's not more like his father. Jake was an upstanding citizen. He should've taken a stronger hand with his son."

"My nephew needed some good doctoring. Not any advice or lecturing from you. Aren't you too old to be practicing medicine anyhow?" Harlan's face was splashed with red.

"Aren't you too old to be chasing ladies around town?"

"I've heard enough of this." She tugged on JT's arm. "I'll drive y'all home."

Harlan and Maddy turned into the hall. She pushed past the curtain.

"Savannah, didn't you bury your husband a few months ago? What's it going to do to his memory if you're getting involved with the likes of him?" Doc spit out the last word.

She almost made it. She spun on her heel and cocked her arm.

"Whoa." JT scooped her up and dragged her back.

Her feet kicked the air. "Put me down."

"Easy, feisty. I don't want to end up in jail tonight too." He plopped her down by the emergency room doors and grabbed his side.

"Nice one, Mrs. Montgomery." Maddy snickered and hugged her.

Her heart swelled. She yanked her shirt into place and smoothed her hair down. "What is wrong with that man?"

"He's an old fool," Harlan said. "Don't you listen to him, Jacob."

JT clamped his lips shut and favored his injured side.

She handed her keys to Harlan. "Could you bring the minivan around? We'll wait for you right outside." Harlan and Maddy passed through the automatic doors.

Savannah wanted to be alone with him. "Let's go outside and get some fresh air."

He followed her, but he'd set his jaw and limped behind her. She wanted to reach out to him but waited until the doors slid closed, shutting out the hurtful remains of the ER.

The warm air pushed against her already-hot skin. Except for the slamming of a car door in the distance, the night was quiet. "Your uncle is right. Don't listen to Doc Taylor. He's an ass."

He set his gaze somewhere in the expanse of the parking lot. "He said those things in front of Maddy."

"She doesn't believe them. She loves you. I can tell by the way she talks about you when she's with Grey."

"The whole town believes what he said."

"That's not true. That man is a coward and an ignoramus. Don't let him win."

He gave her an intense, fevered stare. "When the town council awards the Whiskey Bar the black-tie formal dinner, that's when I win."

Her breath stuck in her throat. He had every right to be angry, but the cold glare in his eyes made him someone else. Someone who would stop at nothing to win, and that could mean hurting her to get what he wanted. And what did she want besides winning? She wanted to hide behind a mask because she was afraid. Though after she almost hit Doc Taylor, more people would likely know about her and JT.

Harlan pulled up. He slid out of the car and took the back seat.

"Do you need any help?" She gripped JT's elbow, but he waved her away.

"I've got it, thanks." He eased into the passenger's

seat, but he knit his brows and sneered until the seat belt clicked into place.

This whole night was her fault. She pulled out of the parking lot. If she hadn't said she needed some time, he wouldn't have climbed out on the roof. Hadn't she wanted JT to finally tell her how he felt about her? Hadn't she spent her whole adult life hoping he was someplace thinking about her while she was thinking about him?

Hadn't she imagined him professing his love for her even while her husband slept in the bed next to her? She'd loved two men her entire life, and one sat beside her, taking up her front seat with his long legs and filling her insides like packed tea leaves in a mason jar. Why wouldn't she tell her children, her brothers, even her friend Rae, that she'd finally found the love she was looking for? What was stopping her?

Now that very man she longed to love was going to steal her one opportunity to make her Tea Room a success. Without that dinner she was sunk. She'd have to close the shop. She'd have to tell Jud to come home from school. Where would she get another job? How would she take care of her children?

She pulled into JT's driveway.

"Thank you for the ride." Maddy slid out of the van with a yawn.

Harlan tapped her shoulder. "Drive safe going home. Let JT know you got there okay, you hear?"

She nodded, afraid to speak. The tears threatened to spill. How would she explain falling to pieces?

JT didn't move.

"Do you need some help getting in?"

He stared out the window.

"Is that a no?"

"Are you going to tell your kids about us?" He kept his face turned away from her, but he'd softened his words.

How could she continue this thing between them if he could be the one responsible for putting her out of business? And how could she stop her heart from reaching out to him? What would it do to him if she won the black-tie? He had everything he was wrapped up in winning to prove to the people like Doc Taylor he was far more than the garbageman.

He turned to her with a hooded gaze. The lines around his mouth had deepened. "Savannah, did you hear me?"

His words scratched against her heart, wanting to be let in. She ran a thumb along his scruffy jaw. "Yes."

He leaned over and placed a soft kiss on her lips. "I'll call you later." He eased out of the car and limped up the front steps. He gave her a wave.

She waited until he went inside. One large tear ran down her cheek. She'd said yes, but she wasn't sure which question she was answering.

Chapter Twenty-One

JT groaned as he reached for the box of drink stirrers on the top shelf. The Whiskey Bar's storage closet smelled like cardboard and lemon. They weren't open for another hour, but he couldn't stay at home holding an ice pack to his side any longer. He was too old to be falling off roofs.

Doc Taylor's words still rang in his ears and boiled his insides. He tried to drown them out with work, but they crept back in and poked at his bruised side. He'd show him. But he'd have to hurt Savannah to do it.

She had to understand winning the black-tie wasn't personal. He'd find a way to make her understand because he wasn't letting her go.

He had to win. If he lost the black-tie, how would he prove he'd made something of himself?

Georgia sat at the bar with her head in a book.

"Here are the stirrers you requested." He tried to hide the pain and wasn't sure if it worked.

"Thanks. How are the ribs?" She closed the book and ran her gaze over him.

"Mine or the ones I want to add to the menu?"

"Either."

"Fine. Are we all set to open?"

"My bar is ready. Not sure what your kitchen staff is up to. I leave that mess to Gil."

"What mess is that?" a female voice called from behind him.

Any other day he'd be ready for this visitor, but not today when his ribs hurt even to breathe and when his pride lay tattered and torn in his bushes. He just wanted to get through the day without any unforeseen hassles, go home early to Maddy so she wouldn't be mad at him for working so much, and then convince Savannah to sneak away for an hour so he could make her smile up at him while he made love to her.

Now he'd have to deal with Rebecca Stone. If he wasn't so sure of his staff and his business, he'd be worried about an unannounced visit from the county health inspector. He didn't expect one so soon after opening, but the county was doing its job to make sure the people ate in clean, safe places. He never minded inspections any other time.

She dropped her duffel bag on a chair and pulled out a clipboard. Her hair was fastened back in a big brown barrette. Her bangs curled up into corkscrews on her forehead. She had on the green polo county shirt, standard khaki pants, and black, rubber-soled shoes.

"Howdy, Rebecca. Nice to see you today." The faster

he gave her what she wanted, the quicker she'd get out of his bar and leave him alone.

"You're looking a little pallid. Are you under the weather?"

"I'd never dream of coming to work sick. Bruised a few ribs. Other than that, I'm fine. Do you remember Georgia?"

Georgia shook hands.

"Are you reading something good?" Rebecca hadn't missed the book on the bar, though Georgia had nothing to hide. The bar wasn't open for business.

"Just a little escapism before the shift officially starts. All my glasses are clean, the bar is wiped down, and the taps have been tested and cleaned today. I'm all set up front."

"You'll wipe that bar again, I'm assuming? Your book might be dirty."

A statement like that was unusual for an inspector to make, but maybe Rebecca was more particular. He didn't know her that well.

"I wipe that bar a thousand times a day." Georgia smiled, but her eyes were glazed with worry.

"Do you want to go into the kitchen?" He turned for the back of the bar.

"Can I have your safety-monitoring records?" She followed him into the kitchen.

He kept the records on a clipboard and on file in his computer. He tracked employee illness, training, temperature of food, and refrigeration. Everything was in order, but she had to see that for herself.

Gil wasn't in the kitchen. He could be in the freezer or the refrigerator or maybe the storage closet. Hopefully, he wasn't outside having a smoke because he'd come in reeking, and though smoking outside was allowed as long as he washed his hands afterward, an inspector like Rebecca could frown on it.

"I'm here sooner than I thought I'd be." She flipped through his papers. "We received a call your food-handling standards might not be up to code."

He laughed to show he wasn't worried, but who made that kind of a call? Did one of his employees say something? Had a customer seen something and not said? Usually, a customer would complain before leaving or write a negative review online. He hadn't noticed any for this location. An unhappy customer showed up every-where. His other locations had received some negative reviews, not all justified.

"The Whiskey Bar is a well-oiled machine. Everyone is trained, food-storage containers labeled, and everything is properly cleaned."

"I'll start with refrigeration." She pulled a notebook out of her bag.

He led her over and opened the steel door. The room was cold, below forty-two degrees. He didn't need a ther-mometer to tell him that. He'd been walking inside refrig-erators for years. He knew when the temperatures were right and when they weren't.

"Your thermometer says forty-seven degrees."

"What?" He checked the fridge's built-in thermome-ter. Had it been calibrated this morning? He ran out and grabbed his clipboard. Gil had logged the fridge's calibration and temperature. "The thermometer must be off. I'll take care of it."

"Don't bother. I'm writing you up for a critical violation."

"Check the product first. You'll see the meats are the right temperature."

"Nine times out of ten, the product is hot too. Get rid of it." She marched back into the kitchen, leaving him in the cold.

"I can recalibrate the thermometer in five minutes. You can tell that unit is cold enough just by standing in it."

"I can tell no such thing. Your thermometer says forty-seven degrees. Your food is in jeopardy of growing bacteria. I need you to dispose of all that food."

"Are you kidding me? There's hundreds of dollars of food in there. I won't be able to serve my lunch crowd today, and I open in thirty minutes. My head chef documented the temperature this morning. Not two hours ago. There's no way that food is spoiled. I'm not throwing it out."

"Mr. Davies, the county health department's protocol is to dispose of any foods that may be contaminated. As a county inspector, I have a duty to carry out my responsibilities."

"Who made the complaint against me?" He clenched his fists and made his ribs hurt.

"The call was anonymous."

"It was a bogus call."

"I'm afraid we have to investigate all possible violations. Your refrigeration unit is too warm. Once you remove the food, I'll leave. You'll have three days to fix the problem before I return for another inspection."

The back door opened, and Gil came in with the scent of cigarette smoke stuck to him. He tried to signal to Gil so he'd wash his hands right away. Instead, he walked straight up to Rebecca and held out his hand.

"Hey, I'm Gil."

Rebecca wrinkled up her nose.

"Gil, I need you to help me empty the refrigerator. It appears the calibration is wrong and the unit is too warm, and wash your damn hands."

"What? No way. I checked the temperature myself. JT, I wrote down everything on the sheet. There's a mistake. That fridge is running like a purring kitten. We can't throw that food out. We won't be able to serve lunch." Gil ran to the sink and scrubbed up.

His words exactly. "Just do it. I'll be right back." He hurried up front. "Georgia, we've got a big problem in the back. Keep the doors locked until Rebecca leaves. Don't let anyone in. Put up a sign that says doing inventory. We'll be open at three today."

"That's going to kill us. What's going on?"

"I don't have time to explain." He dug his phone out of his pocket and tapped at the screen until Parker's number started dialing.

"Hey, man, what's up in Heritage River?"

"We've got a big problem. I need you to bring me food and fast."

"That's going to take me an hour. Want to tell me what the hell the problem is?"

"Health inspector showed up. Someone called in an anonymous tip. Critical violation with the fridge. The thermometer isn't working right."

"So recalibrate it."

"Can't. Will you bring the food?"

"I'll send what I can. You'll have to buy the rest. This is going to fuck us up."

Royally.

JT dragged his aching body out of the car and up the front steps of his house. He wanted a cold beer and a hot shower. His lunch crowd had been nonexistent. The dinner rush was a trickle. Word would spread by tomorrow about the violation. He was sunk. He could lose his bar, he would definitely lose the black-tie formal now, and he'd lose whatever dignity he had left. He should pack up and move the hell out of Heritage River while he still could.

His daughter was madder than a puffed toad. He hadn't made it home early. She hated being in the house alone. She went over to Grey's. Savannah would drive her home around ten thirty. The only light in the day was the possibility of stealing a kiss from his sweet Savannah.

"JT?"

His heart nearly stopped. He turned toward the sound the voice he'd grown to despise. Shirley stood in the pool of the streetlight. She edged her way forward until she stopped at the bottom of his steps.

"What do you want?" He had no time or energy to be nice.

"I want my store back, and this house. They're not yours to keep."

He ran a hand over his face and scratched at his beard. "How many times do we have to go over this? For Christ's sake, Shirley, I've had a long day, and I'm going inside. Don't come around here anymore, and don't bother my uncle either. You want to fight me, then be ready for a fight because the only way you'll get this house is to kill me first."

"I'm your mama. You can't do this to me."

He took the steps two at a time. "You are not and have never been my mother." He wanted to fight someone because of what happened at work, and Shirley gave him a good excuse. "Go home."

"I put up with you all those years while you ran around getting into trouble. You used to be such a sweet boy, and then you started hanging out with those Savages, and you found trouble. I tried to guide you, help you. I fed you, washed your clothes, took you to the doctor when you were sick. You hurt your father more times than he would admit with your ways. I tried to love you, but you made it impossible. And then you kick me out of my home. It's not right."

"You couldn't wait for the day I left. You told me that every chance you got. He left the house and the store to me." He pounded his chest with his finger. "I'm going to finish raising my daughter in that house, and you aren't going to come around anymore, or I'll get a restraining order against you."

"I miss him. He's here in this house. Why should you have it? You're nothing. A disappointment." The hacking coughs of a long-time smoker racked her body.

She wiped a tear from her weathered face, and he felt nothing. How much more would this woman try to take from him? She'd spent years comparing herself to his dead mother, hoping or maybe demanding respect from him because she cooked and cleaned, because she thought his dad should forget about his first wife and love the woman trying to straighten out his son, but all she'd managed to do was tell him he was a loser and a burden to their family.

"Don't make me say it again. Go home, Shirley."

"You can't stop me from standing on the sidewalk and looking up at the porch."

"I'll burn this house to the ground if you keep that up. Now get out of here."

"I'll get my house and my store back. My lawyer said I have a good case. You can't win."

The weight of the day was too much to carry. He left her on the lawn, pounded up the steps, and threw the front door open. It smashed against the wall, leaving a hole in the plaster to match the empty hole in his chest. He kicked the wall.

He chucked off his boots, dragged his belt from the loops, and left them. He hurried into the basement. He hadn't been down here since they moved back in because he'd been too damn busy.

He tore his T-shirt over his head and jabbed at the heavy bag hanging from the beam in the ceiling. The basement smelled cold and damp, which did nothing to cool the heat in his veins. He threw punch after punch until he no longer felt his hands. Sweat ran down his face, over his chest and back. His lungs and ribs protested, but he kept throwing punches. The scrapes on his side broke open. Blood trickled down onto the waistband of his jeans.

"Dad?" Maddy's voice stopped him cold.

"Hey, sweetheart." He wiped the sweat from his brow.

She eyed him. "Savannah is here. She walked in because the front door was open."

"Maddy, is he down there?" Savannah's shadow spilled across the wall as her voice drifted down to him.

"He's working out." Maddy went back up.

Savannah's footsteps echoed against the wood stairs. She bent down to see below the wall. Her smile fell off her face. "Are you okay? You're bleeding." She hurried down the last of the steps.

"I'm fine." He backed up.

"Let me see." She came closer.

"I said I'm fine." His breath slowed down, but the heat in his veins continued to burn.

"You're such a man sometimes." She fisted her hands on her hips and turned that gorgeous chin up at him. Her gray eyes smoked.

"Isn't that what you like about me?" He hoped the smile he forced would deflect her.

"Not exactly the point at the moment, cowboy. You broke open the cuts again, and your hands are bleeding too." She tilted his hands up with the tips of her fingers. Her touch was warm, like whiskey's trail down his throat.

Sure enough, his knuckles were cut and red. They'd be swollen in the morning. "I'll put them in ice." He reached for his shirt and eased it over his head.

She helped him get his arm through the sleeve and bruised his pride in the process. "I'm not a child, Savannah."

"You're hurt. I don't give a damn about your pride right now."

She saw past his exterior and knew what had him tied up in knots. He could let go of his hurt and anger when she was around.

"Fighting isn't going to solve your problems."

"No lectures, okay? Not tonight. And for the record, I wasn't fighting. I hit the heavy bag to work out." If his side didn't hurt so much, he'd flex for her. Instead, he leaned against the nearby stool and wiped the sweat from his face.

"You don't do that to your hands in a workout. Do you want to tell me what's really going on? Did something happen at work today? Is it Shirley again?"

"Please cut me some slack. I don't want to talk about my shit. I want you to come over here and wrap your arms around me."

She closed the space between them, hooked her

fingers through his belt loops, and gave him a little tug. She drove him crazy only giving small pieces of herself.

He leaned down and took her earlobe between his teeth, then cupped her bottom between his hands and pulled her against him.

"Dad?" Maddy banged on the basement door.

Savannah jumped back.

He reached for her, but she slid out of his grasp. "Yeah?"

"I'm going to bed. I have to get up early for school, so I won't be coming down for a snack or anything." Savannah covered her face with her hands.

"Thanks for letting me know. Good night, Madeline Elizabeth."

"Good night, Daddy. Good night, Savannah."

"Sleep well, sweetie," she called up the steps and turned back to him. "I think that's my cue to go. Your daughter suspects we're down here making out like a couple of teenagers."

He stood and pulled her close again. "Do you want to make out like a couple of teenagers? It might be fun."

He returned to her earlobe, tugging on it with his teeth. He moved his lips to her neck and tasted her sweet scent. She pressed against him. The contact sent sparks to his brain and his groin. "Is that a yes?"

She ran a finger along his jaw. "I want to."

He stepped back. "I don't understand you and your mixed messages. Do I embarrass you?" He didn't want to ruin the mood between them, but Shirley's ugly words crowded his thoughts.

"Well, if you continue to fall off roofs, you might."

"Tell me the truth."

"JT Davies, how can you ask me such a question? I wouldn't make love to a man who embarrassed me."

"Then how can you want to haul off and hit Doc Taylor in one minute and keep us a secret in the next?"

"I can't hurt my children. Their father hasn't been gone that long. Caroline never stops wearing his sweatshirt. Grey acts out. Jud is mad at me about school. I don't need to give him anything else to hold against me."

"What about what you want?"

He wanted all of her. He wouldn't be satisfied with only part, but she wasn't giving away her whole self. She could lie beside him but not walk with him. He needed to reconcile the confused feelings in his heart, but not tonight. He'd had too much to deal with today. Tonight he only wanted Savannah.

"What I want doesn't factor in."

He reached for her again. "There isn't anywhere I'd rather be right now than with you. Don't think. Just be. Be with me. Tonight. We'll worry about tomorrow then." He searched her face for a response. How did he get through to her?

"You make it sound so easy, as if the rest of the world doesn't matter." She placed a hand on his chest.

He gripped her hand and kissed the tips of her fingers, but the heat of her touch still burned through his shirt and to his skin. "It's just us. You and me. No one else matters."

She closed her eyes and leaned her head against his

chest. He wrapped his arms around her waist, afraid to move much more and scare her away. She placed her hands on his hips and snaked them up his back. Her touch drove him mad, but he waited. She had to be the one to come to him.

"Can you give me tonight and let me go?" She whispered the words.

"I don't know." How was he going to give her up? She was in his blood.

"Why is this so hard?"

"Darlin', if you don't want to be with me, I'm not going to force you. Shit, I want you to want me as much as I want you. But if I'm not it—"

"JT, kiss me."

Confusion beat up his heart. "Are you sure?" Because he wanted nothing more than to kiss her and make love to her and hold her all night long.

"We have tonight, and I don't want tonight to end."

"I'm not making love to you in this basement."

She eased back to look up at him. "You weren't planning on taking me to your bedroom with your daughter down the hall, were you? Because I won't go there."

"I have an idea. Come with me." He gripped her hand and yanked her toward the stairs.

She ran to keep up. "Where are we going?"

"Trust me."

He pulled his sleeping bag out of the closet and grabbed a lantern. He shoved his feet into his boots and took her out the back door. "I haven't been camping in a long time. I hope the batteries still work."

"Using a sleeping bag will be a first for me."

"I love the sound of that." He hooked the bag under his arm and closed the back door behind them.

She stopped halfway across his yard. "You should know something. I mean, I assumed you did, but I'm guessing you don't." She looked away and rolled her bottom lip under her teeth. "I don't know how to say this."

He turned her chin so she had to look at him. "You can say it. Whatever it is, it's okay." "

You were the first."

He dropped the bag. "That night? You'd never? Why didn't you tell me? I'm such an asshole, Savannah. I'm sorry. I didn't know. The way it happened. I just figured..."

She placed her fingers to his lips. "I knew if I'd said anything you wouldn't have touched me, and all I wanted was for you to finally touch me."

"The first time should be special. Not behind your garage with some guy who couldn't keep his hands to himself."

"First of all, it wasn't just some guy. Second, my hands were all over you if I remember correctly. It took you almost ten minutes to figure out what I was trying to do. I thought how dense is he? And don't act as if the space behind the garage was awful. We had that nice little firepit Colton built and those lounge chairs. Not exactly a king-size bed with rose petals and candles, but it was perfect and private. Exactly like I wanted it."

He traced his finger along her necklace. "Those

chairs were awful, and we had to hurry so no one would catch us. Darlin', let me make it up to you. No roughing it this time. I'll book us a room in a fancy hotel."

"You will do no such thing. We have tonight. No thinking. No worries, remember? Take me to your camp-ground." She shoved the bag back at him.

"This isn't good enough for you."

"Every minute with you is special. I don't need a bed. I only need you."

But not always. He had said they would worry about tomorrow then, but he wanted to know she would stay with him now. He grabbed her hand and pulled her along.

The town park met the edge of his property. It was one of the best things about his childhood home. The tree line sloped down to a small brook. When the water was low, the brook could be crossed on some water rocks. As kids, they'd see who could get over the slippery stones first without falling in. One time he, Blaise, and Colton had made it across without realizing Savannah had become stuck halfway. Her brothers laughed and ran on to the park, but he climbed back to help her. She fell in and soaked her clothes. He had to drive her home and lie to her father about what happened. He took the blame so she wouldn't get in trouble. Mr. Savage threw him out. That man had always scared the hell out of him.

Sometime over the years, the ground under the big pines had transformed into hard dirt. He laid down the sleeping bag and turned on the lantern to help Savannah inside.

The gurgling brook gave them their own soundtrack. He kicked off his boots and slid in beside her, ignoring the pain in his side. "I've been waiting to do this all night," he said.

She ran her thumb along his jawline. The simple touch made him greedy for more. He tugged her shirt above her head to feel her skin. He kissed her, pushing her lips apart with his tongue. He cupped the back of her head to keep her close and deepen the kiss. She rewarded him with a soft moan.

His hands explored her breasts over the cups of her bra. He dipped one finger inside to taunt her nipple.

She unhooked her bra and placed his hand over her breast. "No teasing," she said against his lips.

He kneaded her flesh until her breath matched the racing of his. His heart collided with his ribs, causing wonderful pain in his chest. He didn't care if those scrapes opened wide and he bled to death as long as he could go with Savannah in his arms.

She wrapped a leg over his hip and pressed against his erection. Even with clothes on, the friction turned him into liquid smoke. He pulled at the button of her jeans, but he couldn't get the button loose.

She laughed, and his blood warmed even more.

"Let me," she said.

The sleeping bag didn't give them much room to move. She had to turn on her back to slide out of her pants. He held the lantern above them to steal a look at her. "I could watch you all night."

She rolled her eyes. "Please. My skin sags no matter

how many sit-ups I do. My hips are too big. You're just at the age where you need glasses to see close."

He pulled her against him and slid his hands under her silky panties. "I can see just fine, darlin'. And you're beautiful."

"Thank you." She ran a finger along his beard. He gripped her hand and sucked on her fingers.

She held his gaze. "You're very good at that."

He wanted to kiss her everywhere. The sleeping bag wouldn't make that possible tonight, but he would eventually show her how much her words and her touch sent his brain into a frenzy.

"Your turn." She slapped his backside, and this time he laughed.

He took up a lot more of the nylon bag, making undressing difficult. He managed to get his jeans over his ankles without ripping the bag in half. He positioned her beneath him. "Are you comfortable?"

She placed a hand on his chest. "This is perfect."

He kissed her again. His hands found the tight bud of her nipple and rolled it between his fingers. She arched into his touch. He wanted to take his time with her, but his mind and the blood pumping to his groin were steps ahead.

She dragged her hands down his chest, as if she had all the time in the world. He would never stop wanting her touch on his skin. Her hand slid around him and slowly stroked his full length. He tore his lips free. "You're driving me crazy."

"Kind of what I was trying to do."

He wanted her to feel the frantic pleasure he did, and traveled his hand over her hip to her most intimate place. He tested her readiness. "Is that for me?" His voice stuck in his throat.

"Do you see anyone else here? Now stop talking and make love to me."

He took his time to tease her a little for getting the last word, words he wanted to hear. But the last word was usually his. He stroked her heat, and she rewarded him with the arch of her hips.

His thirst for her grew. He didn't know how much longer he could hold out. He wanted to wait, to let her get to the end first, but the pulsing in his groin and the ache in his chest needed to soar with her. This time wasn't a competition to the finish line. He wanted to show her she'd been the woman in his dreams.

He changed the rhythm of his touch to bring her to the edge, and she gripped his hand.

"JT, now, please. I can't wait."

He was a goner and positioned himself against her. She stared up at him with eyes darkened by lust. His lips found hers. He joined their bodies hard and fast because he'd lost all reason. He wanted her again and again.

"Yes," she said against his cheek. Her hips rocked to the rhythm of his.

He couldn't wait. His movements picked up speed. He drank in her scent as his mouth sought her neck, and his teeth took tiny nips of her luscious skin.

She met him thrust for thrust, gripping his backside to push him deeper. The ache in his chest tore wide open. He struggled to slow down and make this last for her.

She cupped his face in her hands. "Look at me, Jacob Tyler."

He dragged his gaze back to her. "I love the sound of my name on your lips."

"You are an amazing man."

Her words pushed him over the edge. He closed his eyes and let the need for Savannah's love swell over him again and again until he had nothing left. Her muscles flexed around him as she came to the breathless end.

He gathered her in his arms, not wanting to let her go. Their bodies were slick with sweat. "You are the incredible one. You're smart, strong, beautiful. Sometimes you scare the hell out of me."

"Me? How am I scary? Even my kids aren't afraid of me."

"You stand up to anything."

She snuggled closer. "I learned to hide my fear. You're the one who isn't afraid of anything. There isn't a dare you won't take." She pushed back from him. "How is your side? Did we hurt it?"

He tucked her hair behind her ear. "I'm better than fine. I have Savannah Savage in my sleeping bag."

"Are you ready to tell me what happened today that had you raging mad?" She eased back down and traced her fingers along his back.

If she kept that up, he'd be ready for round two with her.

"I don't want to ruin the best thing that happened all day. The retelling of my problems can hold."

"You shouldn't keep it bottled up. Was it Shirley?"

"You're not going to let this go."

"Fine. Don't talk about it. I have to go anyway. The kids could wake up and look for me. Are my jeans shoved at the end of this bag?" She squirmed around, trying to locate her clothes.

"Watch the knee, lady." He gripped her hip and planted a kiss on her nose. He would tell her what she wanted to hear if it meant she'd stay a little longer. "The health inspector came by. She gave me a critical." He told her about the thermometer. "Someone called in a complaint."

"Oh, I'm sorry. That isn't fair. Something like that could be fixed quickly. Who do you think called that in?"

"Shirley." The anger returned and pushed and shoved him from all angles.

"Would she really do that to you?"

"Who else?" He unzipped the bag and dragged his pants back over his legs.

She followed his lead and threw on her clothes. He instantly regretted allowing his emotions to wedge between them. She was trying to help.

"Hey." She stood facing him and took his hand in hers. "Shirley is a sad, lonely woman."

"Fuck Shirley."

"She's been living in your mother's shadow for a very long time. She wanted to be the center of your dad's world, but there wasn't room in it because first your mom

249

and then you filled it up. If she called that complaint in, you'll deal with it. You're going to have to forgive her for yourself if you're ever going to move on."

"How do you know all that?" He tugged her close. He wasn't sure if he could ever forgive Shirley.

"I know your family, and I'm a pretty good judge of character."

"She's right about me making my dad's life harder than it had to be."

"You were young. Kids make life hard. You weren't supposed to be perfect, and your dad never thought you should be."

"He tried to get me to pass my classes, not do stupid things like get arrested for drinking at the lake, hitchhike, fight. I never listened to him. He worked all the time, left me with Shirley who hated me. No matter what he said, I thought I knew better. I was a disappointment to him."

"Not always." She placed a soft kiss on his lips. "This has been a wonderful night, and I want to help you feel better about Shirley, but I have to go."

"You're letting the night end?" He didn't want her to leave.

"It's late. I should be home. Part of me feels a little guilty for being out, and the other part of me wants to thank you for reminding me to let go a little."

"It could be like this all the time."

"JT—"

"Savannah." He had to stop her from saying she didn't want to see him again. He didn't care how desperate he sounded. If she walked away from him, she might never come back, and he couldn't lose her again. He searched for the words to say that would convince her. "Something that feels this right can't be wrong. Other people's thoughts about us don't matter."

She placed a hand on his cheek. "I won't make promises I can't keep. The timing is wrong." Tears filled her eyes.

His heart shattered. He ran his fingers through her silky hair and cupped her face to keep her gaze right on him. He had no other choice. If he didn't say it now, he may never get the chance again. He wouldn't make the same mistake he'd made twenty-four years ago when he packed his bags and left.

"I love you, Savannah Savage. Always have. Always will."

Chapter Twenty-Two

S avannah tilted her chin up to the sun. The warmth did nothing to stop the shivers. She carried wildflowers in a basket with a travel mug of lavender-lemongrass tea and two plain scones. She followed the familiar cobblestone path up the hill. The scent of freshly cut grass accompanied her as she stepped off the bricks and weaved her way around the stones carved with reminders of lives lived before.

She'd picked this spot because of the view and the large poplar whose branches stretched and yawned against the sky. The sun set behind the tree, and some nights the pink and orange rays seemed to set the tree on fire. Her visits were too few to appreciate that, but just knowing it happened every day gave her some peace.

She spread out a small blanket and laid the flowers down. Her fingers traced the letters engraved into the black marble. *Adam Montgomery. Beloved father and husband.*

"Hi, honey. I'm sorry I haven't been here in a while." She twisted open the mug and let the scent of the lemon and lavender drift up to her. "Things have been a little crazy. Caroline is still struggling in school. I'm not sure what to do about that. Grey is okay. I think. He met a girl. Our sweet little boy likes a girl. Jud is mad at me. I can't keep him in school." The tears burned the backs of her eyes.

She wouldn't cry. It wasn't fair to Adam. "I spent all the insurance money for my tea shop. It wasn't smart. I know. Colton tried to talk me out of it, but I didn't listen to him. I have a bit of a mess on my hands, but that's not what I wanted to talk to you about."

She tried to catch her breath. "There's something you should know. I'm in love with someone else, and I'm so sorry about that. It didn't just happen. You might understand me meeting someone new and getting on with my life even if it seemed sudden, but I fell in love with this man long before you and I met. He didn't want me then —at least that's what I believed—so I went on with my life.

"I tried to get him out of my mind for years, but I couldn't. He was always there, even when you slept beside me, and I'm sorry for that too. You were such a good man and a wonderful father, and I wasn't completely honest with you. My heart wasn't whole when I gave it to you.

"I didn't love you any less. We built a good life I loved and cherished. Our children are my greatest gift, and I wouldn't change a minute of that.

"But I loved him too. I never sought him out in all our years together, but God or the universe or whatever has brought him back, and I want to be with him. I keep thinking it's wrong to get involved with another man so soon. What will the kids say? What would you think? I don't expect you to understand, but I hope you'll forgive me. I'll never stop loving you, my sweet, and the life we created together."

She swiped at the tears running down her face. It was wrong to love two men at once, and still she could never stop. JT had weaved his way into her heart when she was too young to know how to protect it. She'd believed for so long that she only needed to know he was okay and happy, but when he came home, she knew that would never have been enough. Her love for him seeped into her bones and snaked around her heart.

Adam had worked his whole life to make sure she'd be comfortable if something happened to him. She hadn't regarded that with her hasty business decision. Now she needed to win that black-tie dinner desperately. If JT won, she'd lose not only her shop but Adam's dignity.

What right did she have to crave JT's affection? She should be mourning her husband by honoring his memory and respecting everything he'd done for his family. Instead, her heart climbed into her throat, trying to get to JT.

She had to visit the cemetery today. After JT told her he loved her the other night, she'd had to come clean at least with Adam.

"Savannah?"

She turned toward the female voice and forced a smile on her lips. "Hey, Grace." She wiped at her face again.

"Am I intruding?" Grace pulled her long blonde hair from the holder and retied it high on her head. Her clear blue eyes were rimmed red, but her blouse was crisp and neat.

"Not at all." She stood and smoothed her clothes into place. "Are you and Blaise visiting our parents?" She searched for the sight of her brother.

"Actually, I come here sometimes to talk with my father. Blaise thought it might help me to work through some things with him we couldn't fix while he was alive."

Savannah's heart swelled. She was so lucky to have a family that supported each other. What would they say when they found out about her and JT? Maybe she could tell Blaise first and he could help her ease the blow to her children. "Can I ask you something personal?"

"Sure," Grace said.

"Do you mind if we walk and talk?" She kissed the tips of her fingers and pressed them to Adam's gravestone. She gathered the basket and the blanket. "How did you know Blaise was right for you?"

Red blotches crept up Grace's neck as they passed onto the cobblestone path. "Well, that wink of his had my knees knocking. No man had ever ruffled my feathers quite the way he did, but I think it was the moment I realized I felt more like the person I wanted to be with him than the person I was without him. Does that make sense?"

"A lot."

"Have you started dating?"

"I don't think the kids are ready for me to bring another man around, and I have too many other things to worry about in my life. Adding a relationship would only complicate matters."

"You nurture everyone in the family, not just your children but your brothers and nephews too. Make sure you take some time for yourself. You've earned some happiness."

"I am happy." She was. Wasn't she? Did she have the right to ask for more when she needed to fix her problems first? Her happiness would come in time. JT would have to wait. No more trips to the woods with him.

"You know better than anyone how quickly life can change. Don't wait for life to come to you. Go after it. If I hadn't taken a chance, I wouldn't be with Blaise now, and I can't imagine my life without him. Or without his family." Grace pulled her into a hug.

The tears stung her eyes. It was as if Grace had known what she'd been thinking. "You're like the sister I never had."

"That means a lot. You are too. And Harley. I'm excited to be in their wedding." Grace rummaged around in her bag and pulled out her keys.

"I can't believe my brother is getting married. I never thought I'd live to see the day." And she still had to finish paying for the dresses. The worry of money was a kettle of boiling water about to drop on her head. "Speaking of Harley, I have to get back to the Tea Room and relieve her. She's finishing the mural today for the anniversary celebration. Would you like to come for lunch?"

"I'd love to."

She glanced over her shoulder and said a silent goodbye to Adam. Could she take a chance the way Grace had? Would love be waiting for her when she did?

The Tea Room was packed. Savannah couldn't believe her eyes. Every table had people, mostly women, sitting around laughing, talking, and drinking tea from the colorful teapots she served to every guest. Kiki, the fork stealer, waved from her spot by the window.

Rae motioned her over. She had flour on her cheek and an apron covered in something that might've been soup. "We've been busy since eleven. I don't know what's going on, but I don't care. This is the best day we've had since we opened. I sent Harley home. She got a call from one of her students. Something about dried paint. She was in a bit of a panic."

"Why didn't you call me? I would've been here sooner." She dumped her tote in the back room. "What needs to be done? Do you remember Grace, Blaise's girlfriend?"

"Sure. The girl from New Jersey. Those lunch orders need to be filled, and I'm out of hot water. Grace, can you wait tables? I need some help."

Grace's face lit up. "I worked at a TGI Fridays in college. I lived off those tips."

"Awesome." Rae grabbed Grace's hand and dragged her into the kitchen.

If her place was filled with customers, what was happening down at the Whiskey Bar? She shot off a quick text to JT.

How's your day?

Sucks. Call you later.

Word of the violation must have spread. If Shirley had made that call, she'd ruin him, which was exactly what she wanted. The packed house at lunch suddenly had the bitter taste of tea brewed too long.

She didn't want to win customers at JT's expense. Wasn't there a way they could both come out on top? He was too competitive and stubborn to stop until he'd won, and she was afraid that anger of his would drive him to do whatever he thought he had to, even if that meant putting her out of business.

Her phone vibrated in her hand. She hoped it was JT calling her, but Jud's face popped up on the screen. She took the phone and went out to the back parking lot. "Hey, buddy."

"Mom, the check bounced."

"What?"

"The check you sent to cover the deposit for next semester bounced. The bursar's office called me down today to tell me I can't come back next semester. After finals, I have to pack my stuff up for good. You have to do something."

She could try to get another loan from the bank or maybe another credit card she could take a cash advance on. How she'd make those payments she didn't know, but she couldn't let Jud miss a semester of school. "I need a week."

"I don't have a week. This is embarrassing. Are we broke or something?"

"We're not broke. I'll figure it out. I'm sorry you're going through this, but sometimes there's a mixup at the bank."

"Mom, I'm not stupid. There's no mix-up. You wrote a check that didn't have the money to cover it, and now I can't go to school next semester. Dad wouldn't have let this happen. I have to go." He ended the call.

She paced in front of the back door. How could she let her son down? She should sell the business and see if she could recoup some of the money. She glanced back inside the kitchen. Grace ran around carrying plates filled with salad. Rae juggled three pots of tea on a tray. Her business might have finally turned the corner.

Her heart still ached for JT's loss, but the tailgate was tomorrow, and then the town council would decide who won the big event. She just needed to get through the next couple of weeks. After that she would know for sure what she had to do. In the meantime, she had only one choice.

She pushed her way back inside and catered to her guests. First thing tomorrow she'd apply for a loan.

Chapter Twenty-Three

Savannah forced her face to stay neutral. Normally, she had no problem keeping a smile plastered in place. Appearances were important. That's what her father had taught her. "Savannah Gale, your problems are your business. Don't give the neighbors something to talk about at the dinner table. Your brothers have done enough of that for two lifetimes." But the pitying look in Maria Longstreet's eyes made faking it difficult.

"I'm so sorry, Savannah. We can't give you another loan." Maria reached across her bank manager's desk with her perfectly manicured hand to pat her wrist.

She pulled back, clasped her hands in her lap, and squared her shoulders. "There is nothing to be sorry about. The expansion can wait." She wasn't sure if Maria believed her story about wanting to add an extra room on to the house, but that was the tale she was sticking with.

Maria stood in her designer black suit accented with

a thick gold chain around her neck. She could pay for a whole year of college with that thing. Maria stuck out her hand. The meeting was over.

She gave Maria's hand a solid grip. "It was lovely to see you again. Please say hello to Jeffrey."

"How are you, really? Jeff and I think about you all the time. Maybe instead of adding on to that house, you should think about selling it. You must be very sad there with all those memories in every room."

"Thank you for your concern, but my children and I are fine. I hope you'll be able to come to the tailgate. Have a nice day."

She turned her back, not waiting for another comment. If Maria was going to offer unwanted sympathy, then she would decide when the damn meeting was over. And if Maria said one more irritating thing, she'd tell her old Jeff was screwing his secretary and had been for the past ten years. She had caught them between the stacks in the library five years ago. She even warned Grace about them.

She didn't have time to find a solution. The tailgate was hours away, and she had to get ready. She'd call the college on the way to the Tea Room and ask for more time to pay Jud's bill.

The morning heat smacked her as she pushed out into the parking lot. The inside of the minivan roasted, and sweat ran down her neck. She picked up her phone to call JT, then stopped. He couldn't help her. He had his own problems at the moment. The Whiskey had been empty for days. She could ask Colton to lend her the money, but she would rather die first than admit she needed it.

The minivan drove itself home while her mind went round and round trying to find a way out of her problems. The empty house was a relief. She didn't have to pretend to Caroline and Grey that everything was okay.

She ripped off her long floral skirt and white blouse and left them on the bedroom floor. The bed remained unmade and a reminder of her loss. Three loads of laundry waited to be folded. She tugged her hair out of its knot.

She opted for her wide-leg jeans and black tank top and wound her brown leather belt through the pant loops. She slid her feet into flip-flops. The comfortable clothes allowed her to take the first deep breath since the bank. She didn't want to think about the bank anymore.

She didn't want to think about anything except having JT's arms around her. The anger from making mistakes, the humiliation of being rejected, and the guilt for loving JT propelled her forward like a shot from a cannon.

She tore the sheets from the bed and heaved the mattress off the frame, knocking over the baskets of clean clothes. She raced to the garage for empty storage boxes. In the nine months Adam had been gone, she'd ignored the one small closet of his. Now she tugged open the door that always stuck on its hinges. The wood scraped. She tossed sweaters, pants, and old baseball hats in with the suits, kicked the door shut, and hurried to the attic.

Sweat ran down her face and eyes as she struggled to

get the box up the ladder-style steps. She shoved the container into the corner, past the evidence of her rodent tenant, and next to the Christmas ornaments. Her breath came in short spurts. Her chest heaved. She flopped down on the plywood and held her head in her hands. This time, in the privacy of her stifling attic, with no one home, she allowed the tears to come.

Chapter Twenty-Four

JT kicked over the ninety-six-gallon garbage can in the back lot of the Whiskey Bar and then kicked it a second time, hoping to feel better. He didn't. His head pounded. Two days and his place sat empty. The news of the damn violation spread like a fungus through this town. They couldn't wait for him to fail. People probably took bets to see how fast he'd lose his shirt. Well, fuck them. He wouldn't lose anything. He'd make this location work if it killed him, and it probably would because he'd have to shut down Savannah to win.

Had Rowan McGee's visit been enough to sway the town council? They'd raved about his food and his service. Charlie had gone so far as to leave reviews on the online sites about the Whiskey. Then that damn inspector walked in and yanked the floor out from underneath him.

He shoved the door open and marched back inside.

Georgia poured a beer for Harlan sitting at the bar. The rest of the tables were empty. "Why aren't you at the tailgate?" He ran a hand over his face.

"Thought you might like some company, and Georgia here is the prettiest sight in all of Tennessee."

She laughed and elbowed Harlan's arm. "Harlan, you're a smooth talker."

The front door swung open. He jumped. Colton and Blaise pushed and shoved each other inside.

"We're here to set up." Blaise stopped short.

Colton looked around. "Where the hell is everyone? I'm not playing to an empty house."

"Colton, shut up." Blaise pushed him again. "Do we have the right night?"

He took a deep breath. Time to face the music. Bad joke. His head still hurt. "I don't have any customers. They're all at the tailgate, I'm guessing." Or they were eating and drinking out someplace else. Didn't matter which. "You guys don't have to play, but I'll still pay you."

"Hang on a second." Colton dropped into a seat. "I know I don't sell out arenas anymore, but I can still pack a place this size. No tailgate party in the high school parking lot is going to outperform me and my brother and my son and my nephew. No fucking way. We're Savage, for Christ's sake. What really happened? You poison someone?"

He told them about the bogus violation. "This is going to set me back too far. The Whiskey is too new to recover from this unless I win that black-tie dinner. Who

265

the hell knows if that's going to happen now? Let me get a check."

He headed for the office and wrenched open the desk drawer. He wanted to take it and throw it at the wall. Blaise stood in the doorway, all six feet of him with big shoulders and thick arms. Blaise could take anyone in a fight. He'd seen it more than once.

"We don't want your money."

"I wasted your time. I pay my debts."

"You have no debts with me ever. Put your checkbook back."

Savannah wanted him to wait to say anything about them, and after her hesitation the other night, he should. He couldn't continue to look his friend in the eye and not come clean. "I need to talk to you about something."

Blaise shoved his hands in his pockets. "What about?"

"I want to be with your sister, and I need you to be okay with it." He needed Blaise to know he meant business on this one.

"You like Savannah?"

He held the man's gaze. "I love her. Always have."

"Why wouldn't I be okay with you and Savannah? Is there something else I should know?" Blaise stepped farther into the small office.

He would never tell Blaise how twenty-four years ago he'd slept with his little sister while she was drunk and still a virgin. "She doesn't want us to be a public thing yet, but I can't lie to you or Colton. I need your blessing.

She's worried about her family thinking it's too soon since her husband died."

"Does she feel the same way about you?"

"Shit, I hope so." She hadn't said she loved him back when he said it to her.

"I can't think of a better man for my sister than you." Blaise stuck out his hand, and he gripped it.

"Thanks. That means a lot to me." More than Blaise would ever know.

"If you ever hurt her, I'll beat the shit out of you. Just so we're clear."

"Crystal."

The Savages always watched out for each other. JT envied them that. He didn't have any siblings, but Blaise had let him inside their family, and he had abused that friendship by sleeping with Savannah and then high-tailing it out of Heritage River, never looking back. He figured Blaise didn't need him. He had a brother who would kill for him and a sister who admired him.

"Why don't y'all get out of here and go to the tailgate. She'll be glad to have you there."

"If you need any help with that violation, let me know. Rowan McGee owes Colton. As the mayor, he might have some pull with the county."

He stuck out his hand again. "Thanks. For everything."

"Glad you're back. It's been a long time coming." Blaise pulled him and smacked him on the back.

"Hey, I'm sorry I didn't keep in touch." He should

have been a better friend, but the need to leave pushed him out of town on a strong wind and kept him away.

"You know, I never told anyone this, but I was pissed at you for taking off on us. You were like another brother to me. I thought if something was wrong you would have told me."

"I was young and stupid. My head got messed up, and I couldn't fight back. So I ran."

"You won't take off on Savannah if things get tough, will you?"

"If she wants a life with me, then I'll never leave her again." But she hadn't said anything about that, and when she found out he told Blaise, she'd probably send him packing.

He walked Blaise and Colton out and stood on the sidewalk until Blaise's taillights disappeared around the corner. The night air was warm and thick, but the sky was filled with stars. No threat of a storm tonight. Savannah would do okay at her event. As much as he needed to prove he had the best bar in the county, he didn't want to hurt her business. He walked down to the Tea Room. The inside was dark, and a sign on the door told everyone to come to the high school.

"Excuse me, are you JT Davies?" A tall woman with wavy hair to her shoulders walked toward him. Her high heels clicked on the cement. Her skin was the color of a Bailey's Irish Cream, and her green suit hugged her curvy figure.

"That's me. Can I help you with something?" He

might be in love with Savannah, but he wasn't dead. He could appreciate a beautiful woman from a distance.

"This is for you. Have a good night." She slapped a manila envelope against his chest, turned on her thin heels, and marched back up the street.

"Hey, wait." He flipped the envelope in his hands.

She waved and kept walking.

The return label on the envelope was from a law firm in the next town over. His hands shook as he ripped it open and struggled to get the papers out. His vision blurred. *Cease and desist. Shut down the Whiskey Bar. Contest the will.* Blood roared in his ears.

He ran back to the bar and shoved the door open. "That bitch is shutting down my place."

Georgia and Harlan stared at him with their mouths open. "What happened?" Harlan slid off the stool and hurried over to him.

He handed over the papers. Harlan pulled reading glasses out of his shirt pocket and scanned the pages. "Well, I'll be. We'll fight it, Jacob. I won't let this happen to you."

Georgia stood beside Harlan and read over his shoulder. "Can she do this?"

"She did it." He ran both hands through his hair, trying not to pull it all out. Shirley had managed to contest his father's will and get a court order to close the Whiskey until a judge could reread it.

Blue and red spinning lights spilled through the window and splashed across the walls of the bar. Two officers from the sheriff's department stood inside the doorway.

"We have a restraining order to stop business here. We'll escort all customers from the building and lock the doors until the hearing on Monday at four thirty in the afternoon." The officer was tall and wispy. A good wind would blow him over. He was maybe five minutes past puberty and held up what was probably the court order that would ruin him for good.

"Miss, sir, if you could settle your business with the owner, please." The young cop took a wide stance and clasped his hands behind his back.

"Georgia, count out the register. I'll take care of the kitchen." He hung his head and dragged himself into the back.

He stood in the middle of his gleaming kitchen, frozen in place. This couldn't be happening. A sharp pain pierced his chest. He rubbed his knuckles over the pain and began breaking down the stations. He shoved salad in the fridge and slammed the door. He twisted the knobs on the grill. One snapped off in his hand.

Georgia brought him the moneybag. "Are you going to leave that in the safe here?"

"I'll take care of it. Grab anything in the back you might need, extra clothes you have, whatever."

"You'll beat this. You'll be open Tuesday morning."

He wasn't so sure about that.

"I called Hoke Carter." Harlan ambled into the kitchen on sea legs. His face swirled different shades of red. "He's on his way here right now. He said don't leave till he gets here and reads that restraining order. He might be able to call the judge at home and at least allow you to stay open through this."

"She won. Shirley wanted my dad's place and the house." His stomach dropped. He took the papers out of Harlan's hand and read all the way through.

Taking slow breaths, he grabbed his phone and dialed Maddy's cell. He didn't have the time or the patience to text her.

"I'm doing my homework."

He let out a long breath. "Is anyone there?"

"You said no one could come over. What? You don't believe me? You're checking up on me. I can't believe you don't trust me. You're going to hold that vaping thing over my head for the rest of my life, right? I came home the other night from Grey's, just like you asked. You were the one probably doing stuff in our basement you shouldn't be doing. I didn't look. That would be gross."

Her words rammed him, but he laughed, grateful for his daughter and her temper.

"What's so funny?"

"Nothing. Call me if anything comes up."

"Will you come home early tonight?"

"I'll try."

She huffed into the phone and hung up on him.

"At least Shirley isn't trying to rip the house out from underneath us." He sank against the counter.

"JT? Harlan? Where in land's sakes are you two?" Hoke Carter shouted from the front of the restaurant.

They followed the sound of his voice. The Carter

family had been the local lawyers in Heritage River for generations. Hoke's grandfather started the law firm before all the streets in town were even paved. Hoke knew everyone's secrets, from the amount of money holding up their bank accounts to their dying wishes. He stood with his hands on his hips, his full head of white hair slicked back, and his suspenders straining against his belly.

"Give me that restraining order." Hoke held out his hand. "And you two young men in uniform, go wait in the car. I'm JT's lawyer, and this is attorney-client privileged information." He dragged a thumb over his shoulder.

The two officers went without a word.

"Now what?" he said as Hoke whizzed through the pages.

"Seems air tight, unfortunately. I'll give old Judge Cruthers a call and see if he'll let you operate business anyway. He owes me for representing his good-for-nothing son-in-law, and if I get dragged away from my poker game on a Friday night, he can damn well be dragged away from whatever it is he's doing. I can't promise you anything other than I'll be standing beside you on Monday afternoon. Your daddy wanted this place to go to you, and I sure as hellfire ain't going to let Shirley get her hands on it. Jake left her more than enough money to live out the rest of her years in peace. She had better start giving you some." Hoke slammed the papers on the table.

"I appreciate it, sir." The weight of the night pushed him down in the chair.

"I'll send those two knuckleheads back to the station. You stay as long as you like, and you lock up yourself. Don't open for business until you hear from me."

"Thanks, Hoke." Harlan shook his hand.

Hoke waved the words away. "Thank me on Monday when this is over." He pushed out into the warm air fighting to get in.

The blue and red lights stopped spinning, and darkness settled across the night again.

"Do you need anything?" Georgia said.

He'd almost forgotten she was there. "No, thanks. Go on home. I'll call you. And I'm sorry. I'll pay you for the shifts you were supposed to work. I don't want you running off looking for another job before Monday."

She squeezed his shoulder and left them.

"You should go home too. I'll lock up and wait to hear from Hoke."

Harlan sat opposite him. "I know you're in a bad place right now, and you're probably struggling to keep it all inside you. Don't go doing anything stupid, you hear me? Just lock this place up and go home to your little girl. Monday this will all be over, and you'll be back in business like nothing ever happened."

Problem was, everything had happened, and it would be all over town if it wasn't already. He'd lose money for being closed through the weekend. He'd lost money because of the violation. He'd never had to shut down a bar permanently, but this might be the first. Sometimes pulling out was the only choice. Parker couldn't afford to take the hit either.

And if he lost this business? What would keep him in Heritage River? He and Maddy would have to start over somewhere else. He'd have to take her out of school in the middle of the year, take her away from Grey.

He'd lose Savannah, if he ever had her at all.

"Jacob, are you listening to me?"

"I heard you, Uncle Harlan. I'm fine. Really. Go on home." He stood so the old man would get the message.

Harlan eyed him up, but his uncle put out his arms and gave him a hug. "Call me if you need anything."

"I will." He locked the door after him and shut down the lights so only the small ones over the chalkboards were lit. "I fucked up royally, Daddy. You gave me this place, and I can't make it work. I'm not sure the woman I love loves me enough to take a real chance on me."

He went behind the bar and grabbed the Buffalo Trace Stagg Jr. He'd be drunk in no time.

Chapter Twenty-Five

Cars filled every space in the high school parking lot. Humidity slicked the night, and mosquitos feasted on Savannah's skin, but the sky was clear. No sign of a storm in the forecast. At least they wouldn't get swept up in the funnel of a tornado before the town council had a chance to eat her food.

Guests stood outside their minivans, pickup trucks, and SUVs. Some had set up their own chairs, but her food and drinks would be the main attraction. It seemed everyone wanted in on the decision of who catered the town's big event. Thankfully, only the council had a say as to the winner. Not everyone in town liked her.

She'd been the head librarian for years, directed most committees at the schools, and was the Girl Scout troop leader the whole time Caroline was in elementary school. She had organized every meal chain in the town whenever a new baby shoved its way into the world or a family broke with the loss of a loved one, but in the end none of that mattered.

The people in town often wondered if her efforts were sincere or for show. What was she compensating for, always juggling too many balls in the air?

None of them knew what it was like to have famous brothers. For years, Colton and Blaise had been on every radio station, on the cover of every music magazine, and on all the late-night shows. They'd sold out arenas in minutes.

She needed to be important in her own right because without ever saying a word, she'd promised her father not to be like her brothers. She organized, controlled, took charge. As the only female growing up in her house, she'd slid into that role without a hitch. Her father had leaned on her, and her brothers came to expect her to handle the stuff they wanted no part of because they were too busy making music—without her.

The inside of the tent they'd set up for food preparation behind the school was hot. Sweat dripped down her neck and between her breasts. She pinned her hair up and gulped some of the iced tea.

Iced tea and bottled water would be her go-to beverages for the night, but she'd brought black tea and a cranberry-apple-spice blend since it was fall, even it was warm and sticky out. She had a mint tea and a pear tea as well. She didn't expect to be brewing any hot water, but the metal urns were full and ready.

She kept her food choices simple: chicken, tuna, and

egg salad on a croissant and a field-greens salad. The only scones on the menu tonight were the blueberry lemon or orange cranberry. She'd stayed up all night making them. Grey and Caroline had helped her. All this food wasn't hot dogs, ribs, and beer. She prayed the crowd wouldn't go nuts with her lighter fare and lack of booze.

Rae had had the idea that the servers should wear roller skates like the old-style carhops. She'd hired three teenagers who played roller hockey and took the last of the cash she had in the safe at home. Adam had socked that money away in case the world came to an end and they couldn't access credit cards or bank accounts. She'd been using that money to pay Rae and Harley.

She hated that her winning the black-tie dinner meant JT had to lose. How could they possibly start a relationship with the competition between them? They both had too much riding on this event.

"We should've had entertainment." Rae shook her out of her thoughts. Her friend placed sandwiches on small trays the teens could carry while they skated. She had her hair in the sloppy bun she wore so well and a Savannah's Tea Room apron over her denim shorts and sleeveless tee.

"I didn't think about that."

"Tailgates usually lead to something, like a football game or a concert. These people are going to wolf down our little sandwiches and hit the road. I'm not sure that's going to sell us as the place to cater the black-tie. We need to get them excited about something."

"But the decision is based on the food."

"Food is a complete experience. You went through all that trouble to handpick chairs and tables for your shop. You worried over the chandelier, the teapots, which teas to buy. Now we have a hundred or more people sitting in a parking lot, staring at each other. A bonfire would've been something."

Rae passed a tray to Christopher Clark, one of the hockey players. His big hands almost took the tray to the ground, but he righted it in time.

"Chris, be careful." She wagged a finger at him.

"There isn't anything I can do about it now. Make sure Rowan and the others from the council don't have to wait for their food. Make their sandwiches a little thicker. I'll take them over myself."

Rowan sat on the edge of the truck bed with Fred and Rose. He wrote in a notebook. Was he tallying points for or against her? She wiped her sweaty hands on her pants.

She could have had music, but her brothers were playing at JT's place. A little guilt would've worked on Blaise, who would have tortured Colton to change venues. Only Blaise could ever get Colton to do something he didn't want to, and even that wasn't often. But she didn't want to take them away from JT's night after the violation. He needed the draw more than ever.

A steady clapping built across the crowd until it grew into the rumble of thunder. She peeked out from the tent.

People stood in the bed of their trucks, banging their feet. Others jumped up and down and waved their hands. One of the hockey players lost his balance and fell on the pavement.

"What's going on?" Rae came up behind her and peered around her shoulder.

"I don't know. I'll go find out."

"I'm coming with you."

"Make sandwiches."

"No way." Rae scooted out of the tent with her.

She weaved through a row of parked cars into the center of the lot and stopped. Her stomach twisted into her throat. A pulsing drumbeat came toward her, egging the crowd on. Tears blurred her vision. She blinked them away. How did they know she needed them?

Blaise marched down the aisle with his snare drum hanging from his shoulders as if he were in the marching band. Colton followed, holding up his guitar for all to see. And behind him, like ducklings, Cash and Knox waved to the crowd.

"What are you doing here?" She pushed her voice above the cheers.

"JT sent us." Blaise showed off a drumroll.

"We'll set up over there." Colton kissed her on the cheek. "Give us thirty minutes." He turned to the crowd. "Five minutes, folks. We're going to have ourselves one fucking good time."

The crowd went wild. She shook her head.

"Hey, Aunt Savannah." Cash gave her a high five. He was as tall as Blaise, with the same strong jaw, wavy, dark hair, and Savage gray eyes. He hadn't completely let his guard down around her after the fiasco with Jud last year.

Her once-favorite nephew had become somewhat reserved in her presence. She missed their easy way and jokes.

Knox simply waved. He was all Harley except for the guitar playing. In that area, he even gave Colton a run for his money.

"I don't understand. Why aren't you playing at the Whiskey?"

Blaise lifted the drum off the harness and handed it to Cash. He slid the harness over his head. "I'll be over to set my kit up in a second."

"I'll get it started for you." Cash flashed his smile and sauntered away. *Yup, all Blaise.*

He ran a hand over his hair. "No one was over there. The whole place was empty. There was no point in playing. We were coming over just to see you, but you know Colton. He can't pass up an audience. We had the equipment loaded anyway. We travel a lot lighter. Makes the set up easier. If you don't want us to play, we don't have to."

"Are you sure JT is okay with this?" Having her family play was an unfair advantage. The crowd would forget about the food and get caught up in the music.

"I don't know if he realizes we're playing, but he definitely didn't want us to play to him and his uncle. Colton wasn't going to do that anyway. You should've heard him."

She didn't need to. She could imagine. "Thank you. I need this tonight."

"We're playing the newer stuff. I let Colton get two of

our old songs and his solo. Otherwise he won't shut up. I hope the crowd likes it." Blaise laughed. "I'd better get to work before he fires me again."

In no time, her family had sparked up their music. The crowd cheered and ate sandwiches. Rowan offered her a thumbs-up. The Tea Room would be okay. She'd be okay.

What would happen to JT?

JT stumbled down the street. The sidewalk swayed and swelled under his feet. His head spun. He'd only meant to get some fresh air and call a cab or his uncle. Instead, he'd started walking. Main Street turned into Church Street, and before he knew it, he was a block from the high school. The lights from the parking lot seared the night sky.

Drinking one hundred-forty-proof bourbon had been a mistake. Not like he didn't know that going in. He didn't care.

A voice carried through the breeze to him. Someone on a microphone? A crowd yelled in response. His boots pounded the pavement.

The parking lot was full of cars and trucks. A couple of kids whirled by on skates, delivering food. Nice touch. A guitar ripped open the night. Colton Savage. He was unmistakable. The crowd screamed louder. The rest of the band joined in, and someone began to sing. If his blurry vision was correct, Colton's son had slid into the place of the original singer, Troy Lancaster, and did a damn good job. The crowd sang along with the old familiar Savage tune. They'd been playing that one since the backyard parties before they were famous.

He couldn't breathe. Those guys should have been at his place making his crowd squeal like that. He leaned against a tree. Maybe the world would stop spinning. He should turn right around and go back to the Whiskey and call Harlan for a ride home. Savannah would shine tonight, and he wanted her to succeed. So why did his chest ache so much?

His phone vibrated in his pocket. He fumbled to get it out. A text from Maddy.

Where r u?

His fingers wouldn't respond to his brain's command. They seemed to have grown to the size of shot glasses in the last five minutes.

Home soon.

First, he had to congratulate Savannah on her night.

If he could wrap his arms around her for a second, smell her sweet scent, he'd be okay. That's all he needed. Five minutes in her company would soothe what was killing him. She might be mad he was drunk, but maybe not too mad. He needed her to give him that smile, the smile she gave him when he made love to her and it was only the two of them locked together, shutting out the rest of the world and the noise in his head.

The song wrapped up. The crowd screamed for another. Blaise's voice came over the microphone to wish everyone a good night.

He weaved through some of the vehicles. Savannah stood off to the side, clapping for her family.

Turn to me, darlin'. He bounced off the corner bumper of a black Chevy Tahoe. His feet tangled together, and the asphalt slammed into him.

"Whoa. Man, are you all right?"

Hands grabbed his arms and lifted him. He shook his head.

"Well, if it isn't JT Davies. Lizzy, come look. It's old JT."

The man came in and out of focus. Balding. Fat. Missing a tooth. "Do I know you?"

He didn't want to stand there with this guy. He tried to find Savannah again, but some of the crowd had spilled into the aisles and blocked his view.

A short blonde woman with corkscrew curls and dark roots leaned toward him. She wrinkled her nose. "You smell like booze."

He couldn't place these two. Did they go to high school together? "If you'll excuse me." He tried to push past them, but the fat, bald man blocked his path.

"You don't remember me. Clive Sherman. We had auto shop together junior year. I was in the grade behind you."

"Yeah. Sure. How's it going?" He didn't have a fucking idea who that guy was. And he didn't care. He wanted the spinning in his head to stop and to wrap his arms around his woman. He craned his neck to find her.

She shook hands with some guy. Her long, dark hair waved over her shoulders. Her breasts filled out her white shirt that tied at her full, sexy hips. Desire burned its way to his core. He waved, but she didn't see him.

"You don't look good. Your eyes are all red and half-open." Clive gripped his shoulder.

"Get your hand off me." He tried to shove Clive's hand, but he missed, and Clive roared with laughter.

"Same old JT. Drunk as a skunk. Hey, we were going to stop by your bar, but I heard it got shut down 'cause you had a problem with rats in the food. What you'd do? Serve them up for dinner?"

More roaring that hurt his head. The fucker still had his hand on his shoulder. "Shut the fuck up."

"Hey, I'm calling it like I heard it. You didn't think you were really going to make a bar work in this town, did you? You weren't smart enough to run a business. Didn't you have that landscaping thing a long time ago? I remember now. You used to mow my aunt's lawn. Except you never got there on time, and when you did show up, you did a shitty job of cutting. I always had to go back and fix that mess. You sucked at that. How could you make a living running a bar?"

He planted both hands on Clive's shoulders and shoved. Clive stumbled back, but he tipped forward, then caught himself before he face planted.

"Hey, don't push him." Lizzy grabbed his arm and yanked him around.

He spun, clocking her in the neck with his other arm by mistake. She teetered backward.

"JT." Savannah yelled and ran toward him.

The ground swayed again. The sides of his vision were black and fuzzy.

Clive snarled as his girl hit the side of a car and slid to the ground. He charged with the speed and skill of a professional linebacker. JT threw his shoulder forward to block the moose coming at him.

"Stop." Savannah again. "Blaise, Colton."

Someone shouted, "Fight."

Clive collided with his shoulder and shoved him back as if he were a tackling sled. He couldn't get any purchase with his feet. The back end of a car stopped him. Clive crushed him against the trunk. He thrust the heel of his palm into Clive's nose, making him squeal like a pig and jump back. Blood ran down the guy's face.

His breath came in short bursts. His head cleared enough to catch Clive's return, but not in time to stop the uppercut to his gut. He doubled over. A knee hit him in the face, and he toppled like a dead tree.

"I'm going to kill you for touching my girl. You good-for-nothing piece of shit." Clive's massive frame blocked out the lights.

He waited for a kick to the skull and tried to protect his face, but wasn't sure what his arms were doing. The kick never came.

"You'd better get the fuck out of here before I call the cops." That sounded like Blaise. Ah, his friend Blaise to the rescue. *Thanks, man.*

"You don't scare me." Stupid Clive with the broken nose.

"My guitar shoved down your fucking throat and my

boot up your ass should scare you pretty good. Now get out here." Colton. Always ready to get in on the action.

Soft hands were on his shoulders. "JT, can you hear me?" Savannah's sweet voice washed over him.

"Hey, darlin'." He might have a loose tooth.

"We need to get him to the hospital."

He shook his head. At least he thought he did. He wasn't going to the hospital. He just wanted to lie on the ground for a few minutes. He'd be fine.

"Hey, man, can you stand?" Blaise gripped him under his arms and eased him off the ground. He slipped an arm over Blaise's shoulder.

Colton grabbed his other arm and leaned into him to keep him up. "I've kissed the asphalt plenty of times. We'll get you fixed up, but I'm not going to lie to you. I'm glad it's not me."

He wanted to laugh, but it hurt too much. "Savannah?"

They guided him through the crowd that parted to let them pass. Whispers and stares followed him.

"She's talking to Rowan." Blaise leaned him against the side of his truck.

"No hospital."

"You might have a broken rib or worse," Blaise said.

"Don't care. No hospital, and I can't go home and let Maddy see me like this. Take me to the Whiskey. I'll sleep it off there."

Colton scratched the back of his neck. "You can't let him go to the bar. I'll take him back to my place."

"I'll take him home with me. Grace isn't there

tonight. He can take the guest room. Cash and I can keep an eye on him."

"I'll come too. I'll text Harley."

"I'm standing right here, assholes. I don't need babysitters. If you won't take me to my bar, I'll walk." He pushed past Blaise, but Blaise pushed him back against the truck.

"How much have you had to drink?"

"What difference does it make?"

"Because I'm worried you're going to pass out and choke on your own puke." Blaise opened the truck door.

"Since when do you care about me?"

Blaise narrowed his eyes. "I'm going to ignore that statement because in the morning you won't remember saying it."

He squared his shoulders. "We stopped being friends a long time ago. You two hit it big and didn't need me dragging your shit around anymore." Words he didn't mean to say tumbled out of his swollen mouth.

"You left town before our record deal." Colton crossed his arms over his chest. "I remember it. We'd played Savannah's graduation party. Three days later I went by your house. I couldn't find some of the wires for the guitars. I thought you might know where they got packed up. Your dad said you'd left and joined the army or something."

"He's drunk. He's not making any sense. Let's get him to my house." Blaise gripped his arm.

They were getting too close to connecting the dots of that night. JT stormed Blaise, and he stumbled back.

"Don't ever fucking shove my kid brother when he's trying to be nice to you. I don't give a shit how much my sister likes you." Colton clocked his throat.

He choked. The slosh in his stomach forced its way up, but he clamped his mouth shut in time.

"You're not supposed to know that." Blaise helped him into the truck.

"Like I couldn't figure it out."

"You didn't have to hit him in the throat either. I could handle him."

"Sorry. To you. Not him."

JT leaned his head against the head rest. He was too wasted to fight anymore. "Can you get Savannah?" The words scraped against his bruised throat.

No one moved.

"What? Did I sound funny? Well, maybe that's because Colton shoved his elbow in my throat. Asshole."

"I'll get her. Then I'll pack up our gear," Colton said.

"That's the closest thing you're going to get to an apology," Blaise said. "You seemed fine when I left you earlier. Want to tell me what happened after that?"

"Nope." He closed his eyes and prayed the spinning would stop. He needed to quit drinking.

"Hey, can I have a minute alone with him?" Savannah's gentle voice soothed the ache in his chest and his head.

She'd come to him. He'd beg for her forgiveness and find a million ways to make it up to her. He forced his eyes open. "Howdy."

She gnawed on the charm hanging from her necklace.

Her eyes were the color of storm clouds. She was going to yell at him, but she was as beautiful as a bottle of hundred-year-old scotch, which he'd never drink 'cause he was done drinking.

"Howdy, yourself. Are you hurt?"

"I'm fine. Now. Can you come closer so I can get a better look at you?"

She didn't move.

"I'm sorry. I messed up. It won't happen again."

"How could you?" She slapped her mouth shut and shook her head. "You knew this night was important to me. I might've been able to deal with you drinking. I've had more than enough experience with an alcoholic brother, but to start a fight... Why would you do that?"

"I didn't mean to. That guy was talking shit to me. I couldn't let him get away with it. Please believe me. I'm sorry. I'll make it up to you." He stretched out his hand, but she didn't take it.

The tightness in his chest returned.

"You can't go starting a fight every time someone says something you don't like. You're not a kid anymore. You have a daughter who needs you. What if you were seriously hurt or worse?" She took a deep breath and bit down on her lip.

She was right, but the words stuck in his throat. He'd fucked up in the dad area too tonight. Everything seemed to fall apart at his touch. He wasn't mad at just fat Clive. He was mad at Shirley for shutting him down and mad at his dad for dying when he still needed him. He was mad at the people who judged him and mad at himself for caring about it.

He slid from the seat of the truck. His knees buckled. She reached out to him, but he steadied himself. "I'm fine, darlin'. Always have been, always will be. Tell Blaise thanks for the ride, but I feel like walking."

He didn't wait for her to say anything else. He focused on one foot in front of the other until he was far enough away from the high school he could stop. She hadn't followed him, but what did he expect? He'd embarrassed her on her big night. She wanted to win that competition as much as he did, maybe more. Instead of supporting her by staying away, he'd walked right into the middle of it and blown it up.

The church on the corner came into view with its tall white peaks and white clapboard sides. Small lights lit up all the doorways. Was that an invitation inside or to keep the homeless from trying to sleep on the steps?

His phone vibrated in his pocket. Maddy.

When are you coming home?

He sat on the brick steps of the church. If he leaned forward and turned his head, he could make out the corner of the Whiskey Bar. The library was across the street. Probably not a great place to be looking at because he'd think of Savannah. He would lose her if he hadn't already. Funny how he'd lost all the important women in his life—his mother at an early age, his wife, his bar. He might lose his daughter if he didn't straighten himself out.

He eased against the wood door, careful of all the places Clive pounded, and stared at his phone. He'd call

Harlan and ask him to go over and sit with Maddy. As soon as his head stopped spinning, he'd get up and walk to the Whiskey, where he'd sleep off the rest of his drunken stupor. He needed an hour. That would be enough time to go home and act the way a respectable parent should act, minus the bruises.

He needed to close his eyes for a minute. Just a minute. Then he'd call.

Chapter Twenty-Six

"JT, wake up." Savannah shook him, but he didn't budge. He was out cold on the steps of the Baptist church. *Stupid fool.*

She sat back on her heels and tucked her hair behind her shoulder. *Well, this is a fine mess.* She should leave his sorry ass right here and let Sheriff Jones arrest him for whatever charge sleeping on the church steps fell under.

Her fingers sought the familiar feel of her charm sliding back and forth on the rope chain. Her eyes burned because it was well past midnight and she should be home in bed asleep. Her back hurt from standing on her feet all day. She really thought she had the whole event in the bag until the handsome, sexy, pain in her backside showed up.

Now how was she going to get the handsome, sexy, pain in the butt home to his daughter who was fraught with worry? She had just pulled into her driveway, ready to rid herself of the day, when Maddy had called, crying that her father hadn't responded to her last text and hadn't come home. No one had seen him. Did she know where he was?

She couldn't say "Sleeping it off someplace, sweetheart. Your daddy had a bad day." That was out of the question. And what had happened that got him so riled up? He was a lot of things, but he wasn't an alcoholic. She knew that show better than anyone. Colton had been drinking since he was a teenager. Blaise too, for a long time, but he'd sobered up years ago. Colton, however, couldn't seem to get his act together until recently. JT wasn't a drunk. He hurt over something. She would help him with whatever that was any other night. Tonight he pissed her off because he was passed out.

"Jacob Tyler, get your ass up." She smacked his arm several thousand times.

"Ouch. Shit. Knock it off." He pulled his arm up over his head.

That's where she should have hit him. She stood and crossed her arms over her chest to give her a slight advantage. Once he climbed up off that stoop, he'd have a foot on her.

He peeked out over his arm and blinked. "Hey, darlin'."

"Don't 'hey, darlin' me. You've scared your daughter half to death, and if it wasn't for her, I'd fry your ass for making me drive around town in the middle of the night looking for you." She tapped her foot for good measure and rearranged her face into the mother-knows-best look she gave the kids.

He pushed up and groaned. "What time is it?"

"Never mind that. You need to go home now."

"Is Maddy okay?"

"No, I left her alone, cut, bleeding, and the house is on fire."

"Savannah, could you not bust my hump? My lip is busted, my ribs hurt, and my head feels like a jackhammer is inside it. I know I fucked up. I need to know my baby girl is okay, or should I be running to the hospital or something." He stood and ran a hand over his stubbly jaw and winced.

Something thawed a little in her heart. Damn him. She wanted to stay mad, but his love for his daughter was such a turn-on. "She's fine. I called Grace to sit with her."

"And she went?"

"Of course, she went. You know you can rely on some of us. My brothers were going to take you back to Blaise's earlier. You could've slept it off in a comfortable bed instead of the steps, but you acted like a jerk to them. Do you even remember that?"

"I'll apologize."

"Whatever." She waved her hand in the air. "Let me take you home."

"They know about us."

She stopped at the bottom of the steps. "You told them." It wasn't a question.

"I told Blaise, but Colton figured it out. We didn't do a good job of hiding it well."

"I needed them to think we were old friends until I was ready to tell. I can't believe you went against my wishes. That's not fair."

He hobbled down the steps. She turned and kept walking to the minivan.

"Hiding us isn't fair." He opened the passenger door and grunted. "Isn't that how we ended up apart in the first place? You didn't want your brothers to find out about us."

"Because I'd come on to their friend, not because I was embarrassed by you." Her voice climbed up into the church bell tower.

"But you're embarrassed by me now."

"I'm not pleased with you." She got into the minivan and kicked on the ignition. "Get in, or I'm leaving you here."

"My car is at the Whiskey. I can drive now."

"So fucking drive yourself home. I don't care, but you had damn well better be nice to Grace when you get there, and if she's asleep on your couch, you're going to leave her until Blaise shows up. You got me? Because if you don't, what Clive did to you is going to be nothing compared to what I can do." She slouched down to look up at him through the open car door.

He laughed.

"Are you laughing at me?" Her blood cooked.

He slid into the seat beside her and shut the door. "No way."

"Then what's so funny?" She threw the van in drive and eased into the street.

"I love how you don't take anyone's shit, especially mine."

She tried to keep the smile off her face. "Yeah, well, my brother is Colton Savage. I learned early on how to stand up to the loudest one in the room."

"He's not a bully."

"No." Her heart swelled a little at the thought of her older brother. He was a stupid fool too. The men in her life drove her crazy in one breath and filled her with pride in the next.

"I'm not a bully either." His voice softened.

"I know that. I don't like what you did tonight at the tailgate. Were you trying to ruin things for me?" She turned onto his street.

"Is that what you think? Do you not know me at all?"

"I don't know what I know. I'm tired. It's been a long day. You scared me tonight getting into that fight." She couldn't bear the thought of losing him because he couldn't control his anger. "What if that guy had a gun and he killed you?"

"Fat Clive isn't someone they'd issue a carry permit to."

"Stop making fun. You don't know what that guy was capable of. What would happen to Maddy if something happened to you?" And what would happen to her if she lost another man too soon?

She pulled into his driveway and doused the headlights. He turned in the seat to face her and took her hands. His knuckles were scraped up again.

"I didn't mean to hurt you tonight." His dark stare held hers.

She could drown in the robust heat of him. She eased her hands away. "I need some time."

"What are you saying?" The line between his eyes creased.

She wanted to smooth it away but forced her hands to stay in her lap. "I can't see you right now. I have to focus on my business and my family. My children need me, and Maddy needs you."

"I'm not losing you again."

"Let's see how things go for now. I want to go home and sleep."

"Come inside. You can sleep here. I'll keep my distance. I promise."

Blaise had gone to her house when Grace agreed to help Maddy. She hadn't wanted to leave the kids alone again. She wouldn't be missed until morning, and her eyes burned from lack of sleep. And of course, her heart was jumping up and down, begging her to stay. "My house isn't that far."

"Let me take care of you tonight the way you took care of me."

"I didn't do anything."

"You came and found me. You helped me after Clive knocked me to the ground. Which I deserved. Really, darlin', I'm sorry. Let me make it up to you. Don't get rid of me yet, please. I'll pull it together."

"What happened tonight?"

He squeezed his eyes shut. "Can we talk about it tomorrow?"

"It is tomorrow."

"I don't want to talk about it now. I just want to take you inside." The pain etched itself through his eyes.

She placed a hand on his scratchy jaw, avoiding his swollen lip. "Please tell me what you're going through."

He sat back. "Like you're telling me what's happening with you?"

"What are you talking about?"

"How much debt are you in?"

"It's not that bad. I have it under control." She kept her stare straight ahead, grateful the darkness in the car hid her lie.

"I can help you, but you won't let me because you have to do everything yourself. Savannah juggles all the balls, never letting one drop or handing one over."

"I don't need your help." How was he going to help her? Give her money? She'd rather die first.

"Why do you think you have to do everything your-self?" He pushed open the car door. "I can't keep sitting in there. Everything hurts too much." He slid out and leaned against the mini-van with his back to her.

Did he expect her to follow him? She wanted to lay on the horn, but she didn't want to wake up the entire neighborhood. She could pull away with him leaning like that. It would serve him right if he fell on his ass again. But she didn't want to do any of that. What she wanted was to climb inside his arms and let their strength carry the weight of her troubles for a while.

She was tired of doing everything herself, making all the decisions, worrying about everyone and everything. He wanted to help her, but she couldn't let him.

She pushed open the door and went around to face him. "Go inside. We can talk more later."

"You didn't answer my question."

"You didn't answer mine either. We're at a stalemate. Two people who maybe aren't ready to be in a relationship. We have feelings for each other, but we can't take the leap to trust each other enough."

"You're ending things between us, then?"

She kicked the ground and watched her shoes. If she looked into his eyes, she'd cave and allow him to take her inside that house and make love to her all night. Let the consequences be damned because when she was with him, she felt more like herself than any other time in her life, except when she was young.

She'd watch him grab life by both hands and take off like a rocket. Nothing stopped him. He didn't care about anything. He did what he wanted, full and deep and rich, like a really good black tea.

He tilted her chin up with his strong fingers. "Savannah, please don't end it. I can't lose you too." The circles around his eyes were deep, as if he hadn't slept in a year.

"What else are you losing?"

"I'm losing the bar." He hung his head.

And damn it, she couldn't stop herself. She slid up to him, wrapped her arms around his waist, and pulled him to her. He rested his head on her shoulder and gripped her waist with his hands. His shoulders shook, but he made no sounds.

They stood that way a while. No one said anything. No one had to.

She ran her fingers through the back of his hair. "JT, it's going to be okay. Whatever happened. You'll figure it out."

"But you're not telling me you'll be by my side while I do that."

"Just give me a little time."

"I have. I'm going to get out of Heritage River as soon as I can. You don't want me. I can't live here like that. I can't turn the corner and see you and not pull you against me. I'd kill any man who was making love to you now that I've had you as mine. And I can't walk down Main Street knowing the only bar I ever lost was once my father's deli. The only bar of all the bars I opened that ever really mattered to me."

She placed her hand against his chest. His heart played rhythms against her touch. "You're upset. It's been a bad night, and you haven't told me all the details about the bar. Go inside, get some sleep. Things will look better in the morning."

"It is morning." He smiled, echoing her words back to her.

"We can talk more after you've slept some and spent some time with Maddy. You don't have to make any decisions now." She couldn't lose him, yet she wasn't telling him to stay. What was stopping her? What was she so afraid of? Trusting again? Losing him? Hurting her children because she fell in love with a man who wasn't their father?

He cupped her face in his hands. "Decision made, darlin'. I'll always love you. Never forget that." He placed a soft, sweet kiss on her lips.

Tears stung her eyes, but she didn't say what was on her mind. She loved him too. Always had. There had never been anyone she loved as much, and her heart broke because she'd been married to the sweetest man, and yet she still loved JT.

She wanted to drown in his kiss and in his amber scent. Instead, she kept her mouth shut. She didn't ask him to stay longer.

He limped up the porch step and let himself inside.

The front porch light went out.

And she was all alone.

Chapter Twenty-Seven

Savannah pulled the attic steps down and took a deep breath. She shouldn't do this. She was making a huge mistake. That didn't stop her from taking the first step or the next.

The attic pummeled her with heat. She had thirty minutes before her family arrived for Sunday dinner. She'd better hurry. Now that she was in the attic, her feet wouldn't move.

She had run out of choices. Her son needed to finish school. If it meant selling Adam's antique Christmas ornament collection, then it did. She couldn't let the kids know what she was doing. Caroline loved those ornaments and always asked if she could have them someday when she had a tree of her own.

When she wasn't so broke, maybe even after the black-tie dinner if she won it, she could start Caroline on her own collection. Or she could ask Colton to start one for her. He'd roll his eyes at the Christmas ornament idea, but Harley would love it, and he did whatever Harley asked him to without much complaint.

Selling was the lesser of two evils. She couldn't have Jud come home from college because of her. That would kill their already-strained relationship.

She ignored the chewed insulation and the rat poison she'd left behind. The squirrel was a project for another day. Dust flew up her nose as she pushed boxes to the side. She sneezed twice. Sweat trickled down the back of her neck. She'd need a shower by the time she was done.

She'd have to save some of the money from the ornaments to buy the dresses for the wedding too, and a wedding gift. Since she wasn't taking any money from Colton for the food at the reception, she'd probably need money for that and to pay extra employees to work the party so she could enjoy her brother's special day.

Blaise was standing up for him. Tears burned her eyes. Her brothers were the most loyal men she'd ever met, except for Adam and JT. She needed to stop comparing Adam and JT. It wasn't fair. It would stand to reason both men would have similar qualities. They were both good men, even if she was mad as hell at JT.

She had to shove more boxes filled with the kids' old stuffed animals she couldn't part with, Caroline's American Girl dolls, and her wedding dress. Was there any reason to keep that thing? Caroline would never want to wear it with its puffy sleeves, lacy arms, and long satin train. There must be a consignment shop or website for used wedding dresses. Someone with talent could cut the dress down and use its parts, like an old car. Was that what her life had become? Nothing more than a division of her parts only worth selling off? Was nothing going to be whole again?

She bent under the eave and dragged out the box she wanted. The green top was still intact. She gripped the corner and flipped the lid open. The antique ornaments were stacked inside, all in their original boxes.

Grandma Louisa had no idea she'd created a fortune. Well, not a total fortune. No one was going to retire on these things, but there were enough rare ornaments here to keep Jud in school for the remainder of the year and to buy the dresses.

Adam would have been heartbroken at having to give up his grandmother's ornaments, but he'd do whatever was necessary to keep Jud in school. That much she was certain of. He might have sold a kidney first, but hey.

She lifted the figural from the box. Many of the ornaments showed wear from years of hanging off a Christmas tree branch, but that only added to their authenticity. He had some shaped like people, and others shaped like fruit. The apple held the most value for fruits, but the ones she really wanted were the egg-shaped ones. She gently placed the apple to the side. Adam had ten egg-shaped ornaments that were thick and heavy. Their caps sat flush to the top. The last time he'd checked, they were worth several hundred dollars each.

Grandma Louisa had been a hoarder of sorts. Grace, with her cleaning obsessions, would never have wanted to go in that woman's home. Truthfully, she didn't love going to visit her either. Her house was so stuffy and filled with dust, but Adam adored his old German grand-mother, and she had lived long enough to see Jud being born.

When Louisa had died, the emptying of her home had fallen on Adam and his father. Louisa had had in her possession something no one was sure how she'd stumbled upon, but it didn't matter how she got it. The woman's obsession with old Christmas ornaments had led her to a 1970 Biedermann brass commemorative ornament. Today it was worth thousands.

"Thank you, Grandma Louisa," she whispered.

She replaced all the ornaments and carried the container downstairs. Tomorrow she'd sell them to the buyer she'd found on Barry's Great Finds. Hopefully, the collector who wanted them wasn't a killer. She'd heard too many stories about someone trying to sell something of high value only to have been killed instead.

She navigated the ladder with the box, almost falling in the process. Her shirt was slick with sweat and stuck to her ribs. She didn't have time to shower.

Grey stuck his head out of his bedroom doorway. "Mom, do you have any new razors? What are you doing?"

She jumped and dropped the plastic container. "I needed something out of the attic. In the linen closet in the hall."

"I'll go look in a second." He disappeared back in his room.

She hurried to her room and locked the door. Every-thing seemed okay. The box fit under her clothes hanging on the bottom rack in the closet. She wiped her forehead with the back of her hand. How was she going to get through this?

The doorbell rang. Her family was here. Would they notice the flush on her face? The picture of her and Adam on her dresser stopped her. It was time. She went back into the closet and pulled down a large tote from the top shelf and placed the picture in there. "I'm sorry."

"Mom, Uncle Blaise, Grace, Cash, and Beau Carroll are here," Caroline yelled up the steps.

Beau Carroll? She wasn't expecting him too. She swapped her sweaty top for one that smelled better. She could blame her appearance on the baking she'd been doing. The scones. She'd left them in the oven, forgetting about them in her search.

She ran down the steps to the voices in her kitchen. Grace, in an impeccable peach T-shirt dress and perfect white sneakers, pulled the baking tray out of the oven. The scones were burnt.

"Hey, Sis." Blaise kissed her cheek. He smelled like soap. The ends of his hair were still wet. "Those are for you." Carnations in blues, purples, and oranges were in a tall vase filled with water.

"They're lovely."

"I hope you don't mind me going into the oven. Something smelled like it was burning." Grace held up the tray.

"Hey, Aunt Savannah." Cash nodded from his perch against the counter.

"Hi, Cash. Thank you for taking care of that, Grace. I

forgot about them. I'm sorry, but I'm so glad you're all here. Beau, what a nice surprise." She kissed the air beside his wrinkled cheek.

"Hope you aren't too mad about my dropping in. I stopped by Grace's to check on the hot water heater, and these two dragged me into the car. I told them I'm fine by myself, but they're more stubborn than a bobcat." Beau ran a hand over his aged-spotted, bald head.

"You're always welcome here."

He had kind of adopted Grace as her stand-in father after she moved to town. She didn't have much family.

"Well, I don't know what we're going to have for dessert now, but my chicken-and-wild-rice casserole should be ready."

"Let me help you." Blaise grabbed the salad off the counter and headed into the dining room. They were eating inside because she hadn't had time to clean the patio furniture today. She'd barely had time to clean up before they arrived.

"I've got it." She tried to grab the bowl out of his hands, but he held it above his head.

"Don't fight him." Grace patted her shoulder.

Grey and Caroline came into the room. Everyone filled the seats. The doorbell rang again.

"I'll get it," Cash said.

"You guys don't have to do so much," she called after her nephew.

Colton and Harley joined them. Harley held a clear box of cupcakes the color of the rainbow. "I asked May to whip up some of her famous treats. Oh, Beau, I didn't know you were coming. I would've asked for some donuts too." She planted a kiss on his head. He blushed, which wasn't something that happened much. He was too ornery to get flustered.

Colton shook hands with Beau, fist-bumped Grey and Caroline, punched Blaise in the arm, and hugged Grace. "What's for dinner? Do you need me to do anything?"

"I just have to get the rolls," she said.

"I'll do it." Colton turned into the kitchen.

"You don't have to do everything yourself. We can help." Blaise took a seat beside Grace.

"I'm the host. You're the guests. It's my job to take care of you." She started filling plates with chicken, rice, and salad.

"We're family. You don't have to take care of us, much." Blaise winked. Grace smiled up at him as if he hung the moon for her.

Savannah wasn't in the mood for lovey-dovey eyes right now. Even though the room was filled with noise, talking, and laughing, she missed JT and Maddy. They should be here too.

"Ya'll hear what happened to JT Davies?" Beau buttered his roll.

She dropped her fork. Could the man read minds?

Blaise shot her a look.

"We were at the fight Friday night. Good thing he started throwing punches after we were done playing and not during." Colton passed the pitcher of iced tea to Cash.

"Not that. Shirley is taking him to court. She wants his bar and looks like she might get it. He's been closed all weekend and has a court date tomorrow afternoon with Hoke."

"Who told you that?" She climbed under the table to retrieve her lost utensil and banged her head. "Ouch."

"Hoke got called away from the poker game Friday night. He wasn't supposed to say, but after the others left, I got him to spill it." Beau laughed. "I thought you might've heard since you're all friends with him, ain't you? Figured JT'd tell you himself."

That wicked woman was dragging him into court and stealing his vitality. Her insides burned. That explained why he'd gotten himself drunk and why he didn't want to talk about what happened. Shirley was stripping him of his pride, his dignity, and his connection to his dad.

"Mom, may I be excused?" Grey cut into her thoughts.

"Yeah, me too. I have more homework to do. I hate math and science," Caroline said.

"Sure. We'll call you for dessert."

"You want some help, squirt?" Cash asked.

"That would be great." Caroline beamed.

Cash pushed back from the table. He had his father's big heart. Grey and Caroline scurried out of the room.

"He wasn't in any shape to talk Friday night," Blaise said. "Anybody know how he got home?"

"Is Hoke going to be with him in court?" She pushed her food around on her plate, hoping she looked calm and somewhat disinterested. She didn't want to tell them she'd found him passed out at the church or that Maddy had called her, hysterical. He'd suffered enough humiliation because of Shirley. She certainly hadn't spared his feelings when she'd said she needed time to tell her family about them. And if her brothers already knew, what was she hiding from?

JT shouldn't be in court alone. She could offer to stand beside him, if he'd even let her.

"Hoke is spitting mad at Shirley. He won't let JT go before the judge alone." Beau buttered his bread and dunked it in the chicken dish.

"Hoke's his best chance." Colton leaned back in his seat and patted his stomach. "Great meal, Sis. Maybe you could teach Harley how to cook." He laughed but grabbed Harley and pulled her toward him, trying to kiss her.

She swatted him away. "You can sleep in the art studio tonight." But her lips twitched up, and her eyes shone like the sun on a hot day.

"You can't stay mad at me." Colton wrapped an arm around her, and she leaned into him.

Everyone was in love. She took a deep breath. It was time. "There's been something I wanted to tell you all."

"Uncle Colton, can you come up here, and hurry please?" Grey yelled with a shaky voice from upstairs.

She jumped from her seat and ran to the bottom of the steps. She couldn't see him. He must be standing near his room or maybe the bathroom. "Are you all right? Are you sick? I'll be right there."

"No," Grey yelled again. "Not you. Uncle Colton

only. Please." He seemed to add the *please* as an afterthought.

Colton followed her, his face a mask of uncertainty. "What's up, dude?"

"Can you come up here? I need to talk to a guy right away."

She shoved her brother. "Go. Make sure he's okay." She wanted to run up to her boy, and she wanted to respect the need for a male figure in his life. If Colton couldn't handle what was up there, he'd come get her, wouldn't he?

Colton trotted up the steps.

She didn't let her mind wander to what might be going on. Maybe he discovered hair he didn't have before? Or some male personal issue a boy couldn't talk to his mother about. Had he contracted herpes from a dirty bathroom? Could someone get herpes that way?

"Is everything okay?" Grace started clearing plates.

Harley jumped up to join her. "Savannah, sit. We'll clean up. I might not be able to cook, but I can at least load a dishwasher."

"I think I'd like to stand until Colton comes back down." She grabbed the empty casserole dish just to have something to do.

"Hey, Blaise. Can you come up here?" Colton shouted down from the top of the steps.

"What the hell is going on up there?" She dropped the dish back onto the table.

"Blaise, bro, now."

"You're scaring the hell out me, Colton Thomas."

"Savannah, simmer down. This is man stuff. Blaise, for fuck's sake. Now."

"On my way." Blaise ran up the steps.

"I'm going up there." She turned for the steps.

Grace grabbed her arm. "Let the guys take care of it. Grey wanted his uncle for a reason. I know this isn't easy for you. It wouldn't be for me either, but Colton and Blaise love him like their own. They won't let anything happen to him. It's probably just embarrassing for a boy to talk to his mother about it, that's all."

"She's right," Harley said. "Knox won't talk to me about anything that has to do with girls or anything to do with his body. He'll walk into a room, and before I can ask him what's up, he says, 'Where's Dad?' Colton tells me as much as I need to know. The rest I leave up to him."

Savannah tucked her hair behind her ear. "You're right. He needs a man for some things." She paced the dining room anyway.

"I'm going to get myself some fresh air. Call me when coffee is ready." Beau hobbled out to the front porch.

"We probably gave him a coronary with all that personal talk." Grace giggled. "He knocked on my front door one morning, and Blaise answered it in a towel. Beau yelled at him so loud the Bucknells across the street heard him."

"Did he just get out of the shower? What's the big deal with that?" she asked, and Grace's neck and face bloomed red. "Okay, say no more, please. You know I love you both, but it's hard to have conversations about my brothers' sex lives." She shook her head. She was happy for them all, and when the guys came back down, if Grey was okay, she'd tell them about JT. Even if Blaise and Colton knew.

Blaise sauntered down the steps. He shoved his hands in his pockets and rocked on his heels. A long, thin smile spread over his lips.

"Well? What's going on? Should I go upstairs?" She wanted to grab him by the shirt and shake him. "How can you be so calm?"

"You don't want to go up there," Blaise said.

"Babe, is he okay?" Grace said.

He laughed. "He's okay. He might need stitches, but he's okay."

"Oh my God. How can you sit there and laugh when my son might need stitches? Should we take him to the hospital? I'll get my keys."

He put a hand on her shoulder. "He doesn't need the hospital. We took care of it. Colton is just talking to him now. Man-to-man. They didn't need me for that part."

"Blaise, you'd better tell me what the hell is going on with my son, or I swear to God, I'll beat you up with a rolling pin."

He laughed again. She was going to kill him.

"Let's just say it's a good thing he takes after our side of the family."

"What the hell are you talking about?" She dropped into the chair and hung her head between her knees.

Colton strolled in the room. A smile played on his lips. "I had no idea kids did that kind of shit." He shook his head. "I mean some guys, yeah, but a fifteen-year-old?"

"Is he bleeding to death? What is going on with my son?" She was going up there.

"Sis, you need to stay put," Colton said. "He's embarrassed enough. Let's just say a special young lady made a comment about men and their privates, and a razor was involved." He roared with laughter. "I'm sorry, but this is fucking funny. We patched him up, and we talked. He's okay." His laughter continued.

"You shouldn't laugh." Harley shook her head, but a smile tugged on her lips too.

Grace covered her mouth with her hand. Her blue eyes sparkled with humor.

It finally made sense. "He's too young to be doing stuff like that." Savannah didn't have to ask who the young lady was. "Am I supposed to act like I don't know? Did he tell you if they were sleeping together?" Had they had an opportunity to go that far? She knew better than anyone when you wanted to have sex, you found the opportunity. Back in high school she had planned for weeks how she was going to get JT behind that garage.

"I'd forget about it. I told him if there's a problem to call me or Blaise. We'll come get him and take care of it, but I'm sure he'll be fine. It's just a surface wound."

She stuck her head between her knees again. "Are they sleeping together, Colton?" If they were, what did that mean?

He squatted down in front of her. "I shouldn't tell you this because he doesn't want you to know, but they have not had sex. I don't want you to pass out imagining it, okay? She dared him. He wanted to seem cool. He was going to take a picture. I told him it was a bad idea."

Maddy was just like her father. She didn't know if she should be glad or furious as hellfire. She would have words with Mr. Davies about controlling his child.

Right now.

Savannah banged on JT's front door until her knuckles hurt. The porch light came on, and the door swung open.

"Are you trying to bang the door down?" He stood there with one hand on the handle. His dark hair was brushed back. The top waved slightly. He wore a black, button-down shirt tucked into tight jeans. Several of the top buttons were undone, revealing some of his pec muscles.

She fisted her hands to keep them from touching him. The sight of him made her knees weak, but she had to stay strong.

"Keep your daughter away from my son."

He stepped onto the porch and closed the door behind him. "Do you mind keeping your voice down? Maddy might hear you. Are you trying to tell me you don't want your son seeing my daughter anymore? That maybe she isn't good enough for him since her daddy doesn't seem good enough for you."

"This isn't about us."

"Maybe it should be."

315

"JT, put your ego on a shelf. We have a problem on our hands. They're getting too intimate."

"I don't have a problem with them."

"I didn't care they were hanging out until today. She dared him to shave his privates."

"She did what?" He gritted his teeth and ran a hand over his face. "Jesus Christ, she's trying to kill me. Did he do it?"

"Of course, he did. He cut himself while Colton and Blaise were over. He asked them to help him stop the bleeding. Colton spilled the truth to me to save me from strangling my son. I don't want them having sex. They're too young to be involved like that." She hadn't been too much older than they were when she drank four beers, grabbed JT by the hand, and led him behind the garage to their makeshift firepit.

"Maybe you should be talking to your son. Maddy didn't force him to do anything."

"Your daughter needs her father to pay more attention to her so she stops trying to pay attention to Grey."

"You're blaming me?"

He'd shaved the beard and left the goatee. His lip was still a little swollen. She wanted to run her hand over his jaw and see how smooth his skin would be under her touch, but she needed to stay focused. She had a point here. "You need to control your child."

His laugh made fire burn in her veins.

"With all your experience as a mother, you haven't figured out you can't control your children?" He shoved his hands on his hips and looked around. His shirt moved and gave her another glimpse of that chest. "Of course, you haven't. You want to control everyone and everything in your path. Well, lady, you can't."

She fisted her hands on her hips too. "I do not do that, but I do expect children to act their age and not like children playing adults."

"What you want is for your son to stay a baby who doesn't want to have sex with girls. And you want to be the one to decide how and when the world knows about us. You want to solve all your problems by yourself. Should I go on?"

"You should shut up."

He gripped her arms and pulled her close. "Make me."

That damn competitive streak. "You're behaving like a child." She tilted her chin up. She would not kiss him, no matter how much she wanted to.

He took her chin between his strong fingers and pointed her gaze at his dark eyes. "Tell me I'm wrong about your need to boss everyone around."

"I don't boss." She moved his hand but kept her fingers laced through his. She couldn't control herself. "This doesn't bother you? That's your daughter telling a young man to shave himself so she can see."

"Of course, it bothers me, and it scares the hell out of me. I don't want her checking out some guy's package, but I can't be on top of her every minute. No matter how much time I spend with her, she's going to want to do stuff with boys. It's what kids their age do."

"I didn't do things like that."

"I did." He smirked. "Your brothers definitely did. We had to do it with someone."

"Do you want that someone to be Maddy?"

"No, I want her to stay three forever, when she thought I was a god instead of like now when she thinks I'm uncool and a giant pain in her ass. But if she is going to experiment, I'm glad it's with Grey. He'll treat her right." He pressed her hand against his chest.

His skin was warm against her touch. She locked her knees to keep from puddling to the ground. "I don't understand how you're okay with this."

"I'm not. Believe me. But I know I can't stop it."

"I don't agree. We can forbid them to see each other." She pulled away. Being near him and touching him fogged her brain. They needed to focus on the kids.

"There you go trying to control everyone. Leave it be. If you forbid Grey to see Maddy, he'll just try harder. I know better than anyone how that works, and I believe you said that very thing to me in your store."

She had. "My son will listen to me."

"Savannah, you're making a big deal out of nothing."

"Stop telling me how to feel. I'm worried about my child. I don't want him making mistakes he can't undo. And stop rushing me to tell my family about us. You have no idea how guilty I feel about losing my husband nine months ago and already being in your bed. What kind of person does that make me? And all you can think of is I'm hiding you like I'm embarrassed. Well, I'm not embarrassed, damn it." Tears surprised her, but she blinked them away. She wasn't going to cry in front of him.

Only a few hours ago, she was ready to tell her family about them, but now with this thing between Grey and Maddy escalating, she needed to remember her priorities. Her life wasn't her own. Not really. She needed to be a mother to her children first, then a business owner. She had no time and no right to a relationship with a man.

"When are you going to tell them about us?" He was relentless.

She tugged her necklace hard enough to break the chain. "I was going—"

"Save it, darlin'. Unless your words are 'I did,' there's nothing for us to talk about. I'll talk to Maddy about being safe, but that's it. The rest is up to them."

He turned and marched up the steps. He didn't look back but closed the door on her again.

Chapter Twenty-Eight

J T fumbled with the collar of the dress shirt that scratched at his neck. The only thing he wanted on his neck was Savannah's lips. He'd been up all night thinking about her standing on his walkway with eyes the color of burning coal. She'd been spitting mad, and she was so damn beautiful that way. He'd wanted to drag her into his bed and make love to her until the sun came up.

He needed to think about something else, or everyone was going to know where his mind was. He grabbed his black hat and headed downstairs. Problem was thinking about something other than Savannah just got him twisted up and ready to fight. Shirley would own his bar, and it looked as if there wasn't a damn thing he could do about it. He'd take the humiliation of an erection in public over the angry roar in his ears and the burning in his veins.

Maddy and Uncle Harlan waited in the front room.

His beautiful daughter wore a simple black dress that made her seem all grown up. "You look pretty."

"Thanks." Her smile rivaled the sun.

Uncle Harlan squirmed in his suit. Davies men preferred flannel and jeans. "You two don't have to come with me. Maddy, wouldn't you rather be in school?"

"You can write me a note. I wasn't going to miss this. I think Grandma Shirley is being a big bitch."

"You shouldn't talk like that." He grabbed his keys off the table in the hall.

"She's right," Harlan said. "Might as well say it out loud."

"We're southern. We don't speak our minds." He adjusted the hat.

"Since when?" Harlan patted him on the shoulder.

"Let's get this over with." He locked the front door and started the truck with a push of the button.

"You're going to win, Daddy. It's all going to work out."

"I hope you're right." He backed out of the driveway and drove into town.

The courthouse with its white columns, red brick, and broken clock was across the street from the sheriff's department and as old as the town itself. His boots scraped against the white marble steps as he walked to his execution. He couldn't lose the bar. Not this bar. He'd gladly give up any of the others to keep the one his father had given him.

Maddy and Harlan flanked him. Maddy stuck up her palm.

"What's that for?" he asked.

"High-five me."

"Seriously?"

"Come on, Dad. I can't hug you in public. Someone might see." She rolled her eyes, but a smile tugged on her lipstick-painted lips. She really was growing up too quickly. He'd better have that talk with her to slow down. She had plenty of time to wear too much makeup and get involved with boys.

They followed the guard's instructions to room 204. It was a small courtroom with stained blue carpet and an empty judge's bench at the front. He expected something bigger with a gleaming floor and mahogany railings to take away his livelihood.

Shirley and her attorney occupied the table to the left. She turned at the sound of their entrance and scrunched up her face, as if she'd smelled something that had died three days before. She turned back to face the front of the room, ignoring them.

"Where's Hoke?" Harlan whispered.

"Said he'd be here." JT checked his watch. Hoke still had time, but that didn't do anything to settle his racing heart. He wanted to yell until the roof blew off and the windows shattered.

He wished Savannah could be there to dull some of his pain. He should have told her he understood what she needed, and he'd stay beside her as long as it took for her to feel comfortable. She was a part of his soul, and he didn't want to be without her.

She'd lost her husband, the father of her children, and

she was trying to honor his memory. And what did he do? He went and let his anger and his pride get right in between them, as he'd done long ago. She must think he abandoned her.

"I'm here." Hoke stood alongside him. His white hair was combed in place, and his suit pressed and neat. His red pocket square matched the red tie with the perfect knot. "Let's take a seat."

"Good luck, Jacob." Harlan clapped him on the back.

"Good luck, Daddy." Maddy gave him a thumbs-up.

Hoke spread some papers out on the table and adjusted his reading glasses on his nose. JT took the seat beside Hoke, placed his hat on the table, and clasped his hands in his lap.

"Let me do all the talking, JT. Don't say anything unless I tell you to."

"Sure."

"I mean it." Hoke leveled his clear gaze on him.

A bailiff with a thick white mustache and hair growing out of his ears ambled in from a door in the wall behind the judge's bench. "All rise for Judge Summerford."

He gripped Hoke's arm. "I thought the judge was your poker friend."

"They must've reassigned the case." Hoke dropped his glasses on the table.

"Do you know this guy?" Dread ran its cold hand down his back.

"Must be new."

"Just fucking great." Any chance he had to win evaporated with the arrival of the new judge.

"Hush now. And stand up."

He did as he was told and buttoned his suit jacket. The door in the wall opened again, and a thin man with black, curly hair starting at the middle of his head stepped up into the judge's seat. He had on the expected black robe. His face was vacant of any warmth, and he wasn't any older than JT. Hopefully, he hadn't gone to high school with this guy, and he'd forgotten. Summerford didn't ring a bell.

"Be seated." Judge Summerford plopped a pair of reading glasses on the end of his nose and shuffled through some papers. "We're here to contest the will of Jacob Davies Sr."

Hoke stood. "Your Honor, I have the original will and testament Mr. Davies signed in my office two years prior to his death."

"I have a copy of that as well, Mr. Carter." Summerford held up the document.

Shirley's lawyer stood too. "Judge, Mrs. Davies has a letter signed and dated by her husband and written six months prior to his death, stating he wanted her to have the property known as Eat At Jake's."

He didn't know about any document. Hoke shot him a look. He shrugged.

He and his dad hadn't talked much about his last wishes. Dad had told him the will was in the safe deposit box, the house and the deli were his, and he'd left money for Shirley. Dad had wanted him to come home and live in the old house.

At the time of that conversation, he'd told his father no way. He'd planned on selling it. He had no interest in living in Heritage River again, but then his dad had died, Maddy needed to plant some roots, and he missed Savannah so much his insides ached at times.

He didn't have any right to come back home and ask her to be with him, but even if she'd still been married, he would've asked her, begged her. He'd been a fool not to love her up front and out in the open his whole life.

"Let me see that." Summerford waved the lawyer over.

"May I see that as well, Your Honor?" Hoke moved around the table, not waiting for an answer.

"Certainly."

The coffee in JT's stomach fought against the twisting knot trying to form. Shirley's lawyer passed the note between the judge and Hoke.

"Why would he write this? He could've come to me and changed the will. He didn't know when he was going to die, unless you were holding a gun to his head, Shirley. Something stinks like rotting fish." Hoke handed the paper back to Shirley's lawyer.

Shirley jumped out of her seat, waving a fist. "He most certainly wrote that note, Hoke Carter. My Jake loved me, and he was afraid you'd talk him out of changing things. He didn't want me out in the street, and he wanted me to keep his deli alive. Not turned into some ugly bar." Spit flew from her mouth.

JT pushed out of the chair. Hoke signaled for him to sit.

"That's not necessary, Mrs. Davies," Summerford said.

"Shirley, I don't know what you're pulling, but I spoke with Jake after the date on this note. He came to see me. Said to make sure JT kept the deli. 'Don't let him sell it,' he said."

His father was worried he'd get rid of all he'd worked his whole life for. *I wouldn't have done that, Daddy.* But his dad hadn't known that, hadn't trusted him. His stomach twisted more.

"If we could get back to the point here," Summerford cut into the conversation. "Holographic wills are difficult to prove valid. We'll need to verify the authenticity of the handwriting by an expert. If the validity of the hand-writing is in question, then the original will and testa-ment written by Mr. Carter will be used as Mr. Davies's final wishes. We'll meet back here in one week."

"Your Honor, I wish to request the expert be provided by Mr. Davies Jr.," Hoke said.

"We want an expert as well," Shirley's lawyer said.

"Fine. Until the final decision is made, the property in question will remain closed." The judge stood.

"All rise," the white-mustached bailiff said.

"Your Honor, I respectfully request you allow Mr. Davies to conduct business in the meantime. His liveli-hood is at stake every day that establishment is closed."

"Mr. Carter, I appreciate your client's dilemma. However, should the property revert back to Mrs. Davies, then I don't want to have another visit in my courtroom because she feels he inadvertently damaged said property while it was in his possession. My apologies, Mr. Davies, but I understand you are the owner of multiple—" He flipped through the papers on his desk. "—multiple Whiskey Bars. I hope your livelihood won't be tampered with too much. Now, good day."

JT stood on shaking legs. The Whiskey closed for another week, maybe forever. Hoke led him back into the hallway. Harlan and Maddy followed with grim faces.

"I'll get on that handwriting expert right away." Hoke kept his voice low as Shirley and her lawyer passed by. "Do you have anything written in your father's hand?"

He stared at Hoke's moving lips, but he wasn't sure what he said.

"Son, you all right?" Hoke gripped his shoulder.

"I have a card Grandpa gave me for my last birthday. He only wrote 'Love, Gramps' and maybe my name. Would that be enough?"

"That's just fine, Maddy. Can you get that to my office today?"

"I'll bring her," Harlan said. "I'll check at home too. Jake wasn't one to write notes or letters. Maybe I'll get lucky. Jacob, are you hearing Hoke?"

"Huh? Yeah. Yes, sir. I don't have anything with his writing on it. But that's good, isn't it? If we can't prove he wrote that letter, then the judge has to go back to the original will."

Hoke pressed his lips together. "We need to prove he didn't write that letter. I need something he did write to compare it to the letter. The birthday card is a good start. No one but Jake would've written that to Maddy. It's indisputable. If there's any possibility he wrote that letter, we're sunk. I'm sorry, JT. I don't know how Shirley got him to write it. He wouldn't have, as far as I know."

"Why is she doing this to us?" Maddy's voice took on the same squeaky quality it had when she was younger. She dabbed at her eyes with her finger.

He wrapped an arm around her shoulders. "I don't know, but I'll take care it." He didn't have a fucking clue how, but he'd have to think of something, or he'd look like a fool to his daughter too.

"I need to get back to the office. Harlan, bring me that card and anything you have at home today. I'll get on the phone and find us a handwriting expert." Hoke snapped his fingers. "JT, your daddy must have an old racing form somewhere in that big old attic. Scour your house for anything he touched. This will all be over in a week. Hopefully, it ends in our favor."

Chapter Twenty-Nine

Savannah waited in her minivan in the parking lot of Rivergate Mall. Because the stores were getting ready to close, the lot was mostly empty. A few shoppers zigzagged their way to their cars with bags from major department stores and that cute clothing store she liked so much. The sun had set over an hour ago. She should have scheduled the meeting during dinnertime. The mall would have been busier, and she wouldn't be thinking about all the terrible things that happen to women in the dark.

The Christmas ornaments were in the back. She didn't plan on opening the hatch until she saw the money and the buyer seemed legitimate. She'd watched enough cop shows to at least know to keep her eyes open. Having JT with her would have been good. He would beat the crap out of anyone who tried to pull a fast one on her. Sometimes that angry streak came in handy. God, she couldn't think about him now. She needed to stay focused.

Her phone vibrated on the seat next to her. A text from Caroline.

When will you be home?

Couldn't they do without her for a few hours? She'd lied to Blaise and Grace about a tea seminar she wanted to attend and asked them to hang out with Caroline. Grey was at a friend's house but not Maddy's.

If he wanted to see Maddy, it had to be at their house. She couldn't handle another razor incident or an unwanted pregnancy. Okay, she was being ridiculous. JT was right about that and her need to control everything. But why did her babies have to grow up?

Soon. Ask Uncle B if you can paint his nails. He'll say yes.

She said a silent sorry to her brother. He wouldn't have the heart to tell Caroline no, and Caroline would think his fingernails painted pink would be hilarious. That should keep her from more texting.

A black Mercedes pulled into the spot next to her. Her heart picked up speed and raced into her throat. She took a deep breath. All that was happening was a simple transaction. She wasn't going to get murdered. Still, she should have told someone where she really was in case her body went missing.

The driver waved to her. He clearly wasn't worried about her intentions. He slid out of the big vehicle and walked around the back of his car. She didn't want to get pinned in between their two cars. She jumped out and met him near the back end of the cars where the parking lot spread out before them.

"You must be Savannah Montgomery." He was average height, completely bald as he'd said, had a nice smile and very straight teeth. He wore a brown tweed blazer with patches on the elbow, jeans, and old-style wingtips. "I'm Don Downs." He stuck out his hand.

She swallowed. "Hi, Don. Nice to meet you." She placed her sweaty hand into his.

The pounding in her chest was going to give her away. She'd feel a little better if someone would come out of the building and walk to their car. It might have been better if she had parked closer to the building.

"You've never sold anything on Barry's Great Finds before, have you?"

"What makes you say that?"

"The deer-in-the-headlights look on your face." His nice smile made a reappearance with a soft laugh. "That, and your account. I've done this a thousand times. I make my living this way. Don't worry, I told my wife where I'd be. I'd be the first suspect in a crime."

She gripped her keys, and he eased out another laugh.

"I'm sorry. I've scared you. I have a dumb sense of humor. Why don't we get this whole thing over with, and you can be rid of me for good? I'm very excited to see these ornaments." He rubbed his hands together.

The breath returned to her lungs. "The ornaments are lovely." She popped the hatch and fought the guilt trying to strangle her. "Oh, did you bring the money?"

He pulled a white envelope out from inside his blazer. "Right here."

She lifted the plastic container out of the back of the van. He eased the weight from her arms and used the back of his car as a tabletop. He flipped the lid of the container, and his eyes spread wide. He handed her the envelope.

She gripped the money in her fist.

"This is a unique collection. It's worth every penny." He held up the amethyst berries and turned them around. "This is beautiful. Hardly any wear and tear. I can't believe you're getting rid of them."

She reached for her necklace, but it wasn't there. "It's time." More words stuck in her throat. Better to stay quiet. If she spoke, she risked crying, even if selling the ornaments was for the right reason. Selling still felt as if she swallowed bitter tea.

He closed the lid. Adam's grandmother's ornaments were swallowed up by the trunk of Don Downs's Mercedes. No one in her family would ever see or touch them again.

"Well, then. I guess we're all set," he said.

She dragged her gaze away from the car and to his face. "Looks that way. Thank you."

"No, thank you." He shook her hand and slid into his car.

She stood still until he pulled away and she could no longer see the car as it followed the driveway out of the mall parking lot.

The night had an unexpected chill in it. The breeze

lifted her hair off her neck. She rubbed her arms. The envelope crinkled in her grasp. Don Downs wasn't so bad. He seemed like a decent guy. Her chest hurt as she imagined the ornaments driving away, but at least she had roughly nine thousand dollars in her possession.

She slid into the driver's seat and kicked the van over. Her fingers unsealed the envelope. The money was limp and wrinkled, but enough bills to be the right amount. She pulled it out and counted.

Her hands shook.

She counted again and looked back in the envelope. The money dropped to the floor.

Don Downs had stiffed her six thousand dollars.

Savannah dragged herself up the front steps of her house. She was going to have to put on a good face for her family, but she wasn't sure she had the strength.

Her phone buzzed in her pocket. She yanked it out. JT's name popped up on the screen. She hit the Decline button. She could only handle one catastrophe at a time. He'd have to wait.

With a deep breath, she let herself inside to the peaceful quiet of the front room. The kitchen seemed closed down for the night. Bless Grace. She'd polished the whole kitchen to a high shine. The counters were wiped clean. The stove top sparkled. The mail stood in one neat pile. The empty sink relaxed her shoulders.

The slider was open, and the tiki poles were lit. Blaise

and Grace sat side by side at the patio table, holding hands. Her throat closed up. They were so in love. She wanted that too, and tonight she needed more than anything to have strong arms around her.

She pushed out onto the patio. Grace and Blaise turned in unison.

"Hi, Sis." He pressed out of the chair. Grace followed. "How was your seminar?"

"Great. Thanks again for coming by. I really appreciate it." And she'd appreciate it if they left because she needed to get back in the attic. She had one more idea on how to keep her son in college.

Blaise held up his hands. Every finger was painted bubble-gum pink. Grace snickered. "This is your fault." He pressed his lips together in a tight line.

"Letting her paint your nails is what makes you the favorite uncle." She tossed her keys on the table and dropped into the chair. She was too tired to stand, but she hoped they didn't take it as an invitation to stay longer.

"Or the dumb uncle. I'm not sure."

Grace gripped his arm. "I think it's sweet. You made her entire night. I have nail polish remover at home. You can take it off, but she did take a picture of it and stuck it on her Instagram account. He's getting a lot of likes. Caroline went to bed, and Grey is upstairs in his room. He didn't want to hang with the adults."

"I'm glad she's the only little girl in the family. I can handle my son and my nephews. This girlie stuff I don't get." He waved his hands in the air.

"That's pretty sexist, Blaise," Grace said.

"Damn straight." He winked.

"Are you okay?" Grace ignored Blaise and fixed her knowing stare on Savannah. "You look a little pale. Can I get you anything before we go?"

"I'm fine, but thanks. Just tired. It's been a long day." She checked the time on her phone.

"Did you eat? I could fix you something," Grace said.

"I'm fine, really. I think I'm going to go to bed too." She'd go to bed right after she dug through the dusty boxes and put another ad on Barry's Great Finds. This time she'd count the damn money standing in front of the buyer. And there would be a bigger buyer this time. She kept her gaze away from Blaise.

"If you're sure. Let's go home, big bad alpha male, and let Savannah get some rest. We'll show ourselves out."

"Thank you for hanging out and for cleaning the kitchen. I love you both."

Blaise put a hand on Grace's lower back and led her toward the door. "You couldn't stop her from cleaning if the world was coming to an end."

"No one wants the world to end with dirty bathrooms. Good night."

"Night." Savannah waved.

Blaise slid the slider shut, leaving her alone. Finally. She waited long enough for them to pull away, then went and checked out the window to make certain. Blaise's truck was nowhere in sight. She couldn't risk them coming back to the door while she was in the attic. She'd never hear the bell.

The light in Grey's room spilled out through the bottom of his shut bedroom door. The area around Caroline's door was dark. She had been using that telltale sign for years. Only Jud's room never offered her that same clue. He'd use his table lamp instead of the overhead light. She made a quick stop in there first.

His absence in the house echoed in her heart now that he was in his second year of college. He had made some mistakes in the past, but he had tried to fix them. Knowing he would find his way in the big world hadn't stopped her lips from trembling and the tears leaking from her eyes at the thought of sending him out there. She wanted to keep her children in her fold because she loved them so much it hurt, but that wasn't the way of life. No matter how much she wanted to, she could not control the inevitable. The least she could do was help him finish college.

She ran a hand along the shelf filled with football trophies. His room wasn't decorated with every accomplishment he'd achieved in high school, but he'd kept awards he'd won in the bottom drawer of his desk. The signed baseballs Adam had bought him were the only keepsake on top. She ran a hand along the glass case too.

A photo of him and Adam from a fishing trip they'd taken a few years back sat on his bedside table.

Everyone said Jud looked like her, but he had Adam's smile. She pressed her lips together to keep from crying.

She'd failed her family miserably. What had she been thinking, opening up that tea store? Why hadn't being the librarian been enough for her? Why hadn't loving

Adam been enough too? She had to let her heart and the memories get in the way, and now she couldn't get JT out of her system. She should never have started something with him again, but she couldn't stay away. Adam was a good man, but JT was in every breath and fiber of her being.

Tears shoved their way out, no matter how much she tried to stop them. They ran down her face and dripped off her chin. She needed to pull herself together and get in that attic.

With a deep breath, she pulled down the attic stairs. If Grey came out and saw her, she'd have to think of something to say. For once, she hoped he had his earbuds jammed in his ears.

What she was about to do may be far worse than selling those Christmas ornaments. Adam wasn't here to ask if she could sell his grandmother's treasures, but Colton and Blaise were.

She had no other choice. She had to help her son because she couldn't count on getting the black-tie dinner any longer. And even if she did win it, the timing would be wrong. Jud needed the money now. Everyone would have to understand she needed to make things right.

She dug out the blue box. Her yearbook from senior year sat on top. She resisted the urge to read the good luck wishes from classmates. JT had taken her yearbook right out of her hands the night of her party and with a wicked grin had written in there too. Her heart had flipped a thousand times as he tugged the cap of the pen off with his teeth. He had written something about not falling in the stream unless he was there to drag her out. She had opened the fourth beer after that.

What she really wanted in that box was at the bottom, wrapped in plastic to keep it from yellowing and the pages from curling up. Her brothers' band had played that night for hours. People she'd never seen before had shown up, and her father had been raging mad about the number of teenagers and young adults on his lawn.

Colton was always writing music back then. He'd write notes and lyrics down on anything he could find. While Blaise had been performing his solo, Colton and Troy were scribbling on some notebook paper. She'd walked up to see what they were doing.

"What's that?" she had said.

Colton, with his long hair sweaty and straggly, stared up at her with bloodshot eyes. "Magic."

Troy laughed. "We're just jerking around with ideas."

Those ideas turned into their very first number-one song and the only album that went platinum twice. She had asked if she could keep the pages. Troy had said yes, but Colton had walked away. He had been too wasted to remember even talking to her. She'd wanted them because JT had walked up to her while they were in her hand and had asked her to dance. Colton had been right. Those pages had been magic for them both.

Now she was going to sell them.

"Hey, darlin'."

She screamed and threw the papers. "Are you crazy walking up on me like that? How did you get in?"

JT laughed and climbed into the attic. "Grey let me in. Said you were up here."

His V-neck, black T-shirt hugged his strong pec muscles. His jeans were faded with holes up around the pockets. She squirmed a little. His beard had a day's worth of growth, his smile was easy, and his dark eyes drank her in.

"What are you doing here?" She scrambled to gather the papers.

He reached to help her, but she pulled away. "You declined my call. I wanted to make sure you were okay. I drove by here first and saw your minivan."

"Well, I'm fine, thank you. You can go."

He squatted down beside her. "What's going on up here? Did you decide to do some late-night cleaning?"

"JT, how could you come over here at this hour? My children are going to wonder what's going on." His thigh was inches away from her. She could reach out and touch him.

"Why didn't you answer my call?"

"I couldn't talk. Did that idea cross your mind? Maybe try calling back next time before you waste your time driving around. I don't need you checking up on me." She smoothed the pages into place.

"I was worried about you."

"Why?"

"What the hell is going on here, Savannah?" He reached for the pages, but she yanked them away.

"This is none of your business." She could never tell

him what she was doing. He wouldn't understand how desperate she'd become.

His gaze searched the attic. "You missed one." He lunged for an errant page she hadn't noticed.

He snatched the paper up and moved out of her reach. He read it, stared at her, then went back to the page.

"Please give that to me." Her wobbly voice threatened to give her away.

"I don't understand. Why the secrecy? You have music sheets from your brothers. So what?"

She stuck her hand out. "I need that."

"Are you giving the music back to them?"

His questions made her head hurt. "Please, JT. Give it to me."

"You're not answering me. Are you planning on doing something with them?" His eyes grew wide. "Are you going to sell them?"

"Why would I do that?" She arranged her face into a neutral position. She didn't want to overreact.

"Because you need the money."

"What makes you think I need money?" The attic closed in on her. She needed him to move his big body away so she could get some air. "Can we go downstairs?"

He blocked her path. "Not until you tell me I'm right."

"This isn't a contest. I want to go downstairs, and I want you to go home." She pushed his chest and regretted pressing her fingers to his muscles because she only wanted to touch him more.

"You can't sell these. If you need money, I'll give it you."

The last thing she would do was take money from him. "Thank you, but I don't need money. I'm fine."

"The Tea Room is struggling. You told me, and I can see it. You have more business since I shut down and my stupidity at your tailgate, but it isn't enough. You can't survive on your business plan. No one makes it who can't keep the lunch crowd. How many months do you have left?"

"My store is fine. I'm fine. I don't need you or your help." The lies piled up and suffocated her. She wanted to need him. She wanted to tell him all her problems, but she couldn't. She had to solve this one on her own.

He handed her the paper. Hurt swam in his eyes. "Do your brothers know what you're up to?"

She couldn't look at him. "JT, please. I don't have the energy for this conversation. It's been a long day, and I'm worn out." Her words were a whisper. The whole failed night pressed down on her.

He tilted her chin up. "Let me help you. I can take care of you."

"You can't." No one could help her now.

"Don't sell those pages without talking to Colton and Blaise first. If you won't take my help, then ask them. They'll lend you the money you need."

"I don't need anyone's help. You've misunderstood what you're seeing here."

"Darlin', I may be a lot of things, but I'm not stupid."

He certainly was not that. Dear God, she wanted to

let go and allow him to hold her all night. Her skin ached to be stroked. Her fingers twitched to touch him. She pushed past him, and this time he didn't fight her. Instead, he followed her down the attic ladder and to the front porch. She closed the door behind her so they were alone with the darkness around them.

Would he stay if she asked him? But she wouldn't ask, not tonight. "How was court today?" She needed to talk about anything besides her bad choices, or she'd cave and ask for his help.

"You're changing the subject."

"I told you—I don't need any help. I wanted these pages because I was thinking about you."

"Me?"

"I was holding these at my graduation party when you walked up to me and asked me to dance." Her pride was bruised and battered. She might as well disintegrate it.

"Then all the more reason to keep them." He folded her in his arms, and she went.

His strong embrace warmed her. He smelled like oak and walnut. She inhaled. Just for one minute. She'd stay for just one minute. "You didn't tell me about court."

He stroked her back. "Court sucked. I have one week to prove my father didn't amend his will."

"And if you can't?" His touch lit her on fire. She needed to pull away before she did something she shouldn't. Instead, she closed her eyes as his fingers tangled with the ends of her hair.

"Then I lose the Whiskey."

She forced herself to ease out of his embrace. "I hope that doesn't happen. That bar belongs to you. If you need any help, I'll do whatever I can."

He smirked.

"What?"

"You want to help me, but I can't help you. Now that's not fair."

"I don't need any help."

"Me either."

"Don't be stubborn."

"Back at ya, darlin'." He turned and got into his truck.

He backed out of the drive without glancing in her direction. The tires squealed and kicked up dirt. She watched him drive away. She wished she didn't feel anything, but the pain in her chest took her breath away.

Her heart broke into a million lonely pieces.

She'd make this right.

Somehow.

Chapter Thirty

Savannah sat in her minivan at the Rivergate Mall —again. This time the mall was busy and she'd parked closer to the building. She prepared to count the money in front of the buyer. The pages sat on the seat next to her. She'd made a copy for herself because they might be all she'd have left to remember JT by. She didn't know if she could move forward with him. The guilt was killing her. Being without him was killing her more.

One problem at a time. Get the money. Send it to Jud. Pay off the dresses. Make the mortgage payment. Then she'd worry about JT.

She checked her phone. The buyer was late. Allen Randolph had sent her a text almost immediately after she'd posted the sale. He said he was a collector of musical artifacts, and original music sheets from Savage would be an important addition to his collection. He didn't squabble about the amount she wanted, six thousand to make up for what Don Downs stole from her. She'd tried to reach out to the thief, but his number was no longer in service, and the email address wasn't valid. He'd screwed her but good.

She'd give Mr. Randolph another ten minutes, and then she'd leave. She couldn't wait forever. She had to get back to the kids. Caroline needed help with her math homework again. They had an appointment with an eye doctor next week.

The car beside her pulled out, and another pulled in. Allen had said he drove a blue minivan. A black Audi filled the spot beside her. Her stomach dove south. The driver held up a hand. Colton wasn't smiling.

She pushed out of the minivan. He hopped out, stamped out his cigarette on the ground, and met her halfway. His nostrils flared. A vein pulsed in the side of his neck.

"How did you know?" There wasn't any point in trying to play coy. He knew. He'd only get madder if she tried to act as if she didn't know what he was doing there.

He lit another cigarette with shaking hands. "I have alerts set up every time someone searches my name. What the fuck are you doing?"

"I can explain."

"I can't believe you'd sell my stuff without asking me first. And how did you even have those sheets? When did you take them?"

"I didn't take them. I asked you, but you had been wasted at the time."

"You can't blame this on my drinking. When did you take them?"

"Please listen to me. You scribbled those pages on the night of my high school graduation party. I asked Troy if I could keep them because you were stoned and drunk and high. I didn't think you'd care."

"I wouldn't have if you'd kept them. But you tried to sell them."

"Wait, you're the buyer, aren't you? How did you do that?"

"Fake account, Savannah. That's why I said not to let anyone have them. I'd pay your price so you wouldn't sell them to someone else." He smoked the cigarette down to a stub.

"Why did you wait until now to show yourself?"

"I wanted to make a point."

"Of course, you did." She had no right to catch an attitude with him.

"This isn't about me. If you'd had those pages all this time, why didn't you give them to Blaise when he needed money?" He pounded the pack for another cigarette.

"Are you sure you want to smoke that?"

He raised an eyebrow. "I forgot to bring my Jack Daniels with me. Answer my question."

She didn't want him to drink ever, and as mad as he was, he could start again. Like the time he'd gotten really pissed at Blaise and drank so much he drove into a fence. "I didn't want to sell the pages, but I'm desperate, Colton. I need the money." If he understood her situation, maybe he'd calm down a little.

"Why didn't you come to me?" He took a long drag on the cigarette. His foot tapped out a steady beat.

"Because I had to take care of this myself." Couldn't he fathom what she was going through?

"I'm your brother. I'm here for you. You don't have to go selling my shit behind my back to get money. I have money, damn it."

"I couldn't ask you." She hung her head.

"So you'd steal my stuff instead? Christ, I don't understand you. You make up all the rules as you go along. Don't say shit about your kids because you refuse to believe it. Forgive me when you feel like it because you needed me, and now you go and stab me in the back."

"Colton, please try to understand this has nothing to do with the past. I'm sorry about what happened last year. I thought you knew that. This is about Jud. He can't stay in school if I don't come up with the money."

"Why didn't you ask me? You think I wouldn't give my nephew money for school? Do you believe I hate him or can't forgive him?"

"God, no. I know you love him. All that other stuff was on me. My fault. This is my fault too. I had to take care of my problems alone. I didn't want to burden anyone. I'd made the mess. Now I have to fix it."

"Not by taking something that wasn't yours and selling it."

"Did you even know those pages still existed?"

"That's not the point." He stamped the cigarette out on the ground.

"You made a fortune on that song. What the hell is

the difference if I sell some stupid notes for a few thousand dollars?" Okay, justifying her behavior might not be the best path, but he couldn't lose anything by her selling those pages.

"The difference is some fucked-up idiot will turn around and make a mint on my handwriting, and I don't want that to happen. That stuff is mine. Those are my personal thoughts and feelings. That isn't for the world to see. When I'm dead, you can sell them because then I won't give a shit what people say about me."

She leaned against the car. Colton would forever be the front man protecting his image. She should have thought about that. He had a vulnerable side, but he didn't let it out much, and only to his immediate family. "I have to help Jud."

"You should've thought about keeping your kid in school before you went and opened that tea store of yours. You wouldn't let me invest in it because you had to do it by yourself. You've been trying to take care of everything by yourself your whole life. Sometimes you have to ask for help. Even I know that. Give me the sheet music." He held out his hand.

Her mouth tasted slimy and stale. She'd let her brothers and her son down. She'd let herself down, and worst, she'd let Adam down. She yanked open the car door and grabbed the sheet music. Colton swiped it from her.

"I'm sorry," she said.

He held her gaze. Their eyes were the exact same color, but his smoldered. If she asked for the money, he'd give it to her, but she couldn't and wouldn't. Not now. Shame paralyzed her tongue.

He hesitated, but without another word, he hitched his leg into his car, backed out, and peeled away. The men in her life left her alone and in the dust a lot lately.

Served her right.

She pulled her phone from her purse and hit the Favorites screen.

The phone rang. "Hi, Mom." Jud's low timber came across.

"Hey, buddy." She had to take a deep breath and press her fingers to her lips to keep from crying. "I have some bad news."

He listened as she tried to explain what happened. He yelled and cursed. "I can't believe you did this to me. My whole college career is ruined because of you."

"I'll figure it out. You might have to go to the community college for a semester. We can apply for student loans. I'm sorry."

"Sure you are." He ended the call.

Her head hurt. She should get home, but she didn't have the energy to face Caroline and her homework. With a heavy sigh, she slid back into the van. Her phone vibrated. Blaise's face popped up on the screen. She'd always liked that picture of him holding a tomato from his garden.

"Hi." She braced herself.

"Colton just called me. Are you out of your fucking mind, Savannah?"

Apparently so.

349

Chapter Thirty-One

JT lifted his hat and pressed on his temples. The afternoon sun beat down on him. Sweat ran down his back, making his shirt stick to his skin. He had an hour before he had to be in court, and there he stood on the court steps. His head pounded from the lack of sleep all week. When he wasn't thinking about losing his bar, he thought about losing Savannah. She hadn't called him. She hadn't told her family about them. What *them?* There was no *them.* Christ, he sounded like a girl. Not that there was anything wrong with that. Maddy would get mad at him for making that kind of comment.

He sat on the steps and watched the town unfold before him. A hundred and sixty years, Heritage River had been hanging in there, building businesses, making memories, expanding homes. Heritage River was the kind of town to raise a family in, which was why he had wanted Maddy here. And he wanted to be closer to his dad. He missed him. If he lost the Whiskey for good, what was he going to do in this town? He meant what he said to Savannah. Without her, he couldn't stay to watch her possibly fall in love with someone else. Hell, they hadn't been together for years. Could she walk away from him because they didn't have a history to tether them?

Uncle Harlan ambled down the street, early as usual. He squeezed a finger between his shirt collar and his neck and pulled the fabric away as far as it would stretch. "Afternoon, Jacob."

"Uncle Harlan. That tie giving you a bad time?" He stood and shook the man's hand. He was grateful for his uncle, who had been his second-chance father on many occasions.

"I hate these blasted things, but out of respect for you and the judge, I keep strangling myself with one. Any more news from Hoke?"

"Quiet as a church mouse."

"I was afraid of that. I'm sorry, son. Let's head inside to the air-conditioning."

The metal detector loomed ahead. This time he had opted for jeans with a sports coat instead of a suit. He didn't feel the need to dress up for what would possibly be a blow to the gut. He passed through the metal detector without a look back. His boots clacked against the tile, echoing down the hall. He took a deep breath.

He pulled out his phone to call Savannah, then shoved it back in his pocket. That stubborn woman wouldn't take his help, wouldn't go public about her feelings for him. Had she sold those pages? He should have tried harder to stop her. Still, he wanted her beside him while he waited to hear the judge's ruling.

Harlan held the door open to room 204. Hoke sat inside at the same table as last time. He flipped through papers but turned as they approached. His hair was slicked back, and his suit crisp.

"Gentlemen." Hoke stood. "Are you ready?"

"Ready as I'll ever be." He took the seat beside Hoke and removed his hat. Harlan sat in the row behind them.

The bailiff with the oversize mustache entered from the back wall. He shuffled around, moving papers from one place to another. His paunchy stomach stretched his brown uniform shirt to its maximum.

Shirley's attorney hurried down the aisle and took his seat at the other table without a look in their direction.

"Is Shirley coming?" he whispered in Hoke's ear.

"She was advised to stay home."

"Is that a good thing?"

"For somebody."

"All rise for Judge Summerford."

The judge, with his balding head and glasses, appeared through the door and climbed up to his bench. "Be seated." He kept his eyes on his desk. "We're here today to determine if the last will and testament of Jacob Davies Sr. is in fact his last wishes." He raised his head and searched the courtroom. "Do we have any additional proof, Mr. Carter?"

Hoke stood and buttoned his suit jacket and cleared

his throat. "Your Honor, we employed Marshall Bean, a handwriting expert, to determine the validity of the note Mrs. Davies claims her husband signed."

"Yes, Mr. Carter, I see your notes here in the file. Please state Mr. Bean's findings."

"Inconclusive, Your Honor."

Maddy had found the card his dad had signed. Marshall Bean said a larger example would prove more conclusive. Though he could argue similarities in some of the letters, he could also argue irregularities in others. Since JT had paid a hefty price for this guy's opinion, Bean signed an affidavit stating inconclusive.

He hoped the findings would be enough.

Shirley's attorney stood. "Your Honor, our expert claims Mr. Davies Sr. did in fact write that note. If Mr. Carter and his client only provided inconclusive proof, I wish to ask the court to find in the favor of Mrs. Davies."

Summerford removed his glasses and pinched his nose. "Do you have anything else, Mr. Carter?"

"I ask the court to take into account Mr. Davies Sr. had the foresight to prepare a last will and testament protecting the interests of his only child and grandchild. A handwritten note that may have possibly been forged should not override the clear requests of a man in sound mind and body."

"Your Honor." Shirley's guy stood again, but Summerford held a hand up to stop him.

"Mr. Davies," the judge began, and Hoke tapped JT's elbow to make him stand. "I'm terribly sorry for the loss of your father. I recently lost my own father. I'm afraid holographic wills are very complicated, and I wish we resided in a state that didn't acknowledge them, but that isn't the case. Without undisputed proof your father did not write that last note, I cannot honor the requests made in the will written by Mr. Carter. Believe me when I say I wish I could rule another way, but the property formerly known as Eat At Jake's must return to the possession of Mr. Davies Sr.'s widow."

"All rise."

His lungs couldn't take in any air, and the blood roared in his ears. His fists clenched at his sides. Heat flushed over his whole body.

"Jacob?" Harlan's voice came down a long tunnel to him.

His vision shrank to a narrow pin.

"Sit down, boy." Hoke shoved him back in the chair.

"What do we do?" Harlan spoke over his head.

"I'll appeal it, but he won't be able to keep the bar open. The place will sit dark. I'll find another expert. One that knows what in land's sake he's talking about. Don't worry, JT. We'll get to the bottom of it all. Just sit tight. JT?"

He turned his gaze to meet Hoke's. Through clenched teeth he said, "Don't bother. It's over."

"You can't give up," Harlan said.

"I lost. She won. That's it." His jaw hurt. "I need some air." He pushed past the older men and stormed outside into the heat.

His truck was parked on the street, but he kept walking. He walked away from town because if he went near his bar, he'd smash the windows. He yanked off his jacket and rolled up his sleeves. He didn't know where he was going or what he would do when he got there.

He only hoped he had enough sense to wait before he threw the first punch.

Chapter Thirty-Two

Savannah ushered Kiki out of the Tea Room and locked the door. She had an appointment and wanted the place empty and cleaned up. She even gave Harley the rest of the day off. Working with her the past week had been difficult. No one knew what to say besides table four needed another pot of tea or where were the extra mason jars. She hadn't meant to put Harley in the middle, but she had. She couldn't blame Harley for taking Colton's side. The woman did have to live with him, and in Harley's defense she loved him, plain and simple.

She bused the table Kiki had been at and counted the forks. All there. Ironic. She wiped down the kitchen and emptied the register. Business had dwindled since the tailgate. She had no right to open a tea shop without doing more research or investigating or listening to Colton. Why did he have to be right all the damn time?

She didn't really know how to keep a place like this above water.

A knock came from the front of the store. She opened the door to Dixie Bordeaux, wearing a print blouse straining at the buttons and a cream skirt stretched at the seams. Her smile warmed her full face and puffy eyes. Her hair had that shellacked, right-from-the-beauty-parlor look.

"Well, hello, sugar. Am I late? I didn't expect the door to be locked." Dixie wrapped her in a gardenia-scented hug.

She hugged back because she needed one. "Right on time. We close at four. I didn't want anyone sneaking in while we talked."

Dixie pulled a yellow folder from her bright pink tote bag that matched her high-heeled pumps. "I have the contract here."

"Would you like some tea?" She wasn't ready to sit down and take a look at that contract. "I still have some blueberry scones left too. Have a seat. I'll be right back."

She didn't wait for Dixie to answer. A woman like Dixie would be too polite to refuse her offer anyway. She returned with a pot of chamomile tea. It would settle her nerves and give her shaking hands something to do.

"Here you go." She poured the tea and placed a scone in front of Dixie.

"Thank you, dear. I've drawn up my six-month agreement. I'll do my best to get this place sold in no time, but the market is slow this time of year with the holidays on the horizon. Everyone is thinking about Halloween costumes, Thanksgiving turkeys, and Christmas garland. Oh, that reminds me. How are the plans for your brother's wedding coming along?" Dixie wrapped her pink-polished nails around the scone.

Sometimes she hated living in a small town with celebrity brothers. "Great. Harley has everything under control. Invitations will be going out soon." There was no easy segue out of the wedding planning, so she jumped without looking. "I need to get at least as much as I paid for the building." That amount would have to do. It wouldn't cover everything, but after she paid off the mortgage, she would give Jud another semester at school. Just not the spring semester if Dixie couldn't sell this place in the next thirty days.

"We'll ask higher to have room to negotiate if necessary. Are you certain you want to let her go? She's such a lovely place, and your scones are divine. Why, you could make a fortune selling these at the church bazaar. Do they know to come over here and get some?"

The church bazaar wasn't going to save her. "I'm certain I want to sell. The sooner the better." She didn't want to sell at all, but she was out of options. She'd do anything to help Jud stay in school, and that meant selling.

Dixie grabbed a pen from her bag. "Sign all the places I've indicated with the pink tabs. There's a copy for you and for me. I'll bring some of the other realtors around next week to take a look. A shame this place might turn into a hair salon or liquor store. We have enough of those in that ugly strip mall out on the highway. But you didn't hear that from me." Her smile pushed the folds of her skin up under her eyes. "How long will you stay in business, because I need to have me some of these scones for my niece's bridal shower next week?"

"I'll stay until the end, I guess." If the customers continued to come, she'd be able to ride out the last days. She needed whatever money she could get and didn't have another way to make it at the moment. She had no idea what her next steps would be.

Where would she get a job? Grace might hire her back at the library, but that was before she had gone and hurt Blaise. Grace would take his side too. Understandable. She'd lost her friends and her brothers. She'd also lost JT because he wouldn't continue to wait for her. She'd avoided him all week, afraid to reach out until she fixed her problems. She'd have to call Rowan and tell him she was out of the running for the black-tie event. JT would win if the bar was open, and she prayed for his sake it was.

"Savannah, sugar, are you feeling okay? Your cheeks have a splash of red in them, and I don't think you've heard one word I've said. Do you need to lie down?"

She reached for her necklace. "I'm fine, thank you. Would it be too much trouble to get the contract to you tomorrow? I want to read through it when I have a little time. I have to pick up Caroline from school soon."

Dixie patted her hand. "Of course. Take your time. Say hello to your family for me." She pushed out of the chair that creaked in response.

She closed the door behind Dixie and leaned against it. Her chest hurt. With one more look around, she grabbed her keys and went to fetch her daughter.

"Mom, are you listening to me?" Caroline squawked in the seat next to her.

Caroline had been talking nonstop since they'd left the eye doctor, something about Katie, Kelly, Jason, and the lunch table. She couldn't keep her mind on what her daughter said. Vision therapy to fix Caroline's processing issues would cost over two thousand dollars.

"I'm sorry, honey. What happened after Kelly read Katie's Instagram caption?" That was what they were talking about, wasn't it?

"Mom, you're not listening. Mrs. Silver said I need a math tutor. I think that's a good idea after what the doctor said. I have trouble focusing with all the noise in the classroom. Will you get me a tutor?"

"Can't your math teacher give you extra help?" What was that woman thinking, making that suggestion without talking to her first? Was Mrs. Silver going to pay for this tutor? Maybe if Mrs. Silver did her job better, Caroline could get some extra help after school. *Unfair, Savannah.*

"Mrs. Silver doesn't stay after school. She has to pick her daughter up from day care. She's divorced. She talks about it in class all the time."

Of course, she did.

360

"Will you get me a math tutor? I know I'll never be in advanced math like my friends, but how stupid will I look if I fail grade-level math?"

She stole a glance at her daughter, and her heart swelled. "You aren't going to fail. You aren't stupid. I'll check into a tutor tomorrow." She could donate blood to pay for what Caroline needed.

"Thank you." Caroline went back to her phone, allowing the conversation to fade away.

The quiet weaved the strands of her nerves together. The sun mixed pinks with oranges, like a good citrus tea, as it climbed down out of the sky. She'd get dinner going. Grilled cheese and soup were about all she could muster the energy for. She would read that contract with a very large glass of wine in her hand, maybe in the tub. She wanted one night of peace.

She pulled into her driveway and slammed on the brakes.

JT sat on her porch steps. He leaned his elbows on his thighs and hung his head. His black cowboy hat lay beside him. He looked up as the tires rolled over the gravel. His slow, easy smile spread across his face. He raised a hand.

"What's Mr. Davies doing here?" Caroline narrowed her eyes.

"Not sure. Why don't you run inside and see if Grey can start some grilled cheese sandwiches for dinner, okay?"

"Is Mr. Davies staying? Oh no, does that mean

Maddy is inside making googly eyes at Grey?" Caroline stuck a finger in her mouth and crossed her eyes.

"Good question. Run in and stop them if that's the case."

Caroline hopped out of the car and ran up the steps. "Hi, Mr. Davies."

"Howdy, Caroline." JT high-fived her as she ran past.

"Grey, stop whatever you're doing..." Caroline yelled as she shoved open the door. She slammed it just as quickly, shutting out her loud voice.

JT stood. He wore a white dress shirt with the sleeves rolled up, revealing those strong arms she longed to have around her.

"Hey. You look pretty."

"Hey, yourself, and thank you." She stopped on the sidewalk and looked up at him. A heat traveled from her center out. His dark eyes were lined red. The creases around his mouth had deepened. "Is Maddy inside?"

"It's just me. I was walking, and I found myself here. Grey said you were on your way home. I thought I'd wait." He ran a hand over his face. "Any chance you can take a walk?"

"Looks like you could use a little time off. Why don't you call Maddy and bring her over for supper? We can take a walk after that." An evening with JT and Maddy wouldn't offer her the peace she needed because she couldn't keep him, but she couldn't let him go with all that pain on his face. He was having a worse day than she was. And if she were going to be honest, she wanted his company even for a little while.

"I don't have my car."

She held up her keys. "Is grilled cheese okay? I wasn't planning on anything fancy tonight."

"Perfect." He kicked the dirt. "You always seem to know what I need. How do you do that?"

She loved everything about him the way she loved everything about tea. He was the strong tea fragrance made of amber and leather filling her pretty porcelain tea pot. "It's just grilled cheese. I'll leave the door open when you come back."

He cleared the space between them and tilted her chin up to him. He placed a sweet kiss on her lips.

"Thank you."

"JT—"

"I know. No kissing in public. I couldn't help myself."

That smile of his would be the end of her. He was doing her the favor by being around on one of the worst days added to a list of worst days.

"Hurry back." She placed the keys in his hand.

She went inside and ran to her bedroom. Her side of the bed wasn't made, but she had no plans on bringing JT there. Tonight was just dinner with the kids. Maybe the walk too, but nothing more, even if she wanted to touch him and feel his hands all over her.

She brushed her teeth and ran her fingers through her hair. She swapped the clothes that smelled like the kitchen at the Tea Room for a white T-shirt and her favorite boyfriend jeans with the rips up by the pockets.

The kitchen looked as if a tornado had blown through and dragged half of Tennessee with it. She shoved the mail into a drawer, wiped the counters down, and returned the cereal boxes to the pantry. The carnations drooped over the crystal vase and dropped leaves all over the island. Time to dump them in the trash. Dirty dishes filled the dishwasher. They'd be eating on paper plates. They could eat outside and make a picnic of it. She picked through what was left of the grapes and cut up some celery and dumped ranch dressing into a glass bowl. She yanked scones with vanilla icing out of the freezer for dessert.

The doorbell rang. She'd told him to come in when he got back. The man did not listen. She opened her front door to find JT and Maddy standing there with grocery bags in their hands.

"What are you doing? I'm making the dinner. Hi, Maddy. Forgive my manners."

He pushed past her. "I had this food at the Whiskey, and it's going to go to waste. Figured we could cook some of it up on your grill." He put the bags down on the table. "And I brought this." He pulled out a bottle of whiskey. "For the adults." He pointed a finger at her. "You can't drink too much. You'll have to drive us back to my car later."

"Dad left his car at the courthouse." Maddy unloaded the bags.

Grey skid into the room. His face bloomed red. Maddy ducked behind her hair.

Oh brother.

"Um. Hi. I was... When is dinner going to be ready?"

Grey's words stumbled out and fell on the floor with his panting tongue.

"I'm going to fire up the grill. We'll have some steaks ready in thirty. How's that?" JT pulled rolls and salad out of the bag.

"The grill? My dad liked to grill." Grey tapped on the counter.

JT stopped. "I bet he was great at it."

"He wore a stupid apron every time."

Her children had the power to tug her heart right through her ribs. Her little boy really wasn't so little anymore. How would she go on keeping him safe? Or Caroline? Or Jud?

JT smiled at Grey. "Our dads had a lot in common. My dad liked to grill up everything. One time when it was raining really hard, he dragged the grill into the garage and cooked in there. He almost set the house on fire."

"Do you miss him?" Grey turned a stalk of celery into a drumstick.

Maddy stood beside Grey. He moved a little closer to her.

"Every day, pal. Every day. How about you?"

"Yeah, me too."

"Would it be okay with you if I used your dad's grill tonight?" He stared Grey straight in the eye.

"I think so. Mom? Can he?"

"I don't think Dad would mind." She pressed her lips together to keep her emotions from spilling all over the place.

"I'll take good care of it. My dad taught me how to cook, and he was one of the best damn cooks in the state."

"Do you want to go outside or something?" Maddy tugged on the end of her hair.

Grey shrugged. "Sure."

"We'll call you for dinner." *And please keep your clothes on.* She turned back to JT. "Thank you for that."

"It was nothing." He salted the steaks.

She put a hand over his. "You made him feel better."

"You've done a pretty good job helping Maddy lately. Let's call it even, okay?"

"I wasn't keeping score."

"This time."

"I'm not the one who's always in competition for something."

"No, you're the one who likes to keep secrets. Sorry. No arguments tonight. Let's put our hurt feelings aside for a few hours, okay?"

"Deal." She could do that, couldn't she?

They cooked the food together as if they'd been moving around a kitchen with each other for a lifetime. The kids talked and laughed with them until the sun set and the mosquitos came out biting. He helped her clean up after the kids retired to the bonus room to watch a movie.

He took her hand and led her out to the front porch. "Are your lightbulbs burned out?"

"I keep forgetting to turn them on."

"You feel like going for that walk now?" He didn't

wait for an answer. Instead, he laced his fingers through hers and headed down the steps.

"The park is down the street. We could walk there." She used to take the kids to the park all the time when they were little.

The sidewalk was cracked in places, kind of like her heart. The crescent moon did little to light their path, but JT would keep her safe, and she knew the way. Maybe she knew the way because of JT. He made everything clearer for her.

He took a deep breath and sighed it out. "I lost the bar today."

She stopped, tugging his arm back. "For good?"

He kept walking until they hit the park. The empty seesaw and slide had an ominous feel at night. He dropped down onto one of the swings. She sat beside him and kicked the rubber mulch under her feet, not saying anything until he was ready to tell her what happened.

"The judge ruled in Shirley's favor." He leaned his elbows on his thighs.

"I'm so sorry. Can you fight it?"

"Hoke says he'll appeal it, but I don't want him to."

"Why not? You can't let her get away with this. It isn't fair. That bar belongs to you and Maddy."

He smiled. "I appreciate your passion, darlin'. I gave it a lot of thought this past week and all afternoon while I walked up and down the streets. I'm going to either manage one of my other bars or open a new one in another state. She can have this one."

"You're going to leave?" Again. Before she'd had a chance to fix her own mess.

"Looks that way."

"When things get a little difficult, you just cut and run. Is that it?" She tried to control her tone, but anger shook her voice with two fists.

"Sometimes in business, you have to cut your losses. If I leave, you won't have to worry about winning the black-tie. Rowan will give it to you."

"Don't you dare take pity on me. I planned on winning that competition fair and square, not because you walked out. Stay and beat me. I dare you."

"Can't accept that dare. I'm not falling off the roof in my drawers again."

She shook her head. *Stupid fool.* "I've never seen you back down before."

"Think of it as restructuring my goals."

"You're leaving because you don't want to lose to Shirley. You hate losing, and you don't see a way to win. So you run. Like you ran away from me when we could've had a life together." She didn't regret the life she did have, but what would life have been like with this man? And now he was taking away their chance again.

He stood and pulled her from the swing. "Would you have married me?"

She stepped away from him. "Don't go asking me that. You left without a goodbye, forcing me to get on with my life."

"If I had asked you to be my wife back then, would you have said yes?"

Tears spilled out of her eyes. "I would've gone anywhere with you. Done anything with you."

"You were going off to college, and I mowed lawns. I couldn't give you a future. I wasn't good enough for you. I had to prove myself first."

"Are you done proving yourself yet?"

"I needed to win that black-tie dinner and show the town I mattered, but I can't if Shirley has my bar."

"Don't you see the people around you love you for who you are? Maddy, Harlan, your dad, my brothers, me."

"Y'all aren't enough. I'm sorry. I have more to prove." He turned away from her.

She eased in closer and placed a tentative hand on his back. His muscles flexed, but he didn't move. "Don't let her win. Your father wanted you to have his deli."

"The whole town thinks I'm still the same loser I was as a kid. Maybe they're right." He turned to face her.

"Fuck the town."

He laughed. "Does anyone outside of your immediate family know you curse like a sailor?"

"Of course not. I'm a southern lady. But that's not the point. The point is you are the most stubborn man I have ever met." She slapped his arm.

"Hey. What's that for?"

"JT, you don't have anything to prove to anyone. When are you going to figure that out?"

"I want the town—"

She put a hand over his mouth. "Stop talking for five seconds and listen to me. You already have proven yourself. You joined the army and served your country. You went to college and earned a degree. You opened five Whiskey Bars. You've made money, and you are raising a beautiful, smart, if not a little forward, young lady by yourself. Your wife left you, and you kept going."

"If all that is true, why won't you tell your family about us?"

She dropped back into the swing and stared at the ground because she couldn't look him in the eye. "Confession time. You were right about not selling the sheet music." She told him about getting busted by Colton and how her family wasn't speaking to her. "I'm going to sell the Tea Room for the money."

"You're not going to let me help you either?"

"I don't need you to save me."

"I'm not trying to save you. I want to walk beside you. I don't want to stop you. I want to light the way. You can let go for a little while and let me take the lead."

"Not if you're leaving."

He ran a hand over his face. "You've got me there."

"What does Maddy say about all this?"

"I haven't told her yet. She's going to be spitfire mad at me again. She's been in three schools in the past two years."

"So stay." Her words were a whisper.

"I can't walk around this town knowing Shirley has my bar. I can't. It's not in me. I hardly ever came home because I couldn't live with the looks and the whispers about Jake's son being nothing. 'Poor Jake,' they'd say. I needed to succeed this time, and I didn't."

She stood and met his gaze. "If you don't realize you've already proven yourself to a bunch of narrow-minded idiots, then you're never going to figure it out. You have nothing left to prove to anyone except yourself."

He gripped her shoulders and pressed his lips to hers. Relief drenched her. She had wanted to kiss him for days. She laced her fingers in the back of his hair and opened her mouth to his. He cupped her face and tilted her mouth to drink in more of her. No matter what they did, she wanted to get closer to him.

He ran his hands down her back and cupped her bottom, pressing her belly against his desire. She ran her hands over his chest, and relished the flex of his muscles against her touch. She made him feel that way, and that knowledge sent her soaring.

He gripped her hands as she tugged at the bottom of his shirt. "Southern ladies don't have sex in a park." His breath was as ragged as hers.

"I don't care." And God help her, she didn't. "Do I have to dare you?"

"Darlin', don't go doing that. I'd take you right on the top of that slide, but I'd like to think I have some sense." He came in close and tangled his hands in her hair. "I want to make love to you properly."

He took out his phone and hit a few buttons. An old Otis Redding song came to life. "Dance with me instead."

"You'd rather dance?" She'd offered herself to him, and he turned her down. He drove her crazy.

"I didn't say that." He held out his hand for hers, but the smile was on his face and the dare in his eyes.

She slid her hand into his, and he pulled her against his powerful chest. He placed his other hand on the small of her back. She ran her fingers along the edge of the collar of his shirt. His skin was soft and warm like his kisses.

"When was the last time we danced like this?" He rested his cheek against hers. He smelled like oak—strong, constant.

Her heart beat to the way their bodies swayed. The song changed to the melodic sound of Jennifer Nettles. "At that street fair my brothers played. Two weeks before graduation. The sun had set, and the band switched to a ballad Troy liked to sing so he could give his voice a break. Do you remember?"

"You were standing with your friends with your back to me. I wanted to hold you. That song gave me the perfect excuse without raising suspicion. I grabbed you from behind and spun you around. You squealed like a pig, but when you saw it was me, you gave me that smile."

"I didn't squeal like a pig, thank you. Don't ruin the mood."

He laughed. The song changed again.

"What smile?"

He eased back to look down at her. "The smile you save for me. Only one side of your lips go up, and you sass me with that taunt in your smoky eyes."

"I don't have that smile, and how do you know it's only for you? I could be using that smile at the gynecologist."

He spun her around with skill. "Oh, I know. It's the

way you look at me the moment I'm inside you. I know you're not giving that look to the girlie doctor."

She stopped and stared at him. Her words stuck together. He knew her better than anyone ever had. Their connection had never been broken. All the miles and all the years between them hadn't changed the way her heart craved to be loved by him.

She placed a hand on his cheek. "Make love to me."

He turned his head and kissed her palm. "It will be for the last time. Can you live with that because I don't know if I can?"

"There's nothing I can do to get you to stay?"

"I'm not pressuring you to tell your family. You do that in your time, and if we're meant to be, then we will be."

"You can't wait any longer." She eased away from him and wrapped her arms around her middle.

"It's not fair for me to force you into telling your family before you're ready. But I've got my life to think about too. I want to be out in public with you. I want to walk down the street with my arm around you. I want the world to know you're mine." He pulled her close again. "Hey, I didn't mean for this to get serious. I just wanted to be with you tonight to take some of the hurt of the day away. I don't want to fight with you."

"Once I sell my store, I can focus on me. I have to take care of Jud first, and I have to back out of Colton's wedding, and..." The tears burned the back of her throat. She swallowed them away. "Please wait for me."

It's what she hadn't said last time when they were

young and foolishly thought they had all the time in the world. She had been afraid then that Blaise would be mad at her, and she was afraid now for different reasons. Blaise and Colton would tell her to find happiness with JT. It was her own guilt that stopped her.

"You know that little speech you just gave me about knowing myself?" He twirled the end of her hair around his finger.

"Yes."

"You don't have to explain to anyone what you feel for me, and if you don't know that by now, you're never going to."

He turned off the music and took her hand. They walked back to her house without another word.

Chapter Thirty-Three

J T unscrewed the last chalkboard from the wall and wiped it clean. The only things that would remain inside the Whiskey when Shirley took her would be the four walls and the floor. He took a shot of whiskey to calm the fire in his veins.

He'd stayed up all night after he left Savannah's. Her words had fought against his thoughts, making sleep impossible. Had he proven himself? What was left if he hadn't? He wasn't ready to stay and watch this place belong to someone who'd hated him his whole life. It hadn't been his fault his father mourned the loss of his first wife. He'd been a kid in need of a mother.

Now he was a man in need of his woman, and she couldn't utter the words he needed to hear. Savannah loved him, but she couldn't let go of the guilt that tied her to the past. It didn't matter to him what anyone thought when it came to them. Why the hell did it matter so much what other people thought about him alone? Why wasn't what he saw in her eyes more than he needed to hold his head high? Maybe it was because no matter what her eyes said or how her body responded to his touch, she didn't walk down the street with him.

He downed another shot.

A knock came from the front. He shoved his thoughts aside and unlocked the door.

Rowan McGee stood on the other side with his black, greasy hair and matching smile. "I was hoping to find you here."

He stepped back to let Rowan in. "What can I do for you?"

"It's what I can do for you." Rowan surveyed the place. "Packing already?"

He stepped behind the bar, needing some space from Rowan. "You heard, then?"

"Small town and all."

"Would you like a drink?" He sure as hell needed another one. He glanced at his watch. He'd have to switch to soda. Maddy would be home from school soon.

"Give me one of those specialty beers. I came to tell you the town council would like to offer you the opportunity to cater the black-tie dinner."

"I thought the decision wasn't going to be made for another week."

"We decided. We want you."

He held up his hands. "You're forgetting I'm closed for good. Judge says I can't operate the bar anymore. If it's all the same to you, I'd rather not end up in jail. Kind of need those days behind me now."

Rowan laughed. "You broke every rule put in front of you. I used to think you were the biggest son of a bitch on the planet and still wanted to shake your hand for not putting up with any shit. It was no surprise to me you were friends with the Savages then and now. How come you were never in the band?" He slid onto a barstool.

"Tone deaf." He tapped the side of his head. He poured a beer and handed over the glass.

"The town council decided they didn't care about whether your bar was open in town or not. You're a life-long resident. Kind of. That's good enough for us."

"How am I supposed to cater without my bar?"

"Come on, JT. You're smarter than that. You own other bars. Bring in what you need from them. We don't care where the food comes from. We want you and your whiskey."

"Why?"

"Because you're what this town is all about. Weathering tough times and coming back standing tall. Like the trees it's named after. The vet angle is good for publicity too. I won't lie. Your library lunch was a disaster, but when we came here, we knew you were the one."

"Give it to Savannah."

Rowan drank his beer. "Good stuff. Savannah can't handle that dinner. Don't get me wrong. I like her plenty because if I didn't that pain-in-the-ass brother of hers would come hunt me down."

"Colton?"

"You have to ask? She's too new to the restaurant business, and she only serves a handful of simple foods.

Tea is her thing, and that's what she should stay with. Maybe she'll be ready for another anniversary event, but not this one."

"Here's the deal I'm willing to make with you. Give that dinner to Savannah and tell her she was your first choice, or Colton and I will hunt you down. She needs that night to make her Tea Room a success, and I want her to have whatever she needs. If she decides all by herself she can't handle it, then I'll step in and help her out, but it's still her night. I'll just be in the background, like a safety net. But believe me when I tell you this, she is the strongest woman I know. She won't need me or anyone else to help her. She's the one you want."

Rowan finished his beer and shook his head. "Every time I turn around, that Savage family causes me a sharp pain in my nether regions." He slid off the bar and pulled money from his pocket. "I can tell by your set jaw that's your final answer."

"Yes, sir. Keep your money."

Rowan shook his head and shoved the money away. "Savannah's Tea Room as the caterer. You know I could give it to any other caterer in the county."

"You could, but you won't." If Rowan gave the dinner to another caterer, he'd spend the next fifty years looking over his shoulder for JT and Colton.

"I'll stop by her place next. But you'll be there if she needs you? You'll bring your staff and some of that aged whiskey you kept up behind the bar?"

"Consider it done, but she won't need me."

She never did.

Chapter Thirty-Four

Savannah paced in front of her family. Colton, Harley, Blaise, Grace, Grey, and Caroline huddled in her living room. Colton leaned against the wall with his arms crossed and a scowl on his face. Harley sat in the chair near him with her thin legs in black leggings tucked under her. Grace and Blaise sat together on the couch. His scowl matched Colton's. Grace patted his leg, but he didn't flinch. The kids sat on the floor, staring up at her, wondering what all her pacing was about.

Someone knocked on the door. She went to answer it. Cash and Knox hurried past her—Cash in his signature black attire and Knox with earbuds hanging from his ears. "Sorry, we're late. Dad said a family meeting was happening. I had to get back from my study group. Knox came to pick me up. Did we miss anything?"

She swept her arm wide. "Come on in." She hadn't planned on Cash and Knox, but that was okay. They were part of the family too. They might as well hear what she was going to say firsthand.

"Where's Jud?" Caroline said. "If this is a family meeting, shouldn't Jud be here too?"

"Jud couldn't get home from school." And he'd refused to come home when she called and asked him. She'd told him on the phone what she was about to tell the rest of them. It didn't make a difference. He was still mad at her.

Harley high-fived Knox as he went by. He shook hands with Colton. Blaise stood to hug Cash, and then Cash leaned in to kiss Grace's cheek. Cash ruffled Caroline's hair.

"Uncle Blaise, did you get that Snapchat I sent you?" Knox settled against the fireplace.

Blaise laughed. "Holy hell, I laughed for ten minutes."

"Knox, man, did you send it to me?" Cash said.

"You didn't tell me you got Snapchat." Grace swatted at Blaise, who ducked.

"Could we get this meeting underway?" Colton snarled.

"You're such a grouch." Savannah relished the playfulness of her family now more than ever.

He raised an eyebrow. "Are you shitting me about now?"

"Fine. You're the least grouchy person I've ever met. Better? I do want to thank y'all for coming. I brought you together because everyone needs to hear what I'm about to say." She took a deep breath and let her shoulders drop. "I'm sorry."

"For what?" Grey said.

"Well, for a lot of things, I'm afraid. I need to apologize to your uncles." She met both of their stares.

"Colton, Blaise, I'm sorry I tried to sell your music."

"Whoa." Cash whistled.

"I had no right to do that without asking you. I'm also sorry to you, Harley and Grace. I put you both in a tough spot. I'm not making excuses, because I was wrong, but I didn't think I had any other choice except to sell that music."

"You could've asked me for the money," Colton said.

"I couldn't. I didn't think I had a right to ask you after you offered me sound business advice that would've helped me and I turned you down. Plus, I didn't want you to say you told me so."

"I wouldn't have said that."

Harley gripped his arm and shook her head.

Blaise shot him a look. "Who's shitting who now, bro?"

"What the fuck? This isn't about me."

"He's right." She needed to derail the argument that could ignite. "This is about me making a big mistake and hurting the people I love the most in the world." She paced more. "I'm glad Colton caught me. I think after I had time to sit with what I did, I wouldn't have been able to forgive myself." She turned to Grey and Caroline. "I sold Daddy's Christmas ornaments for the money to keep Jud in school. I'm sorry about that too."

"Wow, that sucks," Grey said.

"Yeah," from Caroline. "I wanted those ornaments when I had a house of my own."

"I know, and I'm sorry. I'm sorrier because I still couldn't help Jud. It's my responsibility to take care of the three of you, and I'm not doing a very good job of it. I've decided to sell the Tea Room to get the money I need. I'm out of options. Selling the store is the price I have to pay for making so many mistakes."

Colton took a step forward. She put up a hand to stop him. "I will not take your help. This is my mess, and I'm going to clean it up by myself. Which leads me to...I can't be the caterer for your wedding. I've done too much damage to have that honor."

"Savannah, that's ridiculous. We're family," Harley said.

"I'm also backing out of the wedding. I can't afford it. Please let Caroline stay in, but I have to take a pass for myself."

"Like hell you are," Colton said.

Harley stood beside him. "I want you in my wedding. Your family is my family now. I've waited my whole life to have a family like this. You can't back out."

Grace stood and straightened her blouse. "I agree. You all took me in as one of your own because Blaise fell in love with me. I'm not letting you out of this. I'll buy your dress for you as a birthday present."

Tears burned the back of her throat.

"I'll pay for your dress," Colton said. "And don't argue with me about it. It's settled."

"It's not settled, but thank you. And thank you, Grace, but I can't accept your offer. I don't think I belong in the wedding any longer."

"You are being ridiculous," Blaise said. "Let him spend some of that money he's got hiding under the floorboards. He can't take it with him."

"Uncle C, you have money stashed in the floor?" Cash said.

"Don't listen to your old man. He talks out of his ass."

"Savannah, you've become one of my closest friends, and you're about to become my sister. The wedding wouldn't be complete if you're not a part of it. I want you to caterer it, and I want you as a bridesmaid. Colton can't stay mad forever, can you, babe?" Harley pressed against his side and looked up at him with expectant eyes.

"Do you want me to tell my sister I'm not mad anymore?" He looked down at Harley.

"I do. I want her a part of our wedding."

"And if I'm still mad?"

Harley stepped away from him and dropped down onto the couch. "You used to like living in the guesthouse."

Knox snickered. Colton glared at him. Knox dropped his gaze to his phone.

"I'm not mad anymore. Happy now?"

Harley planted a quick kiss on his lips. His smile lasted for a second before it disappeared again.

"Say yes, Savannah, before he changes his mind," Harley said.

She laughed with relief. "Thank you, Colton. I mean that. I don't want you to be upset with me any longer."

"What about me? Don't you want to know if I'm still mad?" Blaise crossed his arms over his chest and stretched out his legs.

"He's not mad." Grace dropped down on the couch beside him and linked her arm through his.

"Don't I get to decide that?"

"Are you mad?" She hoped he'd be able to forgive her too. She needed both brothers on her side before she could accept Harley's offer.

"It's okay. I understand why you did it, even if I don't like it." He pouted.

"Thank you. Okay, there's one more thing you need to know. I've been keeping something from all of you." There would be no turning back from this.

Colton dropped down beside Blaise. "For Christ's sake, these family meetings make me want to smoke."

"You can have your cigarette in a minute," she said. "I have to say this. I'm in love with JT."

"That's your big confession? We all knew that," Blaise said. "You two look at each other with those goofy eyes."

"You mean like us?" Grace teased.

"I love you, babe, but I don't make those corny faces JT makes."

"I'm not only talking about what's been happening recently. I've loved JT my whole life."

"But what about Dad?" Caroline asked.

"I loved him too."

"I don't understand. How can you love Daddy and love Mr. Davies too? Isn't that cheating?"

Her sweet little girl might understand some day when someone walked into her life and plucked her heart right out of her chest, but that wasn't going to be today. "I never cheated on your dad, but I fell in love with JT when I wasn't much younger than Jud is now, and I never knew how to stop."

"I still don't understand," Caroline said. "And I don't like it. You should only love Daddy. He was your husband."

"Hey, kiddo," Blaise jumped in. "I loved Cash's mom once, and now I love Grace. You can love two people in the same lifetime."

"That's different. You're divorced. You ended up hating Aunt Melissa. My dad died. I don't want to talk about this anymore. I have homework." Caroline jumped up and ran from the room.

She let her daughter go, even though she wanted to run after her. This battle would be a long one and not settled in front of the entire family. "Grey, do you want to ask me anything?"

"No. I'm hungry."

"How about if we go get some snacks? Grey, help me make some popcorn." Grace headed into the kitchen, and Grey followed. She loved that woman.

"I'll come with you. Cash, Knox, why don't you come too?" Harley pushed off the couch and herded the boys into the kitchen.

She turned back to her brothers. "Caroline is going to be mad at me for a while."

"She'll come around," Blaise said.

"Wait a second," Colton said. "You loved him when we were kids?"

"Yup." Heat filled her cheeks, yet the space in her chest eased with the confession.

"All that time he hung out with us?" He narrowed his eyes.

"Yes, Colton, all the times we were together hanging out back then and every day since. Part of the reason I wanted to be at all your parties was because of him."

"Are you the reason he left town without telling anyone?" he said.

"I think so. I asked him not to tell you about what had happened between us, and he thought I was embarrassed by him."

"But you weren't embarrassed. You thought I'd kick his ass for sleeping with my baby sister, right?" Blaise said.

"I do know my brothers."

"I just might anyway." Blaise clenched his fists. "You were eighteen."

"And perfectly in control of my choices. Don't go near him." She pointed a finger at both her brothers.

"Is it over between you two?" Colton said.

"I've felt guilty and ashamed for loving JT when I was married to Adam. I thought not enough time had gone by since Adam's death for me to be involved with

JT. I lost him for good because I waited too long to admit it."

She sat between her brothers and took one of their hands in each of hers. "He's leaving again because I couldn't deal with what was happening between us fast enough. I don't want the kids to think I didn't love their father. But if JT had walked back into my life while I was still married to Adam and told me he wanted another chance with me, I would've gone. I'm not proud of that, but life is too short not to be completely happy. I see what you both have with Grace and Harley. I wanted that, and even though I loved Adam, we didn't have that kind of love. We were more friends than soul mates. JT makes me feel alive, like myself. I want to feel that way all the days I have left."

"You can't help who you love," Colton said.

Blaise leaned over her and looked at Colton. "You are getting to be a real softy in your old age."

Colton dove over her and grabbed Blaise's head. "I'll show you *softy,* you ass."

Laughter spilled out all over her. "Knock it off you two."

Blaise fought back, sending them to the floor.

"You're going to break a hip," she said.

Grace and Harley ran back into the room.

"What's going on?" Grace said.

"The Savage men are at it again. Can you two keep the fort down for a little while? I have an errand to run."

Chapter Thirty-Five

Savannah climbed the weatherworn wooden steps of the old farmhouse. She had to make a few calls to get the address, but with the promise of scones, she had managed. The front of the property spread out in flat brown grass. At one time the grass would have been deep green and used for grazing. The farm hadn't been operational in a long time.

The clapboard house begged for a coat of paint, but the windows were large. The sunlight would be a welcomed guest in a place that seemed as neglected as an old, forgetful grandmother.

She rang the bell and waited. When no one answered, she jiggled the handle of the screen door. Locked. As she was about to give up and go home, the inside door opened a crack, but the screen door remained closed.

"What are you doing here?" The garbled voice could be heard more than Shirley Davies could be seen.

"I was hoping to speak with you for a minute. Do you have the time?"

The door opened wider. Shirley unlocked the screen and pushed out onto the porch. Her hair stuck up in the back, as if she had been lying on it. Her red velour sweat suit was wrinkled.

She took the gesture to mean Shirley would give her a few minutes. "Your property is beautiful. Do you sit out here and watch the sun set?"

"Why would I do that? The sun hurts my eyes, and I don't have anywhere to sit. The house is too big for just me. I don't like living here. It's too far away from town, but it was the only place available after I got kicked out of my home. I want to go back to my old house. The one my son stole from me."

Savannah squared her shoulders and folded her hands. "JT mentioned Jake wanted him to live in that house with Maddy."

Shirley waved aside her words. "Jake didn't know what he wanted. He should've asked me what I wanted."

"Maybe what his son wanted was also important to him."

"Jakie doesn't want to live in the house he grew up in. He could give it to me."

Jakie. Dear Lord. "Shirley, why do want the Whiskey Bar so much?"

"Is that why you came out here? You want to ask me about the deli? Why do you want to know about that?" Shirley narrowed her eyes.

"I'm trying to understand why you would take your

son's business from him." She knew full well Shirley Davies never thought of JT as her son, but the woman had put it out there. She would use it against her.

"It's mine. The lawyer got it back for me. He can't have it. He didn't do nothing for it. He isn't good enough to have it. He should just pack up and go back to wherever he was staying before. This town and me don't need him."

"He needs that bar, and he deserves it."

"Why did he send you here? Was he too afraid to come talk to me himself?"

"JT doesn't know I'm here. I came on my own to ask you to give him back the Whiskey." He would be pretty mad at her when he found out she came over to talk to Shirley, but it had to be done. He'd have to get over it.

Shirley let out a gravelly laugh that had her coughing and pounding her chest. "Damn cigarettes. I'm not giving him that bar. The place belongs to me. I'm turning it back to the deli, and I'm running it myself. Why do you care so much? Are you in love with him or something?"

She met Shirley's clouded stare. "I am. I love him very much. He's a good man with a big heart. He loves his daughter, and he's doing a wonderful job of raising her by himself. I know how hard that is. If you really see him as a son, then you'd want what's best for him. You wouldn't tear him down or take from him the one thing that ties him to his father. And if you loved your husband for five minutes, then you wouldn't disgrace his memory by taking away his last wishes."

"He wrote the note."

She put her palm up. "I don't care about that note. I care about JT, and you should too. He's a good business-man. He can make the Whiskey a big success for Maddy. He wants his daughter to know he's built a strong busi-ness. On his own, I may add. They both belong in Heritage River, but he's leaving because you took his bar from him."

"And you want him to stay because you love him." She dragged out *love* in a sing-song voice and swung her hips back and forth.

"I want him to be happy. Will you consider what I've asked?"

"Absolutely not. And if he leaves town, then I want my house back too."

"I guess we're done." She turned and headed back to the van.

She'd tried and failed, but she was glad she'd tried. JT deserved that much and more from her. The sun kissed the top of the trees on its way out for the day. The prop-erty really was pretty. She could imagine the kids running in the yard. Maybe she and JT sitting in rocking chairs on the porch and holding hands. She sighed. In another life.

She checked the rearview mirror as she navigated the dirt drive. Shirley perched on the porch, staring off into the sunset.

Savannah unlocked the back door to the Tea Room. She had an hour before she was open, and Harley had taken the morning off, which meant all the prep work for opening would be hers. She didn't mind being alone. If these were her last days, she might as well enjoy them. At least she'd tried her hand at her own business, even if it didn't work out. Hopefully, the place would sell soon and Jud would only miss one semester of school. What was she going to do when it was Grey's turn to go off to college? One problem at a time. She could win the lottery by then.

She prepped the tea urns and pastry case. She counted the money in the safe and put it in the till for the day. She took the temperature in the fridge and freezer and thought of JT. How could Shirley call the health inspector on him? Here she was hurting her family by selling personal items to give Jud money, and Shirley wanted to pull the rug out from under her child. Could it be because JT wasn't really her son? Did she resent him that much? She wanted to hate Shirley, but she only pitied her. She was the one who missed out on the amazing man JT had become and his beautiful, smart, and sassy daughter.

She had a small retail order coming today because she couldn't afford anything too big. New forks were also on their way. She'd have to have a heart-to-heart with Kiki one of these days.

Someone banged on the front door. She still had ten minutes, but it would prove stupid to turn anyone away. "Good morning, oh. What are you doing here?" She stared at Colton. He wore a black, short-sleeved, collared shirt and black pants. He had a to go from Maybelline's Bakery in his hand. "Why are coming here with that?"

"Because you don't serve coffee and I don't drink that colored water you like."

"It's called tea. Shouldn't you be at school?"

"I have one of those periods where I don't have class."

"You mean a prep period?" She blocked his path, forcing him to hug her.

He patted her back. "You know I hate this mushy stuff. But yeah, a prep period. Whatever you call it."

"How is it you're a teacher and they let you keep your job?"

"The kids love me. The parents love me. And I'm me." He puffed up his chest.

She shook her head. "You certainly are. Since you didn't stop in for tea, what brings you by?" She pulled vanilla scones from the case and handed him one. "Mmm. Now this is good. Thanks," he said through a full mouth.

He took out his wallet and handed her a check. "That's for the catering job for the wedding."

"It's too much." She handed the check back. He'd written it out for the full amount of Jud's tuition. "How did you know how much?"

"Jesus Christ, Savannah. Take the money."

She stood still.

"I called Jud and asked him. Consider it a loan. I'll charge you interest if it makes you feel better."

"This is my problem. I will fix it."

"I don't understand you. You'd allow your pride to stop your kid from going to school. So you opened a business, and it tanked. It happens. When you sell the building, pay me back." He shoved the check at her again.

The door opened and put a wedge into their conversation. Colton stuffed the check into his pocket. "Rowan," he said.

"Savage." Rowan McGee nodded. "Good morning, Savannah." The smile returned to his face.

"What can I get you?" She hoped it was to go. Then she'd throw Colton out too.

"I have some news." Rowan rubbed his hands together. "The town council would like to award you the catering job for the black-tie dinner."

Had she heard him correctly?

"Are you shitting her?"

"Of course not. We'll discuss the details with you over the next couple of weeks. If you could come up with a sample menu in the meantime, that would be great. Congratulations." He stuck out his hand.

She stared at it for a second before she shook it. "Thank you." Her mind whirled. She'd have so much to do before then. She'd need more staff. She might actually be able to keep the Tea Room opened if the publicity of the event drove more customers to her store.

"What's your plan on entertainment?" Colton asked.

"We're looking into several bands," Rowan said.

"My family and I can play. I know the schedule is open for the night."

Rowan's mouth dropped. Hers did too.

"What did you say?" she said.

"Blaise will have an erection if he can play his new music all night. We'll keep it toned down. No old Savage stuff, but I think our name on the bill will draw a bigger crowd." He turned to her. "You can't say no to that." He pressed his lips together.

She didn't care that he hated mushy stuff. She threw herself into his arms. "I don't care what anyone says about you. You're the best big brother ever."

"All right, then. Thanks, Savage. I'll be in touch." Rowan hurried from the shop.

"You can't stop yourself from helping me, can you?" Her face hurt from smiling. She'd won the black-tie.

Then it hit her. JT lost. He'd lost too much, and she couldn't fix it for him. She wanted to help him the way Colton always tried to help her, and she didn't have a clue how to do it.

"Do you remember when you were about six and a thunderstorm came up during the night?" He dropped into a chair and drank his coffee.

She sat beside him. "I'd stand in the doorway of your bedroom and bounce from one foot to the other, whispering your name. You'd grumble at me. 'Go to bed, Savannah.' You did a good job of sounding mean at the age of ten."

"You woke me up. You'd tell me you were afraid of the loud booms in the sky."

"That's when you'd raise your covers and tell me to stay on my side of the bed. 'Don't touch me,' you'd say."

He laughed at her imitation. "You'd run as fast as

your little feet would carry you and dive onto the mattress."

"You'd have to grab me by the back of my pajamas and yank me onto the bed." The memory made her heart smile.

"You'd sleep right on top of me the whole damn night."

"And in the morning, we'd find Blaise asleep on the floor."

"Scaredy-cats, both of you." He poked her side.

She wouldn't change one thing about her life if it meant she couldn't be Colton's sister. Blaise's too. She had been blessed beyond belief to have them in her corner. "Thank you for forgiving me."

"Ah. Knock it off, will you? You're my kid sister. And you've had to forgive me more than once. It's what we do for each other. Blaise is the only one who stays out of trouble."

"Middle-child syndrome. He's a people pleaser." She nudged him with her shoulder.

"Yeah, well, he's fucking good at it."

"Can you do something else for me?"

He hung his head but laughed. "What?"

"Would you check on JT and make sure he's okay?"

He met her gaze. "Don't you think you should do that?"

"I don't want to stir anything up. It's too late to tell him I finally told everyone about my feelings for him. He doesn't want to stay in town if he can't have the bar. I think I understand that. I'd like to be enough for him, but he wasn't enough for me to tell you about. I have no right to complain. We just have one of those 'right love, wrong time' things."

"Do you believe that shit?"

"What?"

"If you love him, go tell him. If you want him to stay, make him. You told us you loved him your entire life, and you aren't going to fight harder for him? My sister doesn't give up a fight when she thinks she's right."

"I felt like I was cheating on Adam. I wasn't honoring his memory by being with JT. Being with JT seems as if what I had with Adam didn't count. And I don't have to be right all the time."

When he finished laughing, he said, "You and Adam have three kids. That should count for something. You didn't come close to cheating on Adam. I know about cheating. I'm pretty sure I broke up a few marriages in my day. Adam isn't coming back. If JT showed up a year from now and wanted to be with you, would you?"

"Without hesitation."

"Then go now because you might not get tomorrow. I think I learned that in rehab." He stood and held out his hand to help her up.

She hugged him. "No one would believe what a teddy bear you really are."

"Don't go telling anyone either. I like my image the way it is."

"Our family knows."

He raised an eyebrow. "You people don't count. Take this. It's a loan." He handed back the check.

She took it with a nod. "I will pay you back."

"I better get to school before Joann's head explodes. But for fun, I think I'll cancel the test I was supposed to give." He laughed and let himself out of the store.

Maybe he was right. Maybe she had a right to what she wanted. Maybe now was her chance to start over. She'd won the black-tie. Her brothers had forgiven her stupidity.

Would JT?

Chapter Thirty-Six

"I hate you." Maddy slammed her bedroom door for the hundredth time.

JT dropped onto the sofa and held his head in his hands. He scratched his scalp. The rooms wouldn't pack themselves, and Maddy wasn't helping. She wanted no part of moving again. She liked Heritage River, liked Grey Montgomery, and she had refused to pack a single thing because she wasn't leaving.

What a mess his life had become in a few short weeks. He should have stayed the hell away from Heritage River. Nothing good had ever come from this town.

He pushed up off the couch and headed back into the kitchen. Something good had come from being back. He hadn't expected to find Savannah waiting for him. He thought for sure she'd never speak to him again after the way he ran out of town on her. He'd taken the coward's way out back then, believing he wasn't good enough for her and thinking she'd tire of him long before he'd be ready to give her up. He hadn't wanted his heart broken by the best thing that had ever happened to him.

He wrapped glasses in white tissue paper. Now he had to let Savannah go because she wasn't ready for a relationship with him, and he wasn't planning on staying to watch Shirley turn his bar into a dive. Maddy would just have to get on the damn wagon, whether she liked it or not.

The bell rang, interrupting his thoughts. He padded to the door and flipped on the front light.

"What are you doing here?" Anger strangled the tone in his voice.

Shirley stood on the porch in her matted, red sweat suit. Her lipstick bled into the corners of her mouth and the lines around her lips. "May I come in?"

He didn't want her inside his house. It was still his. "Now isn't a good time. Anything you have to say, you can say to Hoke Carter."

"Jakie—" The look on his face must have stopped her. "I'm sorry. JT. This won't take but a minute." She rummaged in the oversize bag hanging from her shoulder. "Here." She handed him folded pages.

"What's this?" He didn't have time for this visit, and he didn't want to read anything she'd written.

"You can keep your bar." She crossed her arms over her chest.

"You're giving me back the Whiskey? Why?" She was up to something. There wasn't any way this woman was showing him an act of kindness. "Is the roof leaking or something? You want me to pay for it?"

"You should have it, is all. Your daddy wanted you to own his property, and I'll honor that."

"You're admitting to forging that note?" He flipped through the papers. They were the deed to the building on Main Street. She'd written a note at the bottom stating he was the sole owner.

"I'll admit no such thing." She waved her hands at him. "Go on now. It's yours. Take those papers to Hoke, and he'll know what to do."

"You expect me to believe you just had a change of heart? I'm not stupid, even if you seem to think I am. Why are you doing this?"

"What difference does it make why I changed my mind? You've got your bar."

"Admitting you were wrong about me might be nice."

She looked off into the distance. "I might've misjudged you some, but only recently."

"Thanks." That apology would be the best he'd get. It didn't do shit to mend what ailed him.

She turned toward the street. He started to close the door. What would he do next? Could this be for real?

"I wouldn't have come if it wasn't for your friend," she said over her shoulder.

"What did you say?" He stepped onto the porch.

"Savannah Montgomery stopped by my place and pleaded your case for you. Said you didn't know a thing about her being there. I came to see for myself. I thought if he had a woman come do his dirty work instead of him acting like a man for the first time in his life, I'd keep the bar and fight for my house too. But if you didn't know why I was here, then I'd know she came on her own. She meant what she said about you."

"What'd she say?" The kid in him wanted to hear the praise from the beautiful Savannah Savage. He could ignore the jab Shirley threw in there at him. She would never know the kind of man he was. It didn't matter what that old bag thought. Only what Savannah thought.

"Said she was in love with you. You were a good man and good father. Told me I should start acting like a mother." She faced him head-on. "I'm sorry, Jacob. I never was a good mother to you. You were a little boy, and you needed your mama. Only that wasn't me, and I don't think I saw that until Savannah pointed it out. Now go take your bar back and let me be."

He came down the steps in his bare feet and hugged her frail frame.

She patted his back. "That's enough of that. Now shoo." She ambled down the street, never looking back.

He ran inside and up the steps. He pounded on Maddy's door. "Can you open this, please?"

She yanked the door open with a glare in her eye and a snarl on her face. "What? I'm busy."

"I have to go out for a little while. Don't go anywhere, you hear me?"

"Or what? You're going to ground me? Take my phone? Tell me I can't hang out with my friends? Oh, wait. I don't have any friends because you keep making me move."

He kissed the top of her head. "Madeline Elizabeth, stop busting my backside. I'm going to do what's best for us. Trust me." He hoped he was.

"Whatever." She closed the door.

"I'll see you later," he yelled through the wood before he ran to find some shoes.

JT pulled up to the house and parked. The porch lights were on and a few inside. He ran to the door and knocked.

Twice.

"I'm coming" came through the door to him.

His heart flipped over.

Savannah opened the door. Her dark hair was piled up on the top of her head in some messy-bun thing he'd seen Maddy do with her hair. Her face was clean of makeup, but flour dusted her eyebrows. Her jeans were also covered in flour, and her feet bare. Her gray eyes narrowed as she took him in.

Her tank top accented her arms and breasts. Desire stirred in him immediately, and she hadn't said a word.

"Hi. What brings you here?" She wiped her brow with the back of her hand.

He'd planned on playing it cool. He wanted her to admit she'd gone to Shirley for him. Instead, he cupped her face in his hands and kissed her hard on the lips.

She resisted at first, and he almost quit, but she yielded to him and kissed him back. He pulled away but kept his hands on her face. He didn't want to break the connection between them. "Hi." He leaned his forehead against hers.

"Um, can I ask what that was all about?" She eased back.

"Shirley gave me back the bar."

"She did? That's fantastic. I'm so glad." She opened her mouth but clamped it shut. "Come inside. We'll celebrate."

He followed her into the kitchen. The house smelled like sugar and vanilla. Baking ingredients, baking sheets, and more flour covered the island.

She grabbed wineglasses from the cabinet and opened a bottle of riesling. "Sorry about the mess. I wasn't expecting guests. Tell me what Shirley said."

He took the wine from her. "She said I was the worst person on the planet and handed me back the deed to the bar."

"She did not." She laughed for him.

He could spend his whole life making her laugh like that. "She did hand me back the deed."

"Thank God she came to her senses. This means you and Maddy will stay in town where you belong. You have the right to all the happiness in the world. I'm glad it worked out for you. Really." Her eyes shone.

The timer on the oven binged. "Oh, I'm making some cookies. I forgot they were in there. Do you want one?"

"Savannah." He stopped. The words were out of his reach.

She turned to him. "Yes?"

"Thank you."

She placed a textured cookie on a plate and slid it to him. "For what?"

He grabbed her hand and met her gaze. His mouth opened, but no words came. How did he say how much it meant that she'd gone to Shirley and fought for him? She'd stood beside him in a way no one ever had.

He ran his thumb over the top of her hand while his heart raced and his throat closed. He couldn't love her more.

"She told you I went to see her." She tilted her chin up.

"You changed her mind. You did that for me." He tugged her toward him until they were mere inches apart and still not close enough. Her sweet scent drifted toward him. He laced his fingers through hers.

"Oh, JT, I'm sorry I was so foolish about us. I was afraid, and that wasn't fair to you. I should have defended what we had. I know it's over because you couldn't count on me, but I wanted you to have that bar back. And I wanted you to stay in Heritage River even if you couldn't be mine any longer."

"You have no idea how many nights I've waited to love you, do you?"

"I think I do. But I ruined everything. If I could go back and do it all again—"

He placed his fingers on her soft lips. "Stop talking. You haven't ruined anything. I thought I had done that to us. I'm sorry I couldn't give you the time you needed to come to terms with losing your husband and me showing up on your doorstep, wanting to pick up like no time had gone on between us. I've been so in love with you I wanted to hurry up." He wanted to hurry now too.

He wanted to take this woman right in the kitchen on her flour-covered counters. All she'd have to do is look at him with that taunt in her eyes, and he'd be a goner.

"What are you thinking about?" She ran her fingers through his hair.

"I'm thinking if you keep touching me like that, I'm going to throw you over my shoulder and carry you off someplace to make love to you."

"I dare you." Her eyes twinkled.

He growled low in his throat, grabbed her hips, and pulled her against him. "Darlin', your children are here. What would that look like? And I don't want to do it in my car or the woods or behind your garage. I want us to lie on a bed, for the first time, and take our time. Maybe we could plan a weekend getaway."

"I can't afford a weekend away right now. Every penny I have is going to Jud's school." She looked up at him through her dark lashes. "I have something to tell you."

"Uh-oh."

"I won the black-tie dinner." She bit her lip and shrugged.

He picked her up and swung her around. She squealed. "I'm proud of you."

"I've got a chance to keep the Tea Room open now, and Colton offered up the band to play. Things might work out."

He wiped the flour off her face. "They will." Old Rowan McGee kept his word and didn't tell her she was the second choice. The glow on her cheeks was worth her winning and more. The one person he didn't need to compete with was her.

"My children aren't home. They went bowling with my brothers, Harley, and Grace. They won't be back for a few hours."

"Are you ready for the world to know about us?"

She wrapped her arms around his neck. "Everyone that matters knows."

The pressure of her body made his burn. He tucked his hands into her back pockets and cupped the swell of her backside. "I'm never going to let you go, and I plan on making up for all the time we lost. Be prepared. I'm ornery in the morning before my coffee. You might get sick of me and my temper, but I'm sticking this time."

She put her fingers to his lips. "Your turn to stop talking. I don't want to wait any longer. Take me to bed."

"Here? Are you sure?" He wasn't sure if he should make love to her in this house, and he didn't want to pressure her. "If it's too soon, we can wait."

"I've never been more sure of anything." She took his hand and led him up the stairs.

His stomach knotted up into his chest. He hadn't been nervous with a woman ever in his life, except that night twenty-four years ago when a dark-haired beauty climbed onto his lap and kissed him senseless.

That woman was older and more beautiful than ever,

and she glanced at him over her shoulder with a sexy smile on her face. Yeah, he was a goner.

She shut the door to the master bedroom and lit a candle on the dresser. The smell of fruit swept into the room with them. She ran her hands up his belly and across his chest.

His blood flowed to his groin, and his head spun a little. She clasped her hands behind his neck again, and he pulled her to him.

"Make love to me, Jacob Tyler. And never stop."

Savannah's heart pounded in her chest, her ears, and her head. She wanted to touch him everywhere and wanted his hands all over her. JT was in her bedroom. *Her* bedroom and she was ready. She'd packed up her past and redecorated for her future. The new sheets were lavender with tiny white flowers. The new comforter was silver. This space was for her future, free of guilt. She'd never forget her past, but she had a lot to look forward to with the man in her room. Her body shivered.

"Are you cold?" He let her hair down from the bun she'd shoved it into earlier.

She shook out her hair for him. "Not a chance." She should care that she probably had flour all over her or that it had been hours since she brushed her teeth. She wasn't certain she'd shaved her legs this morning, but she didn't care at all. She was with JT. Finally.

"That's good because I'm about to get you out of your clothes."

"It's about damn time."

He laughed and leaned down to kiss her. His hands tugged her hair, just enough to bring her mouth up to his. That shiver ran down her spine and scorched her most sensitive spot. She loved the way he claimed her as his. She wouldn't be able to wait. She needed him inside her.

His tongue darted around her mouth. She chased it with her own, but he was always a step ahead. He sucked on her bottom lip until she moaned. She pulled on his T-shirt, wanting it off so she could explore his body.

He eased out of the kiss and stepped back, dragging his shirt over his head, and rewarded her with a view of his chest. Even at his age, it was still chiseled and strong.

"Now you." His voice was thick and husky.

She hurried to undo the small buttons on the shirt she'd so carelessly tossed on this morning when she'd thought she'd never be with him again and hadn't given a damn about how she looked. If she'd known he was coming over and giving her another chance at happiness, she'd have worn something prettier. Now there would be time enough in the days and months ahead to dress for him.

He pushed the shirt from her shoulders. His hands ran up and down her arms before they rested on her back. "I want to look at you."

"Look later." She pulled him to her and kissed him.

His lips parted for her, and once again their tongues

moved to their dance. She fought with his oversize belt buckle. "I hate this thing."

"I'll get rid of it." He yanked the belt from the loops of his jeans.

"No, you look really sexy wearing it. I can never get it off you."

"You'll have plenty of practice."

"I hope so." She intended to take advantage of every minute with him from that point on. No more looking back. No more second-guessing. Now was the time for second chances.

He cupped her face and stared into her eyes.

"Darlin', I love you."

"I love you too. Now and forever."

He kissed her again, and she couldn't think of anything else except the way his muscles flexed against her touch. He scooped her up and laid her on the bed. *Her bed.* He slid beside her and traced his finger along her collarbone and then down to her breasts.

She unhooked her bra, and he cupped her breast. She pressed her hand against his and arched up to him as he rubbed her nipple between his fingers. Fire burned her skin wherever he touched, and she wanted the feeling to go on forever.

His mouth dropped to her other breast, sucking and nibbling. His tongue drew a line down her belly and circled at the top of her jeans. "You are beautiful."

"I'm glad you think so."

"Nothing to think about. May I?" He tugged at her jeans, and she helped him get the denim out of the way.

He stood and took off the rest of his clothes. She sat up to take him in her hand. He tilted his head back and moaned as she stroked the full length of him. She placed her mouth over his tip, and he gripped her shoulders. He was beautiful, and she wanted him to feel the pleasure he gave her.

He eased away and knelt in front of her. "I want you to feel as good as you make me feel."

"I was thinking that same thing." Their connection was like sweet-tea essence mixed in cakes.

With one finger, he yanked off her lacy panties. He lay beside her and kissed her again while his hands sought her most sensitive place. He set the rhythm, and she moved with his pace. The longing inside her twisted until she might break.

"Let go for me," he whispered against her ear.

"I want you with me." Her breath was short spurts.

"You first," he teased.

"Together." The way they were meant to be.

"Stubborn southern woman." He positioned himself above her so he could look down into her eyes.

She wrapped her legs around his waist because she wanted to feel all of him. He took her invitation and thrust himself inside her, filling her up and quenching her thirst.

They moved together in perfect harmony. Sweat cooled her skin, but her insides still burned. He ravaged her with kisses, and the hunger for him twisted tighter and tighter. She arched her hips to feel more of him.

"Yes, JT. Just like that."

411

He pushed up on his arms and tilted his head back, calling out her name. Her name on his lips—always. Always.

They rode the wave together until it crashed against her over and over. He pulsed inside her as the moment washed up over him. She clung to him while her heart raced.

"Savannah, that was…" He rested his forehead against hers.

"I know." She ran her fingers across his beard and loved the feel of the scruff against her skin. She loved everything about him.

He propped up on his elbows and reached to brush the hair from her face. "I'm shaking." He slid over and pulled her against him so they faced each other.

"You wreak havoc on me." She laid her head against his chest and listened to his heart beat.

"Me too." He ran his fingers up and down her back in long strokes. "I hate to say this, but I'm going to have to go soon. I told Maddy I'd be back."

She pulled back to look at him. "Can I ask you something?"

"Anything."

"Have you ever been over to Shirley's place?"

"How about you don't bring her up while I'm lying naked beside you?"

She propped up on an elbow. "It's beautiful over there. She has acres of property and an old farmhouse. It needs work, but it's big. More than enough room for six."

"What are you saying?"

"She told me she hated being that far from town. And I don't want to just date you. I've waited my whole life for you to come back to me. I'm too old to be your girl-friend. I may be rushing things, and there's the small issue of Grey and Maddy liking each other. They shouldn't live under the same roof if they're going to date, but I stood on Shirley's porch and saw us there. Me and you. Growing older together." Tears filled her eyes. She had to blink them away.

He sat up. "Hey." He wiped a tear away with his thumb. "I like the sound of me and you growing old together, but I don't know about moving to Shirley's place. What would we do with our houses?"

"Sell them. Sell yours to Shirley. She could have her old house back, and we could start our life together. I don't want to do what Grace and Blaise are doing with two houses. I want to wake up beside you every morning because there have been so many mornings I looked out the window and wondered where you were and what you were doing. I don't want to waste a single sunrise or sunset. I've wasted enough time."

He placed a soft kiss on her lips. "When the lady you've loved tells you she wants to wake up beside you every morning, you want that first morning to start right away. But can I think about it? The buying Shirley's place part?"

She nodded, not wanting to speak for fear the tears would betray her. He pulled her against him again, and she snuggled close.

The front door banged open. They both jumped.

"Shit, they're back." He leaped out of bed and grabbed his pants.

"Savannah, where are you? Is that JT's truck in the driveway?" Colton's booming voice shook the walls.

They scrambled into their clothes. "There's no way to go downstairs and not embarrass ourselves," she said.

"I'm not climbing out your window."

"Please?"

"Tell me you're joking, woman."

"My brothers and my children are downstairs. How is it going to look?"

"Like we love each other." He pulled his shirt over his head.

"If we lived together, no one would think anything of us walking out of the bedroom together."

"Living together isn't exactly respectable." He shoved his feet into his boots.

"Are you saying you don't want to live with me?"

"I'm saying I don't want your brothers kicking my ass because I didn't make an honest woman of you."

She shrugged. "Guess you'd better get ready for a fight. Blaise can throw a mean punch." She reached for the doorknob.

He lunged for her and pulled her away from the door. He held her hands in his. "Are you saying you want to get hitched?"

"Savannah, do I need to come upstairs to check on you?" Blaise hollered up the steps. "Are you okay? Slip in the tub?"

"Where are my children? Those two idiots are making things much worse. I should get down there."

"You didn't answer me."

"What was the question?"

"You heard me just fine." He tapped her nose.

She slipped her arms around his neck. "If that was a marriage proposal, Jacob Tyler Davies, you'd better try again."

He wrapped his arms around her waist and pulled her close. "Marry me, Savannah Savage, and make me the proudest man in the world."

"You've got yourself a deal."

Epilogue

JT stretched the collar of his dress shirt away from his neck. Thanks to the tie, it didn't go very far. He wanted to yank the tie off, but Savannah said he had to wear one. The sun had set, and the December night had a chill in it. Outdoor heaters worked hard to keep the guests sitting comfortably in white folding chairs.

White lights twinkled like a thousand stars draped above their heads and around poles placed throughout the yard. The music began, a piano piece Blaise had written for the occasion. Cash played it on a keyboard plugged in on the porch.

Grace walked down the makeshift grassy aisle first. She looked nice in her long dress. Blaise's face lit up like a stage when he saw her. Yeah, that guy was in love.

But he had eyes only for Savannah. She and Caroline came around the last row of guests, and Savannah took his breath away. Caroline ignored his small wave to her.

She wasn't happy about him being with her mother as anything more than friends. Savannah said to give her time.

Savannah's dark hair was pulled back on the sides and curled down her back. Her gray eyes shimmered as she smiled at the people she passed. The dress hugged her curves in all the right places. She was the most beautiful woman he'd ever seen.

"She's a beauty," Harlan whispered in his ear.

Her eyes searched the crowd until her gaze fell on him. His chest tightened when she gave him that smile. She reached out and grabbed his hand as she went by. He was sure his smile wrapped around his head. Savannah Savage loved him and the whole world finally knew it, and he didn't have to fall off the roof to tell them.

Over the past three months, there had been people who pulled her aside and told her she was crazy for being with him. Even though the bar was his again and the customers were coming in, some people's minds could never be changed. He didn't care anymore. Savannah wanted him and had no trouble telling any pigheaded idiot just that. And if he caught someone talking about her behind her back because she was involved with him so soon after her husband's death, he made sure to share that person's most embarrassing moments out loud and preferably on a Friday night when the bar was busiest.

He stuck his hands in his pockets and wrapped his fingers around the surprise he had for her. He hoped this made up for her closing the Tea Room after the first of the new year. Even winning the anniversary event couldn't keep the place open. She didn't know what she would do afterward, but his Savannah would figure it out. He'd offered her a job, but she told him no. Later tonight when he had her alone, he'd give her what was in his pocket. He hoped she'd like it.

Maddy waved to him from two rows back. She wanted to sit with Grey and Jud. He couldn't remember the name of the woman who followed Savannah down the aisle, but the crowd stood when Cash changed the tune.

Harley came toward them in a white dress that hung straight to the ground. Knox escorted her to Colton, who shifted from one foot to the other. He stood beside Blaise under a canopy of white flowers. In the front row were Troy and Patrick from the original Savage. They'd flown in for Colton's big day. All five of them had played poker last night at Blaise's. It was like old times.

Colton took Harley's hand and leaned in to whisper in her ear. She threw her head back and laughed, then settled her hand on his chest and kissed him.

The officiant asked everyone to be seated. JT didn't hear a word of the ceremony. He was too busy watching Savannah.

The bride kissed the groom, and the guests filed out for the reception in the backyard. White lights sparkled under the tent, and the music kicked up, demanding everyone dance. But the only dance he would ever want was the one with Savannah.

She walked toward him with two whiskey glasses in her hands. "Thought you might like a drink."

"What I would like is to get you out of that dress." He took the glass and nuzzled her neck.

"Later, cowboy."

"How about you stick your hand in my pocket for now?" He pulled her close.

She laughed, but he kept his face straight.

"Is that a dare, JT?"

"Maybe."

"Can't pass up a dare. Which pocket?"

"Left. Suit jacket."

"Well, that's no fun." She eased back and put her drink down.

She shoved her hand into his jacket pocket and swirled it around. Even that move had him turned on. He'd need to stay focused. They were in public. "Find anything?"

She pulled out and held up a gold key. Her eyes grew wide. "Is this what I think it is? The key to Shirley's house? When? How? I don't understand."

He'd spent the last three months trying to get his hands on Shirley's old farmhouse. She'd finally accepted his offer. "Our house, darlin'. Our home for our family. Me and you growing old on that front porch just like you want."

"I love you, JT Davies. I've loved you from the first minute I saw you when I was too young to know my heart would only belong to you. You are the essence of me."

He cupped her face in his hands and placed a kiss on her lips. "I love you, Savannah Savage. Then. Now. Forever."

But wait, there's more. Have a sneak peek at the first book in the Heritage River series:

The Risk for House and Home

Chapter One

Grace Starr turned her Subaru Impreza into the driveway of her two-story gray colonial with black shutters and matching black double doors. She loved this house with its oversized deck she sat on at night catching the breeze and drinking tea, the big kitchen with plenty of cabinets, and the gas fireplace that burned clean. Twenty-Five Tudor Drive was the place she started a family with her husband and raised her daughter, Chloe.

She hated the For Sale sign in the front yard.

She had an hour before she had to be back at the library. She should get some lunch, take a walk, clean a bathroom. The bathroom would win, and if she had time, she'd throw in a load of laundry, wipe down the counters, sort the mail into piles. Her favorite pile being the one that went into the garbage.

The extra car was parked in the driveway too. What was Chloe doing home from school in the middle of the afternoon? Had there been a half day Grace had forgotten about? Some kind of teacher in-service thing? Possibly. Lately, she kept returning to the bathroom to touch her toothbrush just to see if it was wet. Her mind couldn't hold a thought if it were a vault. Problem was, she didn't know if the absentmindedness was her age or the stress of the divorce. Better to blame it on the divorce. She wasn't that old...yet. Maybe Chloe felt the effects of senior year ending and was ditching.

The garage door yawned open, and Chloe came out in bare feet, her blue-streaked hair bouncing off her shoulders. Her nose piercing sparkled in the sun, mocking Grace from its coveted place on Chloe's face. Her shorts barely covered the necessary parts, and her shirt showed too much skin.

Grace cringed at the uncontrolled appearance of her almost-eighteen-year-old. She tried to arrange her face in a way that said she was used to seeing Chloe this way. Larry had let her get the piercing. He had bought her the blue dye. Grace was always the bad guy. The boring parent.

Chloe waved something in her hand. "Mom, you've got to see this."

Please don't let it be a letter from the guidance counselor.

"What are you doing home?" Chloe said, slightly out of breath, through the open car window. "I thought you were volunteering at the library today."

"I am, later. I was wondering what you were doing home on a Wednesday. Did you get in trouble for wearing that outfit to school?" What was the point in fighting? But she couldn't keep her mouth shut.

Chloe rolled her eyes with the skill of a seasoned pro.

"No one dress codes in June. School's boring. We're not doing anything. They won't even notice I'm gone."

The same arguments about doing the right thing bubbled inside Grace and died on her tongue. Did it really matter? And look what doing the right thing did for her. She had followed the rules and planned for all possible outcomes. She was the dutiful wife, and she had still been evicted from her life. "Don't make skipping a habit. I don't care that there's only two weeks of school left."

Ignoring her last remark, Chloe shoved the white paper at Grace. "This came in the mail today. I didn't open it, but it looks interesting. Did Dad get new lawyers or something? Did he move out of state and not tell us? It would be just like him, the jerk."

"Chloe, don't call your father names." Even if Larry was a big fat jerk. Grace inspected the envelope addressed to her. A postmark she didn't recognize. A law firm's name and address in the top corner. Pretty official. What had Larry gone and done? She shoved her way out of the Impreza, gripping the envelope. She took a closer look. Tennessee? "This must be a mistake." She handed the envelope back.

"Are you kidding? You've got to open this." Chloe shoved the envelope at her. "Maybe we won something."

"Wishful thinking. I've never even been to Tennessee. Take it inside, please."

"No, Mom. Open it." Chloe gripped Grace's hand and shoved the envelope in her grasp.

Why was this so important? "Oh, all right." She ripped the envelope open and scanned its contents.

A letter on the firm's letterhead. Her hand began to shake. She had to read it twice to make sure she was seeing things correctly.

"Well, what is it?" Chloe's blue eyes had grown to the size of sunflowers. Her face sagged when she stared at Grace. "Dad did something bad, didn't he? He's keeping all his money or not letting me go to college, right?"

Grace shook her head and searched for her voice. "Surprisingly, Dad has nothing to do with this, but it must be a mistake. There's no way this is real." She looked back at the letter. "It says someone has left me a house. Who would do such a crazy thing?" A laugh bubbled up into her throat.

"That's great. Now we have a place to live. You can tell Dad you don't need him anymore."

Grace thrust the letter back in the envelope. Chloe's loyalty was sweet, but it might not last. These days they got along one minute, and the next Grace had said or done something wrong. Having a teenage daughter could be wonderful and exhausting at the same time. "The house is in Tennessee. You don't want to live there. I don't want to live in Tennessee. I like it here, in this town. Like I said, I'm sure it's a mistake. You want to get some lunch?"

"Wait. Who does it say gave you the house?"

Grace folded the envelope. "I don't know. They don't want to be identified."

"And you don't think that's mysterious and want to find out more?" Chloe raised her eyebrows.

She envied Chloe's ability to still believe amazing things happened at random moments. That was a blessing of youth. "Even if it's legitimate, which I highly doubt it is, nothing good can come from an unidentified person giving you a house. It's unheard of and ridiculous. People don't do things like that."

Well, not practical people anyway.

READ MORE

Also by Stacey Wilk

<u>Heritage River Series</u>

The Risk for House and Home

The Bridge Between Love and Lies

The Essence of Whiskey and Tea

<u>Hometown Series</u>

Taking Root

Raising Winter

Defining Chances

Beginning Over

Steeling Hearts

Whispering Christmas

<u>Winter at the Shore Series</u>

No More Darkness

Through the Darkness

Light Upon the Darkness

<u>The Brotherhood Protectors World</u>

Winter's Last Chance

The Last Betrayal

Her Last Word

The Last Days of Christmas

Seduced by Denial

Chill in the Air

Fighting for Tessa

Nash's Promise

Cruz's Watch

Harlan Unleashed

<u>Big Sky Country Series</u>

Time Won't Erase

Stay Awhile

Love Never Ends

Dare to Tell (coming 2025)

About the Author

From an early age, best-selling and award-winning author, Stacey Wilk, told tales as a way to escape. At six she wrote short stories in composition notebooks, at twelve she wrote a novel on a typewriter, in high school biology she wrote rock star romances in her binder instead of paying attention.

But it wasn't until many years later, inspired by her children and a looming birthday, that she finally took her story-telling seriously. And published her first novel in 2013. Since then, she's gone on to publish twenty-eight more so women everywhere can indulge in books that hook them heart and soul.

She isn't done telling stories. Not by a long shot. If you want to read her emotional and honest books about family, romance, and second chances, visit her at www.staceywilk.com

To see what she writes next, follow her Facebook

group for her amazing readers – Stacey's Novel Family
https://bit.ly/2FK8Lae

Or join her newsletter - https://bit.ly/2AojEFk